Lost American Fiction

In 1972 the Southern Illinois University Press republished Edith Summers Kelley's *Weeds*. Its reception encouraged the Press to mount a series that would republish obscure or unavailable works of fiction that merit a new audience. Since 1972 eighteen volumes of Lost American Fiction have appeared—in hardbound from the Southern Illinois University Press and in paperback from Popular Library, the cooperating publisher.

The editor is frequently asked about the basis for selection. Obviously, there can be no clear guidelines, for the decisions are largely subjective and impressionistic. The only rule is that to be considered for publication a book must have been originally published at least twenty-five years ago. Our chief consideration, of course, has been literary merit. Another quality we are looking for might be called "life": does the work live?—does it have a voice of its own?—does it present human nature convincingly? A third test for including a work in the series is its historical value: does it illuminate the literary or social history of its time? The volumes chosen so far do not represent one editor's judgment: some were recommended by colleagues, our cooperating publishers, and by strangers who responded enthusiastically to the concept of the series.

At this point the editor and publisher feel that the Lost American Fiction series has largely achieved what it set out to do. Eighteen novels have been given another chance, and some have found new audiences. The paperback reprint arrangement with Popular Library is making the books available to a wide readership. To be sure, some will vanish again. We cannot claim that all of the titles are lost masterpieces, but we believe that some of them are. There has been considerable disagreement from readers about individual titles. We never expected uniformity of response. That readers would find the Lost American Fiction books worth reading and would be prompted to make their own appraisals is all we wanted.

M. J. B.

Lost American Fiction
Edited by Matthew J. Bruccoli

Afterword by Wallace Markfield

The Landsmen

by PETER MARTIN

Southern Illinois University Press
Carbondale and Edwardsville

Feffer & Simons, Inc.
London and Amsterdam

Library of Congress Cataloging in Publication Data

Martin, Peter,
  The landsmen.

  (Lost American fiction)
  Reprint of the 1st ed. published by Little, Brown, Boston.
  I. Title.
[PZ4.M382Lan6] [PS3563.A7274]   813'.5'4
ISBN 0–8093–0837–1   77–5667

Printed by offset lithography in the United States of America

FOR

HOWARD, SIMON, MICKEY, CHARLES,
DONNIE, HARVEY, KARL, AND DAVID

Contents

The Landsmen

1. *Yeersel*
(1844–1906)

WE JEWS OF THE VILLAGE OF GOLINSK WERE ALL PLAIN TALKERS AND LONG-winded. We spoke as we felt and our hearts were always full and what we said never came out dainty or grammatical; yet our own everyday language, our Yiddish, our treasured private tongue in which we could speak safely, held for us the daily comfort of a mother's song. Because of this, any two Golinsker Jews in a hurry could stop to say hello in the afternoon and still be a-talking until time for evening prayers.

Living as we did among those opposed in principle to our very existence, in a Russia of poverty, pogroms, and self-disgust, we thanked God for our Jewishness and for our Yiddish language, which gave us at least among ourselves the freedom to speak heart-to-heart. To the non-Jews of the village we were undesirable transients, even though many of us were born there, and our use was as pawns in the interest of Squire Konayev, the owner of the village. Truthfully speaking, to the Squire and to the non-Jewish villagers we were usable offal, a kind of special manure to improve the land, and we saw nothing remarkable about this because it had always been so; or I should say since the time fifty years before my birth when the district was opened to habitation by Jews. At that time, I am told, my grandfather Yeersel-ben-Mayer came to Golinsk from his village in Poland, running away from a famine which had quite naturally produced a reaction against the Jewish population.

Golinsk in 1885 held some sixty families of which nineteen were Jewish. A primitive hamlet some forty miles from Minsk, it had neither mayor nor town council, being administered by Selenkov, the postmaster, and Rezatskin, the clerk, under the direct supervision of the Squire, who had inherited the village. The Squire handled them as was usual between men of affairs and minor government officials. Unlike in your time, this was considered no corruption at all but the accepted state of affairs.

Our village lay in scraggly lanes of huts on both sides of the highroad to Minsk, between Pukop eight miles to the east and Svutz about seven to the west. Pukop was larger than Golinsk, had more Jews, supported its own rabbi, contained a military garrison, and was owned by more than one Squire; indeed there were even not-so-poor Jews to be found in Pukop. Svutz was sleepier, dirtier than Pukop, more like Golinsk except that many of the Svutzker Jews had long since taken themselves to America. Those remaining were mostly cattle-traders who lived by stealing not only from the non-Jews, but from each other. We feared and avoided them and cursed them for being bad Jews and good troublemakers. Only when times were very hard and I needed the business very badly did I ever offer to sew a coat or a suit of clothes for a Svutzker. And more often than not, on those rare occasions, I would bring home a keg of illegally distilled alcohol instead of the cash I had been promised.

We liked the Pukopper Jews but unfortunately they did not care for us. The worst of their four tailors sewed a better garment than I, the best of our two; their synagogue had a stone foundation and ours had none; they could support a rabbi, the venerable Sussya-ben-Mordecai, and the best we could do was to wait for some itinerant rabbi or other to come to us, or to snare, from time to time, a student from the rabbinical school in Minsk who would come for the Passover or for the week of the High Holidays and then never be seen by us again. We were too poor to make it attractive to the rabbinical students we invited, but also it was more than that. Reb Maisha, our aged learner of the youth, the teacher of our school in the synagogue, had embroiled himself in a twenty-year-old feud with the head of the Minsker rabbinical school, Rabbi Hillel-ben-Joseph, who was the cousin of Rabbi Sussya-ben-Mordecai of Pukop, and we of Golinsk for the

most part stood together with Reb Maisha in the controversy. We held
that piety had to be more precious than learning, and that to be too
poor to support a rabbi was nothing to be criticized about. The Pukoppers and the Minsker Rabbi both whipped us with the accusation that
we were not so poor as we were stubborn and narrow-minded. But
we Golinskers bitterly rejected anything so demeaning and we affirmed
the purity of our piety. "Pukop is twice our size," we would tell them,
"and you have several Squires to use to play one against the other,
while all we have is Konayev, let him only choke to death before
evening prayers."

But after the Tsar's assassination in '81, when the military garrison
moved into Pukop and Rabbi Sussya-ben-Mordecai suffered his stroke,
both sides quieted down. Each held its position without any attack
upon it. We enjoyed good relations with the Pukopper Jews as long
as nothing was ever mentioned by a Pukopper about Reb Maisha's
"disgraceful ignorance of the Holy Law," or of "the true piety" of a
Golinsker. Truthfully speaking, some of us envied, secretly, the com-
parative well-being of the Pukoppers but we honestly could not puzzle
out ways to live with the Squire any better than the ones we had settled
upon.

To understand how we had to live in Golinsk, let me say something
about the place. The nineteen Jewish families in '85, about one-third
of the village, lived in unpainted log huts to the north of the highroad, on land rented from the Squire's father by our own elders when
they came from Poland. They could build and own their huts, but not
the land. Fifty yards behind our huts stood the synagogue, and everything else in Golinsk was on the non-Jewish side of the road.

This comprised the smithy, the four taverns, the three brothels, the
post office, and market sheds, the druggist's, the church, the shoe-shop,
the feed man, the Squire's warehouse and sheds, and surrounding them,
in a rising slope, the huts of the villagers; then the more substantial
houses of the postmaster and the feed man, and then the church and
Father Semyon's house, and then the stone house of Dr. Ostrov, the
Squire's personal physician, and finally, on top of the hill looking

down upon us all, the Squire's little fortress, half villa and half castle. At the very top of the rise, behind circular tiers of white birches, the Squire's graystone turrets stood concealed in the summer, and from November to April looked like roly-poly sentinels. No Jew had ever gone further up the hill than the doctor's house, excepting by special command of the Squire, so we called Dr. Ostrov's "Halfway-to-Heaven." We stayed mostly on our side except to do business across the road. Gershon sewed shoes in his hut, Naftoli-Dovid made and peddled the yeasty white beer called kvas, I and Aaron-ben-Kalman were the tailors, Hertz made greases, Nochim traded butter and cheese and played wedding-fiddle, Laib-Shmul was our ritual meat-slaughterer, Berel-the-Ox our watercarrier . . . and so on.

We were everyday Jews in a populated place too tiny even to be a speck on the map. None of us ate more than one decent meal a week, and if the week seemed too long to cope with, too dreary and senseless, we would perk ourselves up a bit thinking of the Sabbath to come — the lighting of the candles at Friday sunset, the beautiful ways the wives had of putting their well-worked palms to their temples, covering their faces for a moment as they uttered the peaceful ritual of the candle-lighting — the dignity of our Sabbath tables, the unity of our clean dear joy, the white cloths, the peace of the shared ecstasy of the Sabbath — the thankful pride in our wives' eyes as we smacked our lips over our savory soup, our slab of meat; and the pudgy curves of the Sabbath loaf baked in twists and jeweled with poppy seeds. Often the loaf did for the week and the soup became thinner and thinner and the nightly potatoes less and less filling, but this only meant that the Sabbath again was nearing.

And in the slack of the week our prayers seemed to take longer and feel less demanding of the ear of The One Above. We intoned and cantillated with simpler variations and the smallest item of village gossip sent us into epics of interpretive cross-analysis. We were hungry; we talked to pass the time against the coming of the whispers we never dared listen to as they rose within ourselves, excepting when we prayed: "O God, why hast Thou forsaken me?"

But there was always the Sabbath, and in the summer picking berries and fruit by the day for the Squire, and cabbages and cucumbers too, eating them as we picked; and that was our village, our home, our Russia, where all our suffering and strength started from, all the beauty and bravery our children were to take to America, which most of us would never see. We knew piety amid filth, and the hardship of the Squire. We could be only what we had to be — simple, narrow, unique people. We Golinskers laughed and sang as we beat our chests and cried — so often, so often without any necessity, only circumstance. People can live to be a hundred and never perceive the differences between necessity and circumstance. But the moment you are dead, it is clear.

The Squire's house, if you remember, looked down upon the village. And when we prayed in the synagogue the sounds would seem to rise directly into his face, something never mentioned even by our most rabid tongue-wagger, Tzippe-Sora. We had such a fear of the man, or better to say, of the titular head of the family Konayev, that during the time we prayed we tried to imagine he had never lived. In the depth and purity of our daily devotions we shut out any belief in the existence of such a sniveling nincompoop, such a professional son-in-law whose whole career was to outlive his wife's father and thus inherit the means of freeing himself from his unhappy life as a country squire with nothing better to take up his time but think of ways to squeeze enough money out of his village to go on junkets to Petersburg and Paris. The Squire had taken some education in his youth and had gone as far as to consider the study of medicine, but had fallen into what turned out to be a comical marriage dictated by his father. So the keen young student had become a horseback-riding squire not quite finished with picturing himself the cultivated man buried in the provincial hole. From time to time Konayev would take out his old medical books and pore over them; and in a locked cabinet of his study he kept his collection of badly translated pornographic romances ordered direct from Paris, with pen-and-ink illustrations. When the mood struck him he would bring a few of these books down to the brothel operated by Profim Alexi Buzarov, his steward's brother; he had become used to a girl there named Varya who worked well with him in imitating certain of the pen-and-ink drawings from his Parisian collection.

In such a fashion, rotted by impatience and disgust at his father-in-law's apparent immortality, the Squire tutored himself for the life to be his when he would come into his inheritance. Roweled every day by his dull noisy wife and the two marionettes who were his daughters, and irritated by the inadequate appreciation of his basic qualities on the part of all of us illiterate semi-starved Golinskers and outlying peasants, Jews and non-Jews together, the Squire had applied himself over the years to cultivating a permanent and sour sadness out of which he brewed his aggravating ideas and contemptuous froths of nervous wrath. Like stones flung into a stream the circles of his anger touched all who lived on the many circumferences of his arrogance. With the joyless implacability of a foolish boy poking a stick into a beehive, and with so self-satisfying a bitterness that it often seemed to be not there, this graying little person with the belly of a carrying sow and the voice of a castrated tenor kept himself busy with his village, seeking little ways to make more out of us with the dull persistence of a hungry man chewing a clean bone. Through his steward, Vassily Buzarov, he knew everyone's business, and by the use of the village bailiff, Rezatskin, the Squire quite well estimated how much he could draw from us, linking this through his Vassily to a steady traffic in illegal alcohol, in which at one time or another he involved us all. There was no question of refusing when the word came that Vassily wanted to talk to any of us; we knew he was going to assign us our stations and tasks relative to one of the Squire's schemes; and we knew we would perform our duties as suggested; for together with the regional military commander, Colonel Vladimir Yakol stationed in Pukop, the Squire each year handpicked the Golinskers he deemed ready for military conscription. Since the Colonel's real interest lay in jolly living, by which he meant over-eating and over-gambling, and since the Squire fraternized with him in these activities and made good the difference between what the

Colonel had to spend each year and what he spent, we knew that to defy him was to throw away our sons. For this crazy power over our sons, for this alone we feared him more than we hated him. In his presence we tore the hats from our heads and had he asked it we gladly would have washed his feet and drunk the water. To obey the Squire in all things was of course no guarantee that our sons would be spared, but many of them were. My own Daneel, my eldest, I had early trained to be an efficient wagon-man; at the age of twelve he could take a horse and wagon cleanly through the smallest trail in the darkest night, to load contraband noiselessly, to hide it perfectly, and to sell it at the best price. Buzarov had commended him to the Squire, and when his name had turned up on the '83 list handed over by Colonel Yakol, the Squire had drawn his pen through it. For this I and other Jewish fathers served him well. Not only did we haul and hide and sell his contraband for him, turning over the exact sums down to the last kopeck, but we plowed and sowed and cultivated and harvested for him; and when we busied ourselves pursuing our bread, we sent the wives and children into his fields.

The Squire liked himself on a horse. He took steady gallops across his land. When he happened to pass any of our young girls working in the fields, he liked to slow up sometimes and tease the girls with his riding crop. "I'll bet you have a pretty little crack down there," he used often to say, giggling. The girls would burst into tears of fright, or run away, and then the Squire would enlarge the game, chasing them on his big gray horse, Commander, until they fell to the ground. In this way the Squire studied their temperaments. Then during the winter that followed when the weathers prevented regular excursions to his favorite fun-houses in Minsk and Pinsk, and after he had returned from his gala expeditions to Petersburg or once Paris, he would become depressed by the local prostitutes and remember the girls he had seen in the fields, our girls, our young hard Jewish plums, the summer girls he had chased on his horse; and he would give thought to those who had tried to joke about his sportsman's chasing game, of the ones who understood the value of a smile and an angry shake of the bosom. He would send for Buzarov and sit down with him to study the possibilities. Drinking brandy and nibbling on nuts, Buzarov would pinpoint the likeliest candidates for the exercise of the Squire's sexual play.

"This must be the one who smiled when you flicked her," Buzarov might say, lifting his glass to savor the cognac Konayev stocked by the case. "Dark eyes and a mouth like a curving Japanese bridge, you say? Ah, of course . . . she's Nochim's middle daughter . . . good, good . . . he has a son of fifteen, Nochim. . . ."

And of course the attractive older sister of a fifteen-year-old Jewish boy was the ideal thing. How could a good sister be unwilling to take the trinkets Buzarov would bring as a token of the Squire's friendliness to the family? And, it followed, how could the girl refuse to thank the Squire personally for the boon to the family? Anything less than complete humility in the entire affair was to invite serious consequences.

On the two or three times a winter that Buzarov would come over to our side of the village with gifts from the Squire to one of our daughters, we knew exactly what had to be done. Somebody would immediately be sent to Yushin, the druggist, for a bottle of stomach oil. The neighbor would bring the oil to the girl's house, and she would have it poured into her. Shortly then she would become deathly sick, during which time the father and Buzarov would sit down to methods of conciliation. These usually amounted to two things, the bribing of Buzarov personally with cash and promises of future personal services, and a pledge of added assistance to the Squire in any way he wished it. With a perfectly straight face Vassily Buzarov would march back to the Squire and report that the girl he wanted now had consumption, or had already been spoiled by the peasants, or had begun to grow a mustache in addition to having gone all scaly and having a running nose. Thus Buzarov would play upon the Squire's easily mobilized disgust, running him through his entire repertory of effete renunciations which the Squire persuaded himself were the evidences of a fundamentally aristocratic temperament.

Yet I heard of many cases that had gone the other way, with the

Squire's father, and I myself saw how it turned out with Lenka, Nochim's eldest, and my Squire. The girl of sixteen, charmed by Buzarov's presentations, had got the idea of being herself able to outwit the Squire and still gain protection for her family. Her father Nochim had well earned his reputation for being a seriously airy fool, and Lenka's desire to do something for her nearest family had at least a logical foundation, if not a sensible direction. But her daring profited her nothing. She came down the hill to find her clothes on the step and the door shut to her. We did not judge Nochim to be a good husband nor more than an erratic father, but when she came home with pierced ears and swinging a bagful of walnuts, he flew into a rage, rode her halfway to Svutz, forced her out of the wagon in the middle of the night, and then turned around for home where he started a long fast. We were criticized in Pukop for this, and in Svutz we were laughed at for not having made a good thing out of the Squire's fancy for Lenka. Later that year we received news of her; Lenka had stabbed a sergeant-major in Riga. Nochim refused to believe it. "To begin with," he would say out loud, "what was she doing in Riga? And how could she ever stab anyone, much less a sergeant-major? Why, the girl used to get sick every time she tried to clean a chicken!"

We understood, silently, that Nochim had acted correctly in putting Lenka out of our lives. Acts of surrender like hers endangered our survival. And another thing we understood, all, quite well, so well that we neither laughed nor cried over it; we knew that without us Golinsker Jews the Squire would have slit his throat at the age of forty.

Some considered Mottel-ben-Kalman even more dangerous to our community than the Squire. "From the Squire, after all, we know what to expect," was how Laib-Shmul, the meat slaughterer, said it. "With the Squire you are always looking for the knife in his hand and you are ready to kneel or run at any minute. But with Mottel . . . who eats like a gentile and lives like a gentile and even thinks like a gentile, yet he's a Jew too . . . from such a man who knows what to expect but troubles?"

Mottel-ben-Kalman had long since earned our spitting scorn for having given up his everything, his Jewishness. Since returning from the army, not even once had he behaved like a Jew, not even during the High Holidays. He was mixed in with all the peasant riffraff; he lived in a room in one of the inns, worked in the smithy of Profim Alexi Buzarov, and carried forward a hoodlum's comradeship with Profim's brother Vassily, the Squire's steward.

His contempt for us was clear-cut and wordless. He neither came to the synagogue nor thought to fast on the Day of Atonement; he ate pig, drank anything, and smoked on the Sabbath; and during spring and fall maneuvers when the Pukop garrison would spill over into our village, he kept himself busy night after night, running soldiers into the town's brothels in exchange for small favors on both sides.

Still, some of us were sorry for him. Despite his terrible sins, Reb Maisha and I recognized his profound bitterness — a bitterness known, expressed, and in some way connected to us, a forlorn and sterile state made so because Mottel had been unable to water it with faith and transform it into its opposite. Mottel had shut himself out, had turned his back upon us. He could not say, with us, every morning, "Blessed art Thou, O Lord our God, King of the universe, who has given us the Law of truth, and hast planted everlasting life in our midst."

We had marked him an outcast, burdening our children with punishments whenever they ran into Profim's smithy and talked to him. We accepted Mottel as a casualty in the running war being fought against us through the centuries. And to remind ourselves of this, we remembered to call Mottel to the altar on the High Holidays to read a piece of the Holy Law, even though we knew he was not there.

For the Squire we felt a steady stew of fear, suspicion, and hatred. We wrapped this fear in bandages of philosophic condemnations and epigrammatic demolishments; as Reb Maisha used to say, "The Squire, his tongue should fall out, is a fox who lives like a tiger and who will die like a dog." But the scorn we held for Mottel pitched itself on a lower, more fundamental key, rarely stated and always felt, like a theme simmering in its variations, rising and falling. Many a time we would spit at the mention of Mottel's name (as when he would come to us talking for Vassily Buzarov and arrange the details of some risk we had to take for the Squire), but the rule for Mottel was bitter silence and pity for him.

Mottel himself never seemed concerned about whether or not he was worth a spit. Perhaps he thought we had inner reasons to tolerate him; perhaps he believed that by helping us make ourselves useful to the Squire he was therefore prolonging the lives of our sons; or perhaps he held that we feared him. There were grounds for that. In my own case, being the first tailor of the village (Aaron, Mottel's brother, was the other, and two so different brothers you never heard of), I was obliged to buy all my cloth and supplies from agents who paid the Squire fees to trade in the village. Sometimes on my sewing trips I would meet tradesmen who offered me goods and supplies at prices well below what I always paid but then I would have had to suspend buying from the agent authorized by the Squire. And doing this involved an unthinkable risk. By order of Selenkov we Jewish tradesmen had to submit monthly written reports of our business activity, listing all purchases, sales, and commissions; and this monthly revelation of how much could be mulcted from us became an irritating expense in itself; the form printed in Russian had to be filled out in Russian, so we were forced to hire someone to do it for us. The least hostile of Russian penmen in our village was Mottel, who had acquired some command of the language during his army service. And so we paid him thirty kopecks a month apiece to fill out our reports, hoping against hope that somewhere inside of him was left enough decency to write down what we told him to.

Sometimes we would say, "Mottel, with everything you had to do in the army, where did you find time to learn Russian?" He would scowl and say, "And if I told you, would you believe me?"

One day Mottel said to me, "I cannot write your monthly report any more."

"And why not?"

"How do I know you are not lying in what you say you bought and sold?"

"And suppose I am? Where is that your risk?" I demanded.

"I am ashamed of you," he told me, grinning so widely that I could see all his brown teeth lying in the center of his beard. "After all I too am a Jew."

"To the Squire, yes. To us, no."

"And being a Jew," he continued, delighting himself with his words, "you have more to lose by being dishonest with me. For is it not written that one Jew should not involve another Jew in his sins?"

"I am honest in my reports," I said, "only because he owns me more completely than he owns the gentiles. If he decides to hate one gentile, he has him killed. But should he decide to hate one Jew, he would try to have us all in the earth."

"A good answer," Mottel replied. "The answer of a poor man who will always be poor."

He took the printed form then, and made out my report for me. He also took my thirty kopecks. I left him with anger in me against him, for I certainly knew he disbelieved the honesty of my statements in my report. I wanted to go back to him and say, "You think like a gentile. The first thought you have when you see a Jew is that the Jew is cheating. That the Jew wants only to get rich! But have you ever thought, Mottel, of what we would have to do to retain those riches? We would have to throw away the heart of our Jewishness! We would have to put the affairs of this world higher in our minds than our ultimate redemption in the kingdom of heaven!"

Mottel would not have believed me. But I soon forgot the whole thing. I had been born to poverty, knew little else, like most Jews. We had our Law and our God, had gained and lost through the centuries in blood and money, and I really could not see how a Jew could retain his riches and still remain a Jew. Instinctively we in Golinsk smelled something fishy in the stories about great millionaires like the Rothschilds, whose existence we did not doubt but whose Jewishness we certainly did. Naftoli-Dovid, our nearest to a drunkard, once said something we all agreed was not in the least characteristic of him. "If Rothschild is as rich as they say," Naftoli-Dovid remarked, "why doesn't he send someone to Golinsk to see who is too poor to get himself wine and unleavened bread for the Passover? Plain talk . . . Rothschild has forgotten he is a Jew and I am sorry for him. The only person to be pitied more than a rich Jew is a poor one!"

Out of those few words of our village life in the Golinsk of 1885, you can see how our faith and our piety had to be our most precious possession. From our piety we wove ourselves mantles invisible to our enemies but quite simply warm and easily recognized Jew-by-Jew. Everything in our lives, everything we felt in our souls, told us our piety inevitably would lead us to the kingdom of heaven in The Other World, and so it became more than a clean dear joy to us. Through all the centuries of our history we held our piety to be the most important necessity of our lives on earth. But necessity and circumstance are twins, after all, and when we lived on the earth we never knew that when we saw one, like as not we were really looking at the other. Only after you die can you tell which is which; and then it's only like a trick.

Thus (Did I not begin by saying we Golinskers were long-winded?), I conclude my "hello."

Now, of the deaths of two landsmen, Aaron and Leah, man and wife, together. He was Mottel's brother and the second tailor of the village. They died on a Friday in '85 between New Year's and the Day of Atonement.

On the Monday morning before that bad Friday, in the first week of our New Year, Mottel sent a gentile boy to my hut. The boy said, "Mottel wants to see you at the smithy tonight at ten o'clock."

It was September. The grapes had been all in for over a week and doubtless the Squire had reduced much of it to juice and raw mash to be cooked into alcohol. The pressing and barreling was done in the open on his own grounds but the hauling away and the cooking and the selling of the illegal liquor was our job. I knew from experience that Mottel, acting for Buzarov, acting for the Squire, would sit me down when I came to the smithy and explain the who-when-and-what.

Ordinarily I would have gone to the smithy as directed, but this happened to be a holy week, the week of the High Holidays — hardly a time to spoil by galloping down side roads in the middle of the night, holding tightly to the reins, praying nothing would happen to the horse or the barrels, and imagining the sounds of policemen's swords clanking behind me, mixing with the angry words of the dried-up Dansonov, our provincial magistrate, leveling damning accusations from the height of his justice's bench with his eyes rolling meanwhile like a hooked fish's. Then again, what if the order came to haul the contraband on the Day of Atonement itself?

So though my horse needed shoes I ignored the summons to the smithy. Let it wait, I told myself, until after the Day of Atonement; but on that Monday night my sleep was fitful, my head cracking with bothering ideas. What if Mottel told Buzarov I did not appear? And what if Buzarov told the Squire, and what if the Squire happened to be in a bad mood? And if the Squire suspected my absence was because I did not care to work for him during Holy Week, wouldn't that possibly unleash his hatred for us at the most sacred time of the year? All that next day my eyes were as heavy as my heart. I could hardly see what I was sewing, and to make it all the more depressing, I happened to be sewing for a Svutzker. Even my horse, Gritka, could hardly drag himself along for need of two new front shoes, and there was no smithy in Svutz.

I returned to Golinsk in time for evening prayers. Afterwards while we were still standing around together, Aaron came to me, the usual frown on his large tired face, his long chin seeming, as always, to point his little beard right through his chest. By the way he began with me I knew he had something on his mind. He did not step up close to me and begin to talk in the ordinary Golinsker flow, but he stood off a bit and said only, "Yeersel . . ."

"Well, then — what?"

"I don't like to drag favors out of you so soon in the New Year . . ."

"To grant a favor is a blessing at any time of the year," I said shortly, pulling my coat collar about my ears; it had become unseasonably chilly that afternoon, as gray and as glum as November, suiting my mood. I began walking toward the door, knowing Aaron would follow.

Moving down the lane toward our clumps of huts I turned to Aaron. "It must be a tremendous favor you want."

"Yes, doubtless. I'm only thinking, Yeersel. But . . . maybe you're in a position to let me take your horse and wagon for a day?"

Aaron spoke with such a helpless hopeless throwing-away of his words that I became immediately irritated; one would suppose, by the way he sounded, that I was the hardest-hearted person in the province. But in the next second I forgave him; after all wasn't he the second tailor, competition? And he had no horse and wagon of his own, but had to trudge the roads weighed down with goods on his back and his heavy tailor's iron hanging from his pants-belt. I grumbled, "What's the matter?"

"There's business, I can use a few bolts of cloth."

"Is already good." Then more softly, "Far away, eh, Aaron?"

"No, only to the Parsovs'."

"But that's near, right here out of town. What's the horse and wagon for?"

"To get goods. In Minsk. I know, Yeersel, I know . . . it's forbidden to buy goods anywhere but from our piggish agent here, but who can afford to pay a Rezatskin-price? In Minsk they'll wait for the money, too."

"Buying in Minsk is risky."

"Let it then be risky."

"It doesn't pay to go to Minsk, Aaron. Further, the horse needs shoes and — "

"Shoes I'll buy, I'll take Gritka straight into Mottel's the first thing."

"No good." I was about to mention Mottel's summons to me but I thought, "Why give Aaron another worry?" I simply added, "He'll ask questions, and you well know he can't be trusted to monkey up your monthly report."

"Well," Aaron told me gently, "even though to Mottel a brother is like a dog's brother, I don't think he'll monkey it down."

"To begin with, Gritka needs shoes immediately. Minsk isn't just down the hill, you know — "

"I already said about the shoes, Yeersel, I myself will — "

"Then suppose you're caught buying outside goods? And it develops my horse and wagon brought it into the village? Hn?"

"Oh, it's certainly a tremendous favor," he said, sighing.

"Between two tailors in one village," I replied, "is there such a thing as a 'small' favor?"

We kept on clumping down the lane toward our huts. The wind had whistled itself up to a loud warning of something unseasonably sharp to come, and I had an unexpected "winter feeling" up and down my back. My stomach felt tighter, as it always did in the winter, and I felt smaller, and the whole world seemed to swell up larger. Our legs shuffled mounds of fallen leaves away from us, and I peered down the lane to spy the lights of my hut, where all was warm inside and the table set and everybody waiting to say, "Papa's home."

"Of course," Aaron added, "a person considering making tricks in cloth-buying shouldn't drag in other people."

"Minsk isn't Svutz, it's forty miles. You can't carry goods that far on your back, and to think of hiring someone to bring it to the village is only to hire yourself a police agent, I'm warning you."

"Push it here, push it there, it still doesn't fall down . . . I have business if I can get cloth. But I can't pay for cloth."

"All right, Aaron — what cloth and how much?"

"For coats. Black. Three overcoats and four jackets, one for a child."

"Ay, it's a good order, so much I don't have to spare. And anyway I haven't for real winter coats."

"Well, then," Aaron said, throwing up his hands suddenly. "Oh, to the devil with it!"

He turned away and started up the lane toward the synagogue. I went after him. "Where are you going?"

"I'll sit in the synagogue, and something will come to me."

"But home — your wife — the boys?"

"And will they say something I can listen to?"

"Look," I begged, "have a little sense, Aaron. Go to Rezatskin, talk it over, take credit!"

"Take credit?" he flung at me. "Since when am I such a beautiful risk? Since when can I go pick credit like a flower? If I'm such a good credit, go out and lend and give it to me!"

"Aaron-ben-Kalman," I said firmly, holding him by the sleeve, angry with him for being so forlorn. "Be not such an infant, be a man with a brain! Go to your big customer, three coats and four jackets, and grind him into giving you at least a small cash payment in advance — then run with the advance to Rezatskin, put it down against the bill for the goods, and start sewing!"

"That would be fine," Aaron replied. "Very easily fine, only my arrangement with the family Parsov is that for the three coats and four jackets, I am to get two chickens a week for a year together with not less than eight eggs a time."

"Ay," I nodded, when Aaron sighed again after quoting to me from his agreement with the Parsovs. It was a good bargain, two chickens a week for a year, and eggs . . . but no cash, not even a ruble, for the agent. "Come on, Aaron, let's go home. We'll think of something yet."

The sky seemed to hang low, under the wind. There were no stars. I thought again of my wife Bosha and the supper waiting for me, and it passed through my mind with such a rip, "Aaron won't be able to wriggle out safely with the two chickens a week for a whole year." And then as we walked towards our huts together for the second time, it fell into my mind — "How simple! I'll go to Shnipsel the Innkeeper in Pukop and borrow five rubles for Aaron to give the agent!" I had heard that Shnipsel sometimes put out formidable sums at interest (impious to us Golinskers, a sin, but innkeepers were known to live dangerous lives). "Don't worry any more, Aaron," I cried out suddenly, "it's all settled!"

I must have taken him by surprise for he almost jumped out of his foot-rags when my voice boomed at him. "Thank God!" he choked out. "So you're letting me take the horse after all!"

I had nothing like that in my head. I was about to let him know I'd get the cash he needed for his advance from Shnipsel; but exactly in this kind of a crazy way is how a circumstance pushes itself into a matter between living men. Once Aaron had said, "So you're letting me take the horse after all," with such relief in his voice, such a feeling of having been saved by some miracle of reckless generosity on my part, it shot through my head like lightning that Mottel still expected me to appear at the smithy to get my orders for hauling contraband during the week of the High Holidays. But if I could truthfully say, "Mottel, I can't. I haven't the use of my horse and wagon," then I had an excuse; I would then be unable to dirty the High Holidays by hauling contraband. By giving Aaron the horse and wagon I was really getting rather than granting a favor; so I forgot all about Shnipsel in 'a flash. "Aaron . . . and suppose you started out for Minsk right away, tonight, and kept Gritka to a walk until you reached the smithy in Ludva . . . then it wouldn't be too hard on his forelegs, it's only that I wouldn't want him to lose a loose shoe . . ."

"No," Aaron replied quietly, holding back his joy in deference to my worry about the horse. "I wouldn't let him go faster than a walk until Ludva, naturally, and at night the road will be empty and it will be no problem at all."

"And once in Minsk — "

"In Minsk there are a hundred blacksmiths."

"So in hell, Rezatskin. Take the horse."

"Well . . . Yeersel . . . live only to be a hundred, you and your children's children."

"But you'll stop in Ludva's smithy for the two front shoes?"

"Of course."

"You won't wait until Minsk?"

"No. When I mentioned the hundred blacksmiths in Minsk, Yeersel . . . I really didn't know what I was saying. Ay, I'm happy!" He began to weep tears of relief, and as it was in my own nature to bring up tears when another wept, I cried with him. I cried in thanks for the blessing Aaron had unknowingly granted me. "Well," I said finally, wiping my nose, "enough of this or we'll both drown before anything else. When can you bring back the horse and wagon?"

"Tomorrow is Wednesday. Thursday night, easily."

"All right. Another thing, very important. Don't bring the goods into the village, Aaron. Stop off at the Parsovs' and leave it with them."

"Naturally."

"And better take Leah. In case there's to be any questioning, you went with Leah to visit her sister in Minsk, right?"

"Her sister and her paralyzed father."

"So it then becomes entirely a family visit, right?"

"What else?"

We were at the foot of the path. Before us lay the clumps of our huts, and I felt a straining to run home. "I'll tell my Bosha you're leaving your two boys with us. Come for Gritka in an hour. And when you're in Minsk, give a look into the Muddytown synagogue for me."

He went to his hut and I to mine. In an hour his sons, Laib and Shim, were guests in my house, playing games with my children, and Aaron and Leah were on their way to Minsk in my wagon; and I never saw them alive again.

The next day, the Wednesday, passed well. At morning prayers in the synagogue I explained Aaron's absence. I had to use a few lies but this did not bother me to any extent. I knew the landsmen would have approved had they known why. They accepted what I said: "Aaron came to me last night and told me his wife had a dream that frightened her, that her paralyzed father in Minsk had died. He asked me for my horse and wagon. They're on their way to Minsk."

Later that morning, I sent my youngest, Mayer, to Mottel with the news that Aaron and Leah had my wagon until at least the following night, and the afternoon I spent in the house of Yushin, the druggist, making over an old coat of his for his father-in-law who lived somewhere in the Novgorod district. Yushin's wife hovered over me like a horsefly, correcting my measurements and counting the stitches. The coat was to be her Christmas present to her father and she wanted it

sent right away, and a perfect fit. "You understand, now?" she kept
repeating in her grating, nervous voice which made the Russian words
sound even more irritating. "It's for our Christmas, you understand,
and Papa gets so cold in the winter, it must fit correctly the first time,
it mustn't be traveling back and forth between here and Novgorod all
winter, is that understood?"

"Yes."

"They say it's going to be a bad winter, and Papa freezes in winter,
is that understood? I mean about the fit, that his collar must rise very
high, well above the ears?"

"Understood, understood."

With winter work in my hands and the skies holding gray and
gloomy, and yesterday's wind still sending clouds of leaves down in
big circles, the summer was already something far gone. In four days
it would be our most solemn holiday, the Day of Atonement, and I
could not remember so winterlike a High Holiday week. Meanwhile
I kept wondering whether Aaron had really stopped at the smithy in
Ludva; I'd forgotten to make sure he had enough money for horseshoes. But Wednesday passed, much like any other day. It was a novel
thing to have Aaron's boys with us, but then we were used to having
Shim and Laib run in and out of the house. Several years before I had
surprised Laib and my daughter Rochel together, playing a childish
game with their little bodies, and it had been a big upset to me at the
time. But that was all forgotten now and I really felt they were almost
my own, the two boys. Which, of course, actually happened later on
when Shim married Rochel. But at the time of which I tell they were
simply the children of our second tailor who had gone to Minsk in my
wagon for the purpose of gaining himself and his family two chickens
a week for a year, and eggs.

But by nightfall of the next day, the Thursday I expected to see
Aaron swing my horse and wagon into my yard, there was a different
face on me. That afternoon the weather had passed from "winterlike"
to real winter. An angry snow slanted down from the clouds that had
been glowering for two days, and the wind opened its mouth and

showed its teeth. The children of the village rejoiced in snow-fights but at evening prayers my frame shook with the tenseness of my praying, and when I came to the part of the ritual that said, "Forgive us, O our Father, for we have sinned; pardon us, O our King, for we have transgressed; for Thou dost pardon and forgive. Blessed art Thou, O Lord, who art gracious and dost abundantly forgive. Look upon our affliction and plead our cause, and redeem us speedily for Thy name's sake," I took it as a most personal matter of supplication.

When Aaron and Leah failed to arrive at nine that night, I felt annoyance with them for not having come on time; I urged myself to believe that the storm was delaying them, and that they should have had the sense to leave earlier. At midnight I rose from bed, put on clothes, wrapped my feet in winter burlap, and dragged myself through the one-foot snow to Aaron's hut, only to find them not there. On the way back I cursed them for not having come on time, and then in the next minute thanked them for being so smart as to not to have tried to make it through the storm. What a fool I called myself! I went home and slept.

Tomorrow . . . of course they'd come tomorrow.

The first thing that fell into my senses when I opened my eyes that Friday morning was, "I'll go get Aaron and together we'll walk to the synagogue for morning prayers." The snow still fell, but now gently, as I rapped the shutters of his hut. "Still not home?" I whispered. No, not home. Now it became a question of what to do. Should I go to morning prayers and then think of some way to make a search — yes! go to the Parsovs', perhaps they laid over the night there! — or try to catch Dimitri, the postman, who had a horse and wagon, right away? Because of the storm Dimitri was going to start off on his rounds either much earlier or much later than the usual seven o'clock . . . but I didn't know which, and I therefore decided I would have to miss morning prayers. The few times before when I had missed, I had experienced an emptiness no matter how logical the reasons for my absences. There were too few of us for even one to miss; we needed our full strength each time to raise up the vision which was to bulwark us against the onslaughts of the day. We needed, too, the presence of every one of us to heighten the buoyancy of our private contemplations, to give rich volume to our "Amens," to guarantee no lessening in the daily renovation of our faith. We needed every voice of yesterday, save those God chose to take away, as we remembered and considered and sustained each other in our adorations. And what I needed to be sure of on that Friday morning, what I needed even more than the blessing of attending morning prayers, was to know that God had not seen fit to take away Aaron and Leah in the storm. Such a tragedy, I already knew, would not lend itself to easy explanations in my mind. I feared the ordeal of such an attack on my faith and more than all I feared the finger of guilt pointed at me, and the voice of God saying, "Yeersel, it is your sin. Yes, you did commit the sin of Micah."

So I crossed the road to their side of the village in high quick steps, avoiding the drifts and trying to keep my knees dry, for they used to stiffen and become painful with dampness. I had a good chance of catching Dimitri before he carried the post to the district. Dimitri had little use for himself, much less for me, but he appreciated the worth of a ruble and for a ruble he would ride me up to the Parsovs'.

I thought of this as I made my way up to his hut. It was one thing to console myself with the thought that I would find Aaron and Leah at the Parsovs', but quite another not to be certain they were in fact there. Shim and Laib had already begun to miss their parents; and truthfully speaking, I had already begun to feel the weight of the sin of Micah, of having been "pure with wicked balances and with a bag of deceitful weights."

With these thoughts tumbling about in my sleepy and miserable head, I knocked on the door of Dimitri's hut, which sat off the lane behind Father Semyon's house. Waiting for the door to open, I realized that Dimitri must have already gone; there were wagon tracks and hoofmarks in the snow. Without waiting for the door to open, then, I ran down the lane, stumbling in the wettish snow, just in time to see Dimitri passing down the lane to the highroad; he had evidently been around on the other side of Father Semyon's.

"Dimitri, Dimitri!" I gave him my highest call, and he turned his head as he sat under the canvas hood of the mail-wagon, the reins in his hand, startled a bit out of his morning calm by the sound of a voice in the snow. I ran to the wagon, my chest bursting with unaccustomed exertion; without saying anything I climbed up on the seat next to him. He took a good look at me, then. "Hey — get off!"

I put my hand in my pocket and took out a ruble note. "If, please, you will be so good to take this?"

"Where were you coming from?" he said, putting it under his fur cap.

"From your house."

"I suppose you woke Yulga."

"I didn't notice." Without waiting to explain further, I added, "And now, sir, if you will please be so good — "

"How good?" he interrupted. "I'll tell you . . . for one rotten ruble's worth . . . and I'll be the judge of that."

"You pass the Parsovs' on your rounds, just drop me off there, I ask no more."

A look of weary annoyance darkened his face, and he spoke as a child whines petulantly to a harsh father. "So for one miserable ruble I'm to misuse a government conveyance! For one miserable ruble I'm to say 'Yes, my Baron'?"

"Sir," I said to him, tears in my eyes, "I appreciate your joking this way, but relieve me of my troubles, take me to the Parsovs' now."

He shoved me in what he considered was just a light way, but his elbow felt like a club on my chest. "It's breaking rules, I mean taking passengers in an official government vehicle. Here we are side by side. For one rotten ruble you become a guest of the Tsar. Suppose Buzarov or somebody official sees it, what next?" He spit across my face into the snow. "Thoughts . . . they will think Dimitri favors Jews, pursues operations with them, takes bribes. Clear?"

"Clear," I replied, "but the truth is, Dimitri, all I have is one ruble."

"My dear man." He spit across my face again, this time nearer to my nose. "This isn't a money matter."

"Then return the ruble and I'll get down."

"What ruble?"

So Dimitri had only been joking. "That's right. What ruble indeed?"

"You never gave me a ruble, never!"

"No indeed, sir. I simply beg of you the favor. Take me to the Parsovs'. I can't walk in snow, my knees . . ."

"Very well — only — one favor deserves another, clear?" I waited. "You're the tailor, clear? Well, I need a good leather patch on the elbows of this coat, and as you Jews say, one hand washes the other."

"Clear. I will patch you," I mumbled, "only," I added, my voice shaking with a fear I dared not show, "I don't have the leather, you'll have to bring it to me."

"Well, meanwhile . . . if I just can't . . . you'll throw some of your old strong goods into the bargain, then."

"Hit the horse, hit the horse," I replied. I didn't consider it the worst conclusion; what if I had had to take out the second ruble from my other pocket? It was bad enough that it had to cost even the one; with it I could have gotten my wife Bosha a really warm shawl. I thought about my wife as we started the ride to the Parsovs'. I was sitting under the canvas hood, I reminded myself, protected from the snow, while Bosha would be walking the quarter mile to the stream, carrying dirty clothes on her shoulders. The ground was bumpy and in the snow, on the way back, she would have to slip, and the ice-cold wash would burn against her face. Later in the day there would be extra water to carry; Shim and Laib had slept three nights with us and her brother Berel, the watercarrier and my dear friend, would be standing in the market by then. For a ruble, also, I could have been able to get her a smaller axe than mine. When she chopped wood it was always too heavy and dangerous in her hands.

In this way, worried about Aaron and Leah and saying good-by to the ruble, we got about three-fourths of the way to the Parsovs'. Dimitri began to curse because of the deep drifts we found going up the hill to the Parsovs'. Then the horse refused to pull, and Dimitri turned to me. "Well, now I'm supposed to whip the horse, I suppose? You can get off here and walk! Oh, what a day it's going to be on the road, it's freezing!"

I looked away from him, sighing, and then saw the three dark specks in the gully below. I pointed to them, asking Dimitri what he thought they were. "Who cares? Now climb down; and remember about the patches on my coat, right?"

Then, still peering down into the gully, I saw my wagon on its side, and Gritka too, underneath the lumps of drifted snow. Well, I made Dimitri come with me and drag me through the drifts down the side of the gully. Going down we saw what the specks were — bolts of cloth, the cloth Aaron had brought back from Minsk. Gritka lay in the shafts, a foreleg under him; he must have lost the road in the darkness. I saw the new shoe on his smashed leg; in that weather the old ones would have been better.

A few hundred yards away were the bodies. Aaron's legs lay in a split, at right angles, almost, to his torso. Leah was on her back nearby. The snow under their necks was brown-red, and their throats were pierced, as was Gritka's, by the teeth of wolves. The wind had become a nothing, the snow now hardly fell. "Wolves," Dimitri was saying, "wolves and the first snow, see the marks? Yes, winter is early this year, all right."

Thoughts raced through my head. "What a shame to have to be thrown in with a Dimitri at a time like this. Today is Friday, the funerals must be either today or Monday, for tomorrow is the Sabbath and Sunday is Day of Atonement, forbidden. Forbidden to bury on those days. No, wait! What am I talking? Day of Atonement is Sunday? No, not Sunday, Monday, of course! Still, to wait until Sunday for the funerals . . . ay!"

"Well, now what?" said Dimitri, frowning, already annoyed.

"The Parsovs have no wagon. Help me carry them back to the village, Dimitri, and it's another ruble."

"Impossible. I'm late as it is and as a matter of fact I don't know about using a government vehicle to carry bodies, under any circumstances. I'll take you to the highroad and that's all."

"Dimitri, for heavens' sake — "

"They're dead, right? So what's the hurry?"

"They must be buried today, for reasons, and — "

"You Jews," Dimitri nodded, irritated. "You just can't wait to throw yourselves into the ground!" He shrugged and turned away, speaking over his shoulder. "Either stay here or come back now with me. I don't give a dump either way."

"You fool," I cried, running to him. Surprised at the anger in my voice, he stopped and examined my face. "Can't you be a little decent? Two people are dead and all you know is to make filthy talk!"

"Do you want me to cry?"

"They must have a proper burial according to our faith, don't you understand? Before that rotten brother of his, Mottel, can mess everything!"

I turned and looked at Aaron; his lower lip lay curled thickly under his front teeth and it seemed to me that he must have bitten himself in the pain and terror of the last moments. "Forgive me, Aaron," I mumbled hoarsely in Yiddish, "I shouldn't have lent you the horse and wagon. . . ."

"Be still," Dimitri said; something thoughtful in his voice made me look at him. I saw his eyes fixing themselves at the bolts of cloth. "Well, Jew . . . this is an important little thing, right? Very well, then, and we'll gather up that stuff over there, too."

"The broadcloth, yes," I replied quickly, jumping ahead of his thought. "Aaron was a tailor and used only the finest."

"Give me a hand, then."

Together we carried the bodies up to the roadside and lifted them into the wagon. I sat on the seat while Dimitri slid back into the gully after the cloth, which he dragged up and threw into the wagon. I was afraid to mention that one of the bolts had dropped on Leah's face.

Riding down the hill Dimitri asked if everything was now to my satisfaction. "Yes, thank you. Without trouble, that is if Mottel causes no disturbances, they'll be able to get a decent, holy burial."

"Yes, of course. Bury them as you wish." He chuckled. "Even the wolves should be thankful; they'll get a whole horse out of it."

By the time I got to Aaron's hut and laid the bodies side by side in their bed and went to the synagogue and announced the news and returned to my own hut, it was seven. My Bosha had already begun preparing for the Sabbath; and my nose ached with the smell of the warm friendly meat cooking in the pot.

"Was it a good praying this morning?" Bosha said when she saw me.

"I got to synagogue too late to pray."

"What do you mean, too late?"

"Where are the children?"

"Out playing in the snow, where else?" Bosha began to notice my shakiness. "Yeersel, what is? Why are you asking about the children?"

"Shim and Laib are out also?"

"What is, say, say . . ."

Then I sat down and told her. I omitted mention of Dimitri's theft of the goods, and my remorse at having lent the horse and wagon, but it didn't work. "Woe is me," my wife moaned, "the poor children, the poor children . . . and now God knows when you'll be able to buy another horse and wagon; you'll wear out your feet, your feet. Ay, they're already worn out . . . and what will be with the goods Aaron bought?"

"Be so good as to tell Shim and Laib. I can't, Bosha . . . and anyway," I said, getting to my feet, "the Burial Brotherhood is meeting at Aaron's and I've got to go there."

"Wait, put a bite of something in your mouth first."

"Later," I said, leaving.

And such is the way with human beings that walking to Aaron's hut, bowed down and crushed by self-reproach, I could still remind myself that I was freed of Aaron's gentle competition. Now I was the only tailor in the village; it might not be too hard, certainly not quite as hard as the first time, to get another horse and wagon. But I threw this thought out of my mind and concentrated on my being a member of our Burial Brotherhood, well versed in the proper care of cadavers and a dutiful student of the protocols of grief. It was always I who used to be the first to enter the hut of the bereaved and utter the ancient consolations. "What is death, if not a fated thing?" I would demand of the bereaved. "Who can quarrel with the decision of The One Above? Remember, in the book of eternity it stands written on the same line when we shall be born and when we shall pass away. Ay, the years are short, but eternity is long and in eternity we shall meet our loved ones, in the eternal Jerusalem."

And if the death happened to be sudden I would say, "At least, dear brother, it came quickly and without suffering. Thus does The One Above close the eyes of the dearest and sweetest souls." But if the end happened to come after a long-drawn-out sickness I would point out, "At least you knew it had to happen, at least you were prepared, spared the shock of being demolished in one black moment. Be thankful. The One Above granted you a long farewell, a long time of looking upon the dear face of your lost one."

Yet this time with Aaron and Leah, I could bring myself to say nothing to their two boys. As soon as they learned about it, they hurried to their hut with my Bosha, where they found the house full of heartbroken Golinskers. When I came there I saw them sitting together in a corner on the floor surrounded by weeping women all talking at once. They seemed not to be listening, containing themselves in a quiet that was more of a numbness. Only when one of the women remembered to turn the mirror to the wall did they look at each other and begin to sob.

The moment I stepped into the hut I was hailed by our brilliant widow, Tzippe-Sora. She came at me like a horse galloping downhill. "Well, where are they, the Burial Brotherhood? You know what today is? You know what Mottel is?"

"Yes, Tzippe-Sora," I said. "Yes. Hold yourself in."

"And what will you do about Minsk?" she demanded. Oh, Tzippe-Sora was a real darling, a golden person, but she had hammers in her head and if you gave her the slightest chance she'd twist you into a shape of her own liking.

"Minsk, Minsk," I said deprecatingly.

"But Leah's father and sister are there," Tzippe-Sora said, making it sound like a demand in itself. "You mean they aren't to be notified?"

"Yes, yes, yes," I said absently. "The men will try their best to make everything come out right."

"Don't forget, there's a telegraph office in Pukop. Perhaps a telegraph message, at least so that if they'll want to come . . . and the funerals could be in the afternoon, of course, let's say three o'clock, the grave-digging will take a long time, I passed the cemetery on the way here just to take a look, the drifts are piled high . . ."

"No doubt, no doubt," I said listlessly. In order to answer Tzippe-Sora shortly, one still had to say everything twice. That was her talent. Tzippe-Sora dragged the best and the worst out of you.

"The family in Minsk, Leah's," she continued, "a gold of a family, Yeersel, it'd be a sin not to let them know the news, not to allow them to try to come here to the funerals — "

"But, Tzippe-Sora — " and her digging began to arouse me, then — "please don't handle me as you handle peasants buying your alcohol. Say what you say, but to somebody else."

I turned away from her, feeling I must get to the cold air outside. I needed it to sting my ears. Outside the wind began to whistle itself up into a cutting thing and I was wet from the knees down, the damp snow still clinging, and I was inviting a bad chill; but it was better to be outside, away from warmth and comfort and safety, away from people and their voices, away from the familiar signs of everyday life that were to me then only temptations to self-comfortings and self-justifyings. My belief was that I had committed a great sin in which I had somehow managed to involve The Highest One Himself. In the name of true piety, of the adoration of the one and only Lord, I had sent two people to their deaths, saying I was helping them get two chickens a week for a year. But underneath the saying and into the meaning, I had really acted for another reason — to guard my piety, to keep the name of Yeersel-ben-Daneel clean in the book of eternity. The strength of the indictment against me lay in that only myself and The One Above knew of my sin, a terrible weight to carry into the synagogue on the Day of Atonement, so terrible because so secret, so apparently its exact opposite, a good deed; so terrible because so easily explained away, so unimportant a sin compared to sins men commit openly against each other. This, without doubt, was a very high sin, a sin so complete that it had become a world in itself, an evil thing growing and growing and which I could not smash to pieces as I could smash a snake to pieces. "My piety is not the true piety such as I have my life through striven for," I tortured myself. "It is only vanity, vanity dressed in the coat of piety. But why, why have I been so blind, Lord, up to now?"

Shivering to myself in this fashion I stood in the snow outside of Aaron's hut until the landsmen of the Burial Brotherhood came out looking for me. Seeing the tears on my beard little Nochim ran to me. "Ay, Yeersel . . . you were like a brother to him, helped him when he needed, showed him even how to hold the needle in his hand!"

"Even so," said Hertz the grease-maker, "hold yourself in, we have a decision to make."

"The burying," said Berel-the-Ox. "Ay."

"When and how, that's it," added Laib-Shmul, the meat slaughterer. "Let's talk as we walk, the five of us."

"No, let's just walk and wait to talk until we sit down," Hertz said.

"To decide correctly one has to be sitting down," Berel added.

"Sitting, standing, but let it be settled without too much chewing-over," Laib-Shmul said. By unspoken agreement we went to my hut. I was considered perhaps the most pious member of our congregation, and because in the past I always was the first to speak at our burying meetings, they sat and waited.

"Well," Hertz asked, leaning toward me. "What do you think, Yeersel?"

"I think I'm catching a chill."

"And I think," Berel said then with the same concentrated calm in which he spoke, to make us call him the Ox, "that in all decency the funerals can wait until Sunday. After all, Leah has a father and sister in Minsk, and if we waited until Sunday they could be at the buryings. They'll have to be told today anyway, they'll have to sit out the period of mourning. . . ."

"Leah has a sister in Minsk, yes," Laib-Shmul said, "but Aaron has a brother here in Golinsk right under our noses."

"Ay, and what a smell he makes, that Mottel," Nochim said, shaking his head in long twists.

"If all Mottel was able to make was smells, that wouldn't be so bad," Berel interposed. "It's a lot of trouble he can make, too."

"Not too much, maybe," Laib-Shmul said. "After all, they are already dead and they've got to be buried. Where's the argument against it?"

"There doesn't have to be a reason for Mottel to make trouble," I said. "His talent is to invent reasons."

"Listen," Hertz said, "what trouble can he really make? A death certificate we don't need, for to grant us a death certificate would mean they admitted Aaron and Leah were human beings . . . and money for graves we don't ask anyone for. . . ."

"Certainly not," I agreed. "Aaron has paid his head taxes faithfully and well into the burial fund for I don't know how many years."

"So what remains to worry about, then?" Laib-Shmul demanded.

"Something," Nochim said.

"How?"

"If you will recall," Nochim said, a bit pleased now to be explaining this to Laib-Shmul, who had a blunt and intemperate attitude of seeming always to know everything, "Aaron's father and mother lay side by side on the northwest end of the cemetery, and Aaron's father's grave — please follow me carefully — lies one grave from the boundary of the cemetery. Clear?"

"Of course," Laib-Shmul said. "Here is Aaron's father's grave, next to him is an empty unused plot, and next to that is the boundary. Well?"

"Aaron naturally belongs next to his father — but who knows if Mottel would agree to that? Who knows if Mottel wouldn't want to lie there himself?"

"He would have to be asked," Berel said. "After all, he is the brother, and if we buried without asking him he could go to the courts, and the courts would without doubt be on his side. And even further . . . we must ask his opinion on whether to bury today or Sunday."

"Berel is right," Hertz said, his mind made up. "To Mottel's funeral I'd gladly go, at any time, but he still lives and so he must be considered."

"As for the father and sister in Minsk," Berel began, "they, too, must be considered. . . ."

"Only if we can afford it," Laib-Shmul interrupted, finding a good moment to make a strong remark. "And there is only one way to find out what we can afford to do. One of us must this minute go to Mottel and find out a number of things — first, if he knows about what happened; second, if he has any objections to Aaron lying next to his father; and third, would he object to holding the funeral over until Sunday so that Leah's father and sister could attend?" Having said all he wanted to say in one breath, Laib-Shmul stopped, sighed deeply, and looked at the rest of us. "Well said or not?" he demanded.

"Why," asked Nochim softly, "should only one of us go to him? Why not all? Five he can't yell down as easily as one."

"Five he could knock down much easier than one," Berel said gently. "No, it's not a question of numbers but of shrewdness and tact. And for that, we have Yeersel."

"Well, let it be as Berel says," Hertz intoned with a prayerlike rising and falling of his strong voice. He slapped his palm down upon the table. "Let Yeersel go to Mottel and sound him out. Who knows, Mottel might feel something for his brother now. And if Mottel should sound like he's going to enjoy himself in arguments, in threats, in jokes with us — "

"Then we'll ask no questions," Laib-Shmul said. "We'll have the funerals right away, this afternoon!"

"Let's not decide until Mottel is spoken to," Nochim replied. "Or else what's the sense of asking him?"

"Ay, it's a terrible thing," Berel said, "to hold the bodies from today until Sunday morning. They'll change, you know."

"The snow isn't running away," Hertz remarked, sighing.

"But to bury on Sunday morning and then to go into the synagogue that afternoon to begin the Kol Nidre, the services for the eve of the Day of Atonement . . . what a sad, heavy business!"

"And to bury today, then, makes everything lighter, happier?" Nochim demanded.

"Leave off, leave off," I asked them. "I'll talk to Mottel right away."

"I'm sorry, Yeersel, I shouldn't be waggling my tongue that way," Berel told me. "Mottel must be at the smithy now. Shall we all walk with you there?"

"No. No. I'll go alone."

Nochim the fiddler, flighty but goodhearted . . . Hertz the grease-maker, a man of balanced patience . . . Berel the watercarrier, with his bit of beard and stoical word-stinginess (my quiet brother-in-law not yet fully pleased with the sounds of the world and the people in it, even nearly a full dozen years after he had regained his hearing) . . . and Laib-Shmul, the meat slaughterer, rich-voiced and pounding . . . all had agreed that I was best fitted to contend with our contemptible one, our traitor-atheist, Mottel. On the way to the smithy, alone, my feet walked on mountains of shame. Oh, how mistaken, how unnecessary!

I bent an eye into the smithy but found only Profim Alexi Buzarov, the proprietor. A length of rope was about his neck from which hung several new shiny horseshoes; they made me think of Gritka now lying in Parsov's gully. "It's Yeersel," he said with a cold squint.

"A pretty necklace," I said to humor him, pointing to the horseshoes.

"The finest and the lightest." He jingled them. "The Squire plans a bit of moving-about this winter. Have you seen his new sled? Beautiful, solid as a railroad car! Wood covered with leather, all closed in! Real windows!"

"Remarkable. Excuse me, where might I find Mottel?"

"In his room down the street."

"Thank you."

"But better don't go now. He's sleeping and he's been drunk."

"Drunk? Since when, Profim?"

"Since always," he smiled. "One look at him this morning and I sent him to sleep it off."

"There has been a tragedy," I said carefully. "His brother and sister-in-law."

"Oh, yes," Profim replied. "He mentioned being told about it by Dimitri, down the road."

I hurried out. Good, very good. Mottel would be sleeping off his carouse for the next several hours, during which we could attend to the funerals. In my own mind I had come to the opinion that waiting until Sunday would be a mistake. Such a long period of waiting would only extend the ordeal of the two orphans, Shim and Laib; would only prevent us from going to the bathhouse on Sunday and making ourselves clean for the most important holy day of the year; but, also, that Leah's sister and paralyzed father could make the journey from Minsk in this snow was extremely doubtful, and even so, even so . . . there were other questions. Would it be proper to tell the sick old man the news and risk another stroke and his own death? And could Leah's sister get away by herself? Who would care for the invalid?

As my mind opened to these new thoughts, I made my way to the broken-down inn several doors from the smithy, to make my token visit to Mottel. One look at his sleeping form would be enough to say I had tried to talk to him.

The inn was church property managed by two elderly cousins of Father Semyon, the sisters Lukov. Entering into the hallway, I knocked on the door of the main inner entrance. Nina, the younger one (said to have been a beauty and a onetime favorite of the Squire's father), looked me up and down as she stood at the door, and told me to get out. But I put a coin into her withered hand and told her why I had come. She pushed the coin into her purse and showed me upstairs to Mottel's closed door.

I opened it a bit and peered inside. I saw a couch but it was empty. I opened the door just enough to step through; there was the couch, a small round table, a chair, piles of empty bottles in two corners, a pair of shoes, hobnailed and blackened by smoke . . . but no Mottel. I turned to leave and saw him in the doorway, his brows knit, frowning at the unbelievable sight of me. He stood in his bare feet, the rest of him dressed; and in his mouth was the tiny stub of a cigarette. As always with Mottel's cigarettes, it sat in the exact center of his mouth. His straight black hair fell sideways and over his right eye; his beard was clipped close; his nose seemed to spread almost from one cheek to the other, as though it had been pressed out with an iron. As always, he wore his private smile. Now as he looked at me he swayed a little, and put his hand against the side of the doorway to lean on it. "Well, it's Yeersel," he said; and in any other person it would have sounded quite cordial, but once you knew Mottel it was impossible to accept such an impression. The man had been a stranger to us for so long, had so long ago thrown his lot in with Profim and Vassily Buzarov that to think for a moment he was our friend, much less a landsman, was to be out of mind.

"Ay," he said, closing the door, "what a fine surprise to return lightened in the bowels and find a fine Golinsker Jew." There it was, as I expected . . . first the smile and then the sly kick. "Let's sit down a little and solve a few problems of the world, eh?"

"I have but one problem today."

"Sit down, sit down." He lay on the bed and shoved the one chair at me. I watched him as he stretched himself out on his back. "It's been a hard few hours, a hard few hours," he mumbled. Then he closed his eyes. "Mottel," I began, thinking I must at all times be shrewd, be tactful, "the one problem I do have — all of us — is with the burial situation."

"Aaron and Leah?" he asked, as though half asleep, his eyes remaining shut, his breathing coming slow and very heavy.

"Yes."

"To be through with it . . . I don't care to think about the burial situation. Put them into the ground, that's the situation, yes, that's the situation. . . ."

"Well, yes," I continued carefully, "I agree. Now, as you know, they will lie next to your parents, one on either side."

"A grave is a grave. . . ."

"True, only, Mottel . . ."

"Only what?"

"You do not object to Aaron lying beside your father?"

"No."

"Then all I have to mention, Mottel is . . ." I took a deep breath . . . "well, the funerals are today."

His eyelids moved a little and his head turned to me. "Who decided?"

"It's not yet a decision . . . it's only a plan."

"Well, it's a good plan."

My heart gave a happy jump. No objections at all! Even in favor of burial today! "Well, Mottel — perhaps you'll feel well enough to come this afternoon . . . to the funerals?"

"I don't go to funerals." He raised himself on one elbow, spit his cigarette butt out, opened his eyes, and leaned toward me. "Bury them or don't bury them, funeral them or don't funeral them. To me it's the same. To me, what happens to people when they die isn't of interest. You see, I don't believe in God and I don't believe I'll eat pickled herring in heaven." He swung his legs down to the ground and leaned down, gripping his calves in his hands. "I'm not concerned with what's good only to bury."

"People are entitled to have an opinion," I muttered, making myself remember to be shrewd and tactful, not to lose my temper at this sinful kind of talk. "Well, Mottel — I'll leave you to your rest."

"Wait, how often are my humble walls flattered with your presence?"

He laughed, and he missed a breath, or something choked up in his nose; anyway he began to gasp in his laughter. "See how well I know how to speak, how literary-like, and in Yiddish!"

"You speak very well, indeed. Now let me say good-by-and-be-well. . . ."

"But I want you to stay! Stay!"

"No, really . . . you must be exhausted."

"I'm only tired . . . it would be very good to be exhausted. Never mind. But listen, this I want to say . . . oh, sit down, Yeersel . . . I won't hurt you, go take your chair on the other side of the room if I'm near enough to contaminate you. . . ."

"Well . . ."

"Listen, listen," Mottel began. The words fell out of him like stones from a beggar's bag, all piled up and slinking against each other, drunken words, angry words, foolish words, human words. "Oh yes yes yes . . . you can't take away from me that I'm a Golinsker because whatever else, I can still talk anybody's head off, drunker better than any other way. . . ."

"Well, I suppose . . ." (Shrewd, tactful.)

"You're looking at me now and thinking what a terrible crime, what a terrible thing I've done to myself, eh? . . . a drunken worthless piece of flesh to become, no different from any gentile, eh? . . . and there's my brother dead and to be buried and I don't even go to take a look at him, I don't think of watching him go into the ground, eh?"

"The One Above watches for you," I murmured, hoping I could leave quickly, yet guarding against antagonizing him into turning my victory into a catastrophe; so I sat there, humoring him. "After all, it's got to be in your heart."

"All right . . . it's got to be in my heart . . . but if as you say The One Above watches, then why didn't he watch that the horse shouldn't fall into the gully?" He waved his hand disgustedly. "Dimitri told me about it." He laughed. "Oh, that Dimitri, he's sorry now he ever saw me today." Then he pointed his finger at me, shaking it. "Well?"

"Well, what?"

"Explain why The One Above wasn't watching that the horse shouldn't — "

"You aren't really serious? You want an answer?"

"There isn't any."

"Pardon me, Mottel, you are mistaken. It is written of The One Above, 'He will fulfil the desire of them that fear him; he will also hear their cry, and will save them.' "

"Did he save Aaron and Leah?"

"Of course," I cried. "He saved them from a miserable life! He took them to Himself, to eternal peace!"

"If I was so sure of it, I'd kill myself and enjoy life in heaven — only it just isn't the way you think." He stood up and began searching in his pockets for matches and cigarettes. "No, no . . . it isn't that way at all, excuse me. When you're dead you're dead — and when you're alive you're dead most of the time, too, so what's the difference?"

"Mottel, listen," I begged, suddenly wanting, for the first time, to try to pierce into him. "What's the use of being alive if you don't be-lieve in something?"

"Take a smoke?"

"Mottel — "

He lit his cigarette and threw the match to the floor, and in the way he flicked his wrist I could see how angry I was making him. "I be-lieve in something, yes!"

"Well, then, that's good," I replied, starting to edge near the door, "and when I have a little more time, I'd like to — "

"Excuse me," he said grimly, taking hold of my shoulders, "I'm not finished with you." The smoke from his cigarette made me sneeze; he pushed me away. "I shouldn't have started with you at all . . . you don't know what it is to believe anything except the Holy Law. You're not even in the world any more. You think to be a man in the world is to forget to be a Jew . . . and that to be like your father is the one and only all. Yes, I believe in something — in myself and what I'd have done if only I'd been left alone."

"Very well," I replied, seeing him go to the corner stacked with bottles and pick up one that was not empty. "I'll leave you alone now. I'll let you do what you want."

"Don't bother about me," he grunted, uncorking the bottle. He lifted it to drink, then changed his mind. "I'll live until I die," Mottel said, pointing at me with the hand that held the bottle, "and after I die there'll be a difference, people will know I'm dead, understand? But after you are dead, you and your fellow walking corpses, nothing will be different, nothing at all."

"Let it be as you say, Mottel. As for me, I'm going."

"Wait, here's another one . . . I don't care what you do with the two bodies, but the boys, the two sons, Shim and Laib . . ." He stopped to take a drink, a long one.

"Never mind now about the two boys. . . ."

"But I'm their only living uncle," he grinned, "and they interest me. Tell them I'll see them."

At the door I gripped the knob in my hand and found courage. "Never mind about seeing them. We don't throw young souls into the hands of apostates."

"You're interested only in dead bodies. Well, dead bodies you can have . . . but living flesh and blood of my brother, well — "

"Better me to be dead than to watch you press Shim and Laib into your shape."

"Die, die, die . . . what's dying to you?" He breathed upon me, his stench moved past, all the smells of a man floating on top of the garbage of the world, the liquor, the faint sign of women, their perfume and powder, and the stink of horses. "To you dying is easy, Yeersel, as easy as my taking a drink! The quicker you die the quicker, you believe, you will enter heaven. So the piouser and piouser you make yourself!"

"When a person lives like a dog, he thinks like a dog," I said quietly. "Now good-by."

"But how can you stand and be so patient with me?" he demanded. "Why can't I insult you, what's the matter with you?"

"You're a lost one, a wanderer. I don't blame you, Mottel. It was the priests. The priests got into you when you were in the army, those nine long years away. They, the army, the priests I blame and curse — not you!" Then I put my arms out. "Wash your face, Mottel, make a beginning. Come with me and sit beside your brother. Pray for him."

"They don't belong to me — they belong to God, right?"

"Don't make a joke!"

"So . . . they're safe."

"The worst sin is to dishonor the name of The One Above. He will never forgive you."

"Well, that's all right," he smiled, "I'll never forgive Him, either."

I gave up. "Better sleep now." Under my breath I added, "And The One Above willing it, may you never wake up."

For the third time I turned to the door. But again Mottel kept me. "By the way," he shouted suddenly, harshly. "About the goods, Yeersel."

"What goods?" (The goods? Mottel knew?)

"Yes," he said to me over his shoulder as he went to the bed and then threw himself on it, still holding the bottle. "That Aaron had," he added, as he set the bottle on the floor near him.

"What Aaron had," I shrugged, "he had."

"But really, Yeersel, who owned those goods?"

Ay, now the blow would fall. Now the traitor in him was peeping out. He would wring the buying of the goods out of me and twist the blame on my shoulders, and through his connection with the village agent, Rezatskin, he would set a pretty toll and force me to pay it. "Who owned the goods, if not Aaron?"

"Really? Out of the need to help a fellow tailor you loaned him your horse and wagon, your competitor, to buy goods?"

Already he spoke as the inquisitor, yet it was with a tease, with a grin, with a little giggle embroidered around it. Was he really probing, or was he too drunk for anything but toying? Yet our talk began to have the shape of a trial, and next would be Mottel going to Buzarov and Buzarov to the Squire and then the Squire to Selenkov; and then finally the knock on my door. "I didn't ask him what he wanted the horse and wagon for," I cried. "Leave off, I did nothing, I broke no regulations — "

"You knew he was going to Minsk."

"Who asked him where?"

"That's a foolish lie." Mottel sat up in bed. "Not your goods that he bought in Minsk?"

"Not my goods. Well, what do you want of me? I'm in enough difficulties already with losing my horse and wagon."

"True," he said, leaning down for the bottle. "They were counting on your wagon for this week. Something for the Squire, the Konayev, you know."

"So I understood when you sent the boy Monday with the message. But Aaron came to me the same day. He needed help. He had no place else to ask but me. If he could have gone, for instance, to his well-placed brother, and his well-placed brother would have arranged for him to buy goods here in Golinsk through the Squire's agent, on a fair credit, then he wouldn't have had to run to Minsk to try for a living of two chickens a week for a year. But with such a well-placed brother he had to go to Minsk and die."

"Politely said, Yeersel. And true." He laughed his private laugh again.

"Mottel, how can you gain such joy from admitting a sin?"

"I wasn't admitting," he snorted, throwing the empty bottle into the corner on the other side of the room. "I'm just wondering," he added, shaking his head in mock anxiety, "if maybe the whole blame doesn't actually fall on you, Yeersel, the great pious one."

"How on me?" I demanded, but before the words were out my face was beginning to feel wooden with the thought that had been stabbing me since the first opening of my eyes that morning.

Mottel came toward me again, leaning into my face, peering down into my raised eyes. "Listen, little beaver," he said, taking hold rather gently of my beard, "and consider a fact. Aaron and Leah died in your horse-and-wagon, as the result of your favor." He spoke slowly, savoring the morsels of pleasure in each mocking word. "And was it a favor to Aaron — or was it a favor you granted to yourself? Come now, little pious one, answer me." But I could only moan.

He giggled again. "Isn't God the protector of the truly pious?" He leaned down close to me until we were beard to beard. "Now if you won't answer me, I'll have to answer for you . . . right into your teeth, Yeersel. Aaron died thinking you wanted to help him, but you lent him the horse and wagon so you wouldn't have it to lend to the Squire . . . just simply because you didn't like to dirty your piety on Holy Week, and perhaps anger God, and perhaps get crossed off the list of the pious-enough-to-live-in-heaven!" He tickled my beard with his fingers, laughing meanwhile. "Oh, little pious animal, little beaver, aren't you ashamed? And God sees all, you know! And oh, oh, isn't He angry with you!"

Still laughing, Mottel loosened his hold on my arm, gave my beard a last obscene tickle, and pushed me toward the door. I ran out and down the stairs, still hearing his laughing, and when I found myself outdoors I began to shake with a great tremble. Mottel had been having himself a good long drunken joke of a time with me. Yet the joke had an underside with a terrible meaning; both of us, he and I, the atheist and the dedicated son of Israel, still had something in common, something I couldn't bear to think about. He and I had been joined into one sinful soul, for together we had accomplished two innocent deaths, and what had to be his end had also to be mine.

I flew to the synagogue, took out the prayer book for the Day of Atonement, and turned to the section listing the fifty-three separate divisions of sins for which there was forgiveness. There was no mention, no hint, of the sin of vain piety. Convinced that for this sin I could not be forgiven, a great sob sat down in my throat; it would not be moved; in the years to come, the years of my daughter Rochel marrying Shim and traveling to America, the years of Mottel's disappearance and unbroken absence, the years of my wife's death and my children's dispersal and my own decline, the weight of this unforgiven sin of mine grew somewhat lighter, and it became an invisible wen to which I gradually accommodated myself. Still, each year on the Day of Atonement when we came to the list of the fifty-three divisions of sins for which there was forgiveness, Mottel's laughing began again to fall upon my ears. I would cry, and as I cried I would try to fight my tears with the psalm, "The Lord is my refuge and my fortress, in Him will I trust. For He shall deliver me from the snare of the fowler," but the words stood only hazily in my head; I had been my own snare, I would tell myself, and my own fowler.

Thus it was with me in Golinsk, when my hands moved and my eyes saw. But my hands moved only the needle, and my eyes saw only the cloth. My needle was fear. My thimble was prayer. The cloth I tailored was a weave of circumstance twisted together haphazardly. The Squires had proclaimed the necessary weave of my life-goods, and I accepted this lie of the Squires as a blind man accommodates himself to the absence of light.

Who knew I had been driven and hungered into sustaining myself with contemplations of the joys of The Next World? Who dreamed I had fed my piety because only my piety had fed me? Who was there to tell me that the vanity in my piety was no more than a splinter under my fingernail, placed there by the Squires of my time?

To know these things I had first to die.

2. Maisha
(1815–1887)

For FIFTY-SIX OF MY SEVENTY-TWO YEARS I WAS CALLED A TEACHER AND gave learning to the children of Golinsk. I sat with them at the learning-table in the synagogue and taught the alphabet, the Law, the Books, the Commentaries, and the Commentaries on the Commentaries — all in the form of my own commentaries on these holy subjects.

The synagogue was a large hut of logs chinked with tar and clay. We had a floor of split logs, windows, a stove, and in a corner near the altar, the learning-table. I would sit there all day massaging Hebrew learning into little Jewish heads, freezing in the winter and fainting in the summer, suffering chills in the spring and asthma all the time.

Now if you multiply my fifty-six teaching years by the twenty or so children at my learning-table in the ordinary year (with the exception of my first twenty teaching years, when the army and other accursed things took children away from the village earlier), you get some eleven hundred souls who should have passed through my hands and some seven hundred who did. Many died after me, some even before; some stayed in Golinsk, many tried new places both known and unknown to me; some but not many, like Shim and Laib, went to America; more moved only to other similar villages like Pukop or Svutz or Shnavka in our Minsk Province; and too many were taken into the army, of course, never to return, remaining unaccounted for; and some just went away, like Laib's Uncle Mottel. Yet, in my later years I seemed surrounded by the faces of men I had known from their childhood, faces I had seen annoyed by me at the learning-table, faces that would later grow beards and become landsmen . . . faces that often came to sadden me on certain occasions. Take, for example, the

face of Laib-Shmul, our meat slaughterer in '85, the year Aaron and
Leah died. I need to dwell upon him and I shall, but I didn't sit down
only to squeeze a lemon.

Yes, we are now doing something a little more important . . . looking at a certain Maisha. . . .

Ay, hiba, hiba! He's born, he's born! Three years after Napoleon
wriggles home on his cut-up belly, a soul decides it's wonderful to be
born in Russia! Maisha-son-of-Haim, a genius child, hiba, hiba! Look
where he maneuvers to get himself born in 1815, in Karlin, Karlin near
Pinsk, a bit of a hamlet only, as it seems to people! But the infant-to-be
knows better! Yes, he knows what is happening nine months before his
birth and he approves; did you ever hear of such a thing? A genius!
He observes the process of his physical conception, approves of his
father Haim the saloonkeeper, falls immediately in love with his sweet
and warm-chambered mother, Melka, and works furiously at being
born because he knows he is not only going to be a Karliner but a
nephew of Mendel, a true Karliner, O blessed joy! Ay, first he sang,
the child Maisha, and then talked, and then walked . . . and like other
little boys he learned the joys of running in the streets, of chasing the
gentiles' cruising pigs out of the Jewish side of the town . . . and every
day he sat at Uncle Mendel's learning-table until the age of nine, and
then on a day not long after the Passover, Uncle Mendel took him by
the hand and walked with him in the new-blossoming fields, and said
good-by.

"Maisha, Maisha, dear little joy-child, I must tell you something."

"Then tell, Uncle Mendel."

"From the hour of your birth you have shown me the soul of a
Tzaddik. Four years you have sat at my learning-table and I have seen
only the love of God in you. Now, before I go, I want to give you my
last words."

"Where are you going, Uncle Mendel?"

"Over the world, my dear. First to study at the table of the aged
Lazer of Ladi, himself a Tzaddik from the learning-table of the
Master of the Good Name."

"And will I never see you again?"

"As I will see you — in every strange hut, on all roads, and in the life of night."

Uncle Mendel took my hand in his and began his chant as we walked the long line through the apple-tree field on a carpet of new grass, the blossoms hanging above and straining their heads down to hear his every intonation, we passing under and away:

> Why is the Hasid the Hasid? [sang Uncle Mendel]
> And the Misnagid only the Misnagid?
> (Ay, *chie-dee-die-die,* ay, *chie-dee-die-die,*
> Only a Misnagid?)

> The Hasid, the Hasid, the Hasid,
> What carries he in his Jewish heart?
> He carries not the Law, but the Lord,
> And fears not the Law, but the Lord,
> And loves not the Law, but the Lord,
> Enjoys not the Law, but the Lord,
> And lives, lives-lives,
> In the Lord!

> Ay . . . *chie-dee-die-die* . . . *chie-die-dee-die-die-die* . . .
> Love him, O Lord, the Misnagid!

Ay, Uncle Mendel, how we jumped and skipped at every *chie-dee-die-die* that spring day in the apple-tree field, and how we danced to your chanting! And how afterwards we flung ourselves all breathless on the cool green of the ground, tired and panting and humming!"

I said then to you, "Before we return to the village you must tell me something."

"I cannot teach you further, Maisha." (And you patted my head.) "You know everything I know."

"I am nine now. For a very long time I have not spoken as it is said I used to speak, with the tongue of The One Above. These talkings I do not remember, and they puzzle me."

"And why shouldn't one be puzzled when he has spoken like a Tzaddik before the age of four? And if, as you have, why shouldn't you be further puzzled now that you are nine and speak thusly no more?" (And you patted my head.) "Ay, little Maisha, it's only a slight puzzle. You see," (and you patted my head), "at the moment of birth, one is closest to the Lord in the time that one is on this earth. Each minute here is a million years removed from Him. And the older we get the further we fall from the bosom of The Highest One."

I began to cry. "Then how will I ever get near again to Him!"

"You are nearer to Him now at this moment, as you cry out in fear of being distant from Him, than the others at the moment of their birth. Be rested, of joyful faith. Yours is a clean dear Jewish soul. You shall truly know and love Him forever."

And you patted my head, and then you left Karlin and threw your-self upon the world and I never saw your Karliner face again. In my later years, Uncle Mendel, faint whispers of you reached me in Golinsk where I had settled in '31, in my seventeenth year; and when I would hear a news of you from some wandering Hasid — that you had been seen in Podolia, that in Vilna you had disputed with strong Misnagdim, that in Kovno they had stoned you — I would sit in meditation and remember all your sayings and repeatings, and what I felt I could no longer remember I then wrote down. In this way I made myself a short Book of Mendel, which I always treasured. And whenever I wished to make a good learning child very happy, I would always remember our last day in the apple-tree field and pat him gently upon his head.

In my twelfth year (I had begun by then to sit in the chair at the head of the learning-table when our official teacher would be indisposed), the town became terrified because of the new Conscription Law. It decreed a term of military service for Jews of twenty-five years in addition to the years to be served as military students in the Russian military schools to the age of eighteen. The new articles of conscription allowed recruits, on paper, to be taken from the age of twelve up. But six months less or a year and even two years less was not disallowed. We Karliners had deep reason to be alarmed. Our governor had long looked to find some means of shattering the Hasidic fortress of Karlin.

"No question," was the word in my father's saloon. "The new laws give Jewish soldiers a twenty-five-year chance to become Christians."

"It'll help like cupping-glasses on a corpse," my father would say.

"Yes. Exactly. There will be mountains of Christian corpses produced in the army for the next twenty-five to fifty years. Corpses that used to be living Jews."

In our house there was no need to explain the effect of the Conscription Law. Did I not have two brothers who had been taken away to the army before my birth, brothers who never knew me because they had never lived to come home? The official letters, in each case, stated that "your son met a brave end on the field of battle," but from other sources, from fellow Jewish soldiers, we learned of their murders by their own officers, not on any field of battle but in the course of efforts to convert them. Hertz, the older one, had starved to death in solitary confinement after refusing to eat pig's meat. The other one, Shnepsel, had been forced to sit on a cake of ice in the winter, under guard and with his pants off, for neglecting to appear one Sunday at the military chapel. The joke ended with a chill from which Shnepsel did not recover.

One afternoon in the summer of the year of the new Conscription Law I came home from my learning to find a huge pot of water boiling on the stove. My mother said nothing to me but went through the door that led to the saloon and came back with my father, whose usually longish and noncommittal mien now moved with a certain quick twitching. I remembered this happened to my father's face whenever he had sudden trouble. I said immediately, "What happened?"

My father said, "Ask rather what must happen," and turned to my mother, who had fallen into tears.

"Who is dying, Mother?" I cried. "And you mustn't cry so, you mustn't! What is the life of the flesh if not simply the clothing we wear as we walk the short corridor into the house of eternity?"

"Nobody is dying, yet," my father replied shortly. "You're a little early with the holy words of comfort."

Out of her tears my mother wailed. "They were here today, the men with the lists."

My father spat on the stove so that it made a very loud hiss, and the sound of it, quick and hot, was sufficient commentary upon my father's feeling for our Jewish committee through which the civil authorities dealt with us in such a matter as conscription. In older days the Committee had finely and heartfully attempted to represent the entire community of Karliner Jews. But in my boyhood, the Committee kept raising the hilt of its possibilities. They were merchants and Misnagdim, needing to represent themselves more than the whole lot of us; so when the government assigned them to select Jewish recruits to fill the new quota, they turned to the less mercantile, to the plain Karliner Hasids.

"The men from the Committee," I repeated, realizing my mother had meant that they had come about me, to put me in the army. "Well . . ."

"Quickly," my father said, "they come to twelve-year-olds, and with such fine logics! If he goes now, he'll be all through with the army by the time he is forty-three; he'll have half his life all to himself . . . the older he is when they take him, the worse it will be."

"Fat pigs!" my mother screamed. "The Satan plays in them but they won't carry anything out! Not in this house!"

"Of course they are fat pigs, what else?" I said loftily. "Has not the holy Yerachmiel told us that merchants are willing to undergo all trials, all hardships, in order to make a living? These perspirers move on the world without the joy of The Highest One within them, without being able to accept the hardships of life with total indifference. What can we feel for them if not pity?"

"Pity today, pity tomorrow," my father said, turning to my mother. "Is the water hot enough?"

"Soon, soon," she choked out, her head buried in her apron, her body shaking with her sobbing. So that was the plan. . . . With the hot water I would be, so to speak, made ineligible for army service.

Look here, I won't shock you. After all, was it really so terrible? The feet thrust into boiling water long enough to make a good scald, and then two strong hits across the toes with the back end of an axe, and it was over. My father and mother thus spared me thirty-one years of living under the thumbs of uniformed Satans bent on capturing and strangling me forever. The difficult part was not the pain, or the limp you got, or the less fingers or bent-over back (for do you think I was the only boy who had such an "accident?"). No, the really dangerous thing was making the "accident" seem uncontrived, something our Committee could easily explain to the authorities. The Committee, let's give it a due, did not object to "accidents" but only required plausibility in them; and being a saloonkeeper my father had many opportunities to listen and consider, and make use of a certain steady drinker in debt to him. He was one Yalkinn, a serf with a hatred for his master deep enough to keep him in my father's saloon at every possible hour. Yalkinn had made the saloon his real home, and had come to the point of surrendering everything to drink. There were many like him but my father chose Yalkinn for the excellent reason of Yalkinn's total disgust with Jews. This coupled with his debt to my father and his willingness to do anything for drink made him the most dependable one to go to the Committee and say, "I ran Maisha over with my wagon or my horse kicked him. I know not which, I was drunk at the time — so drunk that to relieve him of the pains in his feet, I plunged them into the pot of boiling water I found on the stove in the Jew's kitchen. Or I might have done it because he had no right to be walking in the middle of the road in the first place!"

Seeing such a statement in writing the military authorities forgot about me. True, the bones never healed correctly and walking became the one real ordeal of my life . . . yet my two poor brothers had had good feet and walked without thinking, and where were they and where was I? I was still on the earth — in a position, I believed, to compare its bitterness, injustice, and shame with the gladsomeness and perfection of my certain Paradise.

So it went, with the little Hasid.

I go back to Yalkinn, the peasant who lied for me. In the several months thereafter it became clearer and clearer that the price of his lie would ruin my father unless something could be thought of to stop Yalkinn from dragging great numbers of vodka bottles out of my father without paying for them, and also to throttle his drunken boasting in the saloon about his "having the Jews in my power for life."

One night I lay on my bed-shelf over the stove and heard my parents whispering in their corner. "Be his friend, Haim," my mother urged, "let him drink until he drops dead from it!"

"Him alone wouldn't be terrible," I heard my father say in a strained sad croak, lying in the far corner of their bed. "But he's beginning to cost me fifteen-twenty bottles a week with his friends together!"

"Shh," my mother said. "God will help, you'll see. Now bend yourself in and sleep."

Thus was my father comforted. But I understood. Not Yalkinn but I was the source of my father's trouble. It was not simple for a Hasid young or old to pray for the death of one such as Yalkinn, for whom there was less hope in heaven than on earth, yet that night I managed it. "O Highest One," I prayed, "Uncle Mendel repeated to me the words of the great Koretzker, teaching me that anger is as sinful as melancholy; yet now I wish to feel anger, O Most High . . . for did not the Koretzker say also that after one has learned to put his anger in his pocket, he may take it out when he has need of it? And since the Satan plays in Yalkinn, and since the Satan thrusts at my father, may not, O Highest, I beseech you to make an end of Yalkinn, to strike him dead?"

But the danger of Yalkinn was removed otherwise. Yalkinn's master, the Baron, had taken a young wife after many years of widowerhood and had most apparently succeeded at the age of seventy-eight in impregnating her, which made him love his little daughter as nothing else in the world.

One day that winter the child disappeared. The Baron sent twenty couriers on horseback throughout the region promising a reward of one thousand rubles. All Karlin, and most principally the Jews, needed the child found. Our Committee had hastily collected itself and decided to offer its services to the search; it was agreed also that in the event of the child's being found by a Jew, the reward was to be returned.

At the end of the second day the child was still missing. The weather held very cold, everything was ice, and the Baron demanded soldiers from Pinsk. Two companies arrived in sleds the following morning. The first order issued by the Colonel shortly after his arrival directed every Jew in Karlin to stay within his own four walls until further notice.

"Each in his own house, forbidden to see one another . . . Ay, what next?"

"Shh," my mother called.

"That's right," my father cried suddenly, "sew up my mouth! We're fools, hear? Waiting for them to hack themselves in with their sabers and chop us up one at a time!"

"They'll hear you outside."

"All right," he said in a lower voice. "This is the third day. Not even a strong man could live outside three days in this winter. The child may be found, but if so she will be dead. Joylessness will fall upon us with their sabers, in terrible blows! In three weeks he'll be thirteen, a son of Israel — if not a corpse!"

"Don't be afraid, Maisha," my mother begged, "the father is mixed up now!"

"He is correct," I said. "Only don't weep, Mother dear. As Rabbi Nahum said — "

"Hold in what Rabbi Nahum said," my father shouted.

"Enough!" my mother shouted; and when my mother shouted my father and I always kept quiet, for we knew we had deeply offended her. She made us sit down and listen to her. "I know what we must do. To sit waiting until the end is crazy."

"Thank God," my father shot in, "you're beginning to agree with me."

Such terror in them, such love for me, sitting there planning my escape from the pogrom they saw coming! Ay, the waste . . . working to live if not without fear then at least without hunger, and to what end? To wrap their heaviest burlap rags around my crippled toes, to send me away with some bread and white cheese rolled in a piece of oilcloth, to sew a little bag stuffed with rubles into my undershirt . . . and to pour their last words into me:

"Outside is a soldier. Go to him and take his hand. He'll lead you to a wagon." (*Father*)

"And when it's a little more quiet we'll come to Pinsk for you, Maisha." (*Mother*)

I began to cry and first my mother and then my father begged me not to be afraid and not to be unhappy. "Let me; let me cry, Mother. If I do not know what gives you pain, how can I say I truly love you?"

"Ay, ay, cry, little flyaway," my mother sobbed.

"We'll soon see each other," my father kept saying.

. . . Only the soldier waiting for me in our street didn't put me on the train for Pinsk, but on the train for Kovno, but not before he took the money sewed in my undershirt. In Kovno I found only Misnagdim but they sheltered the ragged little fugitive with his pathetic story of Karlin, and when my thirteenth birthday arrived they made an event of my confirmation ceremony. For my confirmation sermon I embroidered upon the thought of the Rabbi Saras, repeated to me by Uncle Mendel, "The good man should himself be the Law, and people should be able to learn good conduct from observing him," but this made a poor impression.

No word came in reply to the letters sent to my father and it was decided by the Rabbi that for the time being, until at least it could be known that I could return safely, I should continue to assist the beadle. For almost two years I hoped and prayed but no word came at all. Karlin was far away, travelers were few, and news traveled slowly if at all. "Ay, Maisha," the beadle said to me once, "when a father doesn't answer to a son, the father must be without hands."

Misery and lonesomeness drove me back to Karlin, no matter what the risk. In the summer of 1830 I made my way there on broken feet, eating fruit and bread for three weeks, to find my mother in her grave and my father ready for his own. He had broken himself into pieces, letting the saloon slide away from him, never looking to see what he ate and drank, and even keeping away from the synagogue. As for the little daughter of the Baron . . . months after my flight it had come out that she had not been lost at all but had been taken to Paris secretly by her mother and her real father — who, it turned out, was the Baron's middle son. This had so shamed and crushed and enraged the Baron that he had flung the truth of it away from him and announced the "disappearance" of the child, passing from this to the higher nonsense of sending couriers out with the news of a reward and to the calling-in of the military. From all this the Baron had given himself a stroke and died. But then what, a month after? The mother, the daughter, and the real father, the Baron's middle son, come back to Karlin and without a thought live like the royalty they are!

Yalkinn, the Conscription Law, the Baron, my departure, my mother's death, my own disappearance for two years . . . it had become too much for my father. In the synagogue they told me, "Your father has forsaken God."

"Ay . . . what, what can I do?"

"Love him, love him more than ever."

One morning after prayers I came back and found him breathing with chokes. Leaning down to him, I saw thick teardrops in the corners of his heavy eyes. "It's all right, all right, Maisha. Now . . . I know . . . why I . . . I was created."

Thus he sent himself into The Next World. And when the winter melted itself out, I promised myself to find Uncle Mendel, to travel any distance but to find him and be his helper and disciple.

But between what a person promises himself and what he finds in the world is quite often a difference. In Golinsk . . . yes, Golinsk . . . I found myself, as the Proverb says, a wife of worth.

In Karlin the announcement of my intended pilgrimage was received with true Hasidic joy. I would first travel to Ladi, seat of the great Lazer to whom my uncle had gone three years before; and I too would study with Lazer and the more improve the good name of Karlin. My Karliners pledged to send letters to places where Hasids held sway and inform them of my coming and also to forward to them any news of Mendel, the Karliner. On my part I was to write steady letters back to Karlin. In that way, we prayed, Uncle Mendel and I would most certainly be reunited.

For many months in my seventeenth year, I hobbled from town to town asking in the synagogues, "Has Mendel the Karliner been?" When my mission became known, many times I would be brought to food and to a sleeping-place; my comings would be deemed blessings and I would be given things to help me on my way, even ointments for my twisted feet.

But then there were other times, such as in December; when Ladi was still very high to the north I dragged myself into a tiny, miserable habitation. It was late in the day and I had come from Pukop. There I had been angrily directed by the beadle to take myself to Golinsk where I would find other such Hasidic idiots as I.

My spirits were not high, but could have been lower. Passing across the district of Minsk, I expected the scorn I had received from the superior-minded book-learned beadles of that province. They were poor, with not much more to their names than I, and undoubtedly plagued by all kinds of wandering beggars; and when one is not only a beadle but also a Misnagid, and the year is 1831, what else can one be but a Policeman of God — that is to say, a wandering soul?

Well, to make it brief, I sit at the roadside in Golinsk not knowing where to go look for a Jew and too exhausted to try. I am glad to sit. My feet burn like fire and I'm grateful, for otherwise they'd be freez-

ing. The wind blows, it gives hints of snow again . . . ay, I'm thinking, if I sit here much longer I'll have to say evening prayers by myself,
well, so . . .

Then comes a man, looks down at me, speaks. Ay, Yiddish! "You're
a Jew?"

"What else?"

"Where are you from?"

"Karlin," I say, not certain from the voice what kind of heart lies
behind it. He's a big man with a rope pulled around his waist to hold
his coat snug, a coat with a fur collar, and his legs are wrapped with
fur, and it's a fur hat.

"Where are you going?" is his next question.

"To Ladi."

"On foot?"

"How else?"

He takes another look, a long one. "You wish to pray?"

"Yes." I decided I'll not start right off with my question, "Has
Mendel the Karliner been?" I know he's not a Hasid; he's too anxious
to know about me and not very anxious to help; but a good man he
can also be without the Hasid part so I'll be still . . .

"I'm going to the synagogue now. Come."

"Be so good as to lift me by the arm."

He takes my arm and pulls me up. I hobble with him to the synagogue. He tells me I'm in Golinsk, a place of seventeen Jewish families.
He is Lipka, a tarmaker, claydigger, and woodhauler, and who am
I? "Only a student," I reply. "I'm going to Ladi to study with my
uncle."

He is impressed. "Your uncle learns students from as far as Karlin?"

"Yes."

"He's a true rabbi, your uncle?"

"Yes," I reply. According to me he is a true rabbi, and I don't press
Lipka for his definition of one.

He takes me to the synagogue, I pray with the others, all poor peasants and trifle-merchants of the village; and from the way they pray

(looking mostly in the book, and swaying only gently, and without loud singing), I see they are not Hasidic-minded at all. I wonder why the Pukopper beadle called Golinsk a Hasidic place. (Later I understood it was his way of insulting Golinskers; between Pukoppers and Golinskers brewed a feud involving the Minsker Rabbi; but this did not become important for years.)

At prayer I forget where I am and begin swaying and shaking myself as the beauty of the service runs through me like a wine. When I come to the "Holy, Holy, Holy," I begin to sing it and my voice leaps above the routine shouting. And when the last amen is said, Lipka turns to me. "Do you always shake yourself so at prayer?"

"Well, I was a little cold," I mumble . . . and to myself I think, Tonight I mustn't be thrown back on the road!

By now the others are gathered around me in the synagogue. I'm a stranger and the custom is for me to launch into a long account of who and what and where and why, until I am interrupted by one who says, "You'll eat and sleep with me until tomorrow." I look around at their faces . . . plain ordinary faces . . . and I become ashamed with myself. "Why do I have to lie?" I demand. "I'm from the Hasids. All right, give me permission to sleep here in the synagogue and I'll go tomorrow after morning prayers."

Lipka is amused. "So you're something of a Hasid? Because you shake yourself at prayer like a bridegroom without a bride, that means you're a Hasid?"

This Lipka is evidently a big maker in the community for the rest keep quiet to see how I answer him. "Whether a person is a true Hasid is not for him but for others to say," I fire at Lipka, drawing myself up very straight and folding my arms. "The Master of the Good Name, the Besht himself, taught that the man who sways and shakes himself at prayer must not be laughed at. This man prays with fervor to save himself from foreign thoughts which threaten to engulf his prayer. Would you laugh at a drowning man who makes motions in the water to save himself?"

Lipka chews this over in his mind for a few seconds and says,

"You'll eat and sleep with me." Then he takes me to his little stable of a home, tells his wife to give me to wash my hands, and asks my name.

"I'm called Maisha of Karlin."

And at the table (it was potato soup and onions fried in chicken fat), I saw Gitel for the first time. This Gitel changed me from Maisha of Karlin to Maisha of Golinsk, and made Lipka my father-in-law.

The way it came about was through my feet. After supper I could not stand up, and after I told Lipka and Gitel and the mother about the boiling water and the blows of the axe, then about Yalkinn and finally the whole story from beginning to end, the mother brought out a pan and filled it with baking soda in hot water, and I sat soaking and talking until midnight. Little by little we all felt better and little by little I kept noticing the warmth in the mother's eyes and the roundness of Gitel's. She was only fifteen then, yet she had a woman's eyes and she also spoke very little. Three or four times in my narrative I paused to remark, "I've said enough for one night and tomorrow I must be on my way . . . it's late . . . well, so . . ." The last time I said a word about the next day, Lipka shook his head and asked, "Why not rest tomorrow and go the next day?"

Gitel's eyes grew rounder and rounder to me and I stayed not one day but six. And on the sixth day Lipka said, "Maisha, you want my Gitel?"

I began to flush up. "What did I do? What did I say — ?"

"I'm not against it, Maisha. Only you'd have to quiet down a little bit with the Hasidism, earn a living, be a responsible father."

"Gitel is pretty," I said, "and she'd easily do better than just me. Anyway."

"Gitel is not pretty and she knows it," her father said. "But if she's pretty to you I won't argue."

"She wouldn't want me, I know that without asking."

"That's another thing, Maisha."

"But I know — to her I'm just a wandering student — and really, how can I, as you say, quiet down my Hasidism? I must find my Uncle Mendel, he has my life in his hands."

"So?"

"Yes, that is so."

I bade Gitel good-by and thanked Lipka and let the mother kiss my cheek. I set my feet again on the road to Ladi. But I went only as far as Svutz. There I told myself that I had to rest, at least over the winter until my feet could better stand the strain; and as long as I had to rest, why not in Golinsk? When they saw me again, the mother kissed my cheek, quietly, as though she had expected me, and gave me to wash my hands. Lipka threw me a pleased look; his beard seemed to grow three inches when he saw me. And Gitel? Without a word she went to the stove to get hot water to put into the pan, with baking soda, for my feet.

The next day after my return was the Sabbath, and my appearance at the synagogue caused much peering and exchanging of nods. Lipka introduced me to the beadle. I had known he was the beadle before being introduced, and Lipka had not bothered at all to introduce me individually to the congregation. "Why did you bring me over to the beadle?" I asked Lipka on the way home from the synagogue.

"He is a good beadle, Zellik. But he is bad with the children. They learn nothing from him but to hit each other with sticks."

"You have a learning-table for children in the synagogue?"

"A good wooden learning-table," Lipka grunted, "but to tell the truth I don't know what is more wooden, the table or Zellik. Plain talk: you could be the teacher of the children, Maisha, but you'd have to leave off some of the Hasidism . . . anyway, my boy, you see . . ." Lipka waved his hand vaguely by which I took him to mean that while he thought me a fine fellow despite my bad feet, he hoped I was not really too fanatical about my beliefs, at least not so fanatical as to not marry his daughter.

I married Gitel, of course, but not right away. Not until my feet benefited by the resting and not until I tried myself out as the teacher at the learning-table in the synagogue, with Lipka and several of the fathers sitting by, listening. And it went well, my expounding of the Law, and the fathers were pleased, and I said to myself afterward, when I heard the praise, "Didn't Uncle Mendel tell of the Rabbi of Stretin who said that special piety should be kept hidden, otherwise the pious one is guilty of pride?" Ay, I really didn't know what to do!

For two weeks I waited for the answer to come. Then on the eve of the Feast of Lights my Uncle Mendel came to me in a dream. He wore the white robes of prayer. In his hand he held a golden light, and he took me and kissed me. "Maisha, Maisha," he said over and over again, "Ay, Maisha, Maisha . . . he who is a complete Jew at home is only half a Jew on a journey."

"But, Uncle Mendel!" I replied in my dream. "Why then are you without a home?"

"Maisha . . . does not the Talmud tell us that *when the Ark set forth* is a separate book? And has not your Ark found its home?"

"You are my Ark, Uncle Mendel!"

Then he smiled and kissed me once more, putting his golden light in my hand. I looked about me, holding the light up high, and saw Gitel coming toward me in a slow, beautiful solemn dance, wearing the wifely ceremonial wig and long many-colored petticoats . . . and when I looked for Uncle Mendel again, to return the golden light, he had disappeared. "Uncle Mendel!" I shouted, "Your light, your light! You forgot it!"

"Sh," Gitel whispered, her brow knitting, but with something gay and lively in her seriousness. "Stay, grow a beard, and we'll have children! Remember the words of Uncle Mendel . . . 'He who is a complete Jew at home is only half a Jew on a journey.'"

"Ay," I whispered back.

"Don't you see what it means, Maisha? . . . It means, truly, that a Jew without a home cannot be more than half a Jew."

"Gitel . . . Gitel . . ."

"And without bringing Uncle Mendel into it at all, Maisha . . . can a man be more than half a man without a wife?"

. . . What could I do against a dream like that? In the morning before breakfast, even before morning prayers, I went to Lipka. "I had a dream . . . let Gitel be alone with me for an hour today."

"Good," Lipka said as though he read me. "It's going to be a match?"

So that afternoon with the mother removed to a neighbor's hut and Lipka out on a roof somewhere with his buckets of tar, I sat with Gitel at the kitchen table for the formal proposal. Taking a long cold look at her I began to think of all the advantages . . . a devoted wife, a fine home, no other children but Gitel there. . . . "You're not really pretty," I began, "but my feet are no bargain either."

She gave her head a subtle twist and said, "Well, that's true. Let's make up together that you will always keep your feet covered, and I'll walk around with a handkerchief over my face."

"But seriously — "

"What's a face or a foot, Maisha?" Her eyes became full of love for me and I quickly felt ashamed of myself. "I'll be for you, if you want . . . and if your feet should fail you I'll carry you in my hands."

To be loved so . . . the thought of it alone gave me the last push I needed. "Your face, I should say, has . . . the right kind of eyes. . . . Gitel, let the wedding be during the Feast of Lights!"

"Let it be as you say," she smiled, twisting her head a bit, as she always did when she was pleased, like a little bird.

I became a Golinsker husband and sat at the head of the children's learning-table in the synagogue from eight in the morning to four in the afternoon. My father-in-law gave us the customary year's free board and lodging, and then another year on top of it. To pay for our coats and shoes and linens I dragged tiny sums out of the community by selling candles during the time of the Feast of Lights; by disposing of the leavened leftovers in the huts at Passover; by acting as assistant prayer-maker at the cemetery (when the beadle and meat-slaughterer, old Zellik, was ill); but mostly by standing on my feet all day on Sunday at the market-square in the village, selling kvas, a white-barley beer Gitel made during the week, at a penny a glass.

In our second year Gitel began to carry and I looked for a hut of my own. To get it I needed not only cash but the privilege of a lease on the land. In these circumstances I could only go to my father-in-law, himself a poor man. But I had no more than opened my mouth than he said, "Well, of course."

"How do you know, 'of course,' when I've hardly told you more than a word?"

"That's how it is with you deep students," Lipka replied. "Students don't know how much meaning there is in one word."

"A truly holy thought," I observed. "Only — "

"Yes, of course . . . only Gitel is with child and you need a hut and a lease for the land . . . and a little cash. Quite an 'only'!"

The manner of my father-in-law's getting me my hut was a real bit of Golinsker juggling. He went first to the old Squire's steward and rent-collector, Valentin Buzarov, and told him, "Your house needs a roof and your little boys Profim and Vassily could do with fine coats and leggings, leather, this year. These I will provide you with, as a gift . . . if you can arrange a land-lease with your master so my son-in-law can have his own hut . . . and if you will permit him to pay you the first year's rent, in full, six months after he has lived in it."

The steward agreed. Then my father-in-law went to old Zellik, the beadle, and said, "You are too old and rheumy to stand all day in the cemetery, saying prayers for those who cannot be here, be it hot or cold or rain or snow. Your roof, moreover, leaks badly and that's why your cough improves. I'll fix your roof, Zellik, at no charge . . . only let Maisha, my son-in-law, stand for you in the cemetery." Zellik agreed and my father-in-law pressed him further. "Your brother, Yeersel-ben-Mayer, is older than you and more feeble in his eyes, which is very bad for a tailor. Now if you will, as our meat slaughterer, kill Yeersel's chickens free for the next two years, I will not only keep your roof perfectly dry above your head, Zellik . . . but I'll also bring you free wood for two years, and send you free kvas, a bottle a day, for four years. Agreed?"

After Zellik had agreed, my father-in-law then went to Yeersel-ben-Mayer, Zellik's brother, well over seventy-five at the time, and proposed, "If you will sew me two boys' coats, Yeersel, with leather leggings, I'll fix your roof, Zellik will kill your chickens free for two years, I'll bring you free wood for four, and my son-in-law, Maisha, will provide not only a bottle of kvas a day for two years, but also say your cemetery prayers for you at all times you are away from the village in the course of your sewing." When the old tailor hesitated, Lipka added, quickly, "And further! I'll send you a barrel of tar for your wagon wheels!"

"Tar for the wagon?" the old man wheezed. "And who will cook it?"

"Maisha!"

In this fashion I got my land-lease . . . now all I had to do was find the wood for the hut, and the glass, and the door, and the step . . . and build it. How my father-in-law managed all this I never clearly knew for years, except that for the rest of his life he seemed to fix as many roofs for nothing as what he was paid for, and that I dug clay and chopped wood for him and gave away more kvas for nothing than any money I saw, and that my Gitel worked years in the Squire's fields without Buzarov ever giving her a penny. Even the actual building of the hut was done without me. I hardly could hold a hammer in my hand. But my father-in-law enlisted every landsman in the village to throw up the hut with the lumber he had wheedled from the Squire's steward. (Much later in his life I discovered that in payment for the lumber he had become a steady cooker of illegal alcohol for Buzarov and had been thereafter unable to get out of Buzarov's hands.) My father-in-law even maneuvered an iron stove into our hut, and when Gitel saw it her eyes couldn't have become bigger had she seen an extra sun in the sky.

"For these blessings, father-in-law," I assured him, "you shall live eternally near to The Highest One."

"And why not?" he chuckled. "Who else could fix His roof?"

"I would rather have managed to build my hut myself."

"Ay, that would be the trick of tricks. One hand washes the other and that's all, or both stay dirty."

Without bitterness and even without much thought I had already begun to make over, slowly, what Uncle Mendel meant to me. From having been my life's inspiration, he became my support through it. I no longer looked for him on the road to Ladi but saw him "in every strange hut, on all roads, and in the life of night," as he had foretold upon our farewell. Uncle Mendel would come to me regularly in my dreams and I would think upon waking, "We are still together."

Our son was born. He almost killed Gitel but she recovered, though she never conceived again. The years began to spin fast. New faces at the learning-table, new graves in the cemetery, more pains in my feet . . . where did it all go? My son Haim suddenly sprouts long legs, the beadle is dead, I'm the new beadle . . . the old tailor dies, too, and the Squire's son comes and goes from Petersburg and Paris like I walk back and forth from the synagogue . . . and faster, faster spin the years . . . and the slower I walk . . . and my son Haim stands on the altar of the synagogue at the age of thirteen, and is confirmed a son of Israel and a man . . . and Gitel and I stand in the first row and look up at him and with him, sing . . .

"Thine, O Lord, is the greatness, and the power, and the glory, and the victory, and the majesty; for all that is in the heaven and in the earth is Thine."

Now my Haim is a man . . . sits no longer at my learning-table all day but runs up ladders and cooks tar with my father-in-law . . . who comes to my wife into our hut not two weeks after, his hands black with tar, his sweat-wetted hair matted on his brow. . . .

Says my wife, "Father . . . here in the middle of the day?"

"Buzarov tells me he won't be taken until next month . . . as a special favor. . . ."

"Who taken, what taken?"

"They put him on the list . . . Haim."

"Ay. . . ."

"Not until next month, Gitel. . . ."

"The army, ay . . . Haim in the army. . . ."

"Sh. Between now and next month the heavens can turn over, anything can happen. Clear?"

"Clear, what . . ." Then my wife understands and spits to the floor. "Give him feet like his father, cripple his hands . . . ?"

"Hold yourself in, daughter. . . ."

"Ay. . . ."

"Sh. Crying helps nothing! Listen, Gitel." My father-in-law, blunt honest soul, means every word. "Thank God we have time — a month."

"But no feet, no feet," my wife moans.

"Who said feet?"

"Then what?"

"Well . . . a finger will be sufficient . . . the right finger . . . the shooting finger, only."

She cries, what else?

"Gitel, have a head! Listen to your father! Which is better — that Haim should lose one finger, or everything?"

Well, it didn't come out the way my father-in-law wanted it. There were no committees in the hamlets, no agencies good or bad behind which to pull this way and that; to stay out of the army a rural Jewish lad had really to be disabled . . . a shorter leg, a twisted back, a crippled hip . . . and we had them in Golinsk, to be sure. Ay, what it means to cripple a son! Yet many of us chose this wry freedom for them as better than the cripplings of twenty-five years of military slavery.

We couldn't decide what on earth to do. Haim was for entering the army and deserting. But in his time of 1847 where could one hide except America, so far away and so little-known a land? In the time of Shim and Laib and their Uncle Mottel, it was possible to wriggle on well-used secret paths leading to ships for America, where landsmen were waiting to receive them . . . but my Haim was born forty years too soon for such good fortune.

My father-in-law said, "What else is left but to let him fall from a low roof? I'm a tar-maker and a roofer, Haim is my helper . . . how can they say it's a fakery?"

"Look at my feet," I told him. "All my life I'll have them with me.

Take a good second look at them, Lipka, and you'll realize that these feet *are* my life . . . ay, The One Above should help me!"

For the first time I felt stricken with anger. Of course I understood the sinfulness of it; didn't our greatest Tzaddiks agree that the life of the flesh was as the life of a fly, that the flesh was only the coat we wore as we passed through the earth-phase and on to the eternal? And didn't Uncle Mendel say so, and didn't I believe it too? . . . But believe today, believe tomorrow . . . a parent needs to help his child, I kept thinking, not to baggage him up with worldly sufferings. . . .

Then came the night that Gitel shook me out of a tremulous sleep. "Wake yourself, Maisha!" she commanded.

"It's yet dark," I mumbled.

"It just came to me in a dream," she whispered excitedly.

"Tell me tomorrow."

"Maisha," she announced, "listen . . . I dreamed I stood before the Minsker Gubernator himself, the master of the whole province! . . . he wore a long blue coat with tails, and medals with ribbons, and he told me to sit down next to him! . . . and I wept and pleaded for him to save me Haim!"

"And what did the Gubernator do, make Haim a general?"

"Maisha! I told him all about you and your feet, and how I almost died to give birth to Haim . . . and the Gubernator told me Haim could stay home!"

"Very nice," I replied. "Now turn around and go to sleep. And should you by any chance meet the Gubernator of Pinsk, bring me for a present one of his testicles."

"All right. Laugh at me but a present I'll bring you . . . a present from the Minsker Gubernator . . . *Haim!*"

"What are you talking about?"

"I know well what I'm talking about," she replied. "It's a sign, Maisha. With this dream God tells me, '*Go to the Gubernator, Gitel. Your plea will be heard*'!"

All the next day she talked of nothing but her dream and how she would really go to Minsk and appeal to the Gubernator himself. I thought to myself, "Let her talk herself out. She'll see herself how crazy the idea is."

But Gitel didn't stop. She told her father, and Haim, and the wives. And the more she talked about it, so help me, the less idiotic it began to sound to me. If my Gitel wasn't the cleanest, dearest, most joyous little spirit in the world then she wasn't anything; The One Above couldn't have chosen a better soul to send down a sign to. By nightfall of the second day after her dream every Golinsker landsman and his wife would ask me, "Is Gitel going? When is Gitel going to Minsk?"

It began to sound almost sensible.

That night I said to my father-in-law, "Now really, Lipka, what do you think?"

He leaned back in his chair, looked at Gitel, and said, "If she had dreamed a dream that would make her want to go to Minsk and ask the committee there for help, I would have said it was useless. And if she had dreamed a dream that would make her want to go to Petersburg and ask the Tsar for help, I would have said it was crazy. . . ." Here he paused to take a few puffs on his pipe. And then he said, very slowly and with a hammer in every word, "But since she has dreamed a dream that makes her want to go to Minsk and ask the Gubernator for help . . ." And then he stopped.

"Well?" I asked.

"Finish the word, Father," Gitel demanded, but softly.

"He will," Haim said faithfully, his long, pointy jaw moving fitfully.

My father-in-law tapped his pipe against his palm and let the live fire from it drop into his hand. He looked down at the little gleaming spots, nodding and sighing.

"You'll burn yourself, look out," Gitel said. He turned his palm facing down and the burning tobacco fell to the floor. Then he said, "The end I don't know." Pounding his strong fist on the table, he shouted, "Oh dear God, what will the end be?"

"See?" Gitel demanded of me. "Even my father can't say it's useless or crazy and isn't he a standing man of the world?" Her voice rose in a joyful call. "Father! Go to Buzarov, promise him anything . . . but let him see to it that they don't take Haim away until I come back from Minsk! . . . Father?"

"Hnnn," my father-in-law grunted thoughtfully. "The least that could happen, the very least, would be a delay. It could take weeks, even months. You'll have things to prepare, assembling papers, certificates, and so on."

But Gitel's voice rose even higher; she pressed her hand to her bosom as she spoke. "What papers, what certificates? I need no more but what's in my mother's heart . . . what else could I bring to the Gubernator? In my dream he raised me with his hands and told me not to cry!"

"Gitel," I asked, "what face did the Gubernator have?"

"What other kind," she sobbed like a child who weeps while he laughs, "but the face of a King Solomon? A serious brow, a beard with curls!"

My father-in-law turned to me and pushed my arm, his face showing grave wonder, his voice urgent with stubbornness. "Well, Maisha — what it is, a sign or a simple craziness?"

"At the first look," I said, finding my way from one word to the next, chanting, "it appears as only the sorrow of a mother . . . neither simple nor a craziness, but by no means a sign." I became caught up in the melody of my chant, the sweetness and truth and ecstasy of it, and the gates of my heart opened as they had not for many years, and in my heart I was again the happy lad sitting at the learning-table with Uncle Mendel, watching him nod to my chanting, hearing the full richness of his voice joining with mine. There was in me then a great loosening, a great flowing-over, and my veins glowed with the power of my joy. "Yet to look at it not in the way of the nose, the finger, the eye, but in the way of The Highest One . . . when I look upon the world it sometimes strikes me that the universe has died and that I have been left the only living man . . . and from whom else then can I ask help outside of You, O Lord? . . . And since I and my wife are the same, from whom else could she have begged help, and from whom else could it have come?"

"Hold, hold . . ." Lipka interjected. "From where do we know the dream comes from on high?"

"Ay, we know, we know," I chanted, going to my son, Haim. Pressing his face between my hands I sang to him, "Haim my son, didn't the great Sassover Tzaddik teach us? . . . and what did he teach us, my son? . . . that The Most High first uses simple measures to aid His troubled children . . . but . . . if our trouble is of an unusual nature, then He comes to our aid in an extraordinary way. . . ."

"He believes me," my Gitel cried, overjoyed. "Maisha, Maisha!"

"It's a true sign," I chanted. "True, true, the word of God, absolutely true!"

"Ay," my father-in-law sighed, getting himself to his feet heavily. He picked up his pipe and put it in his pocket, thrusting both hands deeply out of sight. "Maybe it's all a dream," he sighed, ". . . maybe I'll wake up in the next minute and thank God I'm in my bed. Meanwhile I'll go looking for Buzarov."

And old Buzarov was found in the drinking-room of the Nikolai Inn, and my father-in-law pleaded with the steward to petition the old Squire to direct the military to hold off Haim's conscription until his mother returned from Minsk. Buzarov laughed but my father-in-law persisted; in desperation he spoke of the mother's dream. And this amused the steward, so that he ran to his master with the story of a mad Jew-woman's fantasy.

"Go tell her," said the Squire upon hearing Buzarov, "that she may have a full month to discover the treachery of her God. And tell through the town the cause of her journey so that after her failure she may be laughed at and spat upon together with her God. It will be a good thing."

"Should I saddle then for Pukop in the morning," asked Buzarov of his master, "and deliver your request to the Colonel?"

"I shall ride to Pukop myself," said the Squire, his fingers tightened now about his goblet, no smile upon his lips. "Between us we shall manage. Take yourself back into the village, Valentin. Say that the

Squire holds the Jew-woman's journey as a test of her God, that her son will be given the month freely."

Then on that same evening which was a Sabbath in the summer did every Jew in Golinsk, man, woman, and child, gather themselves in their synagogue to pray for the happy success of the mother's mission. And they prayed as for a festival, singing, "We will give thanks unto Thee and declare Thy praise for our lives which are committed unto Thy hand, and for our souls which are in Thy charge, and for Thy miracles which are daily with us, and for Thy wonders and benefits which are wrought at all times, evening, morning, and noon." And on the morrow of the Sabbath day did they again all sing, "One generation shall laud Thy works to another, and shall declare Thy mighty acts."

And then on the following day did the mother, Gitel, set her feet upon the highroad to Minsk, spurning all company and conveyance. The strong woman of the fields walked with firm purpose throughout two days, slept peacefully by the roadside throughout two nights, and on the third day came to the iron gates of the Gubernator's castle. Seeing the ragged woman so close to the gates, the guards put upon her to remove herself, and she cried, "I will speak to the Gubernator."

Then the powerful guards of the Gubernator cast her to the street, but the mother lay there, saying, "I will speak to the Gubernator." The guards fell to opening her skin in a hundred places. But when the mother moved her lips she said, "I will speak to the Gubernator."

The crowd gave her spittle and stones until Jews came and took her to a Jewish house to bind her cuts. For six days the mother could not raise herself, saying only, "I will speak to the Gubernator." And when the man of that house had listened to the mother's account, he ran wildly to a man of the Committee. With a number of his fellows this man of the Committee came to the mother's bedside and with his own ears listened to her, afterwards turning to his Committee-members, saying in an undertone, "The poor soul is infected with Hasidic madness. The moment she is well enough to bear the ride, we must carry her back to Golinsk before she loses her life together with her mind."

These words, however, reached the mother's ears, and before dawn she rose and clothed herself in her ragged garment and dragged herself again before the iron gates of the Gubernator's castle. In that early hour there stood but one guard, and when he saw the mother stop close to him he ordered her away. But the mother did not step away and the guard drew his sword to her and pricked her with the point upon the head of a still-bleeding wound. The mother cried in pain, saying to herself in Yiddish, "Ay, God, help me."

Hearing the Yiddish, the guard lowered his sword and said, "A Jew?"

"Deep, deep," the mother cried in Yiddish, "and I will yet speak to the Gubernator!"

Frightened, the guard stilled her with his hand, saying, "They spoke of you in the barracks. I, too, am a Jew . . . only speak in Russian! Or better, be still!" The Jewish guard then pulled the mother into the darkness of the sentry box, pleading, "Go away, mother, run for your life. The day-guard will come in a moment and this time you will be broken into pieces."

"No," spoke the mother. "I will stay and I will not be broken into pieces."

"But if they see you here when they come . . ." the guard replied, "don't you understand, mother? They will order me . . . order *me* to take my sword and . . . have mercy, mother, and go away!"

"Have no fear," spoke the mother, "your hand shall not murder me."

Yet even as the mother spoke, behind them opened the doors of the Gubernator's castle, and the day-guard marched out, four tall men with heavy boots. "They are here already," gasped the Jewish guard. "Ay, mother, mother . . ."

As the sound of the boots filled her ears, the mother looked upon the crying Jewish guard and said, "If you must kill me, my son, do it with one strong push." But the Jewish guard stood transfixed, listening to the relief guards asking each other, "Where is Misch?"

"Probably asleep in the sentry box, the bastard," one of them replied. Hearing their boots now coming toward the sentry box the Jewish guard screamed out, pulling his pistol from his holster, "I'm here." Then the Jewish guard ran quickly out of the sentry box and along the deserted gray street, and one of the others saw and shouted, "Done for him," and began shooting and pursuing.

As they all flew after the Jewish guard the mother ran out of the sentry box; and seeing the door to the Gubernator's castle standing open she ran to it and entered into a large dark wooden-walled hall lit with a single taper. The mother heard sounds of people running down from above her and shrank herself into a dark corner. Soldiers ran past her through the gates, and bullets could be heard from the distance as more soldiers came running down the stairs. A few women came out of doors in the hallway and began to pass flame over the candles. The mother shrank deeper into her corner as the hall grew lighter and lighter. And then at the head of the stairs appeared a livid man wearing a dressing robe with a mink collar and slippers of the finest leather. His eyes snapped with anger yet the mother, Gitel, seeing him at last, ran to the foot of the stairs, her arms stretched up, crying "Gubernator! Gubernator!"

The mother fell to her knees as the women drew themselves about her, chattering, "Who is she?" The Gubernator ran quickly down the stairs, saying something to the women as he passed and headed for the street. They took hold of the mother harshly and threw her into a windowless room, locking the door. There she fainted, with a prayer for the Jewish guard on her lips.

After a long time the door opened again and the mother was once more dragged out by the same women, who took her to a water closet and began to brush the dirt from her garment, and to wash her, and to comb her hair. The mother submitted, asking, "Then the Gubernator will speak to me?" The women made no reply but continued their scrubbing; and when they had done with the mother they put her in the hands of a guard who motioned her to follow after him.

In this manner she proceeded up the staircase until they came to a wide and brightly candled corridor lined with spotless footmen standing on the deepest of carpets. The guard paused before a high door, knocked, and when it opened, motioned the mother to enter. There-upon she came into a festive hall tabled by gentry in the midst of their banqueting. At the head of the long table stood the resplendent Guber-nator, smiling to the mother and holding one hand to her, saying, "This way, my good woman." The mother then walked by the glitter-ing gentry at the table, and knelt before the Gubernator. "Up," he com-manded and she obeyed. "Wherefore come you to me?" the Guber-nator questioned her, glancing warmly at the attentive gentry.

"I come on my feet from Golinsk to speak to you," declared the mother. "I have a son, an only son thirteen years old that they would take for the army. Yet it came to me in a dream that you are wiser than an idiot, Gubernator, and that this being so, you would grant me my son to myself, and no army."

Much chattering rose from the table of gentries at the words of the mother. The Gubernator demanded, yet with a smile, "And wherefore am I deemed wiser than an idiot, mother?"

"In my dream," she replied, "you came to me as King Solomon, the wisest of all, and gave me back my son. King Solomon was wiser than any idiot, and so it must be with you."

"Now tell me, mother," remarked the Gubernator, smiling even more warmly at his gentry, "why Solomon was wiser than any idiot."

"Idiots believe that they are wiser than anybody," the mother said. "Yet Solomon was so greatly wise that he could persuade even idiots to admit themselves fools."

At this the Gubernator threw back his head and laughed with the pleasure of a child, and the gentry dutifully imitated him. "Yes, then," the Gubernator said, composing himself, "you think me wiser than the idiots who told you not to come here?" The mother raised her head and spoke, "My son stands on the list for next month, Gubernator. Spare him for me, I beg you, I beg you." Then the mother fell to the floor and kissed his feet, and the gentry stood up to see, and the Guber-nator stepped back. "Raise yourself, mother," he spoke. "Your son shall be spared. Go now and be fed, and your hurts dressed, and in good time we shall settle this of your son." With a small cry did the mother again kiss the feet of the Gubernator and moan to herself happily. Then footmen led the mother away to be fed and her hurts dressed. Yet at the door she paused and asked, "What of the Jewish guard?" But the footmen replied, "That is over," and brought her to a clean chamber where women came to her with ointments and clean garments.

The mother had not known that the Jewish guard had flown into the Jewish district of Minsk, and that in killing him the guards had fallen upon Jews who had sheltered him. Through that whole day terror lived in the Jewish district, and crowds gathered angrily and sent fire and flame into Jewish houses, and firemen drowned Jewish children, and dead lay in every Jewish street.

To put a clean face upon this, to counter evil with good, had the Gubernator smilingly granted the blessing of her son upon the mother; and until quiet returned to the Jewish district the Gubernator kept the mother within the castle. The days fell into weeks and the mother appealed to the women to bring her to the Gubernator. "I am healed," she cried, "and I must be soon in Golinsk before the time is up." Then one day the women led her to the Gubernator. "It shall be as you dreamed," he told her gently. "Today you shall be taken in a carriage with two horses to your village. And in your hands will be the paper ordering your son's exemption, with my seal upon it."

"God bless you forever," cried the mother, "but give me no paper with your seal upon it. I may lose it or it may be taken from me." She bared her arm to the shoulder and held it out to the Gubernator. "Let the order be written here, with needles, together with your seal. Then I cannot lose it or have it taken from me."

The Gubernator agreed. Men of such craft came to the castle and imprinted the order, with the seal, as the mother had requested. Upon the following day the happy mother set out for Golinsk in a closed carriage drawn by two horses and with two corporals riding on the driver's seat.

The mother sat proudly. They rode without incident until the carriage came within two miles of Pukop, where they met a company coming from the garrison there. The corporal pulled his carriage to the side of the road, allowing the garrison to pass, and exchanged remarks with the garrison sergeant.

"How is it in Minsk?" said the sergeant from Pukop.

"You haven't heard?" asked the corporal from Minsk.

"Everything is as should be," said the second corporal from Minsk loudly, throwing a glance behind him.

"Somebody important in there?" asked the sergeant from Pukop in an undertone.

"Very," said the second corporal from Minsk.

Hearing them, the mother thrust her head out of the carriage window and the sergeant glanced at her once and at the corporals twice, saying suspiciously, "Show me your papers." The corporals showed their papers and the sergeant examined them. Then he spoke to the mother, "Kindly stand outside."

The first corporal from Minsk said, "Sergeant, she had better stay where she is. She is important to the Gubernator."

The sergeant turned and sent the company from the garrison on its way, and the second corporal said, "Well, Sergeant, we'll be going along."

"You will remain a moment," the sergeant replied thoughtfully. Then he spoke again to the mother, "You are from where?"

"Golinsk."

"And your name?"

"Gitel, wife of Maisha . . . mother of Haim."

"You have identity papers?"

"No papers," the mother replied. Then she added, smiling, "But I have this."

Baring her arm, she showed the sergeant the Gubernator's tattoo. "It is the Gubernator's order exempting my son from the army," the mother said. Reading the tattoo, the sergeant's face grew annoyed. He looked at the two corporals again and the first told him, "It is as it reads . . . yes."

"May I, kindly, have another look?" the sergeant said to the mother, climbing into the carriage and closing the door. The corporals in the driver's seat heard what they took for the gasp of a woman whose bare arm was unceremoniously squeezed. But when the sergeant did not soon emerge, the second corporal, becoming curious, jumped down from his place and looked into the carriage. There he saw the mother sprawled limply on the seat, a handkerchief stuffed in her mouth, and the cuffs of the sergeant's blue tunic high upon his forearms.

The corporal said, "What trouble is this?" And the sergeant replied, "The trouble is over." By then the second corporal had jumped down from the driver's seat and the sergeant spoke further to both. "This one had a boy of thirteen on the list for next month. But he was mistakenly taken two weeks ago and shipped far to the east. The thing on her arm says, 'Serious punishment for all disregarding this order.' I had to protect the Colonel."

"Well, the Colonel," said the first corporal. "Yes, but . . ."

"Let us leave her with the sergeant," said the second corporal, "and turn for Minsk as though we had taken her to her door."

They carried the mother into a piece of woods not far from the highroad. The sergeant then said, "Go back to the carriage." The two corporals obeyed, and as the first of them leaned down to pick up the reins, he muttered words of annoyance at the sergeant who had suddenly placed him in this unexpected position; but his companion assured him that neither of them had seen nor heard the act, and that whatever the outcome of the sergeant's loyalty he was only one while they were two. At this, the first agreed and took heart, whipping the horses away.

The sergeant cut sapling wood with his sword to make a small hot fire. Removing the handkerchief from the mother's mouth, he thrust the face and arms into the fire, keeping it hot with more wood until the skin had shriveled, more especially the arms. He drove the sword under her left shoulder blade as an afterthought of surety, wiped the sword with the handkerchief which had been in the mother's mouth, and threw the handkerchief in the fire. Watching the fire burn itself out, the sergeant felt the sudden press of his bowels and he relieved them, and threw stones over the last few smoking embers, and walked back to the highroad.

Of these things I knew nothing while I lived . . . it laid in our heads that my wife had perished in Minsk; we had received news of the little pogrom there at the time Gitel must have been within the city; we learned vaguely of a soldier having run berserk in the Jewish district, and shooting. Making inquiries of the Minsk Committee long after Gitel's disappearance, we were told that one such as Gitel had been beaten before the gates of the Gubernator, only to disappear in a moment of derangement on the day of the little pogrom.

I then began the mourning prayers; and long after that, travelers' gossip told of a woman's burned body found in the forest near Pukop. But who listened? Why should anything have befallen Gitel near Pukop when she had been in Minsk during the pogrom?

The landsmen came and urged me to look about, to find a good woman and live a bit contented. The wives picked Yentl, a widowed niece of old Zellik the beadle. Yentl wasn't ugly and had nice children but I couldn't see myself bothering. I was certain I'd say to Yentl, "What? If it's all the same to you I'd rather have a glass of tea."

My father-in-law at last threw up his hands. "Maisha, I pawned and mortgaged myself for I don't know how many years so that you and Gitel (may she rest) could have a house. If you're going to do nothing but sit for your life, you might as well sit in the synagogue and sleep in a corner of my hut . . . if you don't take a wife, act like a man, I'll take the hut back!"

"Do so right away. I won't marry again."

"You're sure?"

"As sure as I'll be with Gitel in The Next World. Remember — even There a man with two wives has trouble."

"Don't make everything into a joke . . . and about Haim. Who knows he won't be coming home?"

"I know."

"He won't be over forty-four when they're finished with him. But you are a Hasid, Maisha . . . a Karliner Hasid . . . and don't Hasids always say they must rejoice?"

"I rejoice."

"How? By giving yourself nothing to live with?"

"Because I have much reason to die."

So at nearly thirty-three in the year 1847 I was pleased to become old Reb Maisha of the crippled feet and asthma and jokes. The rest of my time in Golinsk, the remaining forty years, were really no more than that moment with Lipka.

One more little story and I'll be finished. I should have come to this long before, but a life without sense is not simple to tell of especially when it has been your own.

I pass to the Friday before the Day of Atonement of 1885, the Friday Aaron and Leah died, the Friday of the big early snow and the Parsovs' hill and Yeersel's horse. I was seventy. My white beard came down to a point, like a question mark; my mouth was always open, an O, because of my asthma; and if I didn't tremble from the heat I trembled from the cold; and if it was neither hot nor cold I trembled from the changeable weather.

Aaron's hut was crowded. Two dozen Golinskers filled it, waiting for Yeersel to return from his interview with Mottel. Everybody had something to say about the terrible accident except the victims, naturally, who lay covered side by side upon the bed. The talk ran like a quick river, each trying not to release his lament until the funerals. Suddenly I felt myself yanked into a corner by our meat slaughterer, Laib-Shmul. "Wouldn't it be a blessing on the two orphans if you sat them down and told them a few holy words at a time like this?"

"I have six things I could say to that, Laib-Shmul," and my tone was plain ice. "But I'll only say one. I don't like to be handled like an unclean cow."

"I don't handle unclean cows," Laib-Shmul barked, correctly taking my remark for an accusation.

"Not by daylight," I said shortly.

I really didn't know if Laib-Shmul slaughtered unclean cows on the side but he had always been, ever since I had him at my learning-table as a boy, one who had remained ignorant of the difference between a chicken and a human being. The man was gross to a fault, and even more irritating was his method of never making up his mind about something until he knew the majority's opinion. In this way he managed always to feel at peace with himself; only he was nothing. He behaved as circumstances required, for the most part; and when he acted perhaps in some way which might have not been the majority's, he fell back upon his favorite phrase, "It's all a matter of interpretation."

Most of us Golinskers had long ago decided to be neither Hasids nor Misnagids, but just Jews. There wasn't time enough both to study into the matter and to bring home bread every day. As a result the landsmen had quite agreed among themselves that though I was capable of sitting at the head of the learning-table, in other matters I had little aptitude and less sense. Laib-Shmul particularly enjoyed disputing with me, especially at our synagogue meetings, on anything from the right time for cutting firewood to the wrong time for cutting firewood.

Yeersel came into Aaron's hut, his face gray with strain. Everybody crowded about him. How was Mottel? Would he allow the funerals to take place that same day?

"Yes, yes," Yeersel muttered, bending to unwrap his soaked foot-rags. "Only he begins to interest himself in the orphans, Shim and Laib."

"Interest, what interest?" came from Gershon, the shoemaker, in his hoarse ringing tenor.

"He wants the boys, plainly."

"Impossible to allow," I said immediately.

Out of the high talk which followed, the voice of Tzippe-Sora rose like the crack of a spitzruten. Her old eyes filled with scorn. "Well, now . . . if Mottel had a tongue for every hair on his head, and every one of his tongues told us, 'The boys are my nephews and I'll do with them as I want,' I still wouldn't think of fighting with him! Have you all forgotten how close Mottel stands to the Squire through Buzarov? Leave Mottel alone, at least until you men sit down and make a plan . . . how the two boys will live and with whom . . . then we'll let Mottel know what we want for the boys."

"That's what I thought all the time," I heard Laib-Shmul saying loudly; and as usual, a little late.

"Well, Yeersel?" asked Laib-Shmul.

"Let it be as others say," Yeersel mumbled. I had never seen him so shocked by death before.

Then one of Tzippe-Sora's sons, Yussel, came running in and shouting, "Did you hear about Mottel?"

Yussel's eyes glittered. I liked him, one of my worst pupils. The man had simple sweetness, though no brains, and seeing him often warmed me. This time, by his glints, I gathered the news was good. "If you want to see something, go to the police! He's there!"

"The police?"

"He went too far this time."

"Killed someone?" from Nochim's Zagzaigel.

"He broke the shoulder of the postman, Dimitri, with one swing of his sledge," Yussel explained with gestures. "Dimitri came back from his rounds needing a shoe for a horse and Mottel promptly broke his shoulder. It's one thing to pick a fight — but this time it was a government employee, no less!"

"Thank you, O Highest One," said Tzippe-Sora. "Only be so good as to keep him there for a good ten years!"

Indeed, a Mottel in jail meant a Mottel without a problem for us. And even as we buried Aaron and Leah that afternoon in the ground behind the synagogue, and heard their sons, Shim and Laib, stand saying the mourners' prayer, the thought of having no contention from Mottel in the planning of the orphans' future gave us who gathered around the brown mounds in the snow a hint of the sweet goodness to come to them and to us all.

Directly following the funeral, the landsmen took themselves into the synagogue and sat down, unwrapping their wet foot-rags. Being the beadle as well as the head at the learning-table, it was my duty to light the fire in the stove. But I had neglected to bring in firewood the day before and it was now completely soaked.

Sitting then in their coats the landsmen began to talk about where Shim and Laib might live and what they would do. Being Golinskers, they started where they should have finished. "Of course it's a simple thing," said Hertz, the grease-maker, shrugging. "Aaron was a tailor and Shim helped him. Shim is now a man fourteen years old and well knows how to hold a needle in his hand. I don't see the problem with him. He does for Yeersel what he did for his father, may he rest. As for Laib, he's eleven, and an orphan, so he'll be confirmed a year earlier, on his next birthday. And as to how they will live and who is to care for them, also obvious. . . ."

A silence greeted Hertz when he finished, not the silence of agreement but the kind wherein everybody disagrees but waits for someone else to make the first attack.

"There are different obstacles," said Gershon, breaking the silence thoughtfully. "Remember they have an aunt and a grandfather in Minsk who might want something to say . . . let's not hurry to a poor decision. . . ."

"The grandfather sits paralyzed and the aunt is no bargain," called out Zisha, Naftoli-Dovid's eldest son, from the benches; a hard worker, quieter than his father, speaking little; a good man, far from bright, unlike his namesake, Zish, the old army corporal.

Yeersel asked Zisha how he knew the aunt was no bargain and Zisha said, "Leah, may she rest, once told me how the aunt never gave milk to anybody from her cow unless they brought her potato peelings first. Not even to the sick did she give milk without potato peelings, and that's no woman to leave orphans with!"

"Wait, think a minute, brothers," Nochim said excitedly, bitten by a sudden idea. "Why, in a word, can't they stay in all our homes, for a month at a time?"

Another silence, and then a harangue capped by Laib-Shmul's empty zeal of spokesmanship. "In the name of your stupidity, Nochim, give yourself a blessing! Go empty yourself of what you're splashing all over us!"

"Hold your mouth in the synagogue," Hertz warned.

"It's the height of foolishness," the aroused Laib-Shmul insisted. "What are they, horses to be dragged from stable to stable every month?"

The truth, it was too cold in the synagogue to do any clear thinking. They were shouting and pounding the learning-table only to keep a little warm. As time went on and they shivered and sputtered in their coats, I began to fear they were freezing themselves to spite me. More than once I announced that I would go around to collect dry firewood from the huts but each time I was waved back to my seat.

I felt my days as beadle were beginning to be numbered. The demands of my asthma had made me careless about things like firewood; and as the afternoon wore on, and tempers kept rising as the temperature dropped, I spurred myself to think of something which would come down upon the matter with the clear sense of a Solomon and make them admire my brilliance. When nothing of the kind occurred I felt shamed in my heart. Me, a Karliner God-child, unable to untie the knot of a blessing upon two orphans! What a failure for one who had once called himself a Hasid!

I sat in the midst of all the useless noise and I said to myself, "Maisha, a piece of wood has more to it than you . . . if it doesn't grow at least it can be made to stand up . . . or it can give heat when it's burned . . . while you can't give anything, you who sat at the head of the learning-table when all but three of these landsmen were children . . . and not only can't you help them now, Maisha . . . how much could they have learned at your table, to be so futile today?"

Finally when it seemed that the meeting must end in an empty uproar, there came to me, as if by special courier from The One Above, a magnificent conception which could lift me into the very bosom of God, a conception gaining me not only new respect from the landsmen but also the services of two pairs of young strong arms and legs in the performance of my beadle's duties. I stood up and hobbled to the learning-table which had been the center of my life, giving myself courage by pretending that they were still my pupils at lesson time. Rubbing my knuckles against the table I said, "Children, children . . . I want a word."

I spoke as one long acquainted with the position of beadle, with just enough of a humble tone to show I considered myself only another such as they, baffled but still stubbornly seeking an answer. "Children," I began. "It's nearly Sabbath-time and the stone we hammer still remains a stone in one piece. Let me look at this stone. Who knows but maybe I'll find the one little crack, that when hit just right will break it?"

"We are now looking at stones?" Hertz said sadly.

"Let him open his mouth," Yeersel told him.

"Let me be pardoned," I began again, "but up to now all of us have been twisting ourselves around like a fart in the borsht."

"Ay, it's late," moaned Laib-Shmul. "We're frozen into blocks of ice and he brings up a good hot borsht! First it's stones and then borsht and in the end he'll serve up a whole German lecture!"

No one answered Laib-Shmul but I felt their mood of limited patience. "To call the nephew of Mendel the Karliner a German word-juggler is very foolish," I said softly, bending low over the table, looking from face to face to find the glimmer of a wedge. Yeersel's was the kindliest and the saddest and I addressed him directly. "Yeersel, look at me. Am I not a person you could truly call an orphan? Alone, old, and getting to be a problem? To snatch the matter by the back of the neck, isn't my heart fitted by experience to know the weight of orphaning better than any of you? I'll only mention Gitel, may she rest, and my Haim, may he rest wherever he is. . . ."

"Oh, let up, let up," roared Laib-Shmul, "why talk of what we know when it's what we don't know that hurts more?"

"Very well, then. I wish to take Shim and Laib and be responsible. I want to be their mother and father."

"But, Maisha," Gershon said, "you don't even take the right care of yourself, I mean . . . ?"

"I'm used to them and they to me. I'm their teacher, we know each others' little habits, and it will work. Shim can be apprenticed to Yeersel, eat with him, and sleep with me in my hut. Laib will be twelve next May and until then he will study for his orphan's confirmation as a man of Israel. Both of them can live in my hut, and Tzippe-Sora can finally have her heart's desire by paying the boys a rent for their hut . . . she'll have a quiet place of her own away from her crowd of family boarders until it's time for Shim or Laib to move back to the hut . . . whoever has a wife first. Well, there . . . plain enough?"

"Plain, plain," said Yeersel, frowning with worry. "Maisha . . . please pardon me . . . but don't you think maybe you're just a little too, too . . . ?"

"Too old?" I replied, trembling. "Yes, without a question! But where is a younger man to say he'll dedicate himself to the boys?" I saw guilt in the eyes that stared at me and I stared back at them, my eyes making a circle around the table. In that moment I saw I had them; allowing myself to breathe more deeply, I spoke in a wild surge of confidence as I had in the years of my youth when nothing I said could be wrong. "Why are we shivering and wasting time? And tell me why in my last years there shouldn't be young sounds in my house again, and warmer walls, and newer jokes? Let The One Above take you to Him for throwing me this blessing, of guiding two sweet children of good parents, may they rest, into a Jewish manhood, into a life of bread and joy of which it will truly be said, 'The Lord became attentive to them, for they sang in the midst of their troubles.' . . . Oh, before I push myself into The Next World, let me leave something of myself growing in two fine young Jewish hearts. . . ."

For a few moments, nothing . . . then beginning with Yeersel the landsmen gaveled the table one by one with their open palms; a decision! And Laib-Shmul too, of course, smacking his palm down louder than any other. They rose and stamped their feet as I turned to the altar and got out the candles, seeing the sun already slanted to twilight.

In the next minute we were at our evening prayers; and on that Sabbath eve the ritual was chanted with more than the usual adoration for the blessing which had been rewarded. In triumphant cantillations which I made soar fervently over all the others', I gave thanks to The One Above for having managed so well.

The next day was the Sabbath. After evening prayers I sat down with Yeersel and Gershon for an hour and we agreed that the boys should sit the full week of the mourning period where they had started it, in Yeersel's hut. Meanwhile Daneel and Zagzaigel would attend to moving the boys to my hut. That same night I changed everything around to make it right for three. I gave them the bed and also the full use of my chest of drawers, throwing my clothes into the horsehair trunk and saving the top lid for family objects . . . Gitel's locket, Haim's first prayer books, and the Book of Mendel written in my own hand. I was happy in my heart as I did these things, imagining how they would look sleeping as I watched them from my pallet above the stove . . . the grave Shim, with his tender eldest son's dignity, and Laib, three years younger and a child compared to the serious other. I made my bed on the stove-pallet and lay long, looking at the empty one to be occupied after their mourning period ended. I thought of Haim and Gitel, and of my father and Uncle Mendel, and told myself, "Why sorrow after them now? They are passed-over, and have perhaps wiped out some of my sins for me. Why shouldn't I feel joy in them as well as in Shim and Laib?" I began thinking of Laib-Shmul and how I might curb my dislike of him. Now that I had risen to make myself guardian of the boys, my every action would be watched and weighed in the light of my pledge. I had no fears of making a bad job of it but I saw the benefit of keeping on good terms with our meat slaughterer; better with him an insincere peace than a sincere quarrel. In this calm fashion I fell asleep.

On the following morning, the Sunday, I thought to make an early visit to the bathhouse, it being the day of the Atonement Eve; I enjoyed bathing in quiet and had yet to overcome the shame of my crippled feet, wishing not to have them seen by too many. Directly after morning prayers I walked down the lane to the bathhouse superintended by Yakov, Tzippe-Sora's, a jolly young curser of nineteen or so, with a big mat of hair, coarse but good-natured. Tzippe-Sora paid Buzarov a stiff rent for the bathhouse plot (which she denied, Tzippe-Sora being superstitious about giving out information concerning her private affairs). She lived as humbly as any of us, yet it was known, for example, that Laib-Shmul had exacted a dowry of forty rubles, gold, for marrying Tzippe-Sora's now departed Hendel; Hendel said her mother borrowed it from Vassily Buzarov, with the mother saying only, when hints were made to her face about her wealth, "With your brains and my money, Rothschild couldn't steer such a world." . . . But walking down to the bathhouse that Sunday morning, exchanging greetings with landsmen and seeing the new deference in their eyes, I thought only of how excellent it was to be seventy and alive enough to command a respect.

As I came to the bathhouse I saw a number of landsmen anxiously grouped around the figure of Sergeant Kuizma Oblanski, his white cap and epaulets high above them, his tunic unbuttoned as usual, and his sword hanging carelessly to within an inch of the ground. The sight of the policeman standing outside our bathhouse on the day before the hallowed Day of Atonement, and the disdainful indifference with which he was spitting against the wall . . . what on earth did he want?

"Here he comes," Yakov called out, pointing, and Oblanski turned and walked toward me in his slow waddle.

"You," Oblanski said in his squeak of a voice that came out so strangely from behind his red beard. I began to tremble.

"What does he want?" I cried to the landsmen standing about — and to Oblanski — "Yes, sir, Sergeant. Please what is it?"

"You are to come with me."

I said nothing to Kuizma Oblanski. He led me across the road and through the dirty doors of the police building with its soiled flag waving outside. In the hall we passed a large portrait of the Tsar wearing an expression of great royal kindness; and without ceremony Oblanski walked me through a door leading to steps and the basement, and thence to a row of strongly bolted wooden doors. He opened one and pushed me in.

Without a window and even without a candle, I sat on the dusty wooden floor unable to see the hand before my eyes. For me the night had already come and I began to mutter the opening prayer for Atonement Eve, "Blessed art Thou, O Lord our God, King of the Universe, who has sanctified us by Thy commandments and has commanded us to robe in the garment with fringes." I was without a praying garment but I made to lift a fringe and touch it to my lips, continuing, "By authority of the Court on high and by the authority of the Court on earth: with the knowledge of the All-Present and with the knowledge of this congregation, we give leave to pray with them that have transgressed."

The door opened and closed before I could turn to see who it was. In the dark I caught the smell of horses and as the man stepped closer the smell grew stronger. "Well, now," he said, speaking in Russian. But no voice in Golinsk was deeper than his; that and the smell told me it was Mottel.

"You? . . ."

"Tell me, Maisha," he said, going into Yiddish, "what have you been teaching yourself lately?"

"Go away," I begged whispering, trembling. "It's enough that I'm here. For the sake of your dead brother leave me alone before they find you and make everything worse for me."

"Hold yourself in," Mottel replied calmly. "You're here because of me."

"What have I to do with you? . . . Mottel! You didn't mix me in with your Dimitri business? . . . How could you!"

"Hey," he said quietly, putting his hand to my mouth. "You think this is simple?" He gave me a little shake and took his hand away. "Listen. What they will do with me is a question. It depends on how much of the truth Dimitri tells and on how much Buzarov will work the Squire for me."

"It's not my concern about — "

He gripped my arms so that I winced. "This has to do with Aaron . . . sh! . . . he didn't want to buy goods here from Rezatskin, understand? So he went to Minsk and bought there. Now . . . Dimitri helped bring the bodies back and so stole Aaron's goods that he bought in Minsk . . . and sold them the same day, you see, while he was on his mail route."

"I know nothing about any goods, Mottel," I whispered fearfully, "and if this is only to mix me up in your troubles, I won't say a word to them about it, I — "

"Wait," he commanded. After a few moments I felt him putting something in my hand.

"Know what it is?"

"Some kind of paper," I replied.

"It's money. Twenty-five rubles I took from Dimitri. It belongs to the boys, Laib and Shim. It's the money Dimitri got for selling the goods."

"I don't understand this, I don't . . ."

"Simply listen, then . . . when Dimitri got back from his route he came to the smithy for a horseshoe. I asked him about the goods in Aaron's wagon and from how he answered I knew he took it. So from one thing to the next, I broke his shoulder and took the money, understand?"

"But from where did you know about Aaron . . . buying goods in Minsk?"

He spoke as though amused. "Maisha, you think I'm still trying to make tricks with you so that you'll end up in Siberia?" And then a pleased tone entered into his voice. "What's the matter? You don't think Laib would tell me why his father went to Minsk?"

"Laib?"

"He isn't afraid of me. . . ."

It was too dark to see, but he sounded pleased. Yet . . . "Why didn't they take this money away from you when you were arrested?"

"Why?" He chuckled. "Because I know how to hide money. Never mind, after it's dipped in very hot water and dried, nobody will ever guess where I hid it."

"But they'll take it from me!"

"No . . . put them in your pocket, the bills. They'll let you go in good time."

"What?"

"Don't act so surprised, Maisha."

"It's a trick!"

"Of course, what else?" He walked to the door and stopped to say, "Oblanski will be back in a few minutes. And whatever he tells you, remember to say only, 'Yes, Sergeant.' Clear?"

I couldn't talk; it was too much for me to understand. Then Mottel had another thought. "Oh . . . where will the boys stay?"

"The boys? . . . Shim and Laib?" I decided to lie. "I don't know."

"Well, Maisha . . ."

"Wait," I said hastily, feeling the anger in him at my clumsiness. "They'll be with me!"

"It could be worse . . . you're better than the rest of them . . . you, at least, are an honest fool."

He opened the door and went out, leaving me twice-fold in the dark. Only much later did I come to the realization that it had been Mottel who arranged the arrest somehow so that the boys would have the money rightfully theirs, should he be sent away for having attacked Dimitri.

Yet even as it opened up in my mind that the apostate Mottel had this goodness in him, to think of the welfare of the orphans to this extent, it pained me to listen to his judgment of his Jewish brothers. He had spoken as our enemy, yet in him was a goodness connected to his own ignorance, it seemed to me then, the one struggling to overcome the other; and in the cell that evening and all that next Day of

Atonement as I fasted and prayed, it was not only for myself that I asked The One Above for forgiveness, but for Mottel also, one whose works were greater than his knowledge of God, as the Talmud tells, "like a tree with many roots and fewer branches, but which all the winds of heaven cannot uproot."

And in the two remaining years of my life when it would be asked of me, "Why do you, his guardian, let Laib run to the smithy ten times a day even though we know it is for a reason approved by the landsmen?" I would reply, "It is better for Laib to know his evil and to reject it, than not to know it and wonder that it might not be evil at all."

This was hypocrisy. After the time he had got me in prison, I loved him. I loved him not alone because of the twenty-five rubles he had sent to the orphans, but also without a reason. And as you know, such a love lasts forever.

There remains only to tell you of my first moment in The Next World.

My Uncle Mendel came to me as in a dream and he kissed me a welcome and said, "Now, dear little Maisha, what do you think?"

"For want of knowledge have our people gone into captivity," I replied. "For that, and from the arrogance of the world which commands them to remain ignorant and suffer."

"But that is an old story," smiled my Uncle Mendel, "up here."

3. *Laib*
(1874–1932)

THEORETICALLY I AM SUPPOSED TO BE RESTING IN PEACE AND MINDING MY own business. But believe me, that is real crap.

I died angry, and I still am.

They named me Laib, son of Aaron and Leah. Then in the U.S.A. I became first Loy Golinsky and then Dr. Laurence Golin, a fiddler and leader of restaurant orchestras, with a Damrosch collar and white piqué edging inside my vest. Never mind what I was called; the big thing was . . . in my whole life I behaved the way I wanted, not the way I was expected. I was true to myself, you follow me?

Wait, please . . . no sympathetic romanticism. You're not on my side, we don't agree at all . . . or I wouldn't be so angry. Not at you, of course. Or at any particular somebody. It's a matter of the State, the entire State, a thing that is not even a thing but yet the greatest enemy mankind ever had, you follow me? Don't take me wrong, I was never interested in politics and always hated politics but unfortunately politics gave me tremendous bothers and aggravations, always coming into my house without knocking, saying, "Who the hell do you think you are anyway and what the hell right have you got to want to be yourself?"

The State gets irritated by such childish people, hunts them down and robs them of love, bemerds their dignity and honor, and puts signs on them, "*I Am a Shnook*." Oh, the State has its good side. If a person likes to buy a little net and go in the fields chasing butterflies, that's okay; ditto chasing golf balls, women, and streetcars; also all kinds of legalized evils. But let a person start chasing the truth, chasing it and not giving up . . . well, ladies and gentlemen, that person is not going to be very popular even among those who mean most to him. I'll go further: the person who remains true to himself so strongly that he runs up against the brick wall of the State can turn out to be a very excluded person if he's not careful.

Wait again, please. Follow me carefully . . . you think I'm in favor of thieves and murderers? No, sir. I am interested in how the State goes against the person whose interests don't fit the interests of the State. Keep that clear, otherwise you will believe I am being sorry for myself alone, which is not correct. The terrible thing about the State is not what it does to the persons who remain true to themselves, but what it does to the innocently corrupted who live out their existence doing what is *expected* of them, automatically; dreams of childhood and youth forgotten and buried long before their bodies. This is the crime, the murder. And in the victimized, believe me, were my own flesh and blood whom I loved without end, who did not understand me, and to whom I could not make myself understood at all. So how can I rest in peace?

Born in Golinsk, Russia. Died in the Bronx of New York.

Observed life in the following places: Warsaw, Vilna, Hamburg, Vienna, Paris, Philadelphia, New York, Miami Beach, Lakewood, Atlantic City, Ellenville, et cetera.

Played the fiddle and was a leader of restaurant orchestras including one entirely composed of ladies.

Married an actress.

Observed the differences between Plato and Hegel, Milton and Gorki, St. Augustine and Spinoza, Shakespeare and Ibsen, Bakunin and Lenin, Pavlova and Duncan.

Took Mozart over Bach. Not excited about Beethoven outside of the Second. Considered Ravel a good faker. Took Rimsky-Korsakoff as the best.

Next to Balzac, Tolstoi and Dostoyevsky were babies just passing time crying. Walt Whitman could have sounded better.

The definite best American was Mark Twain, his Yankee. Also about the two boys.

And two singers . . . Caruso and a colored girl from the gin mills but with a call like the mother of the world, Bessie Smith.

And Vanzetti . . . for him I sat down in 1927 and wrote a whole symphony, which was no good. Out of this my son Lester took a melody and wrote up a song that sold nineteen thousand copies in 1930, entitled, "Oh Boy! What a Wonderful Girl!"

Never liked music as a business but had no better way to make a living than with the fiddle. Wanted to play for myself only, but no money that way. Wanted to play for children, started a music school once in Philadelphia, loved to give the little kids free haircuts . . . everything not covered by the saucer-on-top got clipped off. Mothers didn't like it. Used to teach them notes by cutting up apples . . . a whole note equals a whole apple, a half note equals half the apple, a quarter note equals a quarter the apple, and so on . . . and the whole apple equals all the parts of the note. Mothers complained, said I taught the kids how to play with knives. Couldn't make a go of the music school, went back to playing "Ave Maria" in $1.50 nine-course restaurants. My wife's opinion, "A good-natured feller, but no head for business, never grew up."

I think I went with a little dignity and honor, I think I didn't let the State get its hands on me and twist me into something not myself. I kept the way I was, when I was a child in Golinsk.

The way music got under my skin had to do with the big Squire of our village who was to Golinsk like John D. Rockefeller to New York. This Konayev used to give parties for friends who would come to his castle from all over: all kinds of people, military, government officials, other Squires. All the rooms in the castle on the hilltop would be lit up like for the coming of the Tsar. In the summertime lanterns would be strung along his promenade and in the night music would roll down the hill, and drunken enthusiastic baritones would sing, hitting the top notes like nervous mothers slapping their children's cheeks. This music was the sign of a life much different from mine. It excited me to learn that somewhere was a kind of life in which worries and troubles and praying were not so important. At the age of seven the mixed-up sounds of the music and dancing and free laughter rolling down from the top of the Squire's hill were a revelation; lying in my bed and listening I would think secretly, "It must be good sometimes to be a gentile."

One day in the fall when I was going on eight my mother and brother Shim and I were walking home from picking grapes in one of the Squire's vineyards. My father was an itinerant tailor without a horse and wagon, so you can imagine what he made out of trudging the roads with his goods bundled on his back. Many times he would come home from two–three weeks on the roads with little more than hard-luck stories. The fall of the year was the best time for us with everything to be picked, apples and grapes and cucumbers and all the different things the Squire raised and shipped away; and as we picked we would eat.

That particular afternoon I have mentioned, the sun was already down and it was getting cool and windy. Shim and I understood that the times my father was on the roads he became almost like my mother's third child. As we were walking home that late afternoon from our grape-picking I could see my mother missing him, her eyes calm as she walked silently, unlike the way she had been in the field, in a chatter with the other women.

We had more than a quarter of a mile to go when a junkman's horse and wagon overtook us. He wasn't from our village and we didn't know him but he stopped and let us ride with him. I don't remember what he looked like but he must have been either drunk or just a very jolly peasant because everything he said was with a big laugh. We sat back of him surrounded by pieces of rusty tin, useless chairs, jagged panes of glass, ikons, bed slats, and what-not. My eyes fell on the neck of a mandolin. The belly of it was crushed but two strings were still attached to the bridge. I gave a plunk.

"Look, Mama! It plays!"

"Put it back," she whispered, "or he'll say you broke it."

When we got to the village we climbed out and I said to the junk-man, "How much for the mandolin, please?" Before he could answer my mother said quickly, "Pay no attention to him, thank you for the ride." The junkman said, "Let me take a look at it," and leaned back into the wagon. My mother pushed me again to make me walk away, but I said, "Wait, wait . . . I have two kopecks, you gave me two kopecks," I said to my mother, "maybe he'll . . ."

The junkman had the mandolin in his hands and was looking at it, somehow very amused; with what I can't tell you. "It's no good," he said, as though making a joke, "but take it for two kopecks and give yourself concerts and concerts and concerts!"

"I'll take it," I cried, fishing out my two kopecks. My mother held my hand and whispered to me, "You'll play concerts on that banged-up thing when hair grows on your palm!"

I ran nearer to him and offered him the two kopecks. He began to laugh again, taking the money and handing me the mandolin. I didn't see him drive away, only the mandolin in my hand. "Ay," my mother cried, "you've thrown away two good kopecks!" I felt the sting of my mother's hand on my cheek.

Then my brother Shim spoke. "It's like Tzippe-Sora says, Mama. When a fool throws a stone in the water ten wise men can't pull it out."

"It can play," I said as I wept.

"Ay, well," my mother said, "let's go home."

As we made our way up the lane I said to her, "It can play, Mama, you'll see."

"Don't tell Papa I slapped you," she replied. "After all a mandolin isn't a stone. Maybe it can be fixed."

The next day at the learning-table I told Reb Maisha my stomach hurt, got the mandolin, and went looking for Nochim, the dairyman who fiddled on the side at weddings and christenings. He would know how to begin to fix my instrument. He was nowhere in the village. I sat down outside of Verenka's tavern, put the mandolin in my lap, hunched up my knees, and waited for him to pass. I sat so for a long time. The sun weakened, the wind became like a knife, and every minute that passed made it worse for me. I should have been with my mother and brother picking in the Squire's fields. When I would come home the first thing my mother would do, she'd break the mandolin into pieces. Just as I was deciding to hide it someplace and go home, a voice threw itself down to me.

"You, Laib!"

It was a harsh quiver of a call in Yiddish. When I looked up and saw it was my father's brother, my Uncle Mottel, I almost choked. I had been told over and over again never to have a single thing to do with him. I scrambled to my feet and began running but dropped the mandolin and had to stop and come back to pick it up. He handed it to me, squinting as usual, the stub of a cigarette popping out of the exact center of his mouth. His way of breathing very heavily had a frightening effect and I imagined the devil himself breathed that way too. Why Uncle Mottel was considered so evil by the landsmen I didn't know except that everybody said he'd thrown away his Jewishness since he came back from the army, and that he'd outlived his lung fever only because the Satan himself had refused his soul, spitting him out from hell.

"Where'd you get it?" he asked.

Then my feet finally got the message and I started to run away, but he reached out and pulled me back. "No, no," I cried, kicking at his shins.

"Wait," he commanded. "This damn thing, where did you steal it?"

"I bought it," I muttered.

"A fine purchase," he grunted. He took it and I wailed, "Give me!"

"What for?"

"Give me my mandolin!"

"Tell me, what for?"

"To play!"

"To play? Not to sell?"

"I said give me my — "

"Go home," he laughed. It sounded like the laugh of the junkman, the laugh of a stranger and yet the laugh of a would-be friend. But when he turned his back and started to go into Profim's smithy with my mandolin I did not consider him anything but a robber. I picked up a stone the size of an egg and hurled it at his head, turning and running in the opposite direction without seeing if the stone hit him. As I ran I could hear him laughing again. My ears played a trick on me. Mixed in with the laughing of my renegade uncle was the sound of the music rolling down the Squire's hilltop late at night.

All the way home I cried for what had happened to the mandolin and for what was waiting for me. But when I told my mother the story all she said was, "Ay, that Mottel. Don't cry, Laib. Take a pee and you'll feel better."

"I don't want to!"

"Then don't," said my brother dryly. "But shut up."

"So we've arrived at the town of Shut-Up, have we?" smiled my mother. "Boys, let's climb right back on the train and ride to the town of Quiet-in-the-House." She took an envelope from her bosom and waved it. Before she spoke my brother and I knew. "Good news, boys. Papa's coming home for the Sabbath."

That week we all got ready for my father. The hut was made spotless. My mother took the shears and clipped our hair. She begged a chicken on credit from Stanya Parsov, a farmer my father sewed for, and on the morning my father was expected I took it to Laib-Shmul to be slaughtered according to the Law. Then that same afternoon, when my father was expected almost at any moment, my mother remembered to send me around to the druggist's for three kopecks of dried raspberries which my father always put into his tea to loosen his catarrh.

To get to Yushin the druggist's I had to pass Profim's smithy. Uncle Mottel was just inside the door, leaning against a wagon and arguing with a few peasants. I tried to hurry past but he saw me and called out strongly, waving at me to come to him. Uncle Mottel sent away the peasants, flinging a final argument into their faces, and turned me to the rear of the smithy.

"That's where we're going."

"No, I don't want to!"

"But you do," he said, gripping my arm and dragging me through the dark narrow place with its earthen floor blackened by soot and the walls dirty-brown and smoked-up from the heat of the forge. His fingers felt like hooked nails holding me, and the smithy like a room of the devil. "You took my mandolin, that's why I threw the stone," I cried. "Why did you take my mandolin?"

Uncle Mottel pointed to a stool under the rear window. "There," he commanded. "Now we'll take a little look, eh?"

From a high shelf near the window he handed me the mandolin. He had screwed a piece of bent tin on to the broken belly, and patched the rest of it with strips of thin wood glued together. He handed it to me. "Go on. Play something."

I plunked a string with my thumb. "No, like this," he said, placing the neck of it in my left hand. I mumbled a thank-you and turned to run but he caught me. "Wait, Laib. And when they ask you who fixed it, what will you say?"

Ay . . . what would I say? Could I reveal I had been my renegade uncle's friend, to this extent? Everyone in our community had reason to spit upon Mottel; and besides, how enraged my father would become when he found out this dealing of mine with his heretic brother. "I'll say I fixed it myself."

"They'll make you tell them who."

"I'll hide it. They won't know I have it back."

"If they find out, they'll take and break it."

"They won't find out."

"Where will you hide it?"

"I'll see."

"And who will teach you how to play it?"

"I'll teach myself."

"Listen," he said, taking the mandolin. He plunked it a few times and laid his fingers on one string in such a way that a dinky tune came out. I was speechless; he knew music.

"See?" he said. He wanted me to ask him how to play it, and I wanted to. But I couldn't get enough breath into me to talk. "Very well," he said, breathing in his heavy way, "here, let's try."

Finally I could stammer out, "I can't. I — I have to get dried raspberries."

"Very well. Come back when you have time. I'll keep it right here, good and safe."

"No, I don't want to come back."

"Naturally," he replied with a shrug.

"No, I'm afraid of you!"

"Yes, of course. But do you know why?"

"Yes," I whispered. "They say you're worse than the devil."

He spat the cigarette stub out of his mouth. "I'm worse than the devil, of course," he murmured, smiling. "But did you ever hear this?"

He took the mandolin and picked out a little song, peering down at the neck, picking it out with difficulty. It was an old barracks tune and he sang some of it in the original:

> I gave her a shawl for her head,
> She gave me the half of her bed,
> And we gave each other what her stupid mother
> Had told her she'd get when she wed.

Uncle Mottel sang with a soft quiet voice and very seriously, almost like it was some hymn. But with every word, almost, he put in a smile. He stopped and asked if I liked it. "I don't know," I said. "I don't know what the song means."

"It's what they sang in the army."

"But what did they give each other?"

"A kiss."

"Oh."

"I know better ones. Too bad you're afraid of me."

"When were you in the army?"

"When? Let's see . . . from '75 to '79 . . . how old are you?"

"Seven."

"Well, I went when you were one and came back when you were five."

"My father says they sent you home to die."

"I lay very sick in the barracks. They gave me up for dead. But not wanting to bother with me any more they dressed me in my uniform, put my discharge papers in my pocket, and threw me on the train for Golinsk. 'The devil take him,' they said."

This I considered for a few moments. Then I said, "Please give me back my mandolin."

But he returned it to its place on the high shelf. "Better think over what I told you, Laib." Then pushing me toward the door, he said, "Go — go get your dried raspberries!"

My father came home and the presents he brought were down to the usual, showing how little my father had made out of his long hard trip — a six-inch cut of old cheese strudel from Mrs. Put-a-Patch-in-My-Sleeve, homemade cherry brandy from Mr. Make-My-Pants-Fit-My-Son, and a bag of candle-sugar to be divided by Shim and me. These and something under four rubles cash came from his weeks' walk of the roads. Dogs had barked at him. His best beds had been the hard benches in synagogues. Bread, cheese, and water had been his menu except when he came to a village with Jews there on a Sabbath. Once or twice he brought back stories of his great fortune, of his being allowed to stay in rich Jewish houses with the help, and of eating like from the plate of King David — and once, even, he had come home with three pairs of hardly-used shoes for my mother and Shim and me, the miraculous gift of an innkeeper. Privately (when my father thought Shim and I were asleep), he told my mother the shoes had been stolen and that the innkeeper had taken a ruble for the lot. But this particular trip brought nothing remarkable.

"And what have you been doing with yourself, boys?" my father asked Shim and me when he gave us our candle-sugar.

"The same," Shim said.

"Just the same as always," I added. But how could it be so? Tomorrow, when my father and mother would lie down for their Sabbath afternoon nap, I would give a jump over to the smithy.

He was busy with the postman's horse, at the forge, turning a horseshoe over the flames with expert twists of the tongs. Dimitri was shouting at him, "Come on! Hurry up! What do you think you're doing, making pancakes?" Then Mottel saw me standing uncertainly just inside the door and shouted a Hey. With his tongs he pointed to a broken-down wooden loft behind him. "Climb up, take a rest, boy. It's the day of rest today, remember?"

I climbed the ladder to the dark loft. It smelled like a lot of cats and as I sat there waiting for Mottel to get through, I began to take strong stock of all the things to be done in the future just to play imitation music on a hacked-up mandolin. I would have to listen to jokes about the Sabbath; I would have to be ready to lie about having anything to do with my outcast uncle; I would have to be ready for anything, including a good bundle of fingers against my face from my father. "Why is he my real uncle?" I asked myself as I waited. "Why can't he be just a plain gentile?" Then without warning I felt attacked. Coming to the smithy and sitting in the middle of stinks and climbing ladders and getting mixed up in all the evil doings of a place like the smithy was altogether too strange and dangerous to go through for the sake of making a few plunks on a string. I wanted to climb down the ladder and run home.

But my uncle's foot was on the first rung. The mandolin in his hand rose with his climbing and when he got up he handed it to me. In a few seconds he sat explaining the mandolin; had I climbed down before he climbed up, I would have hurried home and that might have been the beginning and end of music and me.

I did not in the beginning hold Uncle Mottel to be enjoyable; I saw nothing of interest in him except that he knew a talent I had to learn; I told myself, "The minute I can play, I'll take away the mandolin and never come back." With such reasonings my conscience was soothed and I visited the smithy faithfully on many Saturday afternoons that year, far into the winter, until it became too unusual to go out without manufacturing crazy excuses for walking in blizzards.

I learned a couple of songs. It took a dozen lessons to learn to play them badly. I began to think of all the music there must be in the world; I thought I'd need a thousand years. I told this to Uncle Mottel.

"Not so, Laib. Like words have letters, music has notes. You look at the music paper and read the notes, which means that the paper tells you what to play . . . clear?"

"But when Nochim plays a fiddle to weddings he doesn't use music paper. . . ."

"Here, look."

Uncle Mottel played the scale. "These notes are the a-b-c. Everything comes out of these notes, with little differences." He explained further. The musicians who played for the Squire's affairs came with bundles of music paper and played off what was written without having to keep all the music in their heads. My uncle didn't know any notes other than the scale, he told me, but he swore that music existed on paper. This was a relief.

"Well," I said, "how does a person learn to read music?"

"A person," Uncle Mottel replied, "can find no better place than the Petersburg Conservatory. It is a beautiful building. There a person studies music day and night if he wishes, and wears fine clothes and eats the best food, and finds dear friends among his fellow students, boys and girls."

I said eagerly, "It's just what I'd like."

"You?"

"Me, yes."

"Ay," Uncle Mottel laughed, pushing me a gentle push. "Who said you're a person?"

"You're making a joke," I said.

"Yes, what else, it's another joke. Ay, Sergeant Polmonov, such a funny fellow . . . I was a green one, a recruit. Polmonov comes to me in the barracks one time and says, 'Hey, soldier, I heard good news about you.' Well, they all made a circle around me to hear. 'Do you realize,' Polmonov asks me, 'that you are related to a very great man?' I said no. 'Indeed you are," Polmonov says. 'You are related to a great German genius of music, Franz Schubert.' "

"Are we?"

"No, but I was as green as you. I believed him. The fellow swore Schubert was my landsman, wrote all kinds of songs, even one about Christ's mother."

"A Jew?"

He laughed once more. Wrapped around the inside of it lay a leading secret of his character which I didn't fish out until many years later. Once I noticed myself laughing, in a certain way, harsh and not harsh. In that second it jumped into my mind—this was how Uncle Mottel used to laugh—not only against his enemy but against himself for being fool enough to think his enemy was only another man, nothing more.

"It goes without saying that they hit me." He threw me one of his grizzly smiles.

That afternoon a string broke towards the middle and couldn't be fixed; he said he would send away for a whole set.

Then it got too much into the winter for me to make excuses for sneaking away on Saturday afternoons. Once I saw Uncle Mottel in the middle of the street with his coat open to the bitter wind, so drunk he could hardly walk. I started running, hoping he wouldn't see me. "Hey!" he called with a big roar that made me stop and turn around. "They didn't come yet, they didn't come yet," he shouted with big waves of his arms. I kept my secret the winter through, even forgetting about it much of the time. The ice finally started to melt. We began to see the color of the ground again. In the mornings on the way to Reb Maisha's learning-table Shim and I would notice how less frosty the beads on the trees were getting, how more like wood the bare branches were. Everything was with a drip-drip-drip into the afternoon; horses appeared on the roads without blankets; the market square became busier a little earlier each day. The winter was saying good-by.

Peasants sat in their yards in the afternoon, sewing and strapping and nailing together bits of harness that had lain broken through the winter. Axes were being sharpened; T'zippe-Sora's chickens began getting themselves chased through the mud by the bigger boys; my father started mentioning the possibilities of an early start on the roads

("Listen, Leah, maybe it's true about Yitzel from Shnavka making the wedding for his Yalka before the Passover; if I gave a jump over there perhaps Thursday, it could be I'd find a week's sewing for the wedding, between the two families."); but the surest signs that winter was disappearing fast were to be seen in the yard of Hertz the grease-maker, blackened barrels and tin drums arriving and being dumped all over; in the visits of Gershon the shoemaker, with pencil in hand, to find out who might be ordering new shoes for the Passover; and most of all in the longer synagogue meetings of the landsmen on Saturday nights, when they went back to their yearly debates on whether or not to try to hire an ordained rabbi out of the Minsk rabbinical academy.

As soon as the days became mild enough, I went to Uncle Mottel for my mandolin. I said thank you and ran. My father was on the roads, almost a week gone. Shim and my mother bent themselves in some field of the Squire's, plowing and sowing with other families. Life was all spread out again and I headed for the woods. I heard a sound of something running behind me, something making loud swishes in the dead leaves on the ground. The back of my neck felt like a piece of cold marble. Thoughts of mad dogs prowling and wolves still hungry from the winter made me ready as I turned around for the sight of fur and the spring of paws and the teeth in the open mouth.

"Where did you get it?" she cried, running up, pointing at the mandolin. It was Rochel, Yeersel's daughter, three years older than I.

"What are you doing by yourself in the woods?" I said sternly. "Don't you know it's dangerous?"

"See?" she said, swinging a kerchief full of acorns under my nose. She put her arm out to touch the mandolin, a strong little arm. Her hair was jet black as it would remain until the day she died. "Let me hold it — where did you get it?" she demanded, yellow fires dancing in her brown eyes. I pushed her away, angry and worried. "You and your acorns!" I muttered.

"It's beautiful, Laib," she said, making a grab for it. I dropped the mandolin behind me and took hold of her wrists. "Hear me, Rochel,"

I threatened, "don't tell anybody or I'll . . . or I'll . . . never mind, you'll see!"

"You little pimple!" she answered, twisting her wrists free.

"Shut up!"

I slapped the kerchief full of acorns out of her hand and threw myself at her. We fell and rolled in the leaves. I was angry; she would tell about the mandolin, who fixed it would come out, the punishments would be the worst . . . but my anger became something else. Nothing was more important than the unexpected sweetness of Rochel. When she saw I wasn't fighting any more, she started to get up and I tried to hold her. She pulled her hand free and gave me a hard blow on my face with her strong little bundle of fingers. My nose felt all squashed. "That is what you get for being a bull," she cried as I hid my face in the leaves.

She picked up the mandolin and gave it a plunk. I turned over and spoke.

"This has to be a secret, Rochel."

"Why?"

"Because."

"You'll let me play it a little, Laib?"

"No."

"Selfish pig," she cried out, throwing it over my head into some thick brambles. She started running but I caught up to her and gave her a good slap and again we were fighting, and again, you see, the physical experience became everything. "Stop your tricks," she said, spitting at my face as I held her arms behind her.

Without warning a strong sudden pull on the back of my shirt, like the hand of God, lifted me to my feet in one moment. When I looked up I saw Yeersel, her father, with a piece of my shirt in his hand, and Berel the watercarrier running to us from a wagon on the other side of the gully.

"She started," I said, beginning to cry.

"So?" Yeersel pulled her up and shook her by the shoulders until Berel-the-Ox stopped him with a short push. Yeersel raised his hand to me but Berel said, "Worry about your own, let his father worry about him."

Berel crooked his finger my way and I went and stood next to him. Then Rochel began crying. "He wouldn't let me play his mandolin, he wouldn't!"

"That's why we were fighting," I blurted.

"So?" Yeersel said more quietly. "Sh," he told Rochel, "and stand still." He looked at her and then he looked at me.

"Nothing is disturbed," Berel remarked in his quiet way, as though speaking from afar.

"Show me the mandolin," Yeersel said to Rochel.

"He wouldn't let me play it, that's why," Rochel said, accusingly.

"What mandolin? Laib . . . how does a boy like you come to mandolins?"

"I got it from a peasant."

"What peasant? Don't look down."

"It was a secret. . . ."

"A fine secret, a mandolin in the woods." His horror rose to whip him. "You're here and he's here and the woods are here. . . . Ay, it's a secret, yes. But not a mandolin-secret, a different secret entirely!"

He began with his hands on Rochel, weeping. Berel went to stop him but he yelled for Berel to worry about his own, and kept holding Rochel with one hand, hitting her behind with his palm. "Mandolins!" he yelled. "Here," between his teeth. "Lies? Here! . . . Mandolin stories, here again! . . . Tricks with boys? Here!"

I couldn't stand Rochel's yells and Berel couldn't either; he kicked stones with the back of his boot; not caring if my goose was cooked the minute I opened my mouth, I cried, "I'll show you, I'll find it."

This I did. Yeersel could hardly believe his eyes. He took it in his hands, touched the strings. "You play on this?"

"A little."

"Show me."

I took it from him and fumbled my way through one of my two songs. "And that's the whole thing?" he asked.

"It comes with words too," I said.

"Let me hear."

Perhaps because it was the first song I learned, I sang him about the fellow giving her a shawl for her head in return for half of her bed, believing as Uncle Mottel had explained that she had given him only a kiss. When I finished Yeersel murmured, "You speak a nice little Russian," and in one move of his arm he took the mandolin and threw it to the ground, smashing it with several stamps of his feet.

"You broke it!"

"Worry better what your father will do to you," he answered.

"It was broken but I got it fixed and it could play," I sobbed. "Uncle Mottel fixed it and you broke it and now I'll never, never — "

"Mottel?"

Ay, it slipped out. And Yeersel in a wink lost all his anger. "So that's how the snake sneaked in," he murmured. "With such songs to a boy." He gave a great sigh, then squatted so that our eyes faced each other. "Uncle Mottel is your comrade, Laib? A fixer for you of mandolins, a teacher to play with girls?"

"Only songs, only the mandolin, the truth," I cried. "Please . . . please . . . don't tell my father!"

"Hear me, Laib," he said. He took my hands and spoke in such a tone that I knew he was sorry for hitting Rochel, and now quite worried about me. "How can't I tell your father that one of his two eyes, his youngest son, makes himself a comrade to a bit of flesh that isn't Jew or gentile, a friend to nothing, the enemy of everything? How shouldn't a father be told, Laib, that his son is the pal of a zero with hands and feet, with stones in his heart, an animal, a hopeless wanderer in the forest of the world who eats anything, sleeps everywhere, and breathes out poison? Is this a proper comrade, Laib, a piece of wood, a club in the gentile's hand that hits us, that takes our blood?"

"No," I said with a quiver of terror.

Tears appeared in the lids of his eyes. "Better I shouldn't have a tongue in my head than say it . . . but that's how it lays, that's what we are cursed with."

"Don't tell my father," I whispered.

"But with Mottel you're finished?"

"Yes."

"What are you, a dog or a Jewish boy?"

"A Jewish boy," I sobbed.

"The truth spoken?"

"Yes!"

His face fell heavy on mine and his beard felt like a blanket as he kissed me. "Then I won't say to your father. But with Mottels and mandolins you're finished?"

"Don't tell my father."

"And we have a covenant?"

"Yes!"

"You give your hand?"

We walked back to our side of the village, hand in hand. I began to feel saved from a terrible danger. What the ex-danger exactly was I couldn't have said but it had to do with triflings on a mandolin and the sweetness of a girl. One had led to the other, and both were sins to be put at Uncle Mottel's head. Right was right. Everybody in the world excepting Uncle Mottel couldn't be wrong. Yeersel's hand lay soft and warm over mine.

In this way I was kept from him, cheated out of many times of closeness, and thus the State's invisible policemen followed me in my goings about Golinsk until the accident four years later, when I was eleven, when my father and mother died.

That same spring Shim started going with my father on the roads. The rubles they brought home were as few as always but with them now came something new — my father's proud stories of how neatly Shim laid out goods and packed them up again; how quickly he threaded a needle and built fast fires to warm the pressing iron; how well behaved he was in strange houses so that even gentiles noticed and remarked; how every night he washed not only his feet but his shirt; and how in the mornings no matter where they slept, in a barn or on a floor or in a field, Shim would rise before my father and have the pan of clear cold water ready to pass over their hands before morning prayers. It was a comfort not to have to pray alone in places far from other Jews, but with a grown son.

While traveling my father used to try to be near a substantial Jewish community for the Sabbath, and always asked the beadle or one of the respected landsmen to give Shim a reading of the Law when the Ark would be opened and the Scrolls unfolded. My father would describe the goodness of Shim's reading of the Law, the clear seriousness of his inflections, and the sober, pleased comments of the congregation afterwards. Then one day towards the end of the summer my father showed us the rough stitchings of a half-finished jacket Shim had cut out by himself for a tinsmith in Kapula. "About Shim I have no worry," he said in a quiet mixture of pride and relief. "Already he knows how not-to-sew, and from that to knowing how yes-to-sew isn't far."

"Wait, in another few years you'll have a second pride," my mother said with a nod at me.

"With two extra needles working, and with a horse and wagon to carry enough goods about," my father said between blowings on the hot beet soup he used to love, "I could fall into a few good things."

The road from Pukop was full of young officers many nights that August. They would ride into Golinsk in open carriages, their dress uniforms looking brand-new in the twilight, sitting behind and below the drivers two and three to a carriage, smoking small cigars and raising their caps to the indifferent peasants standing and admiring the way their fine horses made the sharp uphill turn to the Squire's. Where the Squire found enough girls for these parties no one ever guessed, but whenever he ran short of the unmarried daughters of the district semi-gentry, he sent his steward to Minsk. Vassily Buzarov would return with girls and their mothers or at least women they called their mothers. These same girls attended all the officers' parties the Squire gave, regiment by regiment.

The heat kept me from falling asleep. From my window I could see lanterns dipping in long sways over the broad lawns just below the Squire's house. Each time a band from a different regiment would play the marches and polkas and attempt the lighter airs. Once in a while there would be a solo, a trumpet or a piano, usually; but the time somebody played a violin is what made itself into an importance for me. It was a tiny faraway sound, this fiddle in the muggy night. I crept out of bed and sat on our cracked doorstep, listening, not knowing what the fiddler was playing or how he felt about it but receiving it as a sound of beautiful secret crying. It was only a restaurantish czardas, but I didn't know that. Something in it was for me and I grew cool listening. The slow roll of the beginning strains, the explosion of wildness in the middle that still stayed sad, then the comeback to the original beginning . . . the sound of these things threw a thrill that lasted for I don't know how many minutes after it was over. "I'm different," I kept saying to myself over and over. "I'm different."

I remembered my mandolin; what a silly thing to call worth playing! From now on it had to be a fiddle to play, and take people and turn their feelings inside out, the birth of the only wish for power I ever needed. Sitting on the doorstep with nothing on but my short summer drawers, I pushed my toes into the dust and played a love with the night. The hut was no more for me, not really; I must not fear to feel new things, even though I was just another Jewish boy expected to obey all the laws of the State, written, unwritten, and not yet passed; I must not take my given rank of a pimple on the complexion of the world. This was for others now; the sound of a nighttime fiddle had told me I was different and I believed it. "You're different, you're different," it told me. It was the seed of my rebellion and everything good that ever happened to me grew out of this, that never washed away.

Long after the fiddling stopped it pulled me like a magnet. I mustn't go back into the hut right away but first do something a little bit different, not for its own sake but for a sign to myself that what the hut stood for was now to my back. I walked down the dark lane to the highroad and sat on a cool stone, looking at the Squire's lanterns way up the hill, waiting for the fiddler to play again and not caring if he didn't.

The first thing that danced into my head when I opened my eyes in the morning was "Nochim." Nochim peddled butter and cheeses but he had some kind of an old fiddle which he played in taverns all around the district whenever he had no butter or cheese to sell. He couldn't exactly play it but he could make it chirp enough to justify his begging and sometimes he used to throw it into his handcart on top of his butter and cheeses and try to make the peasants' children remember him for a jolly fellow and thus improve his standing with his poverty-stricken customers.

I threw myself into my shirt and pants as my mother still slept, and ran to Nochim's. The sun was still down but the air stood heavy with scent, everything so green and thick, even the tall weeds part of the richness. I hoped to catch Nochim before he went to morning prayers. Maybe he would lend me the fiddle or better still agree to sell it. Where the money would come from was something else.

"A good morning," I cried excitedly to Nochim's worried-looking wife, Pesha, as I met her taking a water bucket from Berel on his rounds. "Let me help a bit?"

Pesha said nothing as I followed her inside. "I want Nochim, Pesha."

She pointed to the curtain in the corner. "He sleeps." She turned to the door, shouting, "Children!"

Sholem and Marya were walking in from the woods carrying sticks and dragging a piece of dead birch. Without thinking I drew the curtain and shook Nochim awake. "Hah? Hn?" he grunted in surprise, whining through his nose which had been smashed in an accident and put back into something like an ordinary nose but not quite.

"Nochim," I said. But he pushed me away, sighing like a horse. "Please, Nochim, about your fiddle, a question only — "

"Away now," he moaned.

"Live only to a hundred and twenty years, Nochim," I pleaded, "but tell me if one can buy your fiddle."

"Who's buying fiddles?" Pesha demanded, behind me.

"I."

"What with, your boils?"

"I'll bring the money, I'll bring it!"

"When it's in your pocket we'll talk," she said shortly, dropping the bucket of water to the floor with an extra-hard bang. Again I turned to Nochim, who sat up moaning. His shoulders shook, his eyes as red almost as his nose. "Nochim . . . live only to be a hundred and twenty — "

"Don't do me such favors," he sputtered, his morning catarrh beginning to rumble over his moaning. "Only somebody bring me a pot of water, *wet* water."

"Water I'll give him!" Pesha cried. "A salty ocean!"

Nochim demanded, "I knew I was coming in the middle of one of their wedding weeks? I could help if they saw the fiddle in the cart and told me to bumble on it a little? And when a customer and a gentile offers me whiskey, I'm to refuse? You imagine I enjoy throwing myself between them like a nail on a hammer?"

They flew at each other until Nochim roused himself into a fit of hard coughing that made him go outside. "Pesha, dear," I said politely, as she sat with Sholem and Marya eating pieces of hard bread, slowly and with gall, "I'll pick in the fields like ten people. Sell me the fiddle."

"Such a sin against your father and mother I'd never do. Nochim's fiddle plays joys, you think?"

"Tell me at least where to buy one."

"All the fiddles you want, Laib, you'll find in a little store on the corner of Hell and Damnation Street." Sholem and Marya giggled at Pesha's wit; it showed she was getting out of her bad mood. "A good thank-you," I told the woman, starting to leave, my head working on the next step.

Pesha took hold of my arm. "Hear me. A fiddler, a musician, is a person on the world like cockroaches are raisins. And a Jewish fiddler scrapes more than the bow . . . his nose across behinds . . . before they let him bring his nose home. Remember."

Outside I found Nochim leaning on his hands against a tree, his head down, his moans raising themselves to louder sounds.

"Nochim, excuse me . . ."

"Forgiven, forgiven," he muttered.

"I mean excuse me for annoying you *now* . . ."

"We'll talk later, go away," he gasped, bending himself forward in a spasm of retching. "Ay, herring," he groaned, straightening himself up. "They don't make herring the right way, the peasants." His mind took hold of this particular thought. "You see, they don't bother to soak it in water first, and in my stomach when too much salt mixes with too much whiskey, it turns me into a bomb without gunpowder, completely. . . ."

"It goes without saying," I replied quickly, seeing he was about to go off my subject. "What I'd like to be sure of, Nochim, is will you let me play a little, sometimes?"

"Play, play," he muttered, "go play now, right away."

"On the fiddle? Where is it?" I cried.

"What fiddle, when fiddle?" he grumbled. A new retching grabbed him and as he bent over, he made backward pushes with his hand for me to go away. "What do you think a fiddle is for, pleasure? It's not a toy, it's a thing for business," he said with a last retch. "Business."

"Where did you get yours?"

"The fiddle?"

"Where?"

"Minsk," he said, leaning against the tree and sighing. "In a pawnshop . . . nine rubles . . ."

"What pawnshop, Nochim?"

"Who knows? Let me see . . . his name I think was Bencha-Chaim. Any Minsker can show you the place."

"A thank-you!"

Nine rubles, Minsk, Bencha-Chaim. Good. All the heavy picking would be started soon. I'd go to Reb Maisha with excuses and then pick all day; I'd even put my hands on stuff to peddle at the Pukop Fair . . . even if it had to come all the way from China, I'd get a fiddle.

I ran back to our hut. Seeing me come in my mother turned from the stove with a look of pleasure on her face. "Grabbed yourself a little air? Come drink tea, then see if there's a letter. Something tells me they're coming home this week."

I sat down to my tea and bread. My mother picked up her wood basket and headed for the brush outside in her bare feet, her ankles showing under her skirt as she swung the basket in her hands. Many times in America I used to play stage shows with ballerina types on the bill but I never saw a pair of better-looking ankles than my mother's that morning. They meant I was still young, I had many years to get my own fiddle and play it — not a Nochim-fiddle but the real thing coming out of it, such as had come out of the faraway the night before, adding itself to me and changing me.

To find out how to play such fiddle would take time, but I had it.

From the Friday several quick weeks later when Yeersel brought them home and laid them on the bed everything sewed itself with a different stitch and by spring of '86 the cloth of the day had a different rub under the thumb. My uncle Mottel had been put in jail, they said it would be for four months, out of his fight with the postman, Dimitri, just before the Day of Atonement. No one questioned why, being too glad to have him where he was, and none doubted that he might never again be let out, for it would be like him to continue in prison where he began with Dimitri. Such was our estimate of his violent nature; but much later it occurred to me that in all the relieved comments about him, Maisha kept stone silent.

We soon grew used to living with Reb Maisha. During the week somebody would always come and do a little cooking for us and on the Sabbath night we would eat either with Tzippe-Sora or in Yeersel's. As Yeersel's apprentice Shim did well from the beginning. It lay in his nature to get things done; he especially wanted to show Yeersel the good of his father through his own. Shim could hardly wait to be thought of as a full man. Rochel wasn't yet fifteen but between them an understanding was building. Why this was so they couldn't have

explained but it was obvious. Golinsker girls didn't "meet" boys but
grew up with them; when it came time, couples would pair off and
such was the style of romance in Golinsk. In America I met an actress
and married her after preludes of flowers and private conversations in
cafés and even dancing on the tables with her. But the net result
turned out the same as any marriage in Golinsk.

In the first months of my orphaning it appeared to the landsmen
that I had become Reb Maisha's mainstay, which was taken to be an
extra-fine thing since I would be confirmed as a son of Israel on my
next birthday, my twelfth, a year younger than the usual due to my
having lost my parents — the ancient customs holding that an orphan
rightfully requires and deserves Jewish manhood a year sooner than
the luckier boys.

I ran errands, scrubbed the synagogue floor, kept the prayer books
and praying shawls in order on the shelf under the lectern, cut and
stacked firewood, carried away ashes, and sat listening patiently to
Reb Maisha's semiofficial remarks ("The Tsar sits on his throne day
and night. Why does the Tsar sit on his throne day and night? Because
he is afraid the country will forget he is the Tsar. The Tsar is the
Tsar, yet he can't even go to the toilet when anybody is looking!"),
but when I wanted time for myself I had only to say, "Reb Maisha,
today I'll leave the learning-table a little early. I want to study my
speech." This formal sermon from the pulpit on my confirmation day,
composed, conducted, and arranged by Reb Maisha, was to be a triumphant sign to the landsmen of the spiritual job done on me
(Reb Maisha gave all his students their confirmation speeches, but
mine was with special cherries on the top). Reb Maisha wanted to believe that he could plant a little of himself in me. Therefore he went
deeper with my speech than with what he gave other boys. Of course
he didn't leave out the regular, looked-for expressions such as, "On
this day when I enter the world as a man fully understanding for the
first time the meaning of my Jewish soul, I open my heart to my
father" (how Reb Maisha used to drill me on the exact right way to
say, "May-he-rest-in-peace," so it would come out sad but not like a

show-off), "and make this vow with all my new manhood — to follow in his ways as a server and lover of the Lord." That and the thanks I owed my parents for keeping me clean with their careful love, plus various other sublime realizations supposed to enter me on my twelfth birthday like a secret sunrise — that life is sweet but eternity's wisdom is the real manna, that our enemies' hate would destroy not us but themselves, and that The One Above in his wisdom has already seen to the everlasting salvation of Israel. To say these things as a confirmation boy meant getting and giving proof of the worth of our faith; in this lay the kernel of the confirmation. The words alone stood for little, the ideas accepted not in a thinking way but as waves, yet as more than moving salt water, as something moved and moving at the same time, and true forever.

If the speech Reb Maisha had given me to learn had stopped there, if it had been the same as the other confirmation boys', I would have been sold on the proposition; and probably the few things that had already begun to work on me and open me up — Uncle Mottel, a mandolin, the sound of a fiddle in the summertime, the nearness of a girl — I could have put aside as the foolishness a man outgrows. The luck of it was that Reb Maisha took me more personally. He put a few things into my confirmation oration that were deeper, things I twisted around in my head until it made itself into a meaning I found useful and which in the end upset Reb Maisha's purpose. It confirmed me not so much as a man of Israel as of the world — the world I would love though it did not accept such a stubborn complainer against growing up as myself, the pain-in-the-neck of my family.

The thing he put in the oration was against fear of punishment. "Let us be no more children," he drilled into me, "let us understand why God punishes. Is it not childish to fear the cutting-off of a toe which saves the whole foot, and more? Remember the words of the sage of Mezeritz, 'Having lost a toe you will be more careful in your play not to lose another and suffer again the pain you felt.' Fear the wound, not the cure, and love him who punishes you." This reminded me of Yeersel's curing me of the sinfulness Uncle Mottel had put into me; but the more I practiced the pronunciation of this part, it made another sense. I thought, "If, really, Uncle Mottel is terrible, why do they still call out his name for a reading of the Law on the New Year even though he's never in the synagogue?"

If he was so bad, why wasn't he cut off from the rest of us like a poisoned toe? Why in this case did the landsmen fear the cure more than the wound? . . . One night towards the end of the first winter that Shim and I lived with Reb Maisha, the three of us were undressing to go to sleep and I said, "Reb, tell me why Uncle Mottel gets a reading-call to the Law every New Year's, when he's such a God-hater."

"Who says he's called every year?" Shim asked as Reb Maisha climbed to his shelf-bed over the stove and covered himself.

"What for, what for," sighed Reb Maisha. "Ay, such an asthma I'm cursed with, not to be able to breathe . . . and what for?"

Every time Reb Maisha had to stop and think before answering he always mentioned his asthma, so I said, "No, really Reb . . . the truth spoken . . . he's called to read the Law every New Year's, isn't it so?"

"If you noticed it, maybe so," he murmured, turning to the wall with a quick twist of his bones. "I didn't. A good night."

"See?" Shim said to me, relieved.

"But why then even once?" I demanded. "If Mottel, then why not Profim or Father Semyon or the Squire — if our uncle hates us, as is said, as much as they do, the gentiles?"

Shim said, "Listen, Laib, don't start saying crazy things, you hear."

"Quiet, quiet," said Reb Maisha from the shelf-bed but I kept on, and louder. Some of what Yeersel had frightened me with came back into my thoughts. "A piece of flesh that breathes out poison, isn't that what he is? — a club in the gentiles' hands that takes our blood, isn't that so, Reb Maisha?"

"Ay, quiet," he sighed, turning to face us.

"So or not so?" I demanded.

"Of course, so," Shim agreed.

"All right," Reb Maisha said, sitting up and letting his feet hang down close to the stove; and when he spoke it was with his asthma forgotten. "Laib asks the question, 'Why do we honor the enemy and apostate?' Now, Shim . . . what, let's say, would be your word on that?"

Shim fell happily into the old student way of discourse, his fist held before him with the thumb up. "If," he said, raising his fist slowly as he stated the question, "it is indeed truth spoken that Uncle Mottel gets called to read the Law every year though he is an absolute hater of our God . . . then . . . " and as he gave his answer he started bringing his fist down from over his head, his thumb leading the way, ". . . it must be so only because The One Above asks us to believe that the outcast will, however far away he is, one time hear his name being called and come to the synagogue, and make himself a Jew among Jews again!" Shim finished by bringing up his thumb in a quick curve, a triumphant sealing of the argument.

"Not badly spoken," Reb Maisha murmured. "However, it is necessary to poke a little deeper. First, he is called, you say, the absolute hater of our God."

"Right," Shim said.

"We'll see," Reb replied. "Second, Uncle Mottel carries the name of outcast."

"Again right," Shim said.

"Let's see," Reb Maisha said softly, "if what a man is, and what a man is called, is always the same thing."

"What, you're taking his side?" Shim cried, surprised and a little frightened.

"Taking his side?" Reb Maisha said, looking from one to the other of us. "This worries you?"

"Reb — he has no God!"

"Ay, Shim; so *he* says. But between what a man calls himself and what he really is, is sometimes a difference. I question whether your uncle is a hater of God, an outcast, and without a God." Then he smiled with a nod of his head, and gave his toes a twiddle. "I'll tell you what I don't question. Your uncle says all these things about himself and everybody among us believes him. Yet we call him to read the Law once a year — why is it? Because we don't believe him? Ay, no . . . we believe that when Mottel says he has no God, well, he lies. We believe, in our hearts, that in his own he knows he is a liar and, the truth spoken, that he is one of ours, after all."

Shim said, "How can he be one of ours? The things he doesn't do, and the things he does . . ."

"Ay, Shim . . . a little too deep for you?" Reb Maisha grinned in such a way that I hardly noticed his greenish uneven stumps of teeth. It was the face of a person alone yet in peace, with a gentle scorn about him for those who might not care to look too deeply.

As we climbed into bed Reb Maisha remained sitting on his bed-shelf, still grinning. "Did you hear that?" Shim whispered to me. "The Reb is getting mixed-up."

"He knows what is; he knows more than us," I whispered back.

"The light," Reb Maisha called. "Forgotten."

Shim gave me a poke in the rib. I got up and blew the lamp out. Then Reb Maisha said, "Laib, come here." He leaned his head down and whispered from under his cover, "Today a bird told me your uncle is back from the jail. The four months are over and they say he's even friendly again with Dimitri."

"So?"

"Did you know why they took him away?"

"He slugged Dimitri."

"He also took money Dimitri gained by selling the goods in the wagon."

"He took it from Dimitri?"

"And gave it to me. Eleven rubles remained over, after paying the Minsker for the goods he sold your Papa, may-he-rest. These will be for your confirmation suit, and for your own goods, scissors, needles and tape-measures when you go to tailor. A nice little confirmation present." (But who wanted to be a tailor?) "If he wasn't a real one of ours, you see," Reb continued, "he wouldn't have sat four months in jail for this, but don't say anything."

Back in bed, Shim gave me another poke. "What was the old one chippering about?"

"Beans and raisins, raisins and beans."

Shim fell asleep; my head kept filling itself with pictures one after the other . . . of my uncle slugging Dimitri, then sitting in jail, of Reb Maisha sending goods-money to Minsk, of myself saying my confirmation speech in the synagogue, dressed in my new suit, "Is it not childish to fear the cutting-off of a toe which saves the whole foot, and more? Remember the words of the sage of Mezeritz, 'Having lost a toe you will be more careful in your play not to lose another and suffer again the pain you felt.' Fear the wound, not the cure, and love him who punishes you."

Well . . . Yeersel had hacked Uncle Mottel out of me, thinking my sin with Rochel came from Mottel's hating God. But according to Reb Maisha, my uncle in his heart loved God. Therefore Yeersel's cure mightn't have been correct. If the sin was not my uncle's but all mine, then why should I fear my uncle, who had sat in prison to give me a confirmation suit?

In this way I tapped walls I couldn't see, finding that secret believings hide themselves everywhere, even in the hearts of teachers, and that what makes a wound a wound and a cure a cure did not originate in Golinsk and would remain unsettled there. These things did not lay themselves out immediately in such neat notes. The orchestration I would make later but the melody was in me and it pulled me to Profim's.

The next morning I woke up sneezing and coughing but did the usual, dressing and rousing the landsmen to morning prayers, then sliding on the ice to the synagogue to throw wood in the stove. Later at the learning-table the boys noticed my red face and told Reb Maisha. He sent me home with Yeersel's Mayer who helped me undress and then went for his mother.

Her hand felt like ice. The raspberry tea she gave me made me feel only colder. She put all the covers in the house on my bed but the germ got to its real work and the walls went dark before my eyes with a great zizzing turning in my head like bumblebees. It was a pneumonia; they didn't know the name of it but they knew what to do. Hot bricks were wrapped and put to my feet. The women took turns sitting with me day and night. I saw Bosha's face and Tzippe-Sora's, and Gershon's Faiga's, and Naftoli-Dovid's, and Rochel's . . . and when I couldn't keep my eyes open I heard all kinds of zizzings. Sometimes I would turn words in my head, from the songs Uncle Mottel taught me, around and around . . .

Two, three, my head hurts me . . .

. . . and until a woman's voice would say, "Laib, your head, what?" I wouldn't know I was talking. Then it went into my sides, the pain, and another part of the mandolin song gave itself a turnaround . . .

Nuts are dry, my sides they cry
Nuts are dry, my sides they cry . . .

Yushin the druggist came with his cupping-glasses, placing them hot against my sides to suck the sickness out. Then the fever boiled over; I lay in sweat for a week but began to eat. One evening when the men were at prayers and the women all home getting supper, Shim gave me chicken soup. He sat watching me, his hands ready to help if I dropped the bowl. "I didn't know you spoke such a good Russian, Laib."

"From where, a good Russian?"

"When you were very sick. Russian songs. You didn't stop a minute."

"When I was sick?"

"When you were out of your head. Everybody noticed." He held the bowl from the bottom. "Yeersel said you must have learned it from the Mottel. Is he right?"

"Uncle isn't so terrible. I'm going to talk to him again."

"Still out of your head. . . ."

I told him Reb Maisha's parceling-over of Uncle Mottel, but Shim shook his head. "He's getting like a baby. Don't tell anybody. If they find this out they'll look for a new beadle."

"So . . . he'll be out-beadle."

"Have pity. If he goes out-beadle he'll die from the disgrace. Talk with a little sense. Do you want to put him in his grave?"

"I'll say nothing. But only if you'll say nothing about who I'm going to talk to."

"We'll twist that out later. When you're better."

"Agreed now? Or no?"

"Let's talk it over when you're better," he said, giving his neck a little sideways twist that told me he was beginning to give in. "Now or no?" I pressed him. "Give your hand."

We slapped our palms together good and hard the way they did in the market. Shim never broke his promise. For this I respected him to the end of his ridiculous days.

They kept me mostly in the hut for half the winter, letting me out only when there was sun. I would go with Reb Maisha to the synagogue in the morning and sit with the boys at the learning-table until noon, then go home to eat what the women had warmed for me. After, I was supposed to take a nap but this became very boring. I studied my confirmation speech, polishing my ritual-chanting for the Sabbath services and the reading of the Law, trying new little shadings and finding the best places to breathe — until one afternoon I put my hands in my pockets and crossed to the gentile side of the village.

Through the open smithy door I saw him shoeing a horse and laughing with the peasant holding the horse's head. When he dropped the horse's foot and stood up straight my uncle's face came into the light. He looked like a horse himself now, his chin and cheekbones sticking out more than ever, his beard extra straggly and thin, his body somehow narrower. "Ay, in the prison they must have really hungered him out," I thought.

He didn't notice me until I stepped out of the way when the peasant led the horse past me. Then he said as though he'd seen me yesterday, "Well . . . it's you," sticking a cigarette into his mouth.

Not knowing what to answer, I said, "I was sick."

"Yes, I heard you were better."

"I came to tell you I can't stay long," I said quickly. "I mean about the money."

"What money?"

"From Papa's-may-he-rest-in-peace goods."

"Well, so."

"I'm getting a confirmation suit with it."

"So?"

"A good thank-you."

"For what?"

"For giving the money to Reb Maisha."

"Hah." He sounded not pleased. I felt no connection. The mandolin was long ago, a goner, and suddenly so was he. Thin from prison, with the face of a horse . . . "So this is how things change," I thought.

"What are you squirming for?" he asked me.

"I have to go."

"So go," he gestured behind him.

"I mean home."

"Why?"

"They'll be mad," I lied, afraid to say I didn't like the smithy any more, or him.

"Mad," he repeated with an annoyed bray, "they'll be mad!" He gave me a good-by shove and walked to the back of the smithy. I ran home. I didn't think he would bother with me any more. I didn't want him to.

One morning just before prayers Nochim's fifteenish Zagzaigel came into the synagogue with a run and a jump, his eyes shining with good news. Laib-Shmul thought Daneel's Lippe had twins and Naftoli-Dovid that the Squire had died. "No," Zagzaigel cried, "it's even better! It's our Mr. Poison, our Mottel — last night he got himself thrown out of the second floor window of Profim's brothel, his good friend, and now he's lying like a bagful of broken sticks, waiting for the devil to take him in for a partner!"

The landsmen finished morning prayers in a hurry that day for they had to decide where Mottel would be buried. Finally they agreed he

could be in the Golinsker cemetery but only in the far corner, in the
marsh, an unused part normally thought unsuitable. But after a week
of waiting he still hadn't died and it dawned upon the Golinskers
that he wouldn't. This frightened them. During the four months
Mottel had sat in prison, the rendering of the monthly reports to the
Squire had been attended to by Vassily Buzarov in keeping with the
local law that all such reports had to be written in Russian. Buzarov
drove hard bargains but at least the landsmen could negotiate; now
that Mottel would recover and pick up where he left off as the trans-
lator of the monthly reports, they expected he would make them pay
good blood through the nose for the way they had waited for his death
without lifting a finger to help him; for the way they had planned to
bury his body in the marsh which would quickly have sucked his bones
down deep into the mud.

Tzippe-Sora thought of something. "We'll roast him a chicken and
take it to him with a pot of soup," she said to her worried son-in-law,
Laib-Shmul, "and tell him the men kept away because we heard he
wanted to confess to Father Semyon." Laib-Shmul took this suggestion
to the others as something that would work, but Yeersel didn't like it.
"No, brothers, a chicken and a pot of soup can't answer questions . . .
and he'll have questions."

Then Gershon said, "Maybe if Reb Maisha takes it to him it'll go
better . . . Reb Maisha, you know a million quotations from the sages,
surely you'll think of things to fit questions?"

But Reb Maisha wouldn't do it. "The truth spoken, brothers," he
said gently, "we acted like a bunch of oxen."

"A great help!" cried Laib-Shmul with a dry snort. But the rest said
nothing and they knew why.

In the end Yeersel said, "I think I remember something. There was
a time when Mottel amused himself with corrupting Laib by showing
him tricks on a mandolin, with inflaming songs. If then the boy offered
him pleasure, why not now for a good purpose? If Laib brought him
chicken and soup, say, it might occur to him to have at least a little
mercy."

I found Uncle Mottel sleeping on his back, his head and a shoulder buried in gray bandages. He lay straight like a mummy under the covers. Liniment, bad air, whiskey, and body waste mixed with the smell of stale cigarette smoke struck my nose and gave me a queer pinch between my legs. Clothes, bottles, papers fell everywhere. A mouse ran out. Everything lay broken in the light of the afternoon; the bed a sideways slant and the walls showed dots, stains, where the whitewash persisted. A sour watering rose in my throat and I ran to the window and opened it. Nothing happened; the breeze helped the room, and woke him.

"Hah," he muttered. "Lizaveta."

"It's me."

"Stand where I can see."

I went to the foot of the bed. "I brought you chicken and soup. But she pulled it out of my hands. Downstairs."

He took a cigarette from under the cover with his free hand and lit it with a match against the wall. "Take a little smoke, Laib?"

"It makes me cough."

"I smoked when I was seven. Go on, try."

He lit it for me. I pushed some clothes from a chair and sat next to him, holding the cigarette like a firecracker. By the way he smoked I saw he couldn't move his head. "Are you getting better, Uncle?"

"Why not? The devil didn't want me. . . . And how is your brother?"

"He helps Yeersel."

"He'll be a tailor then?"

"Yes."

"And you?"

"I don't like tailor."

"Take a puff."

"I can't, uncle."

"Then step on it. So if not a tailor?"

"I don't know. Maybe a fiddler."

"Where do you come to a fiddle?"

"I don't know."

"But a fiddler, just so?"

"Not just so. I don't know. The sound, maybe. Like in the summer, when the Squire has music up there . . . the sound when it comes out on two strings at the same time."

"And that mandolin . . . you play it?"

"It broke long ago."

He started taking long puffs, grunting the smoke out of his nose. With the window open the smell wasn't so bad and the mention of the fiddle and mandolin also helped, plus my being there not against the wishes of anybody. So we sat without talking, which is sometimes the best way, until my uncle pressed the cigarette stub against the wall and told me to get Lizaveta.

"You'll eat the chicken?"

"Why did they send soup and chicken?"

"I don't know."

"Let that be your last lie to me. Why did they send soup and chicken?"

He spoke without anger but I couldn't lie any more. "They're afraid of you," I cried, "they're afraid you'll harm them after you get well."

"So," he said, much contented. "Perhaps they're right. Let them be afraid. Are you?"

"No," I lied.

"The truth spoken?"

"I am afraid of you," I said with a choke. "I'm always afraid but I never want to be; the truth spoken, Uncle."

"Now get Lizaveta."

"All right."

"You'll come back tomorrow," he added, as an understood thing.

"All right."

"Tell somebody over there I need what to drink."

"Who is somebody?"

"Tzippe-Sora," he said with the beginning of a smile. "She knows the kind I like."

I ran straight to Tzippe-Sora with the message. "Good," she said with low happy moans and gentle shakes of her head, the wrinkles around her eyes hilly with satisfied squints. "Tomorrow you'll take him half a gallon of my brandy, the day after we'll find something else to stuff him with. . . . Don't worry, he'll remain bought off like the rest."

Yeersel, Hertz, Laib-Shmul, Berel, and Reb Maisha were waiting in our hut. The more I described the visit the more I sensed what side I was on. By the time I came to the finale, my tongue was going like the Chicago Flyer. "I thought he would throw me out with the soup and chicken together but he turned around and ordered me to come back tomorrow. I know better things to do, it goes without saying . . . but if it helps us, why shouldn't I be willing?"

"Wait," Laib-Shmul scowled, "I'm not so willing for the damned one to make Laib into his comrade. To me the thing stands in too much of a tremble. What, after all, did we do? We didn't bury him in the marsh, not yet. How will he know we planned it? Who would run to him with it?"

Yeersel replied, "Forgive me; I'm pleased to hear you disagree for a change."

"What pleases you," said Laib-Shmul, "helps like a syringe to an empty digestion. Let's not please ourselves so much but think what we're doing."

"Not what we're doing, Laib-Shmul, but what's done," Yeersel said. "All together in the synagogue, we came to a burial decision."

"Indeed," said Reb Maisha with a quaver and a nervous sniff, "the words left our mouths and flew like birds into the air, and who knows where they will light and when? Do we not find it written in the Talmud, 'The angry man receives nothing, but anger'? Are we not dealing with this?"

"But the boy," Berel said thoughtfully, throwing his eyes to me. "Are we not also dealing with him?"

"Never mind Laib," Yeersel replied gently. "He knows already, for a long time now, the Mottelness of Mottel."

"The truth spoken," I jumped in. "I know it from Reb Yeersel and also from Reb Maisha. Right, Reb?" Reb Maisha jerked his head at this. Believe me, the way I was handling myself with the Golinskers a Huckleberry Finn couldn't do better. "To me he's nothing but a broken zero," I said with a small spit on the side to show how I was with them. "For my part let him choke tomorrow. But until then I'll sit with him and know everything in his head."

"This spoils nothing," said Berel, making up his mind. "Let it stand, the boy goes there. It won't hurt to have one of our own hands taking his pulse."

In such a way I played to go and sit with my uncle every day from then on, with permission.

I never came with empty hands. The landsmen gave me cigarettes and meat and kvas and candle-sugar when I mentioned his cough. The more I sat with Uncle Mottel the less I thought he would hurt anybody. I believed this from the ways he told me, with such a pleasure and a directness, anything I happened to ask. We acted as two men, two friends. In less than a week the first thing when I sat down was to take a cigarette from him and puff like a ferryboat.

The mouse that lived in the room used to run from its hole in the corner of the wall through the door and back a few times a day. After Uncle Mottel began to sit up in bed and look for different things to do, he used to watch for the mouse and throw what was nearest — a glass or a bottle or a plate — but the mouse ran in quick curves and always got through the door or back into the hole. That side of the room looked like all garbage.

"Maybe I ought to find a broom or something," I mentioned. "It's getting into a deeper smell, around."

"When I go to walk," Mottel said, giving himself a long stretch, "the women will come in and fix-around."

"How soon, maybe?"

"A few days . . . I'll see how my legs go tomorrow."

Just then the mouse came out and Mottel gave it a plate. "Leave it alone, why not," I said. "It asks you to feed it?"

"I had enough of them in the prisons." He gave himself another stretch and cleared his throat. "Did you know I was in two prisons, one because of Dimitri and the other when I was in the army?"

"What did you do in the prisons?"

"What I'm doing now," he shrugged. "Give throws to mice and rats and sit with bandages on me. But in the military prison I gave many a thought . . . yes, to the person who had me put in."

"What was it like in the military prison?"

"Very interesting, but bad."

"What military prison?"

"Odessa."

"Big or small?"

"Big enough." He started scratching himself inside his shirt, yawning. "The bread they brought in was a month old and they left the pot a week in the corner."

"What kind of doors — iron?"

"No, just doors. Doors left open, remember . . . but put your head out an inch and that's all they needed for the nice little game they had."

"What kind?"

"Standing with their guns ready . . . sportsmen."

Until I saw him again the next day I kept imagining him in his cell, the soldiers just outside with rifles in their hands waiting for a chance to take shots. I had heard of bad prisons but never like this one and I wondered what he had done to be put in the Odessa prison. When I asked he said one prison was much like any other, and that in the army he learned about many girls.

"She was a pretty one," he said. The words must have brought the way she looked into his head; he had intended to stop there but went on in clusters of sentences with rests and pickups and quiet stops as I noticed years later in the sonata-form; and what he said to me when I was a boy sitting through a sickness with him, I gave in my own time of big troubles the name of "Mottel's Sonata."

"Her name she told me right away, Vavra. I wasn't rough with her and she liked me. A very small person and she had many ways. A child really, earning from dancing."

"You mean in the street?"

"No, she wasn't a gypsy though she did have an uncle who made his living feeling the heads of people and discussing their futures. Vavra danced in a cellar open for soldiers. Sometimes with her brother but mostly by herself with her shoes off. She brought me to her room many times. We used to eat and drink there . . . what she brought home from the cellar. She had me put in the prison."

"Because she found out you were a Jew?"

"No."

"Because her brother didn't like you?"

"He didn't like anybody. Maxim . . . he lived by himself and long times passed until she would see him. This was after he stopped dancing with her in the cellar. My company remained part of the Odessa garrison over a year but after the first few months Maxim did not dance in the cellar . . . the Last Resort, they called it. Vavra didn't mean to put me in the prison, we were fond of each other, she would sit teaching me Russian in order for us to carry on conversations. She could understand a little Yiddish after a while. Certain things in Yiddish amused her. A child, really. Vavra was very in love with her brother Maxim and after he went away she would explain about him, how he took affairs very seriously and how he believed in going around with others like himself, protesting affairs by blowing up trains. Vavra would describe Maxim's pride when once a train with some generals on it was blown up. The brother got himself in with a whole crowd, you see, which didn't care for the ways the Tsar held the reins, and with this bunch of people he went about making noises and explosions to arouse attention and, as Vavra said, to give courage to the oppressed. I asked Vavra if her uncle had ever felt Maxim's head. 'Of course,' was the answer, 'and he put it in writing that Maxim's was the head of a genius.' Well, there are such families. . . ."

"Weren't they caught?"

"Every one of them. The brother they put in the Odessa prison, asking him many questions with their rifle butts and pointed sticks. I heard them on my guard duty and didn't want Vavra to know about it, but it came out anyway between us in her room. I supposed it would make her feel better to know I had my eye on him but as it turned out this was a big mistake. She had her own ways of asking questions."

A half a glassful of Tzippe-Sora's liquor stood on the small shelf near Uncle Mottel's hand. He picked it up to drink, lifting it slowly to his mouth. But with a strong wrench of his sick shoulder he threw it high against the wall behind me, his cry of pain mixing with the crash. "Ay, that mouse again," he breathed. "Such small feet she had and nice, dancing without shoes."

"But, Uncle, she put you in prison."

Rubbing his shoulder he continued. "Not she, exactly. The minute I told her where he was and that I was on guard duty near his cell, she bothered me the whole night. I started shaking her but in the end she made me say what part of the prison they had him in; then she ran to the other crazy ones and with them made a plan to pull him out. Such a child, really. . . . The bomb was thrown. It broke the wall outside, the crazy ones came running through the hole, shooting guns. What fools, they didn't know the least about shooting properly . . . the soldiers gave them, yes, the way the elephant gave the flea on his tail . . . one blast, that's all."

"Uncle?"

"Well?"

I tried to make it sound unimportant to me, but I had to know. "And you too had to shoot?"

"Guard duty is guard duty. All right, so I shot high. . . ." His breathing came and went in harsh little sips through his mouth with what anger only he himself knew. "It helped like diamonds cure the blind. And these great heroes, these idiots, left Vavra outside in the carriage with a bundle of women's clothes for Maxim to wear to freedom. However, not Maxim but soldiers came out and dragged her into the Odessa prison, the same fellows that used to throw her a few kopecks when they liked the way she danced in the cellar. And of course the officers were regular Frenchmen, so polite in their questions . . . in between times the specialists jabbed her with little pointed sticks, plus the rifle butts and delicate whips that found all the tender places . . . in order to make her describe her brother's small society of crazy ones."

"But how does that come to you?"

"To who else then? She knew about her brother's society the way you know about evil. She could not be blamed; it was 'say something or be left for dead.' They nudged it out of her, the way I told her what side of the prison Maxim's cell was. So I sat two years in steady bandages inside the Odessa prison before they sent me home to die. I got good strong good-by claps, figured-out ones."

"Ay . . ."

"They threw her away some place," he added, more to himself. "I never heard where. Idiots."

"And Maxim?"

"Tomorrow we must surely make an end to the mouse." He gave his shoulder slow rubs with his open palm. "Bring ten or twelve flat stones. They'll do it."

"But the brother."

"They ended him where he stood." He spit across the room. "The stones must be flat, remember."

He began to try short walks in the afternoons. I visited him in his room as he rested, answering his questions about who talked against who, who had hard livings and who the hardest ones — anything that came into our heads we talked out. My fear of him was fast asleep, if not dead. The Holy Law taught me that one bitten by a snake forever fears a rope — but what kind of snake is one who fixed my mandolin and sat in prison for my father's goods-money, and two years more before that out of trying to get Vavra's brother free? In the three weeks he readied himself for the smithy again, I parceled out what the landsmen had said of him, how they worried about if he knew they wanted to throw his body in the marsh, and how it had been explained to me, now that it was getting close to my confirmation-time, that I should be a tailor like my brother and father."

"And what reasons did they give?"

"That in a few years Shim would be a tailor for himself and that it fitted for us to be partners. And that wherever in the world I would go or be pushed, I could always carry my living with me on the tips of my fingers."

"And you had answers?"

"Plenty," I replied, telling him with wavings of my hands and in all the tones I had tried — pleading, stern, amused, disgusted — how my eyes were unsuited to sewing, being crossed and teary in harsh light; that there were too many tailors on the roads already and not enough customers; that Reb Maisha was getting older and more feeble and needed me to help him stay beadle; that when I grew old enough to have a wife, I wouldn't want her sitting and waiting for me weeks and weeks to come home with a capful of kopecks, as my mother had waited for my father; and finally that personally I didn't want to be a tailor. To end my case, I told Uncle Mottel I had offered to agree to the decision of one in authority such as for instance Rabbi Sussya-ben-Mordecai of Pukop. But this only made Yeersel and Reb Maisha angry: "And if the Pukopper should tell you to walk with your behind in the open air, would you do it? . . . Listen to him! He thinks the Holy Law was handed down from Pukop! . . . Lions are before him, yet he thinks to inquire of a fox!"

"Ay, lions," said Uncle Mottel with a laugh. "Your case was weak, you dragged in too many arguments. You should have stamped your feet and said no, no, no . . . and that's all. But if not tailor, then what?"

Then I went back to the mandolin. The story ran out of me like water from a broken bottle. I said, "It never stops pulling me, to be a fiddler."

"Fiddlers are fools," he said, spitting.

"I can't help it."

"If it's in you to be a fool," he said quietly, "then be a big one. Be a doctor, a millionaire, a smuggler, a lawyer, a rabbi . . . but a fiddler, a runningness in the nose of the world? What for?"

"For pleasure."

"What pleasure fiddlers give and get," he said in a slow muse, "remains only to themselves and helps nothing. In a body which is a nothing, and has nothing, and belongs to nothing, what can a soul draw from sounds that live for a minute in the air and fly by like crows?"

"But, Uncle . . ." I stumbled how to say it. "My fiddler that I heard at night, from the Squire's hill . . . I remember; I hear him."

"Ay . . . what can be the end of such pleasure? You'll fiddle, sitting in one whole pampering of your ear and live by yourself away up on Soundy Mountain with the winds. Ay, Laib, it's a world of more than pretty sounds. If it's only sounds you want, better be a monk before a fiddler. Together with all kinds of pretty sounds the whole day, a monk gains a free lifetime of eat and sleep." His hand put itself under my chin; he spoke with a harsh and bitter voice, but that was just the outside. "Don't fiddle for them, Laib. Don't give them a soothe, don't rub their kittens' necks. Don't be the dog that brings back the bird and gets only the bone. Be the hunter with the gun in the red coat."

"But how do I come to a red coat?"

"If you're going to be a fool, it means . . . be the right kind. Put strong wheels under your feet. Run out of this Golinsk, to where it's allowed to touch the world with your finger. Look into books, into . . . ay," he said with a thinking turn, "I'd like to be drinking with many grandfathers, to love a wife . . . to listen to engines, to fart in palaces . . . and it would please me to be crossing over oceans, criticizing peace treaties, turning enemies into friends, to walk followed by children . . . ay, eat, drink, laugh, cry . . . but the best pleasure, Laib, is to look under the skirts of the world, and see."

I tried to answer. "If the whole trick of these things is only to run out of Russia, why didn't you?"

"Why-didn't-I-yes, why-didn't-I-no," he said, very dry, pointing with his cigarette. "And if Grandma had what hangs, she'd be Grandpa."

"Uncle, the fiddler I heard from the Squire's hill . . . it was long ago but I can hear him like the first time. Like traveling to places."

"So?"

"Even this minute."

"Then let it be," he said, his eyes looking to the wall. "Let your feet lead you to the place you love."

"This summer," I said eagerly, "I'll go to the Pukop Fair and glue myself to the wandering musicians and they'll make me a fiddler."

"You're not such a small fool," he said, giving me a shove. He sat puffing his cigarette for a minute. "And since it is in your nature to want to give pleasure, go to the Burial Brotherhood and tell them I demand fifteen rubles silence-money in three days or they'll hear thunders."

"For what, silence-money?"

"They'll think of something. Let them know you are to take the rubles and give them to me. This is how you'll get yourself the best fiddle in Minsk."

"What?"

"Your fiddle." He leaned his back against the wall, making a gentle end. "I'll send to Minsk for it. We'll see how big a fool you'll make of yourself."

I should have been happy; I should have exploded. "Ay, but they're so poor, Uncle. Fifteen rubles!"

"Poor today, poor tomorrow."

Then he gave a sudden angry roar for Lizaveta, his call echoing. "We'll see what wriggles out. Meanwhile it's late. Go home. Lizaveta must try again with the liniment."

That night at the supper table Reb Maisha looked up from his plate and saw me just sitting. "The soup doesn't please you?"

"Soup is soup," I said.

"Don't waste time," Shim said. "Yeersel sews your confirmation suit. He wants you to come for the fitting tonight."

When he was finished eating, Reb Maisha went to his trunk. From under some old prayer books he took the bundle of rubles and counted off three. "Here, tell Yeersel this is for the suit."

"Wait till you see it, Laib," Shim said like an expert. "The finest twill in the market, here, rub it between your fingers."

I rubbed the three rubles in my pocket. They were from the eleven from my father's goods which Dimitri had sold. For them Uncle Mottel had beaten Dimitri and sat four months in prison.

It took the night. In bed next to Shim, after coming home from the fitting, I parceled the thing out in my mind and before my eyes closed I had my plan. Of the eleven rubles remaining, half was mine and half Shim's. After paying for the confirmation suit, two and a half were still mine. I decided to take three. No one would know about it until Reb Maisha would give Shim his share to start his own tailoring business. Meanwhile I would let Uncle Mottel think this was all the silence-money I could get. It would not be enough for the best fiddle in Minsk, as he had said . . . but still enough for a fiddle. And when it all came out who could say I had stolen what had been only my own?

I took the three the next day when Shim was with Yeersel and Reb Maisha went to see how the graves looked now that all the ice was melted. "Quick work," my uncle said, giving my arm a pleased shake. "But three is all?"

"All they had."

I kept my head down and my behind tight, ashamed and excited.

It was a real fiddle, and a problem. I didn't know the first thing about it and I had no place to learn. Uncle Mottel hid it in the loft of the smithy and would rub it with a clean rag each time he handed it to me. I wanted to play so his eyes would shine but all I could create were squeals and bumps. "Ay, it doesn't go," I said miserably.

"All beginnings are hard."

"Better sell it back," I said sadly.

"Remember your Holy Law," he replied. "Didn't Reb Maisha ever mention the part that says, 'A person will have a bad mark against him for everything he sees and refuses to enjoy?'"

"But all I make is ugly scrapes," I cried.

"Well . . . the thing is, the notes. That's how to learn, by the notes. The Squire has a piano."

"Ay," I said bitterly.

We sat in a long silence. When my uncle spoke, a new twist showed in his voice. "There is one other piano; in our little Golinsker Heaven."

"Where?"

"In 'Heaven.' The house behind the last tavern on the Svutzker side of the road."

"Oh . . . where the prostitutes . . ."

"Profim's." He took it for a settled thing. "You'll learn notes in the afternoon when the girls are sleeping. One of them plays piano not well but at least carefully. She'll show you the notes and teach you tunes. I have an influence with her."

"But didn't you almost die getting thrown out of one of their windows?"

"Yes, but not Varya's."

"Varya? Is that the one from the Odessa prison?"

"No, you mean Vavra."

"It's a queer place to play fiddle," I said.

"We cannot always cook the way we like. Why treat it like any piece of wood? Why not grab it by its neck and make it play? Leave things to me. I'll tell you when and how."

In years to come, jokes used to be made around my house about "Papa's conservatory." Sundays in the afternoon we'd be listening to the symphony concert over the radio, my wife Gitel (who liked to be called Trudy) and the two girls Ethel and Marsha with their husbands, and my son Lester if he wasn't still sleeping; we would put the loudspeaker on the dining-room table and all sit around it. A few times a year somebody would say, "Tell us about your conservatory, Papa." They'd always laugh in the same places. But I let them. They missed the best parts. I stopped putting them in when I realized they had no ears for the underneath-truth. My "conservatory" in Profim's brothel lasted only the eight or nine weeks until my confirmation. Varya's piano was strictly amateur; I had no way to practice from one Saturday to the next except by fingering a stick with marks on it where the notes of the C-scale were supposed to be (the fiddle remained in "Heaven").

I never had to worry about Shim on Sabbath afternoons because he'd be with Yeersel's Rochel talking over the week like a little boss (and later, in troubled times, they married). The minute Reb Maisha started his deep snores in the hut I was on my way to the woods, to the house, the hidden way. Varya would be watching for me at the back window and have the door open. She was small and always tired-looking but younger than my mother. Her long face and large mouth and full lips reminded me of red rubber stretching when she smiled; at one time she must have been quite a puzzle to men. She always wore the same blue slippers with pompons and a greenish velvet robe down to her ankles, buttoned with a loop at the neck. She would lead me, with a nod of her head, through a hall with closed doors on both sides like one of those cook-for-yourself summer boardinghouses around Monticello, New York, to the small sitting room in the front where she locked the door and closed the shutters. The summer I had the string ensemble at the Beachcrest Hotel in Arverne there used to be a Mr. Frumkin every night with a request to play "Just a Song at Twilight." As I did the solo part, I would think:

> Just a song at twilight, when the light was low,
> Into Profim's "Heaven" softly I did go.

(This was a joke to the family.)

But when Varya handed me the fiddle she kept locked in a chest and then sat down with me standing next to her, to her right, the room became nothing. Fiddle in my hand, it was night all around and I was standing so high up that the sky almost touched my head. Once I said to her, "I'd like to stay longer," though I knew it was time to go.

"Soon it will be different. The spittoons will start filling and by nine o'clock we'll be drunk enough."

Varya had a careless way of running her words together. I could understand and speak Russian not too badly but wasn't always sure I got her meaning. "Is that what's here, drinking?"

"Yes, darling one," she said, her mouth stretching and the tendons of her neck sticking out. "You don't know what fancy drinkers we have here. Come to me in a few years and what a drink I'll give you, darling one." (Big laughs from Ethel and Marsha. Wisecrack from Lester: "Come on, Pop, admit it! You fiddled around a little!") Then I asked, "Does my Uncle Mottel ever come here?"

"Not lately, no. Let it not go further but Mot is a fool. He'll get himself killed yet. Uh, he's crazy."

"How so?" I said. "Is it true as he says . . . that he has an influence with you?"

"An influence, yes, to get me killed." Then she spilled out what made her angry. "I like him once in a while, I'm sorry for him and it's nice. But he gets crazy; that's why the Squire's Buzarov, the boss's brother, you know, threw him out of the window." Then she went into a business about "Mot's" ruining her chances with the Squire himself. "He came around a few times," she said, nodding her head to show me how important such visits were, "and once the Squire picked me. After that he stayed mine twice a month on the dot. Not too charming but for five rubles a drink, you understand, it was fun. And presents. See this?" She pointed to the robe she wore. "Direct from a fancy place in Petersburg. Expensive. Then Mot jumps in one night swimming in vodka, slaps my face . . . screams the Squire is not to drink from the same bottle as he does! Then Mot yells how no Squire must dirty his own little Vavra, Vavra, Vavra. He's so drunk he can't even say my name rightly! I told him to go drink himself to death and warned him to lower his voice with Vassily Buzarov, just then in the next room with Rena. That's all . . . he went after Vassily and when Vassily heard enough he picked him up and in one toss dropped him out of Rena's window . . . and now I don't know where I stand, the Squire's overlooked me twice and I can't worm anything out of Vassily."

It was all Greek about the "drinking" and this-and-that. But the

"Vavra" stuck in my mind. Something told me Uncle Mottel knew what he was saying when he called Varya by the name of the girl whose brother Maxim had made a career of blowing up some generals; that Uncle Mottel understood it was impossible to allow the Squire of Golinsk to "drink" with the girl who opened his memory of the other one for whom he had sat in prison. I didn't get the entire point, but Varya's complaint gave me two things. Uncle Mottel didn't belong with our landsmen, but neither did he belong in the Squire's corner; he belonged to some corner beyond my imagination but still the one I would belong to myself sometime. (This part of the story I soon left out, with my family. They enjoyed themselves with the "drinking" joke; that's all. "Let them have pleasure," I told myself.)

The next time I saw Uncle Mottel, I said, "She's very angry with you, Varya."

"As long as she does what I say," he shrugged.

"She blames you because the Squire doesn't visit her any more."

"She stated that?" he said. "The truth spoken?"

"The truth spoken."

He laughed. "She lies. She's sent the Squire away three times. It's the talk of the house. Tell her to stop lying or I'll put soap in her mouth. Tell her I said that."

"Then you do have an influence there?"

"Tell her one more thing," he ordered. He wasn't in a temper, just amusing himself. "She's to talk to you not with her tongue, but only with her fingers on the piano. Clear?"

I said, "Clear," but I was afraid to mention such things to her. As it was we spoke only when my hands were tired. Once she said, "I know where I saw your face . . . how strange."

"In the market?"

"No, in Berlin."

"I was never in Berlin."

"It's a face on a picture. In the Berlin Museum."

"What's Berlin like?"

"It's as Herr Immen used to say. He was a good friend, a jewelry salesman. 'Varya,' Herr Immen used to say when we were at dinner, 'Berlin is a very stuffed city.' Well, you've rested enough; let's continue, but with the whole bow."

She dropped other remarks about "the maniac of a sergeant in Hamburg" and "the weight I gained in Riga," and "the fun we had in the traveling circus." One time she became so interested in remembering that she added details. The bear they had in the traveling circus, a little dancing bear, broke loose and entered the tent where a Herr Glockmann was delivering a lecture on "The Pitfalls of Paris." Varya's rubberlike lips pulled themselves wide as she remembered, and she breathed fast. "Ah well . . . Herr Glockmann completely hated the French and it showed in his lecture which told why many French girls go into houses. Herr Glockmann went to the trouble of having charts made and pinned on the wall, like a medical lecture, you know, and with these charts he used to prove that the French girls went into houses because so many Frenchmen were only peanuts. At this moment in the lecture the little dancing bear walked in and stretched himself out on his side . . . just a baby one, you know. The people began to yell fearfully and run before Herr Glockmann could make his offer of verified photographs, but Herr Glockmann called out, 'Don't be afraid, ladies! Look and see, it is only Monsieur Peanut!' "

When Varya saw me laughing, she stopped. "Wait, that's silly." Then she started lecturing me. "And another thing. You're a boy. In a year or two you'll start looking. You'll want girls and you'll think of going to houses. Very few have your luck, to be told." She bent down and took my arms. "When you wish to have that kind of fun you must remember to come to me. Otherwise you may be very sorry, understand?"

"No," I said, the truth spoken.

"There is a thing," she said, "between a girl and a boy. All girls and boys, yes?"

"Thank you," I said. She shook my arms again and I smelled her perfume. "Such a smell," I said, "so sweet."

Bending her ear low she said, "Here, take a good sniff." I did and she pulled me to her. "Yes, with a little bit of luck, a little bit, I might have had one like you." She pushed me back far enough to see me, her lips stretched in her smile. "In my own little house not far from Riga, I could have waked early every morning when the day was beginning . . . and found a baby sleeping in the crook of my arm . . . had the cards fallen differently." She changed her tone back to an ordering. "Remember, you're to come to me."

When I told this to my uncle he fell back on the bed and shouted, "She's crazy, also as filthy, believe me, as her competition." I mentioned how sweet her perfume was. He told me not to go by the smell, women weren't flowers.

"But she does remind you of Vavra, Uncle. Isn't that right?"

"That could be. However, she's far from the Queen of Sheba, keep away from her except as your teacher. By the way . . . your confirmation is in two weeks. Take no chance, people will be noticing you more now. Tell her next Saturday is your last for a while."

Varya didn't mind. "I wanted to start you on Chopin. Well, it'll wait a few weeks. But practice the fingerings on your piece of wood." At the end of the lesson she kissed me. As she let me go she whispered, "Am I your friend?"

"Your smell is sweet."

"Then wait." She came back in a minute with a small glass tube in her fingers. "This is so you won't miss me too much." I thanked her and took the cork out. It was her perfume. "Careful, keep the cork in," she said.

"Well, until later."

"Until later, boy." She pulled my nose a little and smiled almost her whole face away. "Strange," she said, "that he should be your uncle."

All the way back to the hut I held her phial in my fingers. As soon as I could I hid it between the leaves of an old raggy prayer book of my father's I never used. Going out early in the mornings to wake the landsmen to prayers, I took her phial with me, thinking of her and wondering how soon I could go back to my lessons; but I never saw her again.

On the Thursday before the Saturday of my confirmation, I went to the smithy with a purpose. I found Uncle Mottel banging an axle on the anvil with short sharp hits of the hammer so as not to hurt his sick shoulder. "Ay, it's the confirmation-boy," he said with a grunt, the axle jumping under his hand. Happy he was in a good mood, I blurted, "Are you coming to it?"

"To the confirmation? To the synagogue?"

"Are you?"

"I'll think it out." He banged the hammer down so hard that the cigarette in his mouth twisted quickly with the hurt to his shoulder.

"Don't you want The Everlasting One to forgive you?" I whispered, worried about him.

"For what?" (I was afraid to say.) "It's up to Him," Uncle Mottel went on indifferently, rubbing his shoulder. "If He wants, He'll forgive even if I don't go to the synagogue. However," he added, his brows wrinkling in long thin furrows as he spit his cigarette to the black dirt floor, "ask rather — will I forgive Him?"

For nearly a year I did not see him again, and then it was for the few hours of our permanent good-by.

I have more on my mind, but let this be enough until later.

Once in a nickel magazine I saw an advertisement for safety razors. A small boy was standing on a stool before the bathroom mirror, giving himself a shave. For a peppy eye-catcher they took a poetic saying, "The child is father of the man," and put it above the picture. But opening the heart is not selling safety razors, so don't think I delude myself. You are not on my side, but start with this:

Remember that when I came back to my Golinsker hut with the dried raspberries after I had seen the way Uncle Mottel had fixed my mandolin, I had then begun to change into a more important version of myself, for I came home with a secret worth lying about, the possession of a playable instrument and a teacher for it. The connection with Uncle Mottel in all its past, present, and future whys and wherefores had changed me into a learning-cadet in the permanent and invisible war between man and the State. And thus the anger that did not die. Why such anger? What was under the wrinkles of speculations, between veins, behind knuckles, hidden in curves of eyes or under beards or in the middle of throats? A plain wanting to walk in airs, to sleep under oceans, to be a piece of electricity; anything to explode the insanity established by no one man. I think of my father with such bitter tears that they can never be wet. I think of him as a bug lying under the rock of the State, a bug personally not in the least wanting to be a bug but a person with a pride, a use, and a valuable history. I think of my father standing beside the lamp on the table, his face down to blow the lamp out with one tired puff of air . . . a face that if painted by the right artist would have made a rock blow its nose. But the State has other plans for the artists, connected to the selling of safety razors — the opening of the heart becoming the unadvertised miracle, the guarded secret, the message taking centuries to deliver and even then it doesn't always arrive.

Maybe I shouldn't have kept it all in. Maybe I should have sat in cafés and drunk tea and knocked the government, or hung around a lot of Union Squares and given the revolution my permission to go ahead, or made free love with philosophical girls and in such pastimes sweated off the anger. But I was a musician and played a musician's pinochle. I did not fool myself into believing I could buy every meld and that a Turkish bath fixed everything. No bluffs or baths could wring "Mottel's Sonata" or "Papa's Conservatory" out of me because these were in the marrow; all the sweating in the world couldn't have dissolved them. Nor by the method of thinking so fashionable in self-complicated circles, where anything is taken and chopped up for eating with fancy forks, could I have employed my Golinsker heritage in recipes from romantic cookbooks to try to win the prize for the most original treatment of a left-over. This was more in the line of my nephew Leon, the professor, and my son Lester . . . but not me. Right here, ladies and gentlemen of the world, appears the only victory a person can permanently win, to leave the world with the same sweetness he brought, to keep himself clean of the dirt of the State with all its ridiculous recipes for "growing up," for sitting through life as through a play, waiting for the intermissions and the end; for fearing not your wounds but their cure, for seeing your food but not your prison.

Let experts argue; I claim I did right (though in my family this remained my personal opinion, no more). For instance one night in 1928 or 1929 I was doing a stage show in Newark with the all-girl orchestra and my son Lester, who by then played sax in a big hotel band, came to take me to a special party of musicians. They were going to play without music for their own pleasure, improvisations. "Come on, Pop. Climb out of 'Poet and Peasant,' everything ain't 'Kiss Me Again,' " he nudged me.

We were riding in his big second-hand Marmon down Broad Street in Newark on the way to a place in Harlem where the boys were meeting. We passed a Hebrew National delicatessen and stopped off for a bite. Between the hot pastrami and the pickles and an argument with the house manager in the Newark theater, I got a little gas and didn't feel like hanging around all night listening to jazz so I said, "Lester, go alone. I'll take the subway."

"But Pop," Lester said, "Bix is going to show up. You can't miss Bix."

"I got gas tonight, Lester, also a headache. Anyway I'm not such a jazz baby."

"Pop," Lester said, his mouth full of pastrami, "you're in America now, for crissake. Melt yourself down an inch."

"America is not a pot and I'm not tin."

"Aw, Pop, again?"

"Just like going to play with Bix doesn't yet make you an American, your sitting here in the Hebrew National eating hot pastrami doesn't make you a Jew either."

"Ok, Spinoza, take it easy!"

"Don't worry, Lester," I said, and went home.

With me the anger was too deep to come out to my own — except once. It kept me home alone in the apartment the day of the fire; the truth spoken, it burned me to death. Had I been doing what was expected of me, had I been sitting on the witness stand reciting a few lies to help save my nephew's twelve-story building in New Roseville, New Jersey, I wouldn't have been burned, physically, in the slightest.

At my funeral three different rabbis pronounced words about how I lived like some giant bird of the skies, soaring on lonely wings to places few spirits ever knew; about how I lived in the mantle of the gentle prophet, Hillel; and about how my household sang with the beauty of my violin. Nothing was said of my wife Gertrude's disappointment when I told Aaron to keep his five-thousand-dollar bribe; that he could go save his building without my help. Nothing was said of my son Lester's dutiful pity of me. Nothing was said of my failure to be to my nephew, Aaron-the-success, what my Uncle Mottel was to me. Nothing was said about my having no one to give my Mottelness to, that surge of a life lived free and full to the extent allowed by the arrogance of the State. And not even the slightest hint was there of the love and grief I had for my own, betrayed by the invisible enemy; so "mature," my own, so "practical."

My love and grief and anger are for them.

4. Nochim

(1834–1886)

At sixty inches I stopped growing; year after year in my youngest manhood the recruiting clerks would measure me. Some tried to stretch me; one of them made a change in my nose with his pistol butt and I never wore the Tsar's uniform.

I made the most of my caricaturish appearance. It invited openings for conversations leading to possible sales of the dairys I peddled in my cart all around the Golinsk district. Without dairys, when my credit with the farmers had returned to zero, I would go about the different towns with my fiddle, and set myself up in the market places and at fairs. Peasants would stop to insult me, yet they often left coppers the more my figure became familiar. (This, only when I needed cash; and never in Golinsk itself.)

I developed also the ability to seek out a wedding feasible for me to make an entrance as an uninvited supporter of the celebration offering the joy of my fiddle for a hatful of coins or a bag of leftovers. To learn of weddings, I would jolly with postmen, listen long hours in taverns, pester housewives, and look to see which boys smiled at which girls. On such wheels I rolled to Pukop the week of Laib's confirmation, intending to return to Golinsk in time for the ceremonies. Laib's gentle father had been my good friend; were I six feet tall, Aaron could not have spoken to me more respectfully.

It being after Passover, cows ate the new grass, seeds pushed, the sun baked my face, chickens walked around like policemen and my stomach was as empty as my purse. The charm of the season did not therefore lie in my head. I stood in the Pukop market square near some gypsies, round confident people from the south who swore to the gathered peasants that the contents of their green bottles guaranteed sons. I stood doing nothing, fiddle in hand, busying myself with four principal thoughts.

First, though I needed any coins the peasants might throw me, I had good reason not to interfere with the gypsies. I wanted to ask one of the women if she had ever met a redhead of twenty-seven with a mole as wide as a thumbnail high on her right cheek. This was my daughter Lenka, whom I had disowned twelve years before when she had allowed herself to become a piece of the Squire's entertainment. I had kicked Lenka away from me and the landsmen had upheld the piety and wisdom of the sacrifice. But I could never after stifle my love nor mourn her as a dead soul. The religious command was just and true; there must be no harlots in a clean Jewish house; the Law had been satisfied yet not I; nor could I ever expect to be. My condition simply demanded that I accept the fated thing. Earning hardly enough to keep my family alive, Nochim the sometimes-beggar could send no agents to search for Lenka; I would never in the world see her again, never tell her the biggest secret — that I loved her anyway — unless by some fortune, news of her would come my way. Therefore, I did nothing to annoy the gypsies.

Second, I hoped to meet someone who might drop a hint of a soon wedding. But it was already Tuesday, the day of Jewish weddings in our district; if I hadn't known of one by then, there wasn't any. I knew of a gentile wedding there that Sunday but I had to be in Golinsk Saturday for Laib's confirmation.

Third, I waited for a Jewish Pukopper to notice me and offer an invitation to evening prayers and supper. But the Pukoppers held us Golinskers to be half-Hasids, pathetic dwellers in the air as irrationally pious as we were ignorant, looking down our noses at them as though we were transplanted Galicians. The fear of being corrupted into our simplicity made them avoid us. The Pukoppers had a saying, "If a Shnavker walks with you, be careful of your coat. If a Svutzker kisses you, count your teeth. If a Golinsker says hello to you, go elsewhere at once."

face, a dirty pillow slept on too many times. "The boy sits in your wagon to go on his journey," I whispered. "In your wagon."

"In the wagon," she said, turning back to her customers. I stood wondering how to ask my question. Wildly I thought to go back to Maruska and beg a bottle on credit for the gypsy. I felt a hand from behind, which picked me up and threw me to the floor. Rolling over, I saw Yegor's two hands plunging down like the front feet of a frightened horse, his fingers lifting and tossing me in the air. He performed this trick, cleanly, with no show of anger.

I lay on my side where I fell, beginning to want to cry not simply for the pain; also was the pain of having been unable to talk to the gypsy woman about Lenka. Yegor's toe turned me over on my back. Seeing my hand protecting the damaged side, he kicked the fingers away and caved the side in further with other sharper kicks. I lay still awhile, fearing he would kill me if I tried to move away. But so to hold myself was unbearable. I made myself crawl to the door, turning for a last look at them. Yegor had already gone toward Maruska, who held her back to me. Arms like upright snakes waved at me from both sides.

In the coolness of the rain, I seemed to come to the end of a journey. My side had opened and was bleeding. High sounds came through the tavern's door — muffled bleats, the screams of a woman in quick pain but with an anger in it. Maruska's were like the screams of other beaten women I had heard, their past hurts returning in the pain of the latest. In that moment I felt a warmness under my shirt where the side was bleeding. Pressing my hand to it I ran up the road toward where I had left the rabbi. Weights lay on my chest. Knives whirled over my head. I fell. I seemed to hear close sounds, the gallop of horses, new screams, a near excitement of some kind. I wanted to lie still, nothing else. The rain fell on my back. I felt the oncoming of sleep and heard something familiar.

> Father, come take a bath,
> The Tsar bathes all day long.

When next I opened my eyes it was to see the face of Maruska by the candle in her hand, her broad loose body in a squat. She wiped her bloody cheek with the bottom of her skirt as she looked at me. I lay on straw, shivering in my wet shirt.

"Keep still," she whispered, "the police may return."

"Police, what . . . ?"

"Those gypsies." Wiping her cheek again, she started in fear, then blew out the candle. "The police came for them. In and out with them. I'll go now, I had to wait until you opened your eyes. Yegor could have killed you."

Maruska, my friend of the while . . . both of us knowing the iron in Yegor's hands. "You'd better be out of here early," she said in the dark of the barn.

"Wait." The meaning became clearer. "The police were here?"

"Their horses ran you over on the road. I carried you in. They made the gypsies drive their wagon back to Pukop."

"Back to Pukop?"

"With them behind it. How you weren't killed as you lay there, under the wheels . . . but your bones are straight. I felt."

"But my side . . ."

"You can walk. You'll have to. It's lucky I ran out, or otherwise . . ." In the pitch-dark barn her voice changed to a gentle child's. "Good rest, Onion-Nose. Be away early. Yegor mustn't see you."

She stamped out, closing the door. Kalman, the rabbi, police, gypsies . . . for what? I had wanted a drink; there had to be an Itzik and a rabbi and a Kalman.

On this I slept. In the early morning of the next day, Friday, I found the world as usual outside Yegor's barn. The bleeding of my side had stopped. A small piece of rib lay exposed like a bit of fat in dried gravy. I could walk; the low sun gave me the shadow of a tall man; the quiet made me remember the fiddle I had left in the rabbi's house; but I had to be for Golinsk now. What remained in Pukop I would learn later.

Moving my feet on the Golinsk way, I saw, in my fever, Pesha and the children before me on the road; they pulled me to the comfortable boredom of my hut and I tried to pace more quickly. "Tomorrow is Laib's confirmation," I told myself, "a twelve-year-old becomes a man . . . someday another Kalman, another prize for them . . . if only," it came to me humorously, "The One Above would arrange for Jews to be born at seventy and grow down instead of up, with the wisest years lived first, with conscription to be worried about at the end instead of the beginning . . . ay, peculiar arrangement, you are not sensible — for in such a harness would not our children suffer for us? . . . Let it be the way it is. . . ."

With such musings I numbed the thought of the nine miles until I would be home. I came to where the highroad turned and ran between clumps of trees taken fire the year before, now gray and bare. I ordered myself to examine the lifeless trunks. "See how they still try to be trees . . . without sense, Nochim . . . take a lesson from them . . . lie down . . . it's a solution."

I sank to the road. Warmth spurted anew from my side. I waited for the smell of the last night's rain, for the feel of damp earth on my tongue, for the blackness. I supposed this to be the end of my nonsensical circlings, all fights for pennies finished, the seeking for Lenka over. "It is better now," I thought in the underpull.

I heard Pesha say, "He opens his eyes."

Pesha? My passage into the Next World interrupted? Yes, it was Pesha. What other voice could manage to squeeze such sadness into her relief? Ay, my ticket not yet stamped; I lived!

Yushin barked, "Good, I'll keep on." Yes, my acquaintance the druggist, happy with his cupping-glasses, eagerly saving my life at his price. He never wished anyone dead, just dying; save the life and take out the mortgage. But not this time, Mr. Druggist. "Go try," I urged myself, "open an eye."

Reb Maisha was first to see. "A good thank-you, God, my Dear!" he chanted with a lift. "One joy at least on this terrible day!"

I knew I was home. Reb Maisha, the crack in the wall stuffed with putty and tar, Yushin, Pesha. Yes, home, but how? My thoughts began to gather themselves; I heard Berel-the-Ox, then Yeersel, and also Laib-Shmul, the entire Burial Brotherhood. "Wait," I whispered to Yushin, "stop the cupping-glasses, they burn. Let a man . . ."

I opened my eyes again to Pesha crying, but where were Marya, Fendel, Sholem, Zagzaigel? "Ay, I'll live," I thought. "I want to know everything." And I shouted quite clearly, "Rabbi, have you seen Kalman of Pukop? Do you hear me, Rabbi?"

"Kalman," I heard Reb Maisha say. "Ay, a Sabbath of Satan's!"

Laib-Shmul leaned over and promised, "Later, Nochim. Everything."

What, the Sabbath? It's tomorrow; what happened to yesterday? I shouted to them, "Where's yesterday, Kalman, the Rabbi, Maruska, the police?" They held me down but I kept shouting. "Send the druggist away, let me gather myself! Say what is, open your mouths . . . Mama, Mama, make them!"

Yushin commanded them to hold me. Yeersel said, "No, he is going; let him speak."

"Wait, Nochim," Reb Maisha said to me. "Hear me quietly."

He spoke of the Svutzkers finding me on the road under a high sun that morning and bringing me home in their wagon, riding on the Sabbath but pardoned by the emergency. The police, they said, had taken Kalman out of the gypsies' wagon, bound and buttoned for the soldier's funeral he had wanted to flee. The Svutzkers had heard the shots and the shouts, "Reprisal against the Jews' conspiracy." After all the bribes! Ay, so; the gypsies in two pays, the rabbi's and the police's! And so ended Kalman, bribe-today, bribe-tomorrow; and of the rabbi, not known except arrested.

Yeersel interrupted Maisha. "Enough for now."

"Ay," from my shrilling wife, "the rest let wait!"

"What rest, brothers?" I shouted, trying to rise up. "Run. Leave me and run. They've made a conspiracy and from Pukop they'll stitch it to Golinsk and sew our own lads into Kalman-coats!"

"The fever," Yeersel said.

"Tie him down," from Berel-the-Ox.

"Don't stand here," I screamed. "Be birds!"

"He believes a pogrom's coming," Laib-Shmul decided. "Tell him of Laib's confirmation, Maisha. It'll quiet him."

This morning, Nochim [chanted Reb Maisha],
In the synagogue, on the Sabbath, into Laib's confirmation,
It came a fragrant thing-a-thing, like the festival bough a bit,
Ha-hi, such a pain to my laughter!

Solemn in the synagogue, solemn confirmation day,
Laib-ben-Aaron born, praying from the altar,
Grown into twelve years, the orphan soon a man,
And comes to the end of the service, Nochim,
A big "Amen," you know, you know,
Blessings, excitements, kissings, ha-hi!
But what is it? What smells?
On Reb Maisha, what smells?

Disgrace, scandal,
Only from a frenchy-woman such a smell,
Ay, brought into the synagogue!
Put in the prayer book, a small something-in-a-glass,
Broken and such a dripping; but how to me?

Then Laib comes back from running away,
Calling "Mine, mine," with trembles,
"She gave it, a present, I hid it in the book
She's Varya from Profim's."
And again Laib with a quick-away and again on me names,
"Such a guardian,"
"Laib with a whore before confirmed in Israel,"
"A fine teacher, Reb Maisha,"
Ay, this in our synagogue today, Nochim,
Today.

See how we joke,
Ha-hi, ha-hi,
Such a pain to my laughter!

So hearing I thought, "Ah, you again, Mottel; again the bad uncle of the confirmation boy." I knew Varya from hearing in the taverns; stories of her and the Squire, and of how she was Mottel's private playtoy, a badhouse romance. But next to my Kalman-thing, a small evil, Varya. Small, indeed.

So closing my eyes I heard Yushin say, "Now he'll sleep."

In my sleep I met Lenka. We sat in a calm field looking at two cows nibbling grass. "Daughter," I said, "it took you so long to come. Was it from far?"

"I waited for you to bring me home. But it is a visit only. I cannot stay."

"You are beautiful."

"As the wheel must be round, so must I be beautiful."

"And such a fragrance to you, Lenka."

"On my shelf are many bottles."

"You are sweet without bottles."

"Then I please you?"

"You are the daughter of my soul."

"But look at my body, Father. Is it not beautiful?"

"Forgive me, Lenka."

"And smell me. Not sweet?"

"I made you a whore."

"Silly Father. You should see me in Riga."

"Then you were yes-in-Riga?"

"All the time. It's nothing like Profim's, no peasants in stinking blouses. One officer or merchant a night, ten rubles; anything unpleasant extra. Ask for the Queen of Sport Street and they'll bring you to me. For freeing me, Father, a blessing on you."

"Don't make such jokes, daughter."

"Let me make you wider and longer with pleasure. Be the master of my body, Father. Die like a king."

"Dear One Above," I cried, "cut me and then burn me."

"But first you must be pleased. Well, now." She brazened herself then to me. "Be a merchant, an officer, a Squire, Father. Just once."

I turned away.

"I am ugly to you," she accused. "A beauty from Profim's you'd rather take, a Varya, but not your own daughter."

"Stop your knives, Lenka. It's my end now."

My daughter said, "You despised me. Even before the Squire. Even before. Go to Varya. Make with her. Die with her."

A wind blew. When again I looked for Lenka she was not there.

I began to moan and cry, "Varya, help me. Varya, I'm dying. Come here, Varya."

With these fine chops I came to the close of my human condition. Hearing my cries for Varya the attending Burial Brotherhood put their confused heads together. "How bring a woman of filth here?" Yeersel wondered.

"All the same," Berel said, "how deny a last earthly wish? How let him remember us in The World Above with such salt?"

"These things are not new," Laib-Shmul said. "Didn't my own father-may-he-rest call for a plate of pig the day he died?"

"Why your father-may-he-rest wanted to eat pig on his deathbed is clear," Reb Maisha said. "Your father did many sins, but as he lay to die he remembered he had never eaten pig. He knew the Smiting Angel would read the list of his sins . . . ten smites for this, twelve smites for that . . . a long list. So he ate pig, knowing that when the Angel would call out his smites for eating pig it would be the last of them. But this is not the same."

Yeersel guessed, "Wait. Maisha told of Varya and Laib. Perhaps it's from that corner."

"Why look further?" Laib-Shmul pressed. "The man dies away. Who will go to Profim's and bring her?"

"Not a man," Reb Maisha said. "Let it be Tzippe-Sora."

The rest tells itself quickly. They brought Varya; Tzippe-Sora stood holding a candle over my bed. I heard her crackly voice. "She is here, Nochim. The woman."

"I can't see her. Give her a candle. You go away."

I next saw a nose and a mouth, her eyes and a fringe of hair; all else dark. "Alone, alone we must be," I whispered.

"Alone," she whispered fearfully. "Why am I here?"

"Varya, you must go far away."

"But I did nothing to the boy!"

"You must go and it will be good for you there."

"I only showed him to play the fiddle," she sobbed. "Please don't curse me . . . it was the fiddle, only the fiddle."

"If you do as I say," I whispered, "I can only bless you. I beg you, woman, go to Riga, to Sport Street in Riga, and ask for the 'Queen' there. They will take you to my daughter, Lenka, and tell her this . . . I wanted her with me always. I dreamed and sorrowed and regretted. Tell her these things, in Sport Street, Riga . . . she's the 'Queen.' "

"I did not harm the boy, you hear?"

"To Riga?"

"Do you hear?"

"Say to her only that you come from Nochim, her father. You will be treated like a queen yourself. Your hand. Give. Don't fear."

The fingers, cold, small. Lenka, Lenka . . . "Now . . . Call them in."

The fingers still in my hand . . . Yeersel, Berel, Laib-Shmul, Reb Maisha . . . the Burial Brotherhood about me; and the final prayer, to Varya's gasps.

"Thou who are the father of the fatherless and judge of the widow, protect my beloved kindred with whose soul my spirit is knit. Into thy hand I put my spirit. Amen, and amen."

Fathers of daughters, think of all the pens broken and bottles of ink consumed in the writing of matters that never happened, and remember a Squire's conspiracy against my flesh. But not with pity. For such a trophy one does not strain from heaven.

5. Berel
(1846–1887)

Now here it is, looking at it with a simple quick eye . . . our boys were being conscripted before their time against no enemy of theirs and it was either to accept it with gall, or give a try for a push-away towards ships going over the sea.

Now this is how I came to be Berel-the-Ox in Golinsk:

Father was a butcher in Minsk, I was born there, every few years some kind of small plague would come there, and all of a sudden the officials would concern themselves about our health and charge into the ghetto with inspectors and in 1851 they inspected Father's meat, of course burning his shop together with many others in defense of the general health and this public activity helped reduce the ghetto quite legally. And of course in their zeal they directed Father to leave Minsk.

Now my father spoke of a dislike of all cities and ghettos, he did not go for Pinsk as the other banished but for a little village he had come from as a boy some forty miles to the east of Minsk, called Pukop. We had a cart in which I rode, I was five then, and with my father and mother we had Gershon and Bosha left, fifteen and seven then . . . Bosha was all right, Gershon had a weak chest and steady cough, in between them had been two other girls before me whom I knew only from remarks and little stories told about them when my father and mother lit the year-time memorial candles . . . and Mother would not allow Gershon to help pull the cart, she would beg him to stop it and ride with me. Gershon would sit backwards in the cart not to see how Father and Mother were pulling him and the moment he stopped coughing he would jump off and walk with our sister Bosha. Now Gershon lived to be fifty years old, sick every day but dying like a healthy person through the sickness of others.

The first night towards Pukop we spent in a field, we woke and found Father straight on his back, giving shakes with his eyes closed, and we built a fire to put hot stones at his feet. He stopped shaking after an hour, his forehead changed to purple and then a gray and I began to chant, "Papa has it, we must burn him, Papa has it, we must burn him." Mother began rolling herself on the ground with such a terror that it frightened brother Gershon into stopping my chant with a hard fist, it struck my ear with all his power, it felled me, it hurt with knives, I pressed it to the cool morning grass. Gershon went to help Mother, he picked her up, she quieted, they talked on a side . . . then he came to me and said to stop my crying. ". . . Because Mother says we should take the cart up the road a way and wait for her."

Bosha and I did not like to leave her, we cried come-with-us, she said, "Don't let Gershon pull," and did not move a step to us. On the road we turned and looked at her, the way she waved good-by too quickly, the way she said "Go, go, go," the way Gershon did not look at her twice at all; it made me ask Gershon after a few minutes of pulling the cart, "Gershon, who'll bury Father?"

"Mother."

Bosha said we should go back and help, Gershon said no, we pulled the cart a long time, the sun went lower and lower. I became frightened, we rested, Bosha and I kept asking Gershon when Mother would be coming. "When she comes and not a minute sooner," he said with a twist-away of his head, with his eyes wet, and Bosha said, "Gershon, do you think Mama caught it too?" and Gershon said, "If she didn't, she'll find us," and I began to cry and that evening by the roadside it was Bosha cooking our potatoes, and Gershon putting on Father's praying shawl. My hurt ear pained all the night and Gershon let himself make sounds of his grief when he thought Bosha and I were sleeping, and two days we walked the strange roads towards Pukop, eating all our potatoes and retching and gasping from the unripe fruit and berries we took on the way.

We met no Jews and Bosha and I kept worrying Gershon why we met no Jews, and we passed around villages too close to be Pukop because we feared the gentiles would know about Minsk and put the plague on us and treat us as if we had it. And on the second day along the roads a peasant in a wagon came by us and asking no questions robbed us of the cart and we had no blankets or cooking pots. A thunderstorm gathered itself to break, frightening woods lay all around the road there, I thought I saw high fur running through the thicket across the way. And then the lightning pointed down close, thunder hammered my paining ear . . . in the middle of the rain we saw a brown spot coming from down the road, a wagon, Gershon ran to it anyway, waving his hands. It stopped down from us too far for Bosha and I to hear anything but we saw joy when we saw Gershon jump on. Nearing us, Gershon shouting over the thunder, "A Jew, a Jew," we also jumped to sit on planks laid over open barrels of wheel-grease sickening to smell, and as we rode Gershon sat up with the wagoner and acquainted him with our condition.

The wagoner was Naftoli-Dovid in his good years, later my father-in-law, and he said to Gershon many times as we rode, "Your father-may-he-rest should have done like the others running from Minsk . . . nothing's here this way, Pinsk is better."

"He wanted no more cities," Gershon told him, "and my brother coughs."

"He'll cough anywhere, right?" said Naftoli-Dovid, slapping the reins with the wet on him, "Look at me, the old Squire hears of cheap wheel-grease in Bobroisk, does he send a friend where a plague is said to be? Certainly . . . his old friend Naftoli-Dovid, his loyal helper in all times . . . gladly going to Bobroisk where they're killing livestock on suspicion of plague there . . . so for the old Squire wheel-grease comes cheap, a blessing on friendly Naftoli-Dovid, his useful Jew . . . well . . . make way, Ocean," Naftoli-Dovid laughed, shaking the rain out of his beard, "crap is swimming."

After the rain I shivered with chills, my ear ached, Gershon laid me on the planks and held my head. The smell of the wheel-grease went to Bosha's stomach, the wagon swayed over rougher roads, she sickened, and with one thing and another we were brought into Golinsk where Yeersel's father of great respect, Daneel-ben-Boruch, said we should be kept. My shrieks of pain made Daneel-ben-Boruch probe my ear with his longest tailor's needle, and the pain soon stopped but brought spells of dizziness and in three weeks the ear went deaf. Meanwhile Gershon was put next to Yeersel's uncle Lazer to be a shoemaker with the old man whose hands were trembling his living away. Bosha learned to run happily down the lanes of the Jewish side like the other children and we accustomed ourselves to our corner of Daneel-ben-Boruch's hut, sleeping under the same cover with Yeersel.

The hearing of my other ear also decreased and mothers comforted me, often showing envy. "Just think, Berel, they'll never want you for the army."

At the age of nine I became both all-deaf and an uncle, Gershon having married Tzippe-Sora's Faiga; and four years later Yeersel married Bosha. They had always leaned to each other, to marry early was a common thing, Bosha was new blood, the landsmen feared too much intermarriage . . . meanwhile Daneel-ben-Boruch ate something and died, I became confirmed and was made the watercarrier, a labor that least needed ears, and when Yeersel and Bosha had their first, Daneel, I helped build them their own hut and remained wifeless with them until sixteen when I took Hannah of Naftoli-Dovid's childless bunch, living in Yeersel's hut, the two families, another seven years. Half the day the whole year around I carried waterbuckets yoked to my shoulders (they widened me out and gave me a broad trunk), from the stream to the huts a quarter of a mile away, the Squire forbidding us a well as was his right as landowner. The other part of the day I either fished for the market or helped my father-in-law dig clay or sell kvas in the market. Hearing nothing I had little to say. I felt blessed in my quiet, seeing what turmoils came from all the tongues around me; whatever turned out to be God's plan for Berel-the-watercarrier, I would accept.

In the second year of my marriage, 1864, they sent a bad recruiting officer during a big snow one afternoon. With two soldiers he visited every hut, every Jewish male from twelve to thirty he marched down to the highroad where he made us into a line and spoke to us holding a pistol in his hand. Only Jews this time, no gentiles, the other peasants of the village standing to the performance and well satisfied to be shown as more free than we, especially since three years before they had been freed officially by a big decree posted on the porch of the village hall which in the end came down to their being permitted, if they liked, to go starve elsewhere. Now this recruiting officer ordered us to take off our coats and shirts in the bitter cold and my brother Gershon's Faiga could not stand to see him bending in half from his coughing. So she went to Gershon and gave him her shawl, a soldier pushed her away; Mottel who stood next to her picked her up, and the soldier took it as a right to push his rifle butt against Mottel's bared chest. Just sixteen and tall, Mottel gave a spring under the soldier's thrust and sent him to the ground, which made the recruiting officer go to Mottel and hit him on an eye with the barrel of his pistol. Since I stood near where Mottel lay the recruiting officer began to open an angry mouth to me, his face getting quite red the more I shook my head and pointed to my ears. In a rage he put the pistol to one ear and pulled the trigger, I heard something like a wetness rushing, and that day they took Hertz, Laib-Shmul, three of Lipka's and Yeersel into their army.

Then a few days after they went, buzzings and ringings went off in my head when I stood praying in the synagogue or sat in the market and once for a joke I told Hannah, "Call into this ear," and it sounded like something . . . and soon after during our Feast of Lights I could hear my own name through the ear the pistol shot had opened . . . and the time came when I could, if I wanted to, hear conversations. Now this was held up by Reb Maisha and all serious elders as a proof that The One Above worried for us, but it was only a short-quoted proof; for a greater miracle touched us a month later, when Yeersel came home with a genuine discharge paper.

I had longed to hear my wife Hannah's voice, to speak to my boys Ellya and Nasan, to experience full prayer; these joys were brought to me. Also with them the hack of boiling angers, the wail of haranguing melancholies now invaded my special calm. These sounds of mothers and fathers and children tearing and biting at each other through their ears made me wish often to be deaf again. I spoke of this to Yeersel one time we sat fishing together by the streamside. "There's much to cherish," he answered, "or why should we ever open our mouths?"

I made no reply, remembering the worm who jumped into horse-radish and thought it was pear preserves because he was used only to bitter tastes. With me it was otherwise. I cherished the sweet silence. The noise of people clashing held the useless violences of beasts — in this simplicity of mine I yearned for even a false calm; so when old Yessel-the-candlemaker died I managed ways of moving my family into the empty hut where at least within my own walls I established quiet, where no turmoils were permitted not even by visitors, where shouters and foot-pounders and long-winded criers were told to go outside, even my father-in-law, Naftoli-Dovid; and when our synagogue meetings turned into contests of insult, as often happened, I would leave. The stream helped me and the quarter mile from it to the huts that I walked thirty times a day and sixty before the Sabbath, the waterbuckets hanging from the yoke across my shoulders, the pipe never out of my mouth; and it would be into a hut with the buckets for the day and out quickly from the clamors and shrieks called conversation from one hut to the next — Berel-the-Ox became an accepted piece of the landscape. "What's to be said," they understood among themselves, "of one half-deaf to begin with, in whose own house to the bargain they walk with their mouths sewed up as if it costed a ruble a word in his presence? Not a bad one, Berel . . . but still an ox."

Stubbornly wherever I could, I set thickets of calm about me and watched them grow higher and wider each year until 1886, when the passing of Nochim placed an axe in my hand.

The Saturday night Nochim went stayed hot for May. Only a splinter of moon showed; most of us lingered outside the bereaved hut. Some still inside were not finished with their consolations of Pesha and Sholem and Zagzaigel and Marya, or were adding their own embroideries to the remembrances of Nochim made by the ring of wives sitting with the suddenly important widow.

Pipe in mouth, standing on a side, I was trying not to hear my father-in-law asking why everyone turned their faces away from him.

In past years Naftoli-Dovid had been what we called a "person," a granted member of the community, a husband and father of value. My father-in-law's lowering began with the death of his wife Masha. He tried to become a matchmaker, made enemies, became a claydigger and brandydrinker, looked without success for great money-making schemes and in time he developed the annoying skill of asking long chains of pointless questions in synagogue meetings.

I moved away from him; the less he knew what had passed at evening prayers, the better. Naftoli-Dovid jumped in front of me and demanded to know where I was going. I took my pipe from my mouth and growled, "Home." He understood I was not to be followed.

Hannah had tea waiting. I sat down and lit my pipe. The boys came running in, Ellya twenty-two, Nasan eighteen, with a strong clatter of feet and both talking high at the same time. One look at them from me and Hannah said, "Time for tea, not talking."

"All right, take a needle and sew up my mouth," Nasan cried impatiently, "but — "

"Quietly, Nasan . . . spoons and glasses to the table."

Ellya gave Nasan a push-be-quiet but he said, "I'm eighteen and married, Mama!"

"So Baylah you gave a contract and me a divorce?"

"Papa," Nasan begged, "it's big trouble!"

"Let it be quietly," I said, "and also with a little tea."

Nasan curbed his irritation and went for the spoons and glasses, Ellya reached up and unwound the string carefully from the rafter, not to disturb the piece of sugar at the end of it. Hannah poured the almost colorless tea, we took turns sucking the piece of sugar hanging over the middle of the table, the boys kept up their thin silence for my sake . . . they knew how I liked nothing said during the first half-glass. Ellya was always the more patient, he'd already lost a wife, Laib-Shmul's daughter Klava, and the child she could not bear. The hot one was Nasan, a little husband of eighteen, very fiercely married to Hertz's Baylah less than a year and she already three months carrying, a girl of beauty that Nasan called "Plum." Baylah called him "Driver"; a genuine love-match.

I mention this because it was my last quiet. Now came many hurried steps on my boards, Laib-Shmul, Yeersel, Tzippe-Sora; a real bursting-in, Laib-Shmul's wild hair all over his face, and his gross greeting . . . "Ay! Everybody's peed-out with worry, and here they sit drinking tea!"

"I got the whole story from Buzarov himself," Nasan told them, "only — "

"Not here," I said, rising. "Not here."

"Not here, what?" Hannah asked, suddenly frightened. "What are they doing now, who are they looking to murder?"

"Make an ending of this chewing-over," Laib-Shmul roared, "we didn't need to come here at all! I'll know how to handle with Mottel, don't worry!"

Laib-Shmul turned to run out but the sharp-tongued Tzippe-Sora threw at him, "It's the quiet fellow here we need to talk to Mottel, not one pickled in angers!"

A bitter argument began, I walked out toward the path leading to the stream and in the next minute Yeersel overtook me, saying nothing. At the streamside we sat on buckets, I annoyed to have forgotten my pipe, Yeersel silently understanding and handing me one of his cigarettes; then we together smoking. "Well, already . . . what?"

"Berel . . . two hours after she sat with Nochim the whore vanished."

"Good."

"Not-good. Varya told Profim how Nochim made her promise to deliver some kind of message for him, she didn't say where. Knowing of course the Squire has a special use for her, Profim goes and sends for his brother Vassily to come and threaten her in the Squire's name that no, she dare not go, and no, she cannot. . . well, that's how she leaves it with Vassily . . . she promises she'll stay but what happens at eight o'clock when she's supposed to come downstairs there? A nightly day, she's not downstairs and she's not upstairs! And in her room everything off the hooks! Understand, Berel?"

"Does the Squire know, or not yet?"

"He's in a rage, according to Vassily . . . but I don't believe it."

"Then what's the worry?"

"Pukop," Yeersel said. "Nochim came from there, the Squire could make a bad stew about 'messages from Pukop' . . . well, I don't know . . . maybe it's half and half . . . but if the woman is overtaken and brought back we'd be safer on both sides."

"And I'm wanted to go ask Mottel to bring her back?"

"Not go ask him, go bribe him."

"Why him?"

"He was with her after she came back from Nochim's. She likes him, she'd tell him where she went. Don't say no," he urged. "We can't let them squeeze us into the Pukop tragedy. And we mustn't lose the chance of getting the woman back for handy to the Squire."

"You're the one," I said slowly.

"Offer him anything, Tzippe-Sora says she'll go to forty!"

"Why not you?"

"His laugh terrifies me," Yeersel said. "With him I'm a coward. When he laughs at me I'm demolished; I couldn't get him to listen to me. Please, I'll mention why another time."

"Tell Hannah I'm sitting here."

"Good."

Now that's how it made itself with Yeersel and me. It could be "no" till the skies fell down; still such a tailor was this Yeersel, mind you, that he could sew a button even on an ox . . . and what is more, let the ox sew a button on him.

Now their side lay at the foot of the Squire's hill, the town for his toes, the stream running between the Squire's and the Parsovs' smaller hill to the east, the water still giving jumps of white in early May, edging a slope and curving down under the highroad and then flowing to our side with less tumble. I followed the stream back from our side where I kept my yoke and buckets, climbed up to the road from under the bridge, headed for the village to look for Mottel first in the smithy; then came near Profim's "Heaven," and stopped . . . go in for a minute, I thought, take a chance, he might be there, and to the bargain, after all I would have liked to have seen what such places looked like, once. As I stood, a distance away, the door opened, he came out on the landing walking backwards and cursing at the brown lights inside; a woman screamed, the door slammed and I saw him holding a fiddle in his hand. I had found my customer, quickly but badly, with no faith in my goods. He turned for the village. With a feeling of making an impossible charge I ran to catch him.

He heard me at perhaps ten yards and met me growling drunkenly in Russian, not seeing my face in the dark, winding himself into a quick run at me and without hesitation meeting me with a powerful kick into my groin, I falling too surprised to say my name. Two, three kicks found my head as I lay until I gave myself a shake and said, "It's me." The Yiddish surprised him, he lost all interest. He went to the side, I heard him drop down all in one muttering, his thumb monkeying with the high string of a fiddle. I was bleeding from the head, the groin was stabbing, he was telling himself about the postman's brother, Kluzanov; nothing to me until he mentioned Laib, the confirmation boy. "Kluzanov, I'll kill him," Mottel was promising himself in Yiddish, very tired under his drunkenness, "dead as his little goat, his little sweetheart with the whiskers . . . what sweetheart? They're married, he married it, he's a widower now, a widower, Kluzanov, hey girls?"

Crawling to him I said, "Mottel, it's me, Berel. . . ."

"I killed it, killed his wife, he brings it to the girls back there, offers to pay them for a show. . . ."

"Enough," I said, sitting heavily up, "Mottel, hear me. . . ."

"Yes, and when the girls wouldn't work with the goat . . . that's when Laib came in, just a kid," now he shouted, "just a kid after his fiddle!"

"Listen, Mottel — can you?"

"That's for you to do. Listen why I almost kicked you into your Next World . . . now he brings this goat of Father Semyon's into the front room, that's where Laib comes looking for the fiddle . . . you see? . . . I thought you were Kluzanov following me . . . well, I was upstairs sleeping all right, Rena wakes me about Kluzanov having the goat there and pushing the boy to the goat . . . I ran down and absolutely yes . . . so I threw the kid into the hall . . . where is he, Laib?"

"Stop it, let me say a word, something's happened. . . ."

"And then I gave it to the goat with the piano stool, with the side, one crash down in between the horns. . . ." He rose. "The kid must be in there, I'll get him now and if I see Kluzanov . . . !"

"What fiddle?" I said in any effort to hold him. "How does Laib get to a fiddle?"

"It's this one, his . . . I got it in Minsk. . . . She says he'd play well but now he won't have a teacher . . . whatever got into her!" The way he began to curse it became plain the teacher was Varya. I waited until he stopped to breathe. "Varya showed him only fiddle-playing?"

"The perfume in the synagogue — I'm sorry I missed that one!"

"Why did she go?"

"That's how it is with these bedpots," he said, calming enough to put the fiddle under his arm before lighting a cigarette.

Then boldly, "But where could a Varya fly to like a bird?"

"Ah, these plowed-out Varyas," he replied more to something in his own head than to me, "when they don't get themselves pensioned in jails or nunneries they begin listening to themselves like to fortune tellers . . . one night they'll call themselves Cleopatra and the next, Josephine . . . and if it's nothing lower than a half-ruble tip, it's enough to persuade them they're Catherine." And then an angry spit, "Yes, all these Varyas; they finish up playing with themselves! 'Any time you're in Riga,' she tells me as a favor, 'just walk down Sport Street there, don't forget it, Sport Street in Riga, and ask anybody to take you to the Queen and I'll be where they take you.'" A laugh now, a splittingness, a mix . . . a laugh and also not . . . "As if they don't have enough stale ones in Riga!"

"Mottel, hear me out." I gave him a quick account of the Pukop affair, of Nochim's end, bringing in Vassily Buzarov about the Squire's rage over Varya's leaving; when I stopped he said, "Let the Squire be lucky and break a vein in his head and let Varya go to Riga or hell . . . to me it's the same."

"We need to find her, Mottel."

"Take a walk in the morning, look at the trees. Maybe she's only hung herself."

"How much?"

"How much what?"

"To bring her back for us, Mottel."

"You offer money?"

"Perhaps forty . . . good?"

He spat his cigarette into the road. "Forty won't catch your mice."

"Not enough for you?"

"Forget her. . . ."

He began to walk away with nothing said, like any gross bargainer. Running, I cried, "Wait, have mercy. . . . Forty is the most we can do!"

His feet stopped moving, I had hopes; but the word turned him full drunk again. "Ask that God of yours for mercy! And also what He's been doing since He finished the world! The Squire's got a mirror in his house from the floor to the ceiling, did you know it? Any time he wants he can look at his bare behind . . . but you'll all die and never see your bare behinds! Very well, you've forty? Then keep it, don't look for Gods and whores to help anything! Look from where your feet grow, idiots — disappear!" He pushed me away from him. My groin gave a twist and I fell again. Meanwhile he turned toward "Heaven" and ran, pulling at the fiddle strings just any way, flecking such a mockery that as I lay in the road the thing in my head was Yeersel saying, "His laugh terrifies me."

In that living, what a mix of friends and enemies, what blind traffics under stars so easy to see, so hard to read!

Now I dragged myself home, Hannah put wet cloths to my groin, I sent Ellya after Yeersel. He came with Tzippe-Sora, I acquainted them with my failure. "Don't say it's a failure," Tzippe-Sora replied quickly. "Varya went to Riga, he said? Well . . . we'll send someone there, one of our own!"

"Tomorrow," Yeersel said. "Berel, you did well."

"I'll go, let me," Ellya said.

"We'll decide after the funeral," Tzippe-Sora told him.

We buried Nochim following morning prayers. Sholem and Zag-zaigel chanted the mourners' prayer firmly and loudly, their heads to the sky, trying to be like strong men for their mother's sake. Pesha crouched at the grave. Now that the blundering little man was gone she loved him again, her open scorn of him and her bitterness forgotten, all his intentions remembered and itemized as she begged Nochim's first wife to care for him in The Next World and not to hold it against Nochim that he had remarried so soon. With the heartbreak proper to such a demonstration she promised the first wife that when she herself would be lifted up into The Next she would bend humbly and adore them both; she pleaded with them to be good askers for the Lord's grace to fall on her and her children and all who loved in misery (here we noticed how she seemed to be depending more on the first wife than on Nochim), after which she signaled the depth of her loss by trying to fall into the grave. But hands ready for this restrained her and we made a circle around her as we said our last words to the dairyman. In our grief we failed to see Vassily Buzarov and the Squire until they were upon us. Their horses had made a straight run across the cemetery, ignorant of where they put their hoofs.

The Squire's steward ordered us to make a line. Both remained mounted. Vassily Buzarov looked even bigger on a horse, the curve of his belly pushed up by the saddle, the eyes under his broad cap still dull with sleep. The Squire sat on his handsome gray son of Commander and wore a high hat and frock coat for Sunday. I had not seen the boyish-footed little man in several months. The beard struck me as being less pointed, the eyes wider apart and not so prying, the hips softer and puffier in the saddle; but the way he held himself stiff remained the same as ever, and also the way he had of giving a horse little kicks and pulls with the reins, from moment to moment making the animal move and stand still in proud alertness to commands as though from a general viewing his troops. The Squire looked at the line before him; something else crossed his mind. He gave Buzarov a sharp look. The giant (so unlike his needle of a brother, Profim) had forgotten.

"Caps," called Buzarov, and we took them off, waiting. The Squire still disliked something and looked at Buzarov again, speaking in an undertone. Buzarov ordered us to make our line "straight." It forced us to trample many graves. The Squire had not wished it exactly, it simply pleased him to address a straight line. Now this was a self-disgusted individual living in hope of spitting Golinsk good-by at any moment, yearning to enter the higher existence for which he felt fated, that of a graceful lion of the western boulevards, of a witty loiterer in purple saloons, of an accepted member of many cliques of imposing parasites discussing in French matters great or small with the same bows or the same sips from the thinnest of glasses, and always under crystal chandeliers and surrounded by mirrors on all walls to multiply their presence. To achieve this apex, however, the Squire needed his wealthy father-in-law dead but this holy day had so very long postponed itself that desolated by impatience he drank steadily when not inviting invalidism in other ways. By manipulating the hundred Jews or so at his command in the hamlet he owned, he supplied himself with the means of making occasional pilgrimages to the most fashionable "Heavens" in the larger cities, and once in a crisis of bravado at a nobly attended shoot in Poland he had forced himself to down thirty-one pork dumplings. The hour's notoriety thus gained left him a stomach thereafter called "delicate" but which remained an organ of massive strength, groaning with all kinds of colics at its outrageous burdens but nevertheless performing its labors as we performed ours — for him — "somehow."

The Squire began at us with a deep sigh which led into a squealing address of imagined crispness. "I am just to leave for Petersburg," he announced as a complaint that we were delaying him. "Out of duty alone I show myself here, I'll be short about it. You haven't enough graves, it's a fact, to accommodate the results of the honest anger of the district if you people continue with your usual stubbornness in the outrages being committed against the regime — and not only in Pukop, let it be known and understood. Let it be known and understood," the Squire repeated; no disturbance of feeling, no tinge of grievance or heat of threat showed. "I have given my word of honor to the Colonel Commander of the Pukop garrison that this year there will be unaccounted for not one single conscript from Golinsk. Nothing, no conspiracy, nothing but death can cause me to break my promise to the Colonel Commander. Such is my warning, let it be known and understood."

He threw his eye from one face to the next, searching for signs of provocation. To frighten us was easy; the Squire had bothered to come on no such simple errand; what he wished and waited for were denials, protestations, anything he could twist into an avowal of "the conspiracy" we had just learned we were part of. Had he told us the day was night and had we not then immediately begun lighting torches against his proclaimed darkness, he would have accused us of thinking him a liar. Accustomed to his style of reasoning we said nothing nor glanced at each other. "Go further against this year's conscription," he continued, his eyes moving past me, "and I will dam up the stream and put you to work turning this cemetery into a grain field." The Squire pointed to Laib-Shmul, a known hot one. "You — do you deny your corpse was in Pukop Friday?"

The meat-slaughterer mumbled, "He didn't say."

"Do any of you deny it?" He waited until the silence grew heavy. "Then you know the corpse was an ally of the Pukop rabbi." Again he waited. "Yes . . . his fiddle was discovered in the rabbi's house." A moaning rose from our line and the Squire allowed a stir of hatred to pierce his mantle of high-toned boredom. "Let it be known and understood, we are not deceived. We know your corpse spoke to the whore and we know what he said to her, where he sent her, and why! We know she's one of your bought couriers, bribed, a messenger! Sending Mottel to bring her back was shrewd but not shrewd enough . . . you think she won't confess?"

At this I stumbled one step to him, saying "Squire, Squire . . . bake and burn me a thousand times if I didn't ask him to go for the woman and if he didn't refuse!"

"Indeed," he murmured coldly, glancing sharply at Buzarov, who spit over his horse's head and said with effortless resonance, "Mottel left during the night in a fast rig borrowed from my brother, saying he would bring the woman back . . . that's refusing you?"

I wanted to swear that Mottel had laughed at the money; for him to have gone after her was unbelievable . . . I bit my lip, what good was it? Their plan was clear, to "discover" some "conspiracy" of ours against them and in the guise of thwarting it to do with us as they wished while posing as our protectors from "the honest anger of the district." As this rose in my mind I became aware of the Squire's boiling eyes on me. He seemed to be pushing himself to some bursting act, he looked at me as though into a mirror of some devilish nature which had abolished his image and now reflected my own. His gloved fingers tightened over the reins, he sipped air through his mouth, his lips thickened, puffing it out again, his eyes swelled with the melancholy glaze of a dog in hopeless heat. In the next moment he would have kicked at the horse and run me down; but I stepped back to the line between Ellya and Nasan and it helped him; he coughed and breathed through his nose again. He gave a sharp pull of the rein which sent the beast's tail curving. "I return in two weeks," he shouted, "listen well to Buzarov, his words are mine."

With this imitation of a masterly farewell (he tried for a baritone and ended in his natural squeal), he headed for the highroad and his holiday in Petersburg.

The Squire felt cheated, life had played a trick on him, he felt he should have been born in a time better suited to nobility. Instead he had to suck a living out of one small village when his grandfather had measured the estate by the time it took to cross it in a fast carriage, counting the family fortune in souls as well as rubles and requiring little more of the Jews than to apply them as sponges to the bitterness of his serfs. Relieved of his aberration the Squire might have been the happiest man alive, deeply in love with himself and without a rival in the world.

With his departure our line lost its straightness. Buzarov said it was not over yet. From under his cap he pulled a paper. "To the Jews of Golinsk," he read with a schoolboy emphasis, his jowls shaking like fish-jelly under the challenge to his dignity, "by authority of the Colonel Commander, countersigned, and with the approval of the landowner. Until permitted otherwise, Jews of Golinsk may not walk outdoors later than one hour after sunset. Until permitted otherwise, Jews of Golinsk may not cross the highroad at any time. Until permitted otherwise, Jews may not circulate in places other than their own portion of Golinsk." He stopped to sweep a large fly from his cheek. Tzippe-Sora called to him, "Hey Buzarov, forbidden to stand in the market and work in the fields?" He nodded and the line broke, we surrounded him on his horse, he took pleasure from it. "There is more," he said, holding his hand for order. "Jews of Golinsk are commanded to gather themselves at noon tomorrow on their side of the highroad to hear a new enactment. Those Jews who absent themselves will be punished properly."

"Say what enactment, Buzarov," we all shouted. He shrugged and turned his horse to follow the Squire's path across the cemetery and this ended Nochim's funeral.

I walked from the shrieking and crying into the next field. Threats, accusations, an enactment . . . I could not set them in order. One question stood like a tree in my mind, it would stay a long time before it would be uprooted — why Mottel had indeed gone for Varya after refusing me. A hen lost from somewhere came near me as I stood in the field, it saw me and jumped to a little fly in the air like a bride's mother happy of the day; the world in a mix entirely.

Now through that day of the big Sunday market in which we had been forbidden to stand, a day we waited for, the elders kept a council going in the synagogue, looking for ways to grab our fate by the neck. We wriggled through dozens of damaging moods. In the afternoon my father-in-law's brother Zish brought his axe-man's hand down upon the learning-table and spoke for making a market on our side of the road, at least. We sent Yakov and Hertz's Avrum to see if we could get an audience with Selenkov for permission.

Waiting for them we distilled gloomy portents out of Mottel's going for Varya. The final remarks here were made by Tzippe-Sora's aged brother, Asher-the-Sour, who slept in a corner of Tzippe-Sora's hut and collected manure in a cart. He cooked the manure into small bricks that burned not well, like some kinds of peat, which he peddled to the peasants. "Let the Jew-turned-pig never show us his eye again unless he holds it in his hand. Let him be dying of thirst and drink vinegar for water. Before he finds the woman let him be rended into small pieces by a forest of knives. And let the pieces be left for the wolves. And let the wolves sniff and not eat them. And let the pieces of him all grow together again and leave him blind, paralyzed, deaf, dumb, and with every opening in his body sealed. And let him fall to the bottom of a latrine. And let him lie there until the Messiah passes, sees him, does on him, and walks away."

When Yakov and Avrum returned, Avrum held his hurt hand in his blouse. Soldiers, we learned, were guarding the road; while explaining to them why they had come down there Avrum had bent to pick up a stone; a soldier took his rifle butt to the hand, saying Avrum wanted to break the regulation and cross the road. He was sent to have the hand bound and Gershon said to the father, "It could be worse, Hertz. Now with such fingers they might not take him for the army when the list is read in October."

Such proof of their venom threw us into children's logics. We smoked as we spoke and made bigger fogs with our words than with our pipes. When there was nothing else to wonder about we began to ask ourselves timidly if after all there wasn't something going on in the villages around us, something similar to the Pukop accident which had led them to the charge of conspiracy. That so trembly a man as my brother Gershon should ask whether this mightn't be proofed out in some way threw us into a debate beginning with whispers. "I don't say must," Gershon made clear. "I don't say . . . but if Jews are indeed heating them up in other places, wouldn't it be better to know instead of thinking it's all made up in their own heads?"

None of the elders spoke for this, Naftoli-Dovid gave a fall on Gershon with, "Very nice, proof it out, he says . . . but who'll crawl to other villages between soldiers; does Gershon offer himself? A man with blood so thin he bleeds a week every time he gives himself a scratch! Yes, it's understood Gershon won't go himself but stands for sending our best youngers on such killingnesses! Proof it out, Gershon? Then go yourself, please, you're not such a great loss! I'm older and sicker than you but I can't be kind enough to go in your place, my head isn't the dried-out pickle yours is!"

The youngers off to a side, listening dutifully, now leaned forward to hear who might come to defend Gershon. But only gentle Maisha spoke. "I am also a little old and unhealthy," he said. "And I don't give strong slaps like Naftoli-Dovid to another sick man. Don't feel insulted, Gershon. The reason why he's Asher-the-Sour is because, as we all know, Asher thought he had married a woman with a strong back and a weak mind (may she rest), but soon found how it was just the opposite. Such a mistake could cause sourness even in a plum, which Asher is not."

By evening prayers a hundred suggestions had been made and discarded. The women came with bread and tea; we tried through the night to find something that looked like a plan, our senses dulled by poverty of facts and a fear of putting up any search for them. When to the last we stirred for home, Tzippe-Sora came in and read our failure in the silence. "Well, brain-men," she said with a cackle, "have you arrived at the Sensible Station?" We said nothing. "Silence, as is said, is a fence around wisdom," she remarked. "But I think not now. Open windows, it stinks here. That's all you've been doing, brain-men, smoking and sitting on your eggs?"

"All right," spoke Laib-Shmul. "Tell us your word, Mother-in-law."

"What other but bribe?" she demanded.

"Bribe?" Laib-Shmul threw at her, roaring. "You didn't hear the Squire making his entire case on accusing us of bribe?"

"Fools," the little woman shrilled, "a day and night you sit and can't count a two-and-one! The Squire opens the door and you don't go in! He travels to Petersburg, no? But Buzarov and Selenkov are here, not so? At Buzarov and Selenkov rubles must be thrown like pebbles and in two days we'll be standing in the regular market, and that's all!"

"Nicely smeared, Tzippe-Sora, " said Laib-Shmul, "only remember the Squire at the cemetery saying they'd first fill it up and then make a field of it if — "

"Such whistles they've blown before," she shouted. "It's May and conscription time is in October! It's how they bargain!"

"What, to you it was only the Squire giving hints he'll take bribes?" Gershon's Hatzkel asked, not believing his ears.

"And why not?" she demanded of him. "How long since he's taking? How many harvests have we made him for no pay and how many barrels of alcohol cooked and sold for him and how many times the dam fixed and how many times wine out of his grapes for him, and his trees cut down and his roofs fixed?"

"Wait," Asher-the-Sour commanded, triumph growing under his

eyelids, "it's all neat as a wedding to you, but one thing, my sister, you forgot. Didn't they bribe in Pukop? And where did it leave Sussya-ben-Mordecai and who knows how many more? If bribing in Pukop helped like a pillow under a barren bride, how will it be otherwise in Golinsk?"

"Caught, caught," Naftoli-Dovid cried at the widow.

She threw at him, "How I'm caught, we should all be so sick! . . . The Svutzkers who brought Nochim said there were gypsies mixed into it in Pukop . . . therefore why shouldn't the Pukopper police take the boy from gypsies bribed to ride him away? Fools! Open your heads! If the boy had gone free, the next time the gypsies would have gotten a bigger bribe and the police less!"

The only answer to her was Yeersel saying gravely, "Tzippe-Sora . . . God should have made you a man."

"Better an insult than such praise," she told him. But how couldn't she be pleased? We were waiting for her next words. "To the first, I say nothing should be done until after the assembly tomorrow when we'll hear what's their 'new enactment,' which can be what? Only the latest excuse for making a big price for the bribe! To the second, we'll bring what's easy to carry to the highroad in the morning and stand with it on our side, making a show of a market . . . not to do business, only to show them we need every penny; it'll help the bribe-price."

"A good word," Yeersel agreed. "It's a market and yet not a market, and there won't be any need for permission."

"Wait, not a little thing," Laib-Shmul said with false thoughtfulness. "You said we're to throw rubles at them like pebbles . . . where does one find such pebbles, Mother-in-law?" he added in a sly. "After all there's only one Rothschild, and he's not here."

Now, we knew how brazenly she traded and how shrewdly she managed to sell her own illegally cooked alcohol (made in the woods somewhere by herself and her sons, and sold and hidden in ways well concealed from the agent Rezatskin and from Selenkov and even Vassily Buzarov); and where the widow hid her rubles, and how much, was an old topic with us. In times past when a bribe-purse had to be made up Tzippe-Sora never failed to supply the difference. She gave Laib-Shmul one of her dry cackles, fixed her spectacles more firmly to her nose, and told him, "After their assembly tomorrow I'll sit down with Selenkov and make a price. Then we'll look to see if we'll have to bother Rothschild." She pointed to me. "Berel, come. I need you."

Spry as she was, she had a rupture. I thought she wanted me to help her down the dark path. "I think you'll take out my rubles," she said without an introduction, softly.

"Not your own sons?"

"Sons shouldn't know everything," she told me.

Home, Hannah waited for me, she sat me down and washed my swollen groin. I soon slept. After a long time my eyes opened, it had to be morning. But the height of the moon and the brightness of the stars showed how far morning still was. Perhaps like this death began; we died every night but The One Above opened our eyes for the morning, and each had his time to be skipped.

"Berel?"

"Hn?"

"Sleep."

"Slept . . . I'll walk, take a smoke. . . ."

I thought to sit by the stream, maybe fish. Passing Hertz's . . . someone sitting on the step. She lifted her head, my Nasan's Baylah, and made a whisper, "It's Nasan . . . not here . . . not him, and not Avrum."

I woke Hertz, he shook Baylah by the shoulders. "I should know where?" she whispered in the lane — a tall girl, one of our beauties, her face in one shine with the softness of three months' carrying.

Hertz and I woke Yeersel and told him, and sat on his step. "That's a boy, my Avrum," Hertz said quietly. "Always looking for squirrels on the top of a mountain."

In time a whiteness approached us, Avrum. By woodland paths without a lantern he had gone three difficult miles to Kapula. "And they also, Papa . . . at noon tomorrow like us, an assembly."

"For what?"

"They don't know."

"And Nasan?" I asked.

"To Shnavka. The Kapuler rabbi said not to try tricks but do as they say and leave all to The Most High. In Kapula, according to the rabbi whoever is taken when the time comes will be given money to use in escaping."

"No good," Yeersel said. "I saw how soldiers are searched. They'll never be able to keep money hidden."

We took Avrum into Yeersel's and made him lie down there next to Yeersel's Velvel so that Baylah would not see him, since her Nasan was still absent.

Bosha sat with us, she took my hand. "Don't worry, Berel, Nasan is a careful one."

I said, "A careful one would have remembered his carrying wife. And stayed home."

Bosha saw the wonder in Hertz, that his Avrum should be so brave; and also with it the pull of his anger. "Go, Hertz," she said, "you put your head down a bit also, I'll watch him."

"I'll remain here the while," he said.

"Enough now, Bosha," Yeersel said, knowing his wife meant two things — Hertz needed to rest but also she didn't think she could stand the smell of wheel-grease that never left Hertz though he scrubbed himself summer and winter once a week steadily. With a friendly flick of his fingernails against Hertz's arm and a cheerful-looking snap of his wrist Yeersel said to Hertz, "Come, let's the three of us sit a bit down at the stream, it's the best time to fish now."

"I'll remain here the while with Avrum," Hertz said much more quietly, but greatly annoyed. That was Hertz to the bones. If you liked him you also had to like his smell.

"Remain," shrugged Bosha, but with a slow lift of her shoulder and a twist against wheel-grease. Yeersel rose. "Come, Berel . . . you and I, then."

To be left just with Bosha was too much for Hertz. "What's the matter," he said as a statement, "is I stink better to men than to women, right?"

"Sh, you'll wake people," Yeersel reminded him.

I walked out followed by Hertz and then Yeersel. With no good-by Hertz went back to his hut. Yeersel and I found ourselves headed up the lane toward the synagogue. As we walked he said, "In Kletsk they're musical, in Kapula they're hintful, in Svutz thievish, in Pukop educated . . . and here we're stubborn!"

Without having to say, we took the path to the stream down alongside the cemetery. The wind made little noises in the dark, the stars still shone with a hardness. Then came a sound from the cemetery, from behind the bushes, a quick thrust of it. We stood listening, our hands went looking for each other's, wondering. . . . "No," Yeersel whispered, "it's a living person."

To find him took a whole minute. He lay against a footstone, we lit matches. His head held to a side, he smiled up at us, Nasan. "Your head, your feet, what . . . ?"

"Sh, Papa . . . not so loud!"

"Nasan, what . . . ?"

"We'll carry him to the stream, the cold water," Yeersel said.

"No," quickly from Nasan, "I mustn't."

"Sh," I said, bending to lift him.

"No, Papa," he shouted. "Ay, you've made me noisy, no one must find out I did it. . . ."

"Are you broken somewhere?"

"No, Papa."

"To the stream, then."

We lifted him up and took him there, listening to him meanwhile. "I couldn't help it, Papa . . . others mustn't be punished for me . . . I thought I'd wait until light to come home."

At the stream we helped him wash, then sat him on a bucket. "Well . . . say quickly, what?"

"Things are doing, Papa. I went to Shnavka the woodsway, and first I saw the beadle there, and then others . . . they have soldiers there also, and an assembly at noon today. We spoke in their cemetery, they were glad I came . . . they gave me their news and on the way home near Shnavka in the woods . . . two soldiers . . . from the back of me."

Yeersel then grimly, "You were seen?"

"I don't know if my face . . . but a fight, then . . . one I kicked quiet, the other with a stone, then running . . . with their pistols shooting."

"Ay, Nasan . . ."

"And what news?" from Yeersel.

"Here, it's written down in Yiddish," he said, putting a paper in my hand. "They read it out, I know what it says . . . Papa . . . Papa . . ."

"Well, what?" Yeersel pressed.

"It's on the paper . . . and it's yes, yes-a-conspiracy."

As if flecked with a whip Yeersel put a match to the paper, saying, "Who needs it written as long as you know what's there?"

Nasan said, we seeing him now the few moments it took the paper to burn, "It came from Minsk, they say on the top of a keg of nails, a week ago . . . how Jews should run from the villages well before October . . . to hide in the Minsk ghetto and from there to take wagons to Bialystok and how they'll be hidden there until a wagon from Warsaw, and then the same to Stettin and Hamburg . . . to ships, they say on the paper."

"Who's they?"

"No name, Papa . . . just 'Emigration Society.'"

"What kind of ships?"

"Not said, Yeersel."

"Over the sea, doubtless," Yeersel said with irritation. "Ay, go give a jump to Hamburg only God knows how many hundred miles!"

"Wait," Nasan said with an eagerness that made me cold, "the paper says places in wagons can be bought, it's a regular business like train tickets . . . wagons going from ghetto to ghetto over the borders . . . and in Shnavka they say they're starting to do it!"

"Ay, surely," Yeersel groaned, "just buy the ticket!"

"No, through the woods to Minsk," corrected Nasan.

"So smoothly?" Yeersel said; for the first time I heard a little snarl out of his gentle nature. "Don't you see, boy? It's their trick on the Shnavkers, letting out such papers so Jews will run and be caught and slaughtered!"

"But in Shnavka they're doing it," he insisted.

The light was coming, mist showed, the stream appeared. We sat with Nasan, telling him what to say when he got home . . . that he had remained in the synagogue to clean up after the others had left, that he had fallen asleep on a bench. Sending him on his way, I began with the day's carries of buckets and Yeersel helped, we talking of this paper. In the end I said, "Well . . . Shnavka is Shnavka and Golinsk is Golinsk . . . and October is far away." He grunted, relieved, then Ellya came to help me and Yeersel went to his hut.

Ellya and I made eight carries before morning prayers; meanwhile I couldn't push it out of me that, yes, Shnavka was Shnavka and Golinsk Golinsk — but the Shnavka paper was no inflammatory brief of the government as Yeersel believed but a genuine agitation. Other Jews were running against the conscription time in October believing that running was a better per cent than bribing. As well as I knew my own five fingers I knew the best month for running out of Golinsk should be July, good for night-traveling, well before conscription time and not too near to now when they were heated against us. Let it cool down, let them take a bribe meanwhile . . . and then we'd fix our run . . . not to some corner of a ghetto to stay there, but to begin an exploration, a run of seekers of new places by way of wagons through many nights over borders not seen twice. July, I thought. This was May.

Now here is how July arrived in May.

First, the rain. Neither loudly nor gently it began falling during morning prayers, in the way of a settled thing, without stopping until night when other settled things had fallen on us and had still to fall. Everybody put out pots and pans, this saved me some carries; yet with different things happening to everybody, and everybody so unprepared, we all went about as wet as in the bath. The weather fitted the day; one of cleansing for some, of drowning for others; the last day I lived in Golinsk.

By nine o'clock something like a market was made on our side across from the carriage stop. Because of the rain Shmelke-the-Helper, Hertz's youngest brother, brought some ancient fence posts and Zish some boards; together they hammered up a frame for a shed, roofing it with boughs and whatever pieces of tin and canvas they found lying about in the yards behind the huts. Under such leaky protection (the posts were short, you had to crouch under), Gershon brought shoes, Yeersel woolens, Laib-Shmul a box of nervous chickens, Daneel some bricked clay, Hertz a barrel of grease, Zish a few window frames, Yakov a keg of nails; and in one large box everybody threw whatever could be taken for a novelty — a skinning knife, a tambourine, a cane, a Cossack's cap, bellows — in all a sorry market but good enough as an exhibition of our poverty, to keep the bribe-price down.

Somewhere around ten that morning Ellya and I finished my last carries. The swelling in my groin had made itself into a hard knot by the time we came down to the market.

We went under the shed, a crowdedness of sellers without a buyer. Hannah was sitting on a box next to Gershon's shoes. She had made him go home. Hannah said, "And you too, Berel. And it wouldn't have hurt Nasan to help you!"

"It's nothing," I said.

"Nothing that a son sleeps while the father drags himself with buckets, soaked?"

"Baylah is a bit sickish," I said, thinking it wise to turn Hannah's temper that way. The discovery of Nasan's bad night would have made her tear hair from her head.

"She thinks she's carrying the Messiah, she's so delicate," Hannah mumbled. "Well, go . . . take a little tea."

"You too, Mama," Ellya said. "I'll stay with Gershon's shoes."

"Hn," Hannah complained, "and what's the matter with his Faiga? Such a lady, where is she?"

"With Gramma," my nephew Hatzkel shouted over from where he crouched as he fitted a board to a hole in the covering. "The rupture came out again."

"Come, Hannah, you'll make tea," I said. Moving out into the cold sheets of wet, I heard Hatzkel give a shout, "Uncle, Gramma wants you . . . I forgot!"

We stopped off at Tzippe-Sora's. She lay in bed with warmed stones in a sack put to the rupture, a shawl tight on her head. "Put a few more pillows," Hannah said, seeing the old woman's head straining as she was sorting out some things into a box from a pile between her knees.

"Mama," Faiga begged her mother, "leave the box alone."

With calm indifference Tzippe-Sora told her daughter, "It helps to throw a junk or two into a trade," and continued reaching into the pile of whatnots, examining them one by one before she put them into the box — pins, combs, homemade rings, bits of fur, old calendars, obscene verses in Russian on faded paper, buttons, key-rings. But Faiga needed to exhibit her worry and snatched the box away.

Hannah said, "Be a good daughter, let her live," with a sharpness that made Tzippe-Sora smile.

"Out of here," Faiga shrilled, "with those thin lips of yours!"

"Don't worry, Faiga, shrouds have no pockets!"

"To your funeral I'll cry my eyes out, but with joy," she shrieked.

"Two things weaken the eyes," Hannah threw back. "Crying too much and looking to count other people's money . . . both such pleasures of yours, you'll go blind without God's help!"

Faiga went to scratch Hannah's eyes; I stood between them and waited until Hannah was out. "Ay, women," Tzippe-Sora said from her bed, not disturbed. "Come, Faiga dear," she said sweetly, "be so good, bring me a few pillows . . . and I'm not finished with the box, daughter dear."

Obediently Faiga brought the box and propped the pillows to her. "Thank you," the little widow said with a nod of pleasure, "my dear one, my good one. Go cook something for Gershon now. He must be coughing in such a rain."

"And leave you alone?"

"Is Berel nobody?" she smiled. "And won't you be back?"

"Let it be as you say," Faiga agreed, sniffing, suddenly quieted. When the door closed I said, "Well, Hannah didn't have to open such a mouth."

"Lies she didn't speak," Tzippe-Sora whispered. "Faiga's not bad . . . but a good person and not-bad are different."

"Too much insulting, too much screaming . . ."

"I let them get rid of themselves . . . you and I have business, Berel."

"What business in such weather?"

"This assembly of theirs at noon," she said, pointing to where a place in the roof began to leak. I took a pot from the stove and put it on the floor, watching drops fall into the center of it as Tzippe-Sora spoke. "I'll make a price with Selenkov. Meanwhile, Berel . . . you'll go and take out my money."

"Why me?"

"You're better for this than my sons. It's hidden near the stream, it won't look strange, you being there, and the best place to pay it over is away from everyone . . . down at the stream, clear?"

"If they'll take, only," I said.

"Was it ever hard for them?"

Saying nothing I kept my eyes on the pot, the drops falling in the center, a picture of Mottel rising in my mind; the way he smoked, the cigarette always in the exact center of his mouth . . . a puzzle. Had he refused my bribe or had he been too drunk to hear it and in either case, still, why had he gone for Varya? Or had he? Was it, as the landsmen said, his way of stealing a horse and rig?

"Hear me, Berel," Tzippe-Sora called, "don't fall asleep there. Listening?"

"Listening."

"You'll go down the side of the water there, the left side. About thirty yards from the bridge there's an old big tree, dead on one side.

Go eight feet up to the dead side of the trunk, you'll see a piece hacked out and put back with clay. You'll take out this piece, clear?"

"Clear."

"Inside will be an old boot, and in the boot wrapped in canvas . . . forty rubles."

"Clear."

"Tie it around you, inside your drawers, and after I see Selenkov I'll tell you where to pay it over."

"I'll do it later."

"No good," she said. "Go now. Take a fish-pole. Who knows, maybe their new enactment is a water-tax and they'll keep you the whole afternoon in one questioning."

Seeing how I didn't stir, she said, "Don't look at the pot, look at me." I turned to her. "Say what, Berel."

"Supposing," I said slowly, "it was something true, a bit . . . what the Squire said . . . about landsmen from other villages commandeering themselves."

"To what, commandeering?" she said suspiciously.

"Just so, commandeering. Who knows to what? But enough for them to say it's a conspiracy. Would a bribe help, then?"

"Fool that you are," she said but with softness, "if others are giving trouble and we are giving a bribe . . . ?"

"Let it be as you say, Tzippe-Sora."

I got to my feet with a heaviness of which my painful groin was but a part. Seeing my discomfort, Tzippe-Sora told me to be done with getting the money and then to lie down. "And don't worry," she ended, "the more we bribe them, the more we own them."

"And when we can't bribe any more?"

"Ay," she said with a smile, "that's when we'll have to rob them."

". . . Why look to make ourselves into thieves?"

"It's a thieves' world, no?"

"But we'll end in jails, not they!"

"And today, Berel, we're not already in jail?"

"All right, Tzippe-Sora . . . you're the smart one, I'm the Ox.

Tell me why we can't go for something better, a bit? Must we stay as we are, always?"

"Ay," the widow said without a smile this time. "This is what you mean by commandeering, I see. So . . . you've heard something from other villages. . . ."

"Well . . . that they're running."

"Where?"

"To ships . . . over the sea."

"Who?"

"The Shnavkers."

"From Shnavker wisdoms let The One Above protect us!" In a tremble of anger the little woman let out a bitterness. "Over the sea! Why not better over the moon? And if we had wings of iron to fly a hundred years without stopping even to drink the rain, you think we'd arrive where a Jew could live? We mustn't look for heavens, we'll find only worse hells! Here we know how to work with our bastards! Over the sea," she spat. "It's a different world there, you think, over the sea?"

"Maybe," I said, "we should find out."

"Turn it around, better," she said. "If Jews can yes-live anywhere, it will find *us*."

"Well . . . I'll go."

"Wait — who came from Shnavka?"

She meant, "Who went?" I put my finger to my lips. "Well, who?"

"Nasan," I told her. "Be quiet about it."

She pushed the box away from her. "Those Shnavkers," she said with disgust. "See what they've done . . . they've raised the price."

Sobered by the widow's criticism, I headed towards the stream for the bribe-money. In a mix of rain and my own peltings I hungered for a sign of what to think. Passing the synagogue I saw all the boys fixing the roof with Reb Maisha's direction; among them was Laib and I remembered his fiddle. Varya was gone, there was no one to teach him further; the fiddle was worth a good few rubles; after the bribe we would be needing every penny, all of us.

I called to him and he came down the ladder, small for a lad of twelve but with a serious old-man face, his nose spread out like his father's, his chin pointed, his head held as though waiting for the next to happen — a quick thin fellow. He ran to me with some push of fear in his legs, his eyes staring as I bade him follow me a way toward the stream. When I mentioned the fiddle he said quickly, "Yes, I was in Profim's looking, but there was trouble."

"I know. Mottel had it. I think he brought it back there."

"Well, it's gone."

"Was it worth anything, Laib?"

"Yes."

"Maybe you'll find it and let us sell it?"

"It's my fault, everything," he said gravely. "Without the fiddle they wouldn't have smelled the perfume, and without that Nochim may-he-rest wouldn't have sent for her . . . and she wouldn't have run away, the Squire wouldn't have angered himself . . . and Mottel wouldn't have gone."

"Don't sadden yourself, Laib. Maybe he didn't take the fiddle with him at all."

"If he took it he had a reason." He made as to go. "Well, I'm sorry."

"And for what?"

With a curl-up of lips, a shadow of annoyance darkening his eyes, he said with a sigh, "It's as Reb Maisha advises. I'm to follow the word of the Bratzlaver rabbi now that I'm a confirmed man."

"Well, then . . . fine."

"Reb Maisha says the Bratzlaver said a man should reprove himself every morning."

"True," I said, pushing him with a joking gentleness, "but if here and there you miss a day, the Angel Gavreel won't write it down."

"I'm helping fix the roof," he said, and ran back to the synagogue.

We had confirmed him to manhood in Israel; this had not dried the boyhood out of him, nor something more, hidden from me at the time, the need of his runaway uncle.

I went deeper down the path, turned east at the stream and found the half-dead old oak Tzippe-Sora had picked for her bank. Now here the stream narrowed itself to about ten yards, the trees stood high on both sides and rich with new leaves, the lower boughs sending branches over the water to make a great umbrella under which I many times sat. The spot was one of my best friends; a jutting rock provided a place to sit holding a fishpole, the quiet making a trifle of the world around. One caught few fish there in the spring, the rush of water running white through the narrow channel from under the nearby bridge and carrying the perch and carp fast through; but I kept a pole there anyway for when I went to sit. Now the rain made splashes in the trees and dropped only a thin sheet to the middle of the stream; my rock-throne was merely speckled, like some side of a huge fish. Standing under the widow's oak I took my blouse off and wrung it damp.

About eight feet up on the dead side, as Tzippe-Sora had said, I spied the thin gray circle of clay and looked for a few heavy stones. A dozen throws and the piece was loose enough to be pried off with a length of dead bough. To get at the boot inside the trunk became a harder thing. A ladder was needed or a shoulder to stand on. To raise a hand and jump was simple, but to reach in at the same time and grab the boot was impossible. I took the fishpole kept in the brush and tried to work with the hook; but no good. With an axe I could have hacked myself a foothold; but no axe. Removing the hook I probed for the boot with the end of the pole, found it, lifted it out, then took the canvas-wrapped roll, about the size of a thumb, into my fingers. I thought first to put it in the crotch of my drawers, but this would have aggravated my sore groin as I walked. Instead I used some of the string to make a chain for about my neck and put the roll under my shirt.

Turning from the tree to my blouse which I had left on the rock — there he was, a high black shiny boot crossed over his knee, his heavy campaign tunic opened at the throat, the imperial-eagled cap pushed up to his brow — sitting and watching (of course an officer by the quality of his boots), as though at the exercising of some caged animal. He was a tall one but young and wore one of those hazy mustaches trimmed down to nothing, the kind worn to the whim of somebody else, missing fastidiousness. His eyes played upon me as he sat on the rock; they showed an interest disproportioned to what he needed to know of me. Bending a bit forward he asked what I had been doing, in the way of a traveler's gambit to a fellow passenger, not certain the stranger wishes to be disturbed.

Puzzled by the friendliness and apparently "equal" tone I could only strive to seem as harmless and "peasantlike" as possible. "Well, sir, we've quite a forest here," I said proudly, inserting a giggle to assure him I understood my own foolishness. "Boots grow in our trees, you see, the way money should in bushes!"

"Oh," he said with a gentle smile; and then with refined diffidence, "Now whatever did you hang about your neck there?" He waved at me, generally, still leaning forward with rapt eyes, still so *interested* in this forest phenomenon of a peasant fishing for boots in trees, the educated glance of a student in discovery. Strange — gentleness, interest, shy curiosity! From an officer! "Really, now," he smiled again, a bit more broadly. "Don't be embarrassed."

Ah, well . . . perhaps I remind you of some peasant baba's son on father's estate, perhaps you're homesick, lad, for amusing simplicities. I said the first interesting thing I could drag out of my head. "Well, sir . . . it's only the foot of a fox," I said, patting my chest.

"Really?" he replied, almost in a squeak of *so-interested*.

"Yes, sir." I tried to go along as if not making it up word to word. "We believe if you take the foot of a fox, wrap it well, put it in one of your oldest boots, and place it in a dead tree for six months . . . well now, after the six months you take it down and wear it. And that makes bad luck impossible to catch you."

"You believe that? Truly?"

"Sir, I don't lie." His smile stayed, his eyes drilled into my chest. "We Jews have been believing it for at least hundreds of years. My father never went without his fox's foot, and he lived to an old age and like an ox."

"You're a Jew?" he cried, amazed, rising. "Never! But in Odessa they don't grow such broad strong ones!" All intrigued, he stepped near. "The foot of a fox, you say?"

"Yes, sir."

Then as though not to startle me he pulled, very carefully, the little canvas roll from under my shirt, using a light probing pressure to turn it between the tips of his fingers as though it lived and must not be hurt. "Remarkable." A calculated wryness peeped from under his diffidence now. "Such great strong arms on you . . . how ever?"

"From carrying water-buckets, sir."

"And a Jew, you say." He put his palms to my arms and pressed not unlike the way he touched the roll of bribe-money. A light flew from his eyes like birds into the morning. Then I began to see how he was in fact making coquettings. Never having met any of those who must commandeer themselves into such ways and habits I had nevertheless listened to Zish's stories of army commandeerings, of how soldiers put on dresses to make mock weddings and honeymoons, many times forcing Jews into playing this with them; and to everything else which came to glue itself onto a person this too I had to handle.

"Well," he said, becoming further drawn. He took the "fox's foot" into his hand and with a light move placed it under my shirt, letting his fingers bend against the hairs of my chest, giving me the feel of lice walking. Seeing how I shook a bit he frowned into my face as he removed his fingers and stepped back. "And what were you about to do when you saw me?"

"Put on my blouse and perhaps fish, sir."

"Very well, then. Go, let's see you fish."

Now I wanted nothing of the kind, I wanted to go back but feared giving any offense. With the bribe-money hanging on my chest, an assembly at noon, and affairs generally on the march, I had in the midst of all to be a fox for this hound. He watched me put on my blouse, fix the hook to the pole, dig a few worms . . . a good few warm minutes crawling by until he decided to sit on the rock next to me. "Married?"

"Yes, sir."

I moved the pole a bit. The string lay on a slant toward the rushing water. "So am I," the officer said unhappily. He looked away, struck by a mood. "I left her in Yalta." He sighed, still glancing away from me. "Do you know what it's like there?"

"No, sir."

Looking straight ahead at the water, I listened to him. "The sea is almost green, the sky is blue with white in it, the sands are very fine. But she'll die there."

"So, sir . . . so."

"Yes," he sighed, "the doctors agree. Married only three months, you understand. I've just come off furlough and I'll never see her again."

"A pity!"

"The good-by," he continued, "so typical of her . . . no cries, no words . . . simply, in her formal way . . . 'Fiodor Antonovich, stop and think of me when you are walking close to a river.'" He took the fishpole into his hands. Shaking with pity, whether for her or himself a question, he spoke down to the water. "She's dying, she's gone. The only one, the only . . . and I'll never see her again, the one woman I saw no misery with. Yes, I'm the steady companion of unhappiness, he's with me everywhere." He let the pole drop into the water, it floated away, it was a good pole.

The officer chose the moment to break into slow tears, to drop his head to my shoulder. "Don't grieve so, sir," I said. He heaved himself into more sorrow, holding me to him, his head to my chest, pulling me to him. "She was the only one," he sobbed. "You see how I don't make myself this way easily," whimpering, "be good, give me a treat. . . ."

"No, you mustn't grieve so," I replied with an imitative gentleness.

"But you're a Jew," he urged, his head down, his ear pressing the bribe-money, "you know suffering, anguish, the cruelty of life!"

"Well, yes, sir. . . ."

"Be human, then," he begged, holding my arms, looking up at me, his chin a wobble, his eyes a despairing glaze. "It's hard for me, every-where I go. . . ."

It happened that in trying a tactful wriggle-away I gave my injured groin a bad twist, and it popped into my head to say, "But, sir . . . understand . . . let me be really kind to you, I beg you. . . ."

"You don't," he pouted, "you're lying, you don't wish to be kind. . . ."

"On the shore," I said. "Allow me."

This he permitted. So standing at the streamside I exhibited the hard blue knot that rose high on my groin. He peered at it, interested.

"You see, sir? It wouldn't have come out if I'd had my fox's foot last winter. It will go away now . . . and I'll surely be protected against other ones, their sickness won't get me like this whore's . . . but mean-while, sir. . . ."

"I touched you," he breathed, horrified.

"Yes, sir."

Rubbing his hands against his uniform, his eyes to the knot, he backed away. "I had to take a walk along the river," he accused him-self, stumbling away, more and more merging with the green, toward the bridge. And when the last sight and sound of him was no more I whispered, "Thank You, Dear God of Israel, for the kick."

Now coming up from the stream, wet through the boots and my beard flat to my face, the two days' troubles and the nights of bad sleep summed themselves — I needed to be out of the rain, in bed with hot bricks, giving myself a hard sleep. My romantish time at the stream forgotten, the knot yelling, "Rest me," I hobbled to the top of the path. Maisha's hut stood nearest, down some yards from the syna-gogue. I had no attention for it but the noise was rare and I looked in, seeing a singing of three. My second look showed me the platter of herrings on the table, a high heap; a feast was being made, a bottle stood at Naftoli-Dovid's further foot; and they sang, on the same words and on different words, but understood as together.

> *Now this is how the Tsar, the Tsar, eats his potatoes —*
> *Into a butter-wall, with a cannon,*

Shoots a soldier hot potatoes,
And into the Tsar's mouth they go,
The way he eats potatoes . . . !

Naftoli-Dovid saw me in the doorway (another annoyance, men over sixty sitting in foolishness without bothering to close the door when it was raining), and threw me a loud half-sincere greeting, "Come in, son-in-law; take something for a warming!"

"What's the big holiday?"

"Don't hold yourself so stiffly," my brother Gershon said, "we're making our own holiday. Ay, did we give them a good trade!" He pushed the plate of herring toward me. "You never tasted such fine saltiness!"

"That's your reason?" I demanded. "Better stand praying in the synagogue!"

"Berel, Berel," Maisha grinned, "what are we doing if not preparing to pray? We're following a teaching of the Master of the Good Name."

"Yes, who else?" said Naftoli-Dovid with a wide wave of his hand that ended in a reach for the bottle.

Gershon pointed to a keg in the corner, saying, "A hundred herrings, Berel, for a few of my shoes, and Naftoli-Dovid's broken watch, and Maisha's old chest without hinges!"

"Who gave?"

"A peasant from Kletsk, an angel," Maisha testified. "No haggling, no insults, just a one-two-three! A hundred herrings . . . take, Berel, make yourself dry inside at least!"

"So early in the day in such a drinking?" I asked. "Nothing else fits before the assembly? Not even to ask The One Above for a blessing on us?"

"Ay, don't be an ox," Naftoli-Dovid said, somewhat depressed.

"And should one pray without joy?" Maisha countered. "If prayers are to bear fruit, if blessings are to come, they must be offered with joy and would you deny that?"

"Instead of asking me to deny," I said, "why don't you admit,

Maisha . . . that if silence be good for wise men, how much better for fools?"

"Angry, you?" Gershon demanded. He took the bottle from Naftoli-Dovid and pushed it to me. "But so wet, Berel! Take a little for your own sake."

I downed a few swallows of Naftoli-Dovid's homemade. It burned but I wanted it to.

"You hear?" Gershon said in amazement. "*My* brother, *angry!*"

The calms I had built about me were splitting, winds were in the thickets, brinks were nearing; as I went out, they resumed their song.

> *And here's how the Tsar sleeps, how he sleeps, the Tsar,*
> *His bedroom filled with feathers, the finest —*
> *And into it himself he throws, the Tsar,*
> *With a regiment of soldiers outside shouting —*
> *"Shhhh!" "Quiet!"*
> *So he sleeps, how he sleeps, the Tsar!*

At home something else; in the guise of trying to make peace between Baylah and Nasan, Hannah was reminding the girl of a few things a wife should understand. "Enough! If Nasan says he fell asleep in the synagogue it's as true as the Holy Law! A wife believes her husband!"

"Lies," Baylah replied quietly and therefore more disrespectfully.

"The more you keep on the more you'll be sorry," Nasan said anxiously, looking neither at the mother nor the wife but shrewdly between them.

"I'll give you sorry," Baylah flung at him. "Let the child choke in my stomach than have a liar for a father."

I said, "Put up bricks," and then they saw me. Nasan jumped to the stove, Hannah cried, "Look, he fell in," and Baylah burst into tears. Seeing me throw off the dripping blouse, undressing, they turned their backs to me and continued with each other. I put on a dry undershirt, careful not to show Nasan the roll of bribe-money hanging on my chest, and got into bed.

Baylah turned with a point at me. "You're his father, tell me, did you believe it? He *didn't* sleep in the synagogue, he's up to something! But his mother, anything her Prince says *must* be the golden truth!"

Nasan tried to quiet them but said the wrong thing, "Mama, let her talk herself out." Baylah showed her temper, I could see why Nasan was crazy for her. "Look out, lad," she flew at him, "you didn't marry any pot of water, I don't empty out so easily! The way we were married we can be divorced, in ten minutes!" The tears flowed, she couldn't stop, she loved him. "You stood with me before Rabbi Sussya, you were then willing, you said, for us to be made into a one, you swore it! But there you lied! You've hidden yourself from me, you don't let yourself be with me a one, you do what you do and you don't tell me — to hell with such a life!"

"Don't rear yourself so, it's bad for the baby, Plum. . . ."

"Your Plums I don't need," she cried, her hands pressing her stomach, "but the truth!"

"Wait," Hannah said, "think a bit! If he didn't sleep in the synagogue, then where?"

"Nowhere! He slept last night? Like Avrum slept!"

"She hacks Avrum in again?" Hannah cried with furious impatience.

"I don't want a liar!"

"Nasan," Hannah appealed, "don't let her wipe her feet on you, give her a few words!"

Nasan couldn't. Scratching his head, he looked at me to fish him out. "Baylah," I said, working to postpone, "why can't you believe him?"

"Do you?"

"Did he say he saw a camel dancing on a pail? Why shouldn't I believe him?"

"I know better," she trembled.

"Yes, better than his mother," Hannah threw in.

Baylah put her shawl over her head, told Nasan not to come home, and went out with a great bang of the door. Nasan hung his head. I told him to go after her. "How can I, Papa?"

"All ugly and beautiful ones come with tempers. Go to her, Nasan."

"What can I say to her, Papa?"

"Don't say anything. Remember, sometimes a man listens to his wife with a profit and sometimes with a loss, but he listens."

"That's all, Papa?" he asked with a special meaning.

"Entirely."

"I'll tell her you're sorry, Mama?"

"Call me names, anything," Hannah said, calming. "Do I have to live with her?"

With this Nasan left. Hannah got the hot bricks ready, wrapping them in a piece of old cover and putting them to my feet. "Ellya looks for you."

"I had to go to the stream."

"Finished the carries and you 'had to go?'"

"You, too, Hannah?"

"What, me?"

"The same as Baylah?"

"It's so bad you don't say what, even to me?"

"Stop fishing."

"I see something to fish for."

"Hear me, Hannah. The truth spoken, I'm sick; I haven't the strength to parcel out upsetments."

This quieted her. She soothed the groin with hot wet cloths and I waited to sleep. My head wouldn't let me, my feet a bit warm and the rest ice. She sat next to me. Now Hannah wasn't anything in the beautiful line, the face too broad, the lips thin, the cheeks bumpy. However, it possessed a great gift, it was a face that informed with an accuracy putting years on a man of my constitution. So with one eye open I said, "It's not so terrible. It won't be anything until perhaps July. And by then the world could overturn itself a dozen times." In small bits, slowly, I explained Nasan's trip to Shnavka the night before. When I got to the part about secret wagons riding for Hamburg she clasped her hands, her lips grew thinner with doubt, her right cheek began tremoring pictures of disaster.

"But how else then, Hannah? How much longer to bind ourselves together with bribes? I came here a boy of five, there were twenty families then. And today still only nineteen or twenty, the best going to the army, few coming back. And what's left? The old, the sick ones, the cripples."

"But at least we're planted here . . . it's our own land a bit. The truth spoken," she said, "I like sitting on the step talking with the women while you're at last prayers. It's nice to look up and see what kind of day tomorrow . . . and everywhere a familiar face. If we dragged ourselves to the other side of the world we'd have to learn to stand it all over again and with us it's no longer six o'clock in the morning."

"Should the children stay because we're too old? Could you send them alone? If they're running from Shnavka they must be running from all over. That's the thing . . . I don't say to be the first, but if it's truly an exodus . . ."

"I'm afraid."

"Of course. But be afraid only to me. Say nothing. Between now and the October conscription we'll find out more. Be nice to Baylah."

She kissed me and said, "Your head is hot. Try, sleep."

I closed my eyes, made bits of talk to myself. Carry, carry. Coming here, getting deaf, hearing again, Mottel's kick, the lieutenant, what next? Will it stop, Ox, will He send a little richness better than Rothschild's, a pinch of quiet in the heart? Something lighter a bit, Ox. Not the yokes of Gershon, Maisha, Naftoldi-Dovid. Elders again children becoming, with herrings. You too in time if allowed, old hay in their barns, Ox; dry for a fire, the what's-left. When the head's hot. Wait, Ox, for sleep. Go down, knot. A good month, July. Come in, Mr. July.

In my sleep I felt three times bigger, and into it a babble thrown, a large hand shaking my eyes open — "Up! Up!" — Kuizma Oblanski, pencil in ear, ledger in hand, the sergeant of police.

"He's sick," from Hannah anxiously. And hovering near, Tzippe-Sora.

"He's avoiding the assembly."

"No, it's my fault," Hannah told him. "I should have waked him."

Oblanski slapped his arms against his flanks, a big man making his impatience larger at every opportunity, his whole pride in his shovel of a beard. "You know the order. I'll report him if you want."

"Kuizma," the widow said, "help take him to the line."

"Am I his servant?"

"For a bottle of the right stuff?"

"Two . . . one for respect."

Hannah dressed me in dries, took my winter coat down. When the bottles arrived Oblanski put them in his pants and supported me down the path to the high road. The fever was strong; I saw the rain falling in sways. At the road the others had made themselves again into a line, standing in one dripping. "Let him sit in the carriage stop, at least," Tzippe-Sora suggested.

"Not allowed."

"All right. Two more."

A grunt from Oblanski. I lay on the bench, seeing more roof and sky than people, the line a blur of high sounds.

A blessing not to see Rezatskin's face, always worrying into you with its rat's glance, thin between the ears like the undersides of toadstools. It had been his experience that open air endangered the health, he wore his long winter coat in the rain and certainly hated us for getting him out. In a thick voice broken by spits and snorts (he seemed always having tremendous colds) Rezatskin began reading our names from his ledger in a voice freighted with unusual anger. The reading took about twenty minutes. Naftoli-Dovid created an incident. He reeled and waved his arms as he answered to his name, the last, causing Rezatskin to remark loudly, "Leave it to him to add to the stench here." At this my father-in-law found some crazy reason to take off his cap and sway over to Rezatskin, saying, "A thank-you, sir.

Now if you were of our own I might say such a homey curse! But as it's you, sir . . . a good thank-you!"

Yeersel and Zish had by then pulled him away. Zish called back, "He's only angry at his own failures, sir, we all laugh at him." Becoming nervous Naftoli-Dovid began laughing, saying, "Yes, that's right —" Oblanski then called strongly, "Now to the next, follow!"

The soldiers pushed the Golinskers into a little crowd trailing the policeman up the hill. Ellya and Nasan made a seat of hands for me. I was glad to be in the rain. I opened my mouth, it felt drier than a fire. The rest were directed to stand outside the village hall; they permitted the boys to set me down on the porch; the roof leaked. I put out my hand to catch drops, keeping my lips wet. Through the rails I could see faces — Baylah's mother Dena, up close, raindrops flattening her bit of a mustache, the suspicious heavily-lidded Shprinza, a few small boys with pieces of canvas on their heads, and to a side a bit, Hannah with Ellya and Nasan, the boys watching her, she keeping her eyes on me. Meanwhile Selenkov had begun in the slow sharp style of an official with much to develop.

"The movement against the Government which has come to light during the past few days in this District — taking in the Pukop Scandal, also the illegal departure of Jews from Svutz, Shnavka, Tinkavitch, Kletsk, and various other places — is evidence of Jews otherwise devoted to the Throne and Fatherland yielding to instigations of ill-minded persons who fan passions in accordance with the designs of the anarchists. It is to forestall such violations of the public order, and to safeguard Golinsk Jews, that this assembly is called."

Now the lofty tone of this opening and its suspicious familiarity showed that our Administrator was out to play his crudest game with us. We were uneducated, our Russian was limited to everyday needs, yet Selenkov seemed to be saying the same things as five years previous when following the pogrom in Warsaw he had assembled us and made exhibitions of concern wrapped in the reasoning that anarchists had flamed the pogrom to embarrass the government before the world. This cordiality ended with the year, however; and though many ran from

Svutz in 1883 we Golinskers sat still at the insistence of Tzippe-Sora, who had quite well established herself in various illegal handlings.

"In such a light, therefore," Selenkov said, "we have three things. I will read an enactment handed down by the Government two weeks ago, held by the Minsk Gubernator pending decisions on matters to be later announced. Here it is, listen carefully, questions may be asked." The Administrator's voice now assumed its normal nagging cackle. " 'The family of a Jew guilty of evading military service is liable to a fine of three hundred rubles. The collection of the fine shall be decreed by the respective recruiting station and carried out by the police. It shall not be substituted by imprisonment in the case of destitute persons liable to that fine.' This is the main sense of the enactment," he remarked, stuffing the paper in his pocket.

Only the rain was heard for a few moments; then Hatzkel's Vremya, daughter of Zelyeh and granddaughter of Asher-the-Sour, asked timidly that it be read over. Selenkov obliged with the bad grace of an incompetent doctor repeating how his patient died. Again a wet silence. "No questions here?" Selenkov demanded. "Then it's understood?"

"Understood, yes, sir," I heard Tzippe-Sora saying as she came nearer. "Clearly, sir, but one thing."

"What's your 'one thing'?"

"Sir," she said respectfully, "just the meaning there . . . when it says 'the family.' "

"The family?" was Selenkov's startled reply. He decided this was a good place to laugh and I heard my lieutenant joining, lightly.

"That's parents, sir?"

"Parents, brothers, sisters. Family!"

"Grandparents?"

"Family!"

"Nieces, cousins, sir?"

"Family!"

"Take any of us, sir, look closely a bit and you know what you'll see. In some way or another, sir, we're all related. Now does that make us *one* family, sir? That's my question."

"Yes," he said with a tavern friendliness, "if you're all one family it'll be easier to pay the fine should any of you choose to evade service, isn't that so? Each gives a little, you see, and the three hundred therefore isn't a burden on just a few."

I heard a call; Laib-Shmul trying to control his temper. "Pay when?"

"That's good," Selenkov said heartily, "it brings up an important matter. First, the recruiting roll is called. A recruit fails to appear at the station. The authorities issue the order to the family to pay. The police deliver the order. And if there is no payment, or insufficient, the family is judged destitute and the Government sells whatever property by auction."

Now the landsmen began to see the snake unrolling itself. "And if we have nothing to sell?" shouted Pesha.

"You are destitute but not jailed. Only forbidden to leave the village. In that way you have the opportunity, should your position improve, to fulfill the arrears!" He found himself forced to end in as loud a shout as he could make; such cried-out Yiddish was there that Selenkov's commands for order became drowned before they hardly left his mouth. Now came the other, the softly confident voice of my lieutenant, not gently as with me before at the stream, but as the dedicated voice of a sincere protector. Speaking quietly, he made the rest of us gradually listen; near as I was to him I heard only snatches, the fever throwing up its wall.

". . . referring now to the known conspiracy within the Pale of Settlement . . . as a means of forestalling excesses against the Jewish population . . . beginning with today, at least one soldier to be billeted in each Jewish home in the Pukop District . . . for a time not more than . . ."

Soldiers . . . soldiers in Jewish homes, ay, people, yes-moan and yes-cry, we're having guests as in the older times . . . commandeerings, our girls, pig-flesh dirtying us, beatings, burnings. . . . Then Oblanski blew his whistle. Selenkov began speaking quite rapidly. "In connection with the previous, the third and final. In view of the outrages in force against the Government involving exits of Jews from the Pale of Settlement and gross evasions of military service, it has been decreed by supplementary command of the Army that conscription time be changed from October to any time of the year deemed proper by the District Military Commands. We have been informed late Saturday from Pukop that in Golinsk as in all inhabited places within the Pukop region, conscription time has been changed from October to today." He brought his hand down upon the rail. "For all, Jew and gentile!"

After this I heard only snatches. Lying on the porch, the fever dulling me down, I had not been aware of the presence of peasants from the other side or that the assembly would have meanings for them too. Names and numbers were called; it was the careful clear voice now of the lieutenant; some Russian, some Jewish. Boots passed close by, the door opening and banging shut; inside Dr. Ostrov waiting to make the examinations.

In twenty-four hours, new boots.

He called Nasan, a blackness to my eyes, and a few moments later, my cheek kissed and then the banging shut of the door. After that I heard nothing until later awhile, feeling kissed the second time and knowing it had to be Ellya; then again the closing of the door. Many hands lifted me, I lay swaying high, the rain splashed my cheeks; and from a distance, to the last, the honking of Selenkov. "Of course a bath, Lieutenant. Beginning tomorrow, no bugs for them but the best."

The insensibility lasted several hours; then came some imagining of clocks, tiny ones ticking in the eyeballs. The second sign was a smell so thick I feared I lay in the devil's own latrine.

Shouts of soldiers on the other side of a closed door made a sudden cannonade. The smell of feces hung in swirls over the room; a whole revolution of bowels and something more had burst there.

Wood hard under my back; I moved my hand. It touched the side of a boot on the floor and I took it in a hurl-up through the window pane for air.

The door flew open, forms in the half-dark entered and banged it

shut; soldiers, by their rifles and voices. But for the smell it could
have been a dream.

A rifle butt tapped against my chin, the voice seeming to travel a
distance. "Making a disturbance?"

I whispered, "For air."

"Yes, a contamination here," said the second decisively, a youngish
voice, a nervous one, the tongue running like the feet of a small boy.

"Why don't I save the wagon a trip?" the first asked himself, raising
the rifle butt over my eyes.

"The smell," I begged. "Take me out."

"We can't," the second replied. "Be quiet or he'll give you the butt."

Still in a fever I groped for the kernel of my condition. To what
"contamination" was I linked and what stench was this, and why were
the soldiers still shouting, "Away!" on the other side of the door?
Then through the hole in the window-glass a sound of something
better came, the massed call of a praying.

This fixed me a bit; it was evening, the synagogue stood nearby;
this had to be Maisha's hut, then, the nearest to the synagogue. I
listened to the praying with the thoughts of my boys being there
mixing into wonders of what wagon the soldiers had mentioned; what
trick under this, what smell, why this cancellation by the lieutenant;
and what other things had I missed the hours I lay between Gehenna
and Golinsk?

They were at prayers: the landsmen, their boys, mine. I wanted to
be surrounded by young bodies especially, the blood running with
stubbornness through the years of their growth (more of their age in
our cemetery than at the praying), who had been spared the too-soon
rotting; they were standing flesh alive, the hard-grown fruit of our
plowings, spared every last accident which calendared our days — the
drownings, the consumptions, the smites of the elements, the agues
and fevers which had snatched others in epidemics revisiting with the
persistence of starving beggars. Spared, but only for tomorrow; for
tomorrow drawn from wombs and circumcised, confirmed and given
to wed; for that tomorrow we had bribed and twisted ourselves to

sweat in fields we did not eat from, hauled illegal goods never on our backs, brandies never on our table, putting bread away against the next month. For such a tomorrow we had sent the Squire off gaily to Petersburg and for that crab of tomorrow he had paid his little visit to persuade us that his monument of a brain had formed every last claw to be pushed into us.

In the hut I sensed something sharper than human waste and remembered the herring feast before the assembly. I crawled to the stove; it was cold, I pulled myself up, holding and groping for matches. Maisha lay on his side in a corner, his backside exposed, knees to his chin, a heap of his matter about him. The match burnt my fingers; I struck others, solving the secret.

Now as Maisha so in other corners — my brother Gershon and father-in-law Naftoli-Dovid, quiet sacks lying in their matters — but let me go to the brine, it was the brine that showed what to bring near and what to keep far from myself, the brine that fetched anger from deep pockets of burial, the brine that put an axe in my hand.

Now the fault of the three jolly ones? They had haggled themselves unfortunately into owning a keg of herring pickled in a cloved brine, and eating into it with such zest that the saltiness made them look to refresh themselves with long swallows of something wet. As it happened, Naftoli-Dovid in his hut nearby had several bottles of his own recent homemade that he was letting stand awhile before taking them to certain of his quiet customers; but since we were forbidden to leave our lanes and since it was raining and since there was nothing to celebrate, Naftoli-Dovid brought his bottles to the herring and the three drank not only to pour wetness and warmth into them, but to fix themselves into praying with a joy, thinking, "Perhaps the Angel Gavreel will hear the joy in our praying and open his Book of Days to the right page and find our names on them and call us to ride in his wagon under lanterns of stars toward our first sleeps between covers of finest-spun cloudlets not for sale." Seeking to bury in childishness what as men they had wearied of, these three jollies had over-herringed and over-liquored themselves into a stupor and had waked

each with ten kittens in his mouth and a body out of water. The celebration over, they had wished neither herring nor liquor, only to pour
something wet into them; after so many herrings and bottles of my
father-in-law's they needed to rid themselves of their dryness; yet
instead, had taken whole tumblers of thick fatty brine poured from
the keg of herring to end as I found them, their bowels convulsed,
their bodies robbed of the last drop of liquid.

Using one match after the other, striking them against the floor as
I lay on my stomach, I circled the room with flickers of light — the
keg of herring tipped over under the table, a few fish near it, only
a small circle of brine out of it — then two large tin tumblers that we
used to take on our travels, good for water or picking berries — now
I crawled to the tumblers and smelled of them and one had an inch
of brine still in it, brine in a tin tumbler, brine out of the keg of
herring, a killing thing to drink, a thing to make the insides explode;
no wonder the stench there; the product of the soldiers' sport, con-
vulsing their bowels with brine when they cried for water —

I went to look at Gershon. His lips flew up with each breath, his
head had some purplish color, and his eyelids also. Now Gershon had
of late years let his beard grow fuller and this increased the resem-
blance to my father, so that seeing him in that color and in the position
of a goner, the wheel spun backwards and I seemed to be the little
boy seeing how my father lay in the field that day out of Minsk, in
his purple dying of the plague. Father dying in the field, Gershon the
same, the cords of years burst. In such times the senses take their
angriest moves, either toward clarity or animal blindness; here with
me it went the first way; I grasped why I had been hidden with the
three. Here was concerned my diffident lieutenant of the streamside
when I had gone for the rubles; the lieutenant had coquetted until
I had horrified him by showing my blue-knotted groin, tricking up
the fable of getting it from a woman to be rid of him. But he had not
forgotten what he truly believed, he had well swallowed my story of
venery and thought to have me put away from the soldiers; which
was why I had been taken where no soldiers would be quartered,

until "the wagon" would remove me elsewhere. And when it might be found that no disease such as I had informed the lieutenant existed in me, then what? Would I be returned and would the lieutenant then laugh at the great joke played upon him? Or would he contrive a more delicate punishment for my impudence?

Now all this lay in my fever, a broil of anger fired by the sight of what had been done to the three with the brine. The anger clamored to come out, it could not be pounded back with my fists against the floor, with my rolling this way and that; and when my hand felt Maisha's axe in the darkness my strength rose me to my feet and I smashed the axe against the window, the glass in a crash, and this brought the soldiers. The door opened to their shouts of "Order!" but by their lanterns I saw clear signs in their eyes, fear that their amusement had been detected, that this wild fellow with the axe in his hand might crazy-wise bring them to justice. They stood in a pause, regarding me, and now through the broken space I could hear the praying well and this cheered me, to conceive some lance against the poisoned poisoners and for us all.

"Well, you've gotten into trouble," one of the soldiers said, putting his lantern down and poising his rifle butt. He charged at me and I swung the axe, but badly, only deflecting the rifle butt to my stomach, the blow felling me. I felt his boot on my face, waited for the butt to follow, but the second had run up and was saying, "Now if you'll wait and think, Drobnis . . ."

"But he's trying to escape, he's contaminated, it would be obeying orders," Drobnis argued, "and they'd be saved the bother of carting him away."

"Well," the second hesitated, "I suppose . . ."

"Go shut the door."

He did and in that moment I whispered to this Drobnis who'd forced my landsmen to drink the brine, "I'm contaminated, it's possible . . . but so are they and can't be helped."

He said, "Bring the lantern closer, will you, Knyazev? I'll show you a clean job, once and over."

This gave me another few seconds; everything became plain and I said, "There's plague here, you didn't do it with the brine. . . ."

"I'll give you plague," Drobnis muttered.

"No," I cried in acted-out anxiety, *"they'll* give it to you! And don't I bitterly know the look of plague? Didn't I see my own father dying of it before my eyes just as I see you, just as close?"

"No Jew tricks!" he shouted, lifting his rifle butt to smash me quiet.

"Go ahead," I said. I didn't believe the face real, the shadowy holes of his eyes and his dark form before the lantern shooting up to the ceiling as one sees an event with the soothe of a secret fantasy ending when one wakes in his bed. "Now I swear that's plague over there . . . the herring was poisoned, don't you see they would have been stricken even if you hadn't given them brine to drink?"

"How do you come to say brine?" the second demanded, Knyazev.

"I struck matches!"

With this Knyazev's hand began to shake, the fingers took hold of Drobnis's rifle, I threw more wood into the sparks. "Yes, they're contaminated, it's the plague here. That's why I took the axe to the window, it's our death here!"

"Let's look," Knyazev gave a blurt, backing to the lantern and taking it to the corner where Gershon lay. Drobnis poked him on his back with the rifle barrel; I dropped my eyes on Gershon for just a glance at the purple face. It was the soldiers I had to watch to measure the temper of their fear, my mind running to the next gambit. "Now there's the thing, billeted in a town with plague! I tried to warn the lieutenant, I knew the herring was poisoned, I suspected . . . but I lost my senses . . . and now you've kept them locked up these hours and the thing's in the air!"

Knyazev rapped Drobnis on the arm. "We'd better go to the lieutenant."

"And what will he do?" Drobnis replied. "Nothing but get on his horse and run! And of course we'll be told to 'gain control' here! We'll have to bury them and wait around to bury others and then be buried ourselves!"

"You're right, we'll have to touch them," Knyazev shuddered.

"Not I," Drobnis growled.

Now my brother's mouth opened, he breathed with rattles, the lips making an "Amen." Knyazev stepped back and kicked the lantern over, adding the smell of lamp-oil to everything else. Drobnis began to call him a fool and other names, then drove himself into a change. "No, let it! Let's help it, where are matches? Let the place burn!"

And from Knyazev, "We'll make a faggot. Well, it's too bad."

One pulled bed-linen, the other dropped matches into the running lamp-oil. I ran at this; with the last iron in my legs. In the press of their decision they had forgotten me, I was no longer important; whatever, I managed to get down the path and into the synagogue without being pursued, gaining a few minutes alone with the landsmen.

Inside the synagogue door, seeing the backs of the landsmen at prayer before the altar of seven candles, the shadows slanting on the walls, the sound of them going straight up, the whole softly strong moment of such an appeal to me, a moment of so many familiars yet now with no time to have the pleasure of it . . . and out of this the regret, let's say, of never when I had the time, to notice these different things about those who in the market saddened me with their gross scratchings at each other, so grating to my pride their bitings and yawpings in the huts, just in the one running after the piece of bread . . . yet snatched away from it there, all of the same heart together, I with no time for these things, still feeling them in a mix of dearness not attended to in time before . . . and in the next second shouting to them, "Say 'Amen!' It's plague and fire! Run, run!"

Now each moment passed with an explosion of dangerous noise like trainless locomotives chasing each other; first their seeing me and putting me on a bench and making a circle about me; the asking of too many questions; then Ellya making them be still with his screams and letting me say what. "Run to the woods, run," I told Ellya in his ear, all around me listening, "to Minsk by woodland paths, to the ghetto, then to over the sea, the conscripts."

With this the rise of a great cry of landsmen haggling with each other, the synagogue a market-place now of harsh buy-and-sell — to run or not, be crazy or not — and with Yeersel's legs under my head on the bench, his hand in mine, his voice to me, "You'll live, you'll live, Berel, don't be frightened, you'll live." Then up this wall of noise came a fast hard trample of many boots, and cries of Russian into the synagogue, the boards rumbling with hard hits around me. Yeersel and Hatzkel lay themselves over me like a cover, then I ripping the little canvas roll of rubles from the string under my shirt and thrusting them at Yeersel. "Take the lads and run, this is money; to Minsk through the woods, Yeersel, to Hamburg, to over the sea."

Yeersel shook me by the shoulders, behind me the first rifle shot, I begging, "Run with them, be father and mother, take the rubles, go." Then into my face the face of Nasan crying, "Papa, Papa," and I in a harsh yell over the shoutings and beatings, "Plague, plague and fire, lift me." Through the window I saw the flame out of Maisha's hut and soldiers running, more of them, down the lane toward the highroad, and the soldiers seeming then to empty out of the synagogue and join them. In one bellow, I stood to Yeersel. "To the woods, recruits! Look for Yeersel," and Nasan kissing me and I saying, "Kiss Ellya," and Yeersel letting a goatish cry out of him, "Kiss Bosha and the children," then turning to run.

I made to embrace him and was left holding a button of his blouse; never again was anything of Yeersel close to my hand.

Then Nasan's back going away from me; and as though hidden in the ground, curving from behind me, a rifle butt to the side of my head and a second time of nothing.

They carried the Ox to a cellar of the village hall, revived him with needles, stimulated him with pails of water, and plied him with questions. But how could the Ox reply, not hearing a word, nor even their screams? Since the synagogue, since the soldier's rifle to the side of his head, the Ox had become deaf for the second time.

They brought Dr. Ostrov to prove with angry pantomime how the Ox had lied: For the three to have had the plague was impossible, the doctor described; and this pleased the Ox considerably. But the beatings after the doctor's departure swelled his fever through the night so that when they rode him up and down the Jewish lanes as a warning to other rumor-makers, he hardly knew he was alive. Thus the Ox left Golinsk as he had entered it, deaf and fevered in a wagon. Yet nothing else had remained the same, not even his quiet, and this also pleased the Ox considerably; a most elevated Ox, a pleasant fever.

In Pukop, a second cell where for many days they left him unbothered except as a pastime, now and then, of giving him questions and then blows, each night the Ox praying for morning to come a bit later. It came lastly to a thing of their carrying him upstairs to the grand room of the Colonel Commander sitting behind the finest of carved tables, the wood blacker than any other the Ox had seen; at his right, too, the Squire Konayev himself, weary for Petersburg, throwing down a smile to him lying in the stretcher, a soldier from a battlefield. It was the Boar against the Ox, a sniffing bleating Boar believing he was bellowing, a loose-skinned Boar pluming himself over the fallen Ox with glances of eyes rimmed with blood, a condition gained at no small expense in the Petersburg fun-parlors.

With peculiar resourcefulness the Boar described the enormity of the Ox's violations, illustrating the charges with drawings taken from a red leather case—drawings of huge-beaked persons burning children whose tender faces lay contorted in innocent agony, drawings of bestial dwarfs with exaggerated privates waiting to rape a little girl held by a grinning monkey wearing praying shawl and phylacteries, drawings of gowned knife-wielders opening the belly of a prone woman, the blood gushing onto a spread Scroll of the Holy Law—an altogether characteristic performance by the Boar to emphasize his accusation of the Ox's having by his stupidity brought reprisals against his people, who by running away had encouraged the tempers of the long-suffering gentiles.

Now following this presentation, the drawings returned to the case, the case to the Squire's pocket, the Colonel Commander made a long reading from many sheets of thin paper of clauses impossible for the

Ox to guess. But from his carefully curling lips and from how the Squire nodded between the Colonel Commander's pauses, the tip of his beard touching the diamond in his cravat, the Ox began to see that he had indeed gored something, that here was an Ox too important to be slaughtered simply, an Ox who was causing them to read an accusation of many pages in the pose of a trial; if without jury or testimony, still forcing the Colonel Commander to a fifteen-minute reading which, had the Ox been less important, could have been collapsed into a few words. "We have treated you badly," the Colonel Commander could have said to any ordinary Ox, "and therefore you are guilty."

The reading sent the Ox to Siberia, as at the end the fingers of the Colonel Commander showed, for twenty-five years.

A year after "his plague on them," following his escape from Siberia, the Ox almost beheld Golinsk, so nicely hill-up and hill-down, and learned a bit about his July-in-May —

— How the soldiers ran from the Ox's "plague," and how Yeersel and the conscripts, running into the woods for Minsk, made truly for America, which some reached. Yeersel yes, Nasan yes, Hatzkel yes, Yakov no, Daneel yes, Yussel no. Shmelke a question, Bencha a question, Ellya a question.

— How flamed by the lamp-oil and soldiers' faggots, Maisha's hut burned but for the wet roof, which fell —

— And how this began the fall of his Golinsk.

This is how the Ox sat in Siberia:
First he counted the accidents. He made a list.

> how he came to Golinsk
> how he became deaf
> how he became undeaf
> how Nochim died
> how Varya departed
> how her perfume entered the synagogue
> how Mottel came to kick his groin

how he forestalled the amorous lieutenant
how they came to drink brine
how he became the second time deaf

Out of these accidents borne to him on winds from all corners had come a flick of thought to make a one of Gershon's purple face and his father's in the field; and out of this to make a plague on *them*.

And for this to have passed, pondered the Ox, was no less miraculous than from the middle of an ocean a piece of straw should float onto sand.

What coal had lain secretly in Yeersel and in him, against a moment they could not have foreseen, when they would need warming into flaming? What in him, the tailor with the gentle heart; and what in the quiet-seeking Ox? And it seemed to him sitting on his cold shelf that as he had taken the axe, so had Yeersel carried the splits to hammer and nails, and that the name of the forest in which they lived was Accident, and that the true name of the temple they strove to build was Miracle, out of axe and hammer and nail; out of the this and the near, out of the days of their time.

Having no buckets to carry in Siberia, no familiar whiles in his cold imprisonment between tasteless dawns, the Ox began wider thoughts. He would have plucked the underplan out of accidents groping to each other to make crowns; he saw how he and all were as stones tied to strings held and whirled, how strings broke, stones flew free of the string-holders; and how some stones soon fell and how others flew higher and met in the air and did not fall but took from the other new strength.

So sat the Ox in Siberia, urging his thoughts to the farthest rim, then faltering. For the Ox, hovering on the rim, no more than this —

— How fearing their ropes no longer held, the Squires had gone to chains, taking youngers summarily, soldiers thrown among the landsmen as in older times, and a new trick of a three-hundred-ruble fine for each conscript; unthinking that though rope burns, iron cuts; and that from such cuttings came only greater strainings and deeper thirsts —

— How they themselves had made the plague on *them,* how they who called the landsmen misfits were themselves misfits of a higher misfitment, they not able longer to bear the world of their own making. It became too small to be handled by men of subtle mind behaving like beasts, too slippery to hold the lads from running to the ships, too small and slippery for them to have simply slaughtered their trouble of an Ox —

And now his Siberia was not the same old ending of the Jews. "Ocean, make way, crap is swimming," Naftoli-Dovid had said when the Ox was five. Later, the Ox a special man in Siberia, it was no longer plain crap, but polished; the Ox sitting in Siberia for more than his Jewishness, for more than his piety, for more than his remembered dead, for more than his sons alone; for his need to love the new and living and imperishable. And this was the Ox's meaning, that love for the new and living and imperishable lay as a lance against the chests of those misfits of a higher misfitment. They had not put the Ox; the Ox had put them, pushing the youngers to sail over the sea.

6. *Shim*
(1871–1922)

WHEN I WAS TWELVE YEERSEL'S ROCHEL NUMBED ME. I COULD NOT HOLD an easy conversation with her. After my confirmation I went steadily on the roads with my father, took confidence in my advancing manhood, and brought her presents. When Yeersel began me on his wagon after my parents died, I improved myself to the point of being able to amuse her with various appetizing topics gleaned from the roads.

Yeersel praised my needle and my conduct, citing hints thrown my way by mothers of dowried daughters in Tinkavitch and Lekavitch; but my eyes for girls were left at home. I wanted Rochel, and equally important, I would never go to another village and leave my brother Laib in Golinsk. Our parents were dead; Maisha was our appointed guardian until our marriages, yet he hardly fitted to be as a father and I promised myself I would be as a father to my younger brother until he himself became a father. I was a serious fellow; I had respected my father and tried to design myself after him, whom poverty had lessened without coarsening. My mother would have refused riches rather than have missed a minute with him. The more I could be like my father, the more Rochel would have to love me; and the more like him I could be to Laib, the sweeter the rejoicing in The Next World. Thus I molded myself, on the way to becoming sixteen, until the burdens of my particular manhood became first difficult and then insupportable.

My numbness with her somewhat wore off and more than ever I wanted to seize her in a grown-up manner. The winter Laib lay ill she sat quite a bit at his bedside with me. It gave me wonderful thrills which after she left changed into melancholy worries. "What did I say?

Nothing, worse than nothing. She thinks I'm bored with her and why not? Two coats, two coats I boasted about cutting all by myself as if a tailor shouldn't know how! Such grossness! And after that? Nothing. All she'll remember is how I sat without taking my eyes from her bosom! And my mouth was so dry! How couldn't she have seen me licking my lips like a beast? Ay, I'm a beast, plain talk, up and down!" — and so on.

But these things settled themselves during what we afterward called the Three Bad Days which began with the Sabbath of Laib's confirmation in May 1886, the day that Nochim died and Varya disappeared and Uncle Mottel after her.

The light was still gray. Reb Maisha slept on the bed-shelf over the stove, making frightening snores, each breath a triumph. I gave Laib a push with my knee. "Laib, today is here, get up." But he still slept at my side.

Two things struck me with equal importance, whether a sleeve of his confirmation suit wasn't too long and how my parents would have enjoyed that day, Laib safely through boyhood's gauntlet and ready to walk manfully with honor. I gave him another knee-push. It woke him. "Laib, look through the window."

"Sh."

"A good day."

"No clouds," he said, looking out sleepily, leaning on an elbow, then falling back upon our pillows. Watching him I thought that with his eyes and cheeks instead of my own dull face, Rochel might have already encouraged me to kiss her.

Laib sat up in bed, his look of inner busyness returning. "Yes, it's really today!"

Reb Maisha woke up with a cheerful hiba-hiba; people knocked upon our shutters, calling gaily, "Is he ready?" and "Is he beautiful yet?" We had saved father's best shirt. Bosha cut it down; and with father's black bow tie stuffed under the new stiff collar Laib looked like a cabinet minister's son, a very good fit across the shoulders; and Reb

Maisha pointed to Laib's new shiny black boots. "Remember, nobody wears better on his feet today than you!"

"They pinch," Laib said.

Reb Maisha slapped his hands. "How else can boots give their congratulations? The best to take out a pinch is to dance." He made a careful turn with a tight little kick at the end of it.

Laib shook his head gravely. "It'll be dancing without music. Unless Nochim got home during the night."

"Feet before fiddles," Reb Maisha cried, smoothing the air happily with his palms, brooking no obstacles to this happy day. "You're late. Look, the sun's on the leaves already! Take him to the synagogue, Shim, don't wait for me!"

Reb Maisha started hunting for his best shirt and Laib and I stepped out of the hut. A few small boys waiting there ran before us on the way to the synagogue, shouting, "He's coming, he's here."

The landsmen stood waiting outside the synagogue. Some ancient whitewash remained on the door, the wood deeply seamed and softened by many weathers; it hung carelessly on its one hinge at the bottom. The landsmen grouped about it hung also a bit carelessly on their own over-burdened joints, here bent out, there curved in, the illnesses and injuries of past years leaving little monuments of bone over the fractures, dropped shoulders for the dislocations, bent backs for the ruptures, open mouths for the asthmas; and various kinds of gaits, each the result of a combination of pestilences. Berel stood straightest but did not hear well; once a man married and had children limps and bumps and morning aches and swelling hands followed naturally along, with the phrase "Papa's sick today" a frequent distress signal until it seemed that the landsmen had always been old, and their wives always thinner or fatter, quieter or more hot-tempered, smarter or more stupid, but never the same and all in time like the synagogue door, ready to fall off the hinge.

The landsmen always walked the confirmation boy down the aisle behind his parents. This day I walked Laib down in a proud march, the women and children watching from their benches, the moment as holy for the confirmant as his wedding procession and to some even holier, for this was shared with none but The Highest, a joy solitary and ever sustaining. As my father would have, I put my hand to Laib's far shoulder and so led him to the lectern where leaving him to begin the services I kissed his cheek and went back to my place next to Reb Maisha, looking among the women for Rochel and spying her at her mother's side, her milk-white cheeks puffed into a proud oval smile for me.

Hertz nodded to me and I nodded back, and Laib-Shmul also and others; even Asher-the-Sour paid me a nod. Many things make a man's blood rise and his spirit lighter; a woman may be seen trembling for him, and the sky may appear to him in a certain way, and he may hear the happy cry of his child sighting him from afar; all these are balms, but none such as standing well in the place of one's father, which I felt.

Chanting the opening prayer, "How goodly thy tents, O Jacob, thy dwelling places, O Israel; as for me, in the abundance of thy loving kindness will I come to thy house," we lifted Laib with us in a sudden rush of saying to him, "See, you have many fathers and mothers." We are made early, and though we put on many clothes they wear out while the underform persists, growing well or badly but never away from the beginning symmetry; and we knew without thought that the Laib-Shmul who bellowed and ranted through the week was not the real Laib-Shmul, nor the acid Asher, nor the giggling Naftoli-Dovid, nor the temperous Pesha; but that the Sabbath brought us to ourselves again, all mothers and fathers and children into a burst of belongment, of no huddles in a corner, out of the weekday insanities straight and fine back to the best freedom we knew, to stand together in the way of our fathers.

I exchanged glances with Rochel as Laib leaned against the lectern and began leading. When one does not yet possess his own four walls, in surroundings too poor for him to call even a closet his own, much of his deeper life is hinted by tastes of privacy all the more breathless in their surreptitious emergence. The synagogue contained some twenty benches distributed half-and-half on either side of the center aisle. It was unnecessary to look about in order to see where anyone was seated, custom having long since established the main places. By giving my chin a leftward twist and my eyes a strong slant likewise I could see Rochel behind me on the second women's bench, always ready to make a tiny movement of her head or smile with only the corners of her mouth. Such devoted vigilance wildened me to imagine our being joined in a delicious way and I told myself we were fated to be united, as though the future had come for an early visit to make us Laib's "second parents" there in the synagogue. Quickened by the holiday yet aching with missing father and mother, such was my joy.

Very well; the services proceeded unevenly and ended in blasphemy. You must remember this was a great event for Reb Maisha, our old teacher and nominal spiritual leader. He wanted the landsmen to agree as one that he had well merited being named guardian of Laib and me, which would follow upon Laib's inspired ascension into Jewish manhood. For this reason Reb Maisha stood on his feet from the start. Knowing the services by heart he swayed in a stationary dance to every note of Laib's chanting.

At first it went well though not outstandingly. Whenever Laib would drift away from the straight high calls of an enraptured confirmant Reb Maisha would wrinkle up his brow and gyrate more fervently, pressing my father's old prayer book to his chest as if to dissolve any hesitations in Laib. The more he did this with the prayer book the more nervous Laib became. The landsmen took Laib's start for beginning nervousness but their tolerance ebbed as it became clearer that Laib was chanting more out of duty than joy — an unacceptable thing to our half-Hasid syndicate for whom prayer without joy betrayed itself as small assurance of redemption. When Laib came to the part — "Who is like Thee, Lord of mighty acts, and who can resemble Thee to kill and quicken and cause salvation to spring forth?" — we expected him as an orphan of less than a year to let this out with at least a natural passion; but his mind was on something else and he chanted it quite without heart. Asher-the-Sour behind Reb Maisha allowed himself a critical cough. When Laib came to the opening of the Ark for the removal of the Scrolls and the reading of the Law he made no attempt to chant out, "And Moses said, Rise up, O Lord," with anything like the required triumphal climb even though Reb Maisha dizzied himself with the strongest circular sways of his frame, pressing my father's prayer book to his chest like a piece of soothing ice. A puzzled buzz skipped from bench to bench on the men's side and Laib-Shmul leaned forward, growling into Reb Maisha's ear, "Did you teach him? Or did he teach you?"

"Ay," whispered Reb Maisha to me, "and didn't he sound like an angel yesterday, going over it?"

I was given the first reading of the Law. Standing beside Laib at the lectern I began the ritual, touching the fringes of my prayer-shawl to the opened Scroll and then placing them to my lips, when I heard an urgent whisper from my brother, "*Take Papa's prayer book away from Reb!*"

The moment I returned to my seat I took Father's prayer book from the tight grasp of Reb Maisha. Seeing how I held it gently, reverently, Laib sighed. When it became his honor to read the final portion belonging to that Sabbath, his chanting became better; relief gave way to joy in Reb Maisha's standing sways, his joy spreading to the others as Laib's chantings continued to soar. Laib had redeemed himself, regaining the esteem of the landsmen for no reason I could see but that I had taken Father's prayer book into my hands. Then quite without thought, in the simple way of digging deeper into one's self, I experienced a revelation. Through me had my father touched Laib with his peaceful finger, lifting and guiding him; through my holding of his prayer book, the relic and symbol of fatherly devotion, had my father bequeathed his powers to me, his eldest son, to use them with love. I saw my parents in heaven raining thanks upon me; how warm the sun through the window on my neck, how like their secret kisses; yes, how touched I was by it all!

All went soft as butter until the final "Amen." It was a great happy "Amen," happy for the Sabbath, happy for Laib. "Amen, a good Sabbath," we cried to each other, thinking of the peaceful afternoon coming, of our naps after the best meal of the week and of the festival eating and singing and dancing when we would rise refreshed to honor Laib. Very well; but as he added his voice to the "Amen" our innocent Reb Maisha took my father's prayer book from me and opened it, kissing a page, then closing it with a hard press of the covers, releasing happy tears meanwhile. His hands shook; the book fell; I bent, picking it up and kissing it before returning it automatically to him as I saw Rochel going to Laib to congratulate him. I followed, Reb Maisha at my heels. We joined the circle formed about Laib on the altar. Nearest to the confirmation boy stood the three widowers, Laib-Shmul, Naftoli-Dovid, and Asher-the-Sour; remembering their incompleteness in this time of joy, tears bubbled through their congratulatory kisses, the sudden added bond causing them to hold the recently bereaved confirmation boy tightly among them. Seeing me, they joined me to Laib and themselves. My hand went to Rochel and she took it; I drew her to our nucleus, into which Yeersel and Bosha pushed themselves, the others all around. Laib turned to me and I kissed his cheek, he whispering, "The book? The book?" I said, "Reb Maisha, give Laib Papa's book to kiss."

By then Tzippe-Sora had begun to sniff. "What kind of smell," she called, sniffing, "is here?" In the next moment we were all sniffing and discovering the sweetish smell; Reb Maisha also, and clearly the odor was coming from him.

"Something of a perfume?" he mumbled. Tzippe-Sora took the prayer book from him, bent her head toward it. "From here," she said, pointing.

"From the book?" Reb Maisha demanded. "Such a so-fancy?"

Tzippe-Sora's eyes, cold and hard, met his; she shoved the book under his nose. "From where else, Mr. Purity?"

The three widowers broke away from Laib; a new circle made itself around befuddled Reb Maisha. "Perfume, yes," said Asher-the-Sour, as others came closer to sniff and ask questions. In a few moments the inner circle was sending words to the middle and the middle to the outer; and where a minute before the peace of the Sabbath ruled, now was the roar of the angry river, Sambatyon; and what a Sambatyon!

"Perfume, yes!" shrilled Nochim's Pesha, "Ay!"

"Our revered teacher has a fancy lady pupil, no doubt!" cried Asher-the-Sour, shaking his finger under Reb Maisha's nose.

Over everything else came Laib-Shmul's roar, "Wait! See! Wet pages!"

I looked for Laib. He was gone.

Yeersel stepped to the lectern and shouted, "No accusations in the synagogue, please! Wives, wives . . . be good enough to take the children out!"

The uproar continued. Rochel headed the women removing the children. So *this* had been worrying Laib! Ay, indeed; that Reb Maisha would press Father's prayer book with such force to his chest as to break a vessel containing this outrageous perfume!

"See," Zisha shouted, holding up a glass phial the length of a finger joint. "Now we've the thief by his little neck!"

"Hidden in a crack of the binding, hidden!" Shmelke cried as Zisha threw the bit of glass to the floor, crushing it angrily under his heel. "Congratulations, dear Maisha, at your age it's remarkable!"

"Maisha, Maisha," Yeersel begged, "what made you do this?"

Bent and captured, trembling, Reb Maisha sobbed, "I should know so much about the devil!"

"Say where you got it, at least?" growled Laib-Shmul, controlling his temper. "From whom such a smell but from women whose business it is to make everything smell nice?"

"And with a gall, to bring it into the synagogue!" cried Asher-the-Sour with such a crash that Reb Maisha fell to the floor, hiding his head.

I ran to the door thinking only of finding Laib. I needed to be certain of where he'd got it and what manner of consorting with whom, and how. Whose blame, after all, if not mine, mine! Had I watched him well enough? No, I had failed to bind him to me, I had allowed the Evil Eye to win his regard, I who a short while ago had fascinated myself with ideas of having soothed him into a fine chanting by "bring-

ing father" to him — a burlesque! — when all he'd required was that
I hold the book safe from Reb's pressing the glass phial and breaking
it!

At the door I saw him. He had run out by way of the side, through
the small room off of the altar, and had come around to watch. Seeing
him I whispered, "Laib, Laib, where did you get it?"

He stepped just inside the door and shouted, "Leave Reb Maisha
alone! It was I! I hid it in the book!"

Yeersel's Daneel was first to reach us. "All right, where'd you get it?"

"From Varya!" he shouted with all his might as the others came
running.

"What Varya?" Hertz demanded.

"The one in Profim's!" he shouted back, suddenly angry.

"Profim's?" they shouted, but already knowing, their hearts sinking.
"What, Profim's?"

"Yes, the Varya in Profim's 'Heaven'!"

Had my brother shot a gun he could have produced no greater
silence; and in that silence he ran. None followed him. They went back
to Reb Maisha and began to rain deeper criticisms upon him.

Wondering what my father might have done, I ran out hopelessly.
Why should any heavenly advice reach me when I had already failed?
Ay, my brother had been only too well confirmed long before his
confirmation as a man of Israel!

This was my potpourri as I went out again and saw Berel-the-Ox,
alone, nothing remarkable, he always separating himself from clamors.

"Where did Laib go?"

"To the stream."

"What am I going to do?"

"Go to him. He'll feel better." He shook his head. "It's bad in there.
Laib should have something better to remember."

He wasn't at the stream and he wasn't at a couple of gullies nor at
the place where we used to eat walnuts together. I went into the village
thinking he might be with Uncle Mottel in the room he kept. But
the old woman said, "He's not here, he's there."

Neither was he in the smithy. Therefore he must be, I thought, well . . . "there."

"Who shall I say you are?" the porter asked, answering my knock.

"I'm Mottel-the-smith's nephew, looking for him."

"Take my advice and don't come in," he said.

"I must. Go see."

He went back, the one we called Pig-Simple because of his idiotic streaks, Arkady Kluzanov, the middle-aged brother of the postman, Dimitri, and of Rodion, the Squire's coachman. He came back and rubbed his hands against the cleaning rags hanging from his belt. "Well, he's here, your uncle. But I've thought about it, you see, and I won't disturb him."

"Tell him I'm here and I'll give you a tip."

"When?"

"Tomorrow. I don't handle money on the Sabbath."

He went back again. I thought of Uncle Mottel who lived on their side of the village. We looked upon him as one who shat upon his own head and ours also. When Laib asked Reb Maisha why the landsmen called my uncle to a reading of the Law every New Year's even though he never set foot in the synagogue, I saw how Laib sought reasons to put himself closer to the atheist, and I began to wonder if Uncle Mottel's freethinking wasn't in the family. I knew little about my grandparents except that they had come from Vilna. My father's father had been killed in the Crimean War; his wife had remarried and gone South. Meanwhile my mother's parents whom I remembered hardly at all, Zelyeh and Fendel, had brought Father and Uncle to Golinsk where my parents married. Mother vaguely mentioned about Father coming from a line of Vilna cantors and later in America I thought Caruso resembled Uncle Mottel around the cheeks and mouth. Many times I wondered about "Grandmother being taken South"; she had married a second man to leave her children behind and I feared something wild in her had passed to Uncle Mottel, with Laib similarly infected.

Kluzanov came back looking puzzled. "He wasn't angry in the slightest, he says go straight up."

He led me down a dark hall smelling of cabbage, and showed me the stairs. The banister was broad and smooth. A cousin of the sweet smell of the perfume in the synagogue filled the air at the top of the stairs; a door was open there and I went to it. I heard my uncle shouting, "In here, Laib!"

They were sitting at a table in the center of the room, she in a dark wrapper and he in his drawers, drinking tea and playing cards as homey as you'd wish. "Who are you?" Varya said, a small plump woman, pale and sleepy.

"His brother."

"A guest," my uncle said, slapping a card down and taking the trick. "I thought you were Laib coming from the synagogue."

He seemed to lose interest in me, paying close attention to the game. Well, there I was; and this was sin. The room seemed bright and clean enough. A pale blue paper covered the walls, not much of it ripped and streaky. The bed looked well slept in, the linen quite white, with plenty of pillows. Before my eyes I had proof that sin was more than furtive grappling, that people did not meet and slink away; there was even something ordinary about it. They were playing cards; how assuring!

"Only trouble brings me here," I said and waited for my uncle to notice me again. "Close the door," Varya said. When I did not do it immediately she dropped her cards and half-rose, an anxious look on her face. "Play," my uncle ordered and she sat down again.

"What is the trouble?" Varya asked, throwing her cards down; a few dropped to the floor.

"He ran out of the synagogue."

"Good," my uncle grunted as he picked up the cards. "May he never go back."

"Then he's not here, Uncle?"

Varya rose to close the door and her wrapper opened. I saw her thick legs and barrel of a figure; not attractive yet with an exact appeal.

Trapped and wishing to save myself I twisted toward the door. She closed it, pushing me into the middle of the room near my uncle. "As long as you're here," he shrugged.

Up to then I had used Russian out of deference to the surroundings. Now I spoke burstingly in Yiddish about the scandal of the perfume. He scratched his ear with his thumb as he listened. "Your perfume," he said to her, amused. "It spilled in the synagogue."

"How foolish. I'll get him more."

"You'll never see him again," I warned, shouting in my fear. "You don't realize!"

"He'll be back," my uncle said. "He'd never leave the fiddle here."

"Hold your mouth, Mottel!"

"Let him know," he told Varya. "See her, Shim? She gives him lessons how to play fiddle. It's kept here, she gave him the perfume . . . but remember, it's only for you to know it, clear?"

"Is that correct, lady?"

"Yes," she told me. "And I don't like you."

"She's a liar, she'd like anybody," my uncle said, pushing himself up from the table. "Just tell anyone about Laib's fiddle and these two hands will make jelly out of you. He wants fiddle? Let him have it!"

"But if it's the truth why can't I say it? You don't know what they're doing to Reb Maisha, Uncle. They think it's something else!"

"Let them," he growled, and I saw he must be drunk. "The fiddle. Yes, that's the worst, you see! Now remember to keep quiet like a good brother!"

"But if Laib really didn't . . ." I had spoken in Russian when he went into it; now I fell back into Yiddish . . . "If he didn't do you-know-what with her, I've got to let everybody know!"

"To play!" he said with a snap I suddenly saw reason for. "Not for weddings, you understand, but to play! That's the worst! Clear?"

"No."

"It pulls you away," he muttered, his hands making circles in the air before coming down in two hard fists upon the table. "Of course you're not Laib, you don't wish anything but crap, you wouldn't think of going where there's a bit of air!"

"Of course he would," Varya said. "Anyone would!"

"Quiet, you," he said to her. "Shim . . . it's true the apple doesn't fall far from the tree. But the apple can roll far far away . . . all that's needed is to tip the world a bit downhill and then you'll see the apple roll! Clear?"

"It's crazy."

"Then be crazy yourself and say nothing about fiddles! Let him only understand how to begin to play! Then watch him roll down the hill!"

"I'll look for him again," I said, going to the door.

"Nothing about the fiddle," he warned.

"Be so good," Varya said as though she understood our Yiddish, "allow me to explain a few things."

"You said you didn't like me," I replied without hiding my contempt.

"I lied," she smiled, lying.

I ran into the hall. My uncle threw me a farewell warning. "Remember, Shim! Take care of your head!"

On the way out I stumbled into Pig-Simple. "That was quick," he said, holding my arm above the elbow. Pulling myself free I opened the door. "No tip for letting you in?" he complained. I ran ahead of his squealing curses toward the woods.

There was a gully we'd go to, Laib and I, when we were younger, where we'd have feasts of berries and walnuts poached from the Squire's fields on rainy days when no one was about. We'd sit in a rough shelter of boughs, cracking the nuts with stones and burying the shells when we were done, all pleasant and partnerish. I went there hoping to find him but mostly to puzzle out what I'd do. I felt weak and out of my depth, nothing like a father at all. Truthfully speaking, though I didn't admit it I found I hadn't exactly disliked my first glimpse of "Heaven." Within its walls one had no need for imaginings. How simple, one merely paid to commit a sin, a known matter to all parties of course including The One Above, Who after all must have had quite a department for forgiving this particular sin, there being so many sinners in that line. A comforting thought; the sin was no longer solitary, marking one apart; and I wondered how many of our own had been in "Heaven." Even if they had not, how serious could it be, actually, when it was well known that the body often behaved automatically? This shivered me into wanting Rochel more than ever. "Not like in there," I assured myself. "We shall be not like in there; but let it happen soon!"

Everything in the gully was entering its beautiful phase, the sun high and warming, the muds gone, the blossoms beginning. I noticed it and I didn't, sitting in my miserable wonder. Where and how my brother had got himself a fiddle one needed to look no further than my uncle, who certainly would break my head if I let the secret out.

Fear of my uncle made it easy to want to obey him. Still my brother had committed a sin more devious and transforming than lust of the flesh. He had sought and found fiddle-joys under the tutelage of an evil woman believing she was doing something fine (exactly a most dangerous influence). Through her and the music she taught him to play my brother had entered into an alliance with a part of the world which was our enemy. He would be pressed to cast aside his previous life entirely; as Uncle Mottel had said, he and Varya wanted to tip the world a bit to let him roll away from Golinsk. Even Nochim, considered not so much a fiddler as a scraper, was held to have become a running beggar at celebrations only out of fiddle-vanity when he might otherwise have been quite an earning dairyman; but this of Laib was worse, worse!

Other boys fell out of trees and got into fights; I was a sitter and a watcher at my father's side during the Saturday night meetings of the landsmen in the synagogue. Their tight grips on a topic, their pungent sallies, the concern for each other in every hot exchange seemed the strongest evidence of our indestructibility. Whether they decided wrongly or rightly lay beyond me and it did not matter. They were themselves. This super-rightness I took for wisdom.

What kept our stubbornness alive? While we wavered on the brinks our advisers fell in. When I was eight some Svutzkers proposed that we join them in running to America on forged passports. We said no, backwardly preferring the dangers we were used to; and on the ship a cholera took most of them. Once the Lekavitch rabbi begged us to give his son a chance; he was just out of the Minsker academy, the father wanted him near, he made various promises. We said no. The son went to Kletsk, married a German woman, shaved his beard, and became an expert in "purifying" the advanced ideas of Moses Mendelssohn with such ardor that the Chief Rabbi of Minsk voided his certificate; after that he plunged deeper into his "purifying" until he finally agreed completely with Moses Mendelssohn and broke his father's heart. We thanked The One Above for our sagacity. "Better Mendelssohn purified than us," said Reb Maisha.

Also — during my boyhood a famous pogrom befell Warsaw following Alexander II's assassination; it made Jews a good three hundred miles away start running to America by the hundreds and thousands. The left-backs of these families were kicked out of the villages into the city ghettos. But we had said no. All or none of us would travel to America; and so it remained until Berel with Yeersel made the crack which split everything, even our stubbornness, two days after Laib's confirmation.

Alone in the gully after escaping from "Heaven," it clanged in my head that Laib was for going away, for entering willingly into the enemy's world, following the call of their music, this feat of my uncle's overcoming our Golinsker cleanliness and joy, Laib the victim of my own lacks. Thus I would have to risk any punishment by Uncle Mottel and say to the landsmen, "Not for wanting the woman is my brother guilty, but for wanting their world; and I am more guilty than he for I protected him badly."

With this appetizer I made my way back to the huts to see if Laib had returned, if they were eating the confirmation dinner; moving toward a worse matter connected to that other fiddler, Nochim. It was well past eating time. The landsmen should have been at their Sabbath afternoon naps instead of standing in small groups outside of Nochim's. Because of the Sabbath they were not smoking, nor even talking; a foreboding.

My arrival was hardly noticed. It seemed proper not to ripple their silence. Something in their way of standing silently, something about Nochim's closed door made me ask Yakov, the nearest, "Well . . . what doom?"

"Nochim. Brought home to die."

Imitating his self-containment I said, "How?"

"He was in Pukop." Yakov was keeping his anger in, wetting his lips and looking at the ground. "Something there."

"I can't hear you."

"Something there," he repeated without lifting from his whisper. It made no strain to hear. "The Pukopper rabbi tried to steal a boy from the army . . . gypsies, bribes . . . they killed the boy, arrested the rabbi."

"But, Yakov . . . how did Nochim . . . ?"

"Not so loud," spoke Laib-Shmul over his shoulder. For him to advocate quiet was the best proof of a doom.

"You don't have to know everything," Yakov said, looking up and away.

I did not see Reb Maisha there and hurried to our hut, weighed now with the same numbness as the others. Hearing my steps Reb Maisha said, without looking at the door, "Laib?"

"No."

He sat at the table looking out of the window, his hands clasped before him in a prison of his own. How broken, Reb, inside his hardy shell; under two difficult knocks, first Laib and now Nochim; and how even the shell would break when he learned the worst, of Uncle Mottel and the fiddle and the loss of a Jewish soul.

I sat next to him. "Reb, dear . . . what passed with Nochim?"

"Don't be frightened . . . a brave and sharp briber, Rabbi Sussya-ben-Mordecai. But to rely on gypsies? . . . wrong, without sense."

"I heard — but how did Nochim get mixed in?"

"The Svutzkers say Nochim drove the boy to the gypsies for the rabbi . . . and the police, of course . . ." He did not finish his thought. "The Svutzkers found him in the road."

"The Svutzkers brought him?"

"In a wagon, just before."

"They rode on the Sabbath?"

"How better to hide they were Jews?"

"Yakov says he'll die."

"They found him yesterday and hid him in the woods until early."

"Will he die, Reb?"

"In God's hands." He looked at me for the first time. "Are you hungry?"

"No."

"Jewish boys mustn't be loose today. Find Laib."

"I tried."

"Go again."

Rochel's mother sat alone at the table set for the confirmation dinner; no sound in the warm noon but the fading hoinking of a pig and the shouts of children in the lane chasing it with stones. Bosha had taken off her ceremonial wig worn for the Sabbath; she held it in her lap.

"Where's Rochel, Bosha?"

"With the others, looking for Laib."

"I don't understand it."

"There's nothing to understand. He was shamed, he's hiding."

"I mean it's only May. Conscription is October. Why did they start bribing and running so early?"

"Pukopper wisdom," she said. "Hn, if the police themselves told Reb Sussya this was the best time to bribe, shouldn't he believe them? Ay, from such wisdom Nochim lies like a stone. And if a fool throws a stone into the water, can ten wise men take it out?"

"God will take it out, don't fear."

"From your mouth into His ears, only."

"I'll see where the others are. Maybe they've found him already."

I began to run the moment I stepped into the lane, toward the path to the stream, for no reason but to get away from the pall. Death and danger, danger and death again and I felt alone as when Yeersel brought Father and Mother frozen stiff from the Parsovs' gully and laid them on the bed. I ran faster but not away from other morbid thoughts; coming to the stream I took stones and threw them angrily into the water just to do something against this preposterous living. Then remembering in a flash the place where Laib might be, the place I had forgotten until that moment, I went far up the streamside away from the highroad.

The place of last hope was on the other side of the stream where in the summer it became something of a marsh low enough to push barrels across without getting wet higher than the knees. A gully on the other side was used for storing barrels of the Squire's contraband; wagons could reach it from a side road and the landsmen came and loaded according to the instructions of Profim's brother Vassily Buzarov, the Squire's steward. In the spring the water sat much higher; Zish had made two rafts, one on each bank hidden for emergencies. When I got there I saw a raft on the other side in plain view; someone must have crossed for there was no raft under the boughs on my side. The water might be over my head; I could not swim; how to get across?

I shouted, "Laib, Laib!" with all my might; no answer. But the stream had been crossed that day for the raft and paddle on the other side were wet. I took up shouting again and heard a distant cry, not any word, but a cry pitched high; a female sound. Realizing it might be Rochel for she had gone out after Laib I yelled her name again and again "Rochel, is it you?" — but all I got back was more wails.

"Trouble, trouble," I thought, "or is it some trapped animal?" I made up my mind to get across. It was a good fifty feet but it couldn't be over my head all the way. To go back to the highroad and come around on the side road would take an hour. "Walk in and keep walking," I told myself, "and if your head goes under it'll come up again. When the water's to your shoulders take a deep breath step by step." With this in mind I took off my boots, socks, trousers, shirt and Sabbath jacket and laid them on the shore. In my undershirt and long drawers I stepped in, shivering but striding swiftly, sinking in the muck to my neck but kicking my feet forward, making the other side without my head going under, but soaked from head to foot.

"Rochel!" I shouted. "Is it you?"

Again the frightened wail from high and far. My teeth were chattering. "Rochel, Laib!" I kept shouting until I reached the gully. But nothing, no one.

Home to the gloomy shanties leaning which-a-way on our piece of hill (winter clay falling out of the cracks and always new seams opening), I put on dry drawers and went to Yeersel's. Still no Laib; Daneel and his wife Lippe were there with Rochel, the table not yet touched, all the places neat, Yeersel and Bosha at Nochim's.

Lippe; a scary one. "Nochim lies in a dying fever, Shim. What are we standing here for? Wherever he is, Laib, let's find him. Since Nochim is back, they're saying—"

"I don't know where to look any more."

"Wait," said Lippe, "did anyone try the Parsovs?"

"Why there?" Daneel said.

"So let it be without a reason," Lippe said. "A person hides where he isn't expected."

"I'll see anyway, then."

"You'd better not, Shim!"

"Daneel's right," Lippe said. "Don't go to the Parsovs after all."

"But didn't you say—"

"Daneel is right."

"Right, wrong." I looked at Daneel suspiciously. "Very well, and what's the big secret?"

I walked out and he followed. We stood in the lane.

"That wife of mine . . . I told her to keep it to herself. I don't want Rochel to know because she'll tell Mama and you know Mama, she'll take a fit."

"All right. Well?"

"I went with Lippe to fetch Yushin for Nochim. You know, his cupping-glasses . . . and Yushin makes a speech to us on the way. 'It's already quite digested, this Pukop outrage,' he says to us, 'we've an entire report by the Pukop carriage-driver. You Jews again are up to your befouling,' he says. 'And we're quite vigilant here, you'll see! If only once any of you here,' and so on."

"Heating themselves up, is that it?"

"Stay away from the Parsovs. And the taverns."

"It's not good for Laib to be away."

"Keep my words to yourself."

"Where else?"

Daneel went in. Rochel put her head out of the door. "Shim, I'll go with you."

"No," said Lippe, appearing behind her, "we're needed at Nochim's. Come with me."

"Better," I said. "Until later, Rochel."

I started up the lane toward the synagogue. "Where are you going?" Rochel called. Could I answer? Very well, where indeed? According to Yushin they were looking to start something with us; better to avoid the village.

Where else to try again for Laib but in the woods? He might have seen me but let me go on. Perhaps the second time he would call out to me.

I sought him as one patting grass for the needle dropped there, first gently and then carelessly pounding, impatient to feel the needle pricking the finger. But no; a nightly day; no answers to my calls, no Laib, no sounds other than my own or here and there the birds, or the breeze flecking the leaves and changing the light, or different buzzings on and off.

With the turning of the afternoon the sun took a deeper slant; I came to a patch of pine stumps where the Squire had taken lumber the winter past. The stumps sat close together; boughs lay all about and pine needles covered the ground. In my long patrol I had circled fully around our huts to well below the village, perhaps a third of a mile on the Pukop side. Not far from home, then; good, time to rest; the stump I put my back against felt like a cushion; relieved of my weight, my feet on the ground before me tingled pleasantly. Hunger and the weariness which hides itself in the welcoming mind pushed me into closing my eyes, into a lonesomeness at once gloomy and protective, and I thought, "Let me wake up in my own bed, having dreamed this." I made dreamlets of my brother's face close to my parents' as they sat around our table, and of Rochel and myself at the streamside, a longer spell; in a dizzying mix of joy and boyish sadness, kissing her again and again, happily "not here and not there," in this way shutting my eyes against the immediate.

This for a minute or ten; until from behind a new sound thrusting, a rustle in the bushes and behind them a pleasant "Well, we're here" to a clinking of feet softly on small stones; then a "This for you, this for me," as at the beginning of a picnic.

Ah, he alone speaks. The peasant has led a girl into the woods, how shy she is yet, how kind his tone, how he anticipates. Against being accused with short words and hard blows of observing so intimate a celebration, I crawled toward an opposite thicket careful not to disturb the pine needles above the slightest, hearing him talking and eating.

Stooping through the thicket and making the curve to the back-path, I glanced through the trees and saw them in a bit of a grove. My first thought was that Arkady Kluzanov must not see and again idiotically harangue me for his tip; nor might he like to be witnessed sitting cross-legged on the ground with a pot in one hand and a gesturing wooden spoon in the other, meanwhile maintaining the most lively speechifying at a goat tethered before him, paying no attention and eating calmly from its own pot.

"Well, it can't be denied I'm an authority on disorderly persons," Arkady discoursed. "No, Dimitri's not really clever, only shrewd. Now there's where Profim has it over my brother; a villain out and out but he knows what he does. Yes, I might want to choke Profim some morning, which I'd never do to my brother but on the whole I hate Dimitri more. Wait, it follows! Simply, you see, when Profim looks in the mirror and sees his crooked face there is no argument; he blames himself and there is nothing to be done about him; the man sees himself yet doesn't bother! Well, such are always found among the murdered! But my brother Dimitri, he will view himself and curse his crooked face and as we say, blame the mirror. Ah, among civil servants this is called a bold thought, it comes of being a postman too long. Do you think I live in Golinsk? I only loiter here. Sleeping in the loft of Profim's is tedious and cold besides in winter; sometimes I pay for a bed in 'Heaven' all to myself. The women there, I am something French to them, 'spirituel.' False, false, false, and false! Why, even Father Semyon isn't immune, his housekeeper agrees and she's my sister Oulia. When he sees me he says, 'God loves you, Arkady, you are not like the rest.' And what do you think the girls say to the men in 'Heaven'? 'I love you, you are not like the rest,' only so they'll come back again!" — and so on, for some minutes.

I made to lift myself to my feet when a thick black snake with a shining skin swished past where I crouched; the yell I let out made the goat bleat and Kluzanov turned his head around.

"All safe down here," he called, friendly enough, with a wave of the spoon. Well, I'd stay on his good side awhile; going down to him I warned myself not to make a slip and call him Pig-Simple.

"Here, see. It's cider and hash we're sharing today. Have a taste."

"I'm not hungry."

"Well, sit anyway." He pointed to the ground. "The snake is gone. Or is it me, eh?"

"Yes," I said honestly, with a gulp.

"I'm a laugher today," he assured me. To say something I asked if it was his goat. "No, it's Father Semyon's. But we are friends."

"Yes, I see."

"We know, don't we, old fellow?" he nodded to the goat. "Our guest thinks I am defective. Well, it's not worth arguing. Yes, yes," he continued lightly. "All swimming in the same sea . . . each saving himself as he pleases. . . ."

"Kindly, Arkady . . . tonight I'll bring you your tip . . . but now I must go home. . . ."

"As you wish. Yes, I'm a defective," he admitted calmly. With a wide wave of the wooden spoon he demanded, "But did you ever meet up with a convulsionary?"

"No."

"They wander everywhere, boundless ones . . . seeking God in different places. And when believing they've found Him, how they lie down and convulse themselves!"

"Please, Arkady . . . I'll go now."

"You needn't hurry off," he assured me. "I'm not like the rest. Whether it's a Jew or not they'd kill doesn't matter, I shrug equally. Do you know I went into your church once?"

"Yes . . . but . . ."

"Wait, wait! I wanted to make sure I was not like the convulsionaries . . . if God is in the Jewish church, I thought, then surely He must be everywhere and it is nonsense to wander after Him. Yes. and He was there, so I cried happily . . . not wishing to be like the boundless ones." He grinned to himself. "Ah, my brother Dimitri . . . he beats me because he fears I will beat him someday. I see how he lives. . . ."

I took a chance and asked, "Do you know my brother, the fiddleboy?"

"The one who Varya . . . ?"

"Yes."

"Bad . . . very bad that a boy frequents that place."

"I've been looking for him, he's lost. Perhaps here about the woods."

"Oh, looking for your brother. It's simple, then." He got up and untethered the goat. "Come along. It is solved."

Holding his pots in one hand and the goat's rope in the other he led me to the path turning toward the Pukop side. "It won't be long," he said. He did not turn with the narrow path; I saw him pushing the balky goat through some low-hanging bushes.

"But I thought you were sure, where Laib is . . . ?"

"The goat is sure."

"What?"

"You don't believe me?"

"I am not used to these things," I managed to say.

Very well; the goat took it into his head to face the village. With each step I became more terrified; I would be seen; I would be accused of stealing Father Semyon's goat or be jollied with as Pig-Simple's companion. The goat stopped to look at a shanty some fifty yards from the village. "Ah, there it is," said Kluzanov, taking the rope. The goat bleated.

"I don't want to go there, it's Oblanski of the police."

"But that's where the goat is looking!"

"I'm afraid of Kuizma."

He pointed to the goat. "Well, now," Kluzanov said, "you mustn't offend."

The door closed, everything deserted. We went to the back and saw an old woman next to a blackened pot hanging over a fire by a braced hook. The sun, already quite low, had moved behind some clouds; everything lay dreary. The woman looked as worn as a skull, all bones and eyes, no teeth, hardly any lips, a shawl pulled tightly about her head.

"Who's here, Mama?" said Kluzanov easily.

With a patient whine, "You've made the dog bark."

She picked up a stick, waved it at the dog, then stirred the shirt boiling in the pot. "Go away."

"This boy has lost his brother."

"He isn't here."

"Kuizma must know where he is, then."

"Whose are you?" she asked.

"You wouldn't be acquainted," I said.

"The goat," the old woman screeched. The dog had tried to surprise the goat but was in a rage of barking against the alert horns nicking him away. The door opened. It was Kuizma, barefoot, his blouse open. "What's the disturbance here?"

"Be a good fellow, Kuizma," Kluzanov said, "say where his brother is."

"What kind of brother?"

"He had a new suit and shoes," I chattered quickly. "Laib; he was confirmed today."

"Jews, do I have to lose sleep over Jews?" he demanded of the old woman.

"You see how it is," she said to me.

"Well, I'm sorry," I said to Oblanski.

"If you knew what they tried in Pukop you'd be more than sorry! Don't come with Jew-yarns about 'lost brothers' who've run away disloyally! Things are happening, look out for the stick!"

He stepped back and gave us the door in our faces. The old woman murmured, "He was sleeping."

"That way Kuizma won't ever rise higher," Kluzanov said, "though he yearns for the courier's uniform with flaps so that he may legally and dutifully beat and beat with sticks, whips, spitzrutens . . . well, we'll go." He patted the goat's head. "Come, fellow, no more tricks."

The old woman pointed behind the house. "In the fields. Nothing hides itself there long." With a wave of her hand, all bones and hollows: "When Kuizma pulled apples from the trees he was not so fat. Then the uniform, boots, 'orders' . . . and his bowing a good-morning to his wife! Luck, boy."

"Don't fear," said Kluzanov, "he'll be found."

"Some other time," I said with a dig of my feet and flying away, knowing Arkady could not catch me for he had to hold the goat.

Between evening and last prayers all had the same to say. Nochim had passed; toward the end he had commanded the Burial Brotherhood to summon Varya to him. The talk went that the Brotherhood had hesitated yet had feared to disobey a dying wish. Tzippe-Sora had fetched the woman, for what purpose never revealed, Nochim sending all but Varya outside and the woman herself leaping quickly through the door and away; a puzzle.

Everyone told Maisha they regretted their attacks. "His putting the perfume in the prayer book wasn't your fault," Yeersel emphasized. "Berel-the-Ox said a right thing, Reb. The blame lies on us all. We pushed him to spend time with Mottel when we feared what the free-thinker might do if he found out where we would have buried him."

"I most of all," Maisha kept repeating, relieved.

"Come eat with us, then," Yeersel said.

"The matters one allows himself to ignore," Reb sighed, walking with us.

The meal was strange. Terribly hungry for not having eaten since before the confirmation, we hardly touched the good things on the table, only nibbling. "Well, we'll feast another time," Rochel said, putting the soup and chicken away. Once in New Roseville my son Aaron failed to arrive for a birthday dinner Rochel had cooked. We waited, hungry, until five o'clock, but everything lost its taste when it came to eating. I remember Rochel putting the food back into the pots. "Just the same as the day Nochim died and Laib's confirmation, Shim." Well, yes; during such times even food can't fill the space.

Usually on Saturday nights the elders went to the synagogue after supper to discourse on the sayings of the great Hasids and other ancient lores, with or without a little brandy. On this night, however, a vigil needed to be kept at Nochim's and respects paid so the meeting confined itself to particular points of the moment. The mentions of Varya tingled me and I had to restrain myself from telling all about Laib's fiddling, before seeing him first. The meeting decided that Zagzaigel should take over his father's dairy routes and that Sholem be put to work with Zish and made into a lumberman. The Parsovs would be cutting timber and Zish needed the help, after which the two might begin to make harness and whips; Yeersel volunteered the use of his new horse, and Hertz the grease when it came time for tanning; and among all enough would be scraped together to buy the first stock, at least, of raw fur. Laib too would have to settle into something; being Maisha's helper was no good; he would never become the beadle and to try to make a tailor of him was also thought bad, there being neither room for another nor such an inclination on his part. "Let's wait until he comes back," I said. "We'll sit down with him then."

"He won't do what's decided without him," Berel-the-Ox said. They all went to Nochim's. I found Rochel and walked with her toward the highroad. "It's night and he isn't here yet," she said.

"He might not come back at all."

Rochel said, "Shim, I know a place we forgot to look."

"No."

"The bath!"

"He wouldn't be there now."

"Let's see."

Our bath stood near the synagogue down from the huts, in a clearing near the path to the stream. I remember as a boy we' had only barrels to bathe in; and the women, for their periodic ceremonial baths, a wooden tub chinked with clay and kept in Tzippe-Sora's cattle-shed. One year the whole lot of us walked around holding poultices, suffering risings and great scalings all over our bodies because we bathed so poorly. We had had a bath which some years before had ended its long life in a blizzard, collapsing beyond repair; but "in the year of the poultices" Tzippe-Sora managed to get ten rubles together and buy several dozen of the Squire's smaller pine trees, her sons cutting and hauling them with our help; also some peasants worked with us in the splitting and building for a couple of kegs of Tzippe-Sora's homemade brandy. We laid a sloping floor and a corner section for the women's ceremonials, and later some benches, the outside cracks being chinked with good thick moss, and inside we used clay and whitewash; for years afterward we thought of it proudly as the "new" bath.

Well, of course no Laib. I jumped into the tub, felt all about in the dark while Rochel tapped the benches. I kept saying foolishly, "Don't worry, it's us, Laib — Shim and Rochel." Climbing up and sitting, Rochel next to me, I received unexpected thoughts, seeing Varya's thick legs out from under her wrapper again, and then Rochel's white thinner ones. I wanted to kiss her, take liberties, say anything. But she would become angry. This bound itself into the tightness of the whole day and I said, "Rochel, let me sit alone awhile."

She went out. All right; this was how one became alone. I alone, Laib alone somewhere if not worse than alone, with the woman, a double outcast; his feet on the wrong road, without father and mother and away even from my own childish will to be as a father to him. I began to cry in low flows out of pain that had pushed itself slowly and deeply in and would not go away.

How long after, perhaps a minute? Rochel's open hand patted my sleeve. For the first time she called me by my intimate name. "Don't, Shimmel."

"You shouldn't be here."

"I stood outside, and then — it's all right, Shimmel, to cry," she added.

"It does good?"

"Then . . ." she said without finishing; and we sat.

After a time I put a hand to her face, first on one cheek and then the other; against her chin; on her brow; over each eye; to her ears. It was too dark to see but this was the first time I saw what she was. Her eyes were wide, a real half of an O under the pupils. Her nose was strong and big, the lips with small ridges near the corners; but the thing was her hair, curled and not very neat, falling behind her ears but already a little pile staying on top, exactly the hair of one who thinks through feelings; altogether under my fingers, a face tired yet awake, a dignity there. The way she sat quietly, then taking my hand, that moment began a century; she thought only of me.

"I'm no good," I whispered. "My fault about Laib . . . Papa and Mama are dead, and Nochim . . . and I'll die and Laib and everybody. . . ."

She put her hands to me and laid my head to her neck. "Say, say anything," she whispered.

I cried; not as before but knowing she heard, knowing she knew why, and here I took my first step from childishness. This with her came from deeper than a kiss, a fuller opening of the heart letting something not out but in.

"Shim."

"What?"

"Could Nochim lay a curse on Varya? For making you-know-what with Laib?"

"She didn't. Perfume, yes. But that's all."

"Truly?"

"That's all."

"Who said?"

"My uncle. I was there."

"In there?"

"After synagogue. I saw them. She taught Laib to play fiddle there."

"Then it's *nothing,* thank God!"

"They're both away, Rochel. I think Uncle fixed it so. He wants Laib away from us."

"Where away?"

"The gentile world, one of their fiddlers . . . who knows?"

"You're sure?"

"We'll see. . . ."

"Shim, tell me if I'm wrong. If they went away in a two, Laib and Varya, around that place of hers they might be able to say for sure. Somebody . . . even to say where they went . . . then we might get him back, it's not too late."

"Perhaps . . . only . . ."

"Shim . . . let's try; if it's truly a two then they can't say a curse drove her away. Not so?"

"Yes, only . . . maybe my uncle's there. He'll fall upon me with two feet."

"Then let's tell Papa."

"Not him or anybody yet," I said quickly. "It'll only go worse. You know my uncle."

"All right, just you and me."

"You mustn't go near such a place, Rochel."

"I'll wait from far, then."

"It must be full in there. They'd be too busy to bother with me."

"Think what's going around! Let them only believe about a 'Jew-curse' and you know already what."

"The Squire, Buzarov . . ." Yes, from such bitter greens what a hate they could cook against us. It had to be done; she was right. "Well," I hesitated, "let me think what to say to them."

"On the way," she urged.

We went behind the last row of huts, not to be seen, waiting until we passed the village to cross the highroad and approach "Heaven" from the woods the rear way. From just inside the woods we fumbled down to even with the back of the house, seeing the lights and hearing the noises, a piano playing in bad snatches, laughing going up and down, then pieces of quiet. "I'll wait here," Rochel said, giving me a push.

"Let me think what to say at least, instead of going with potatoes in my mouth!"

"Ask where Varya went. Say there's a message you must give Laib, and hear the answer . . . make out you know Laib's with her and listen if they sound the same way . . . then say there's money coming to Varya and where should it be sent? . . . and that's all."

"Good," I said. "Yes, one of the other women there, that's who. . . ."

"Use respect, Shim . . . understood?"

"Such a head I never thought you had."

"Quickly, quickly . . . say more such, later."

Waiting for Arkady Kluzanov to open the back door, wondering what his face would look like when he saw me again (would he suppose I'd brought his "tip?" Another difficulty, not a penny in my pocket.), I knocked. "It's in God's hands," I whispered, knocking a second time. I waited minutes; still no one. A tumult of many in one room rose louder than my final knocks; I pushed the door open and went down the dark hallway to the noise, first going up some short steps.

The light improved, the banisters of dark wood shining polished in a golden splash from the room filled with the hiba-hiba of the debauch taking place on the ground floor. From behind the banisters I looked into the room strongly lit, two lamps on top of the piano and a third from the ceiling, a smallish room overcrowded with more peasants than women, lying on benches, slumped about in chairs, a woman's head on one chest, her rear on another, her feet in a third's face; with all the unmixed laughing and waving of hands and shaking of bellies and kicking of feet, everything pressed together, it was some dream peeped into, exactly someone else's dream. A loud senseless bravado; everything outside loosely forgotten as all lay in one curl around the room like parts of a big twisted snake of light and dark colors, the women's partly dressed white flesh, the men's brown bare feet and dark beards, a green wrapper, a blue around the ripped faded red carpet; all of them playing little by-games and watching the main thing, you see, the show. . . .

In the center of the room, Arkady Kluzanov stood crazily present behind his goat, the same one of the afternoon, pushing its front legs up around my brother Laib's shoulders. I'd last seen Laib in his brand-new confirmation suit but he was wearing old filthy pants too large for him and no shoes, with Arkady clucking and cooing drunkenly, "No, boy, no, boy," pushing the goat closer to my brother who backed away to be again shoved toward the goat by the bare foot of a peasant behind him.

"Don't ever hire a mistress," advised Kluzanov wildly. "No, boy, no, boy."

The goat stood willingly, the beard quite mature, an eagerness in its back haunches pushing it forward with Kluzanov behind it grunting, "Boy, boy," at Laib in the impatient manner of a teacher to a dullard. My brother parried with his knee, shouting, "No"; each time, the women giggled higher and the peasants made urging remarks to him out of their laughing. One put out her foot and hand toward Arkady as if to stop him; the peasant who had her around the middle pulled her back.

I saw nothing evil there, only the other side of the tedium of Golinsk, higher and noisier than the everyday thrash. But thrash-high or thrash-low, it was still with their heads under water; no relief, too much between them and the highest truths; whereas our side knew what not to expect from the world and so looked further. But the main thing; I had found Laib.

From above, a quick pattering of boots down the stairs. Uncle Mottel jumped into the room. With a shout in two jumps he yanked Laib away from the goat and pushed him toward the hallway, yelling, "Out of here!" Thus freed Laib flew past me into the hall, not seeing me, and I followed, hearing a harsh banging of some weight on the keys of the piano and then a wild mix of screams from the women. Passing through the back door I heard the screams continuing and my uncle shouting.

"Stop, it's me," I called to Laib. He headed to the woods; I heard his painful cries as he ran; the stones were hurting his feet; he was without his boots. Rochel heard and ran to him and between us we held him. I put my arms around him. "Good God be thanked!"

"Let me alone, get away."

"Where, where were you," Rochel breathed.

"My feet," he moaned.

"Come to the bathhouse and we'll wash them," Rochel urged.

"No, it must be full in there tonight, I don't want to see anybody!"

"You don't know what's happening," I said. "No one's there."

He kept repeating, "I'm not saying anything," all the way. He insisted on our going far behind the huts to the path to the stream instead of by the easy way, even though his feet were paining him. In the bathhouse we found rags to dip into the water-barrel for his feet. The darkness helped hide each other's fright and misery.

"Dear brother," I began as he sat with the rags to his feet.

He stopped me sharply. "Don't give me your smears!"

"I'm only glad to hear your voice again. I thought you'd done with Varya."

Rochel's voice touched sweetly. "Just that you're here, Laib. . . ."

"Varya. What?"

"You don't know," I said. "Nochim came home from Pukop to die and sent for her on his last bed."

"Ellya and Nasan heard from Vassily Buzarov, she's away," Rochel told him.

"But that's only why I came back. . . ."

"Vassily says she flew from Nochim's curse on her . . . about the perfume."

He said nothing; Rochel and I heard him sobbing.

I took his arm. "It's all right. I know about your fiddle. Looking for you earlier I spoke to her and Uncle. Only Rochel knows and she won't say anything either."

"That's only why," he sobbed. "I came for the fiddle. She has the key. Good-by fiddle, it lies in hell now. . . ."

"You'll get it," Rochel comforted. "Meanwhile, Laib . . . where were you?"

"Tonight, tonight I'll get it," he said, rising. I heard him groan as he put his weight back on his feet. "No," I pleaded, "you can't even walk. Wait a day, let it!"

"No." His mind was made up. "It's the end of me here. So she's gone . . . well, there are teachers in Minsk, better ones. Aunt Yiva's there, too, I'll stay with her. If Uncle's over there I'll still get the fiddle tonight. . . ."

"Let it be as you say," I begged dishonestly, "but with a day later. You're without clothes, your feet can't stand . . . give yourself a chance."

"Where are the clothes?" Rochel asked. "The new ones?"

"An accident," he said, beginning to speak quietly, hopelessly; in the darkness I did not notice Rochel stealing out. "From the synagogue I ran anywhere . . . down the back-path to the road. I'd go to Svutz, sell the new clothes in the market, go somewhere else, perhaps find musicians . . . and send to Uncle Mottel for my fiddle. Don't say anything," he flared, "I'm finished with Golinsk."

"Well?"

"A few miles down I met a wagon of Svutzkers but didn't know they were Jews . . . until I tried to sell them my clothes. They told me about Nochim. . . ."

"Also about the great trouble in Pukop . . . ? About Reb Sussya?"

"Also. So I lied them a story of how police were looking for me, something . . . anything to get to Svutz. They let me out near, not in . . . fearing for themselves. In the Svutzker market I handled with a peasant on my clothes . . . the bargain made, I went into an alley to take them off and put on his exchange-pants . . . he had a bundle . . . and when it came to paying he kicked my face and good-by. . . ."

"With your clothes!"

"What then, without? . . . with walking and a long ride I came back to get the fiddle and maybe a ruble from Uncle, I don't know. But listen," he said pointedly, "my face is to Minsk. I'll still go tonight."

"You can't go back to Profim's. Police must be there, I heard terrible screaming, maybe Uncle's arrested."

"Then I'll go this way! Hear me, I don't want to be more of a hurt . . . let them think anything of me! Be a good brother! Let's kiss good-by, until later. . . ."

"Like this? Think of Papa and Mama, let them rest in peace . . . !"

"They lived. So let me!"

I threw myself upon him. "Laib! If you're really going go like a person, not like a thief! Rest, explain . . . tell them how the perfume got in the book, tell your reasons, at least . . . after all let them know it was a clean thing!"

"A clean thing," he repeated bitterly. "Who would think it's clean? Not even you. Don't lie and make it worse!" I said nothing, thinking, "Let him talk himself out."

He spoke quietly again with a scorn that cut, an echo of our uncle. "Very clean . . . to go from the village, but not to a seminary, no . . . to a music institute, eating gentile food or roaming with musicians! A nightly day, clean! To you and the rest of them, the other thing they believe about me, that's of course cleaner to them completely!"

"Laib, wait. . . ."

"Cry till you drown, it won't help." He spoke in cold hard pounds, with a frozen mind. "I know what I want, I know what I am, I know what I'll do. Tie me, starve me, scream till your teeth fall out, but you won't overturn me. I'm not here any more!"

By this time Rochel came back with Laib-Shmul, Velvel, and Daneel. Velvel held the lamp high. They stood in the doorway, silently. When Laib saw them he muttered, "All right."

Laib-Shmul took his arm, not unkindly for him, saying, "Come to bed, tomorrow will be time," and Laib went with them without looking at me.

"Come, Shim."

I sat down. "I'm dizzy a bit, Rochel."

A little later, nearing our hut I noticed a candle in the synagogue and looked in at the door. Reb Maisha stood praying all by himself. His back was straight; his voice rose and fell quietly. I could see he was saving himself for a whole night of prayer. I wanted to go and join him but just stood listening awhile as he said the prayer for sustenance. "My help is from the Lord who made Heaven and earth. Cast thy burden upon the Lord and He shall sustain thee."

With an "Amen" to myself I left Rochel and went back to our hut, undressed, and crawled in with Laib who was already asleep.

The next morning Nochim's funeral took place and what happened is a separate story all by itself. We entertained two guests there, on horses, the Squire himself and Vassily Buzarov. Together they made terrifying threats. Because through Nochim we were "connected" to "the Pukop conspiracy," we were forbidden to leave our side even to stand in the market; besides which was announced an assembly for the next day when we would be told about a new decree of the government respecting our fates. But the worst of all for me was the Squire's announcement that Uncle Mottel had indeed set out after Varya, which neither I nor Laib believed for a moment.

Immediately after the funeral the landsmen entered the synagogue to hold a meeting. "Come," I said to Laib, "you're confirmed now and supposed to sit at the meeting."

"In a little while," he replied. He waved toward the departing ones. "Go along."

"What are you going to do?"

"Nothing."

"Then come," I insisted.

"You might as well know," Laib said. "If Uncle sends for me I'm going."

"Sends for you!"

"He's not coming back. Never. He must have taken the fiddle with him; I'm going to make sure."

With that he ran, of course, toward "Heaven." To stop him was useless. Until then he had spoken not a word to anyone. I was thankful at least for his having said he'd wait until he was sent for; it gave me time.

In such a frame I went to my parents' graves to say a prayer but couldn't. I talked to them, asking their forgiveness for my lacks. The day was a beautiful one, the air sweet with spring, sprouts of green covering their brown mounds; but in my unhappiness I saw only the mounds and the slanty weatherbeaten gravestones around me.

Then her voice, "Enough." I did not turn. Squatting beside me she said, "Come, Shimmel."

"I'm no good. . . ."

"You tried. They know."

"I tried to be like Papa to him, Rochel."

"Hear me, Shimmel. Who can take the place of a father?" She put her hand to the back of my hair. "You'll be a father to your own," she said stroking.

"My own, yes," I said absently. "Jumping over the sky, that's when."

"All right," she said, "so we'll jump over together."

We walked out of the cemetery arm in arm; and when we came to the huts we did not move our hands. Seeing us from down the lane the women pointed and said, "Look, look," among them, happily amused, understanding we were serious.

Very well, "serious." But other things went with wider seriousness. Bosha opposed us even after the letter from Yeersel came all the way from America.

But wait; let me gather myself here. I am done with everything as it happened minute by minute; time has become money to you and listening quite a paid profession; and besides, I have come exactly to my point.

Know first that Uncle Mottel never sent for Laib but almost a year after Laib's confirmation helped him to America. It was during those eleven months that our stubborn Golinsk gave way. Having withstood many past evils it fell under the fines imposed when the eight youngers ran from being conscripted on the day of the assembly, Berel-the-Ox having cried up a false plague and Yeersel guiding them through the woods to Minsk and illegally for America.

The consequences struck all with equal force. The village changed and we changed; led by Tzippe-Sora we made ourselves into a company of contrabanders, cooking and selling untaxed alcohol for the fines and escape-money until Tzippe-Sora was caught and jailed and the synagogue burned down by the peasants after they found illegal stocks hidden there. Then a vest-pocket encyclopedia of evils: Hertz's Baylah spoiled by the Squire; Laib-Shmul caught trying to steer five boys away, he being made the Squire's pigsticker and the boys drafted from their jail at the next call in October; arrested with Tzippe-Sora was my brother Laib, who despaired of Uncle Mottel ever returning and allowed himself to accept an offer of the Squire to become a protégé, living in his stone mansion, wearing a cadet's jacket and studying violin with a special master brought from Petersburg.

Other things; our side became an unofficial prison, all of us looking in the end to flee. I married Rochel in the autumn, on the last day of the Feast of Tabernacles; she quickly became pregnant; by miracles of tailoring and with great help I whisked her to her father in America.

I could mention more but it is not in me to tally evils. I don't believe in stimulating the listener into giving his conscience a sudden tap as though to his wallet among a crowd. Too much of this has been done by denouncers of evils "against which man stands helpless," evils "difficult to abolish at the present time," with the result that the unbreakable thing about this "man" they are always burying — his way of growing — is completely left out by these nearsighted heart-readers. It is a scandal; speaking broadly, one so lies at the mercy of these self-lifting spiritists that one may almost be pardoned for forgetting that man exists and grows, "*despite*."

Everything we did, Rochel and I, we did "at the wrong time." In the midst of death and climbing danger we fell in love. When life itself made a question mark, we married. I sent her to a strange country thinking I'd never see her again; and joining her there I committed "mistake after mistake," went into the "wrong" business, raised five children on little money and less time; as the saying went, we "didn't catch on."

Even our children thought this. I remember the many times my son Aaron used to send the car down to Rochel and me in New Roseville, New Jersey, about two o'clock of a Friday afternoon. We would ride to the big hotel in Lakewood where Aaron "thought it would be a good idea, just for a change." A room would be waiting for us and I would put on a pair of white pants and a blue coat and pray the Sabbath Eve in a special chapel of the hotel, and there would be a nine-course banquet with a string ensemble costing at least three-fifty a head which didn't taste any better than the sixty-cent dinner Rochel and I offered at our twelve-table restaurant on Front Street. And on Sabbath morning I would put on the English walking-suit Aaron had made for me at Schanz for my thirty-third anniversary and we would go strolling among the pines, father and son — "when do we have a chance to talk together, it's all right to miss one Sabbath in the shule" — and despite the high tone and seeing Aaron and Rhoda and the boys, and the car and chauffeur taking us home at nine o'clock — "come on, Pop, honest, stay over, sit down and take a hand, help me make expenses!" — I enjoyed the Sabbath better in Golinsk. There I had Rochel to look at and smile at me. Those times in Lakewood everything was a worry, whether her dress looked right, whether it was a mistake not to eat the lettuce she called "grass," whether her hands were still too red from the kitchen even after fifteen minutes of smearing them with lotion Rhoda sent to our room with one of the boys; and Rochel didn't play cards like other Lakewood elderlies. When they would pass her in the lobby and say, "Well, Mrs. Golinsky, taking it easy now with such a fine son," she would say stubbornly, "No, my husband and I keep a restaurant, my hands have to do something." Then she would worry; she "said a wrong thing"; people would gossip; "the rich Aaron Golinsky lets his mother get up five o'clock in the morning to make breakfast for truck drivers." Rochel would look the other way when Rhoda would begin with her, "For heaven's sake, Mama," and fuss over how Rochel "didn't have to work worse than a janitor" when she could be "a parlor lady" or at least "something easier, Mama; I shouldn't live to wake up tomorrow if I don't have big fights with Aaron the way you sit cleaning fifty chickens every Friday for the Sunday trade, it's a disgrace." Aaron would sometimes smoke two cigars trying to "open a little store like a department store" for us, where Rochel could "sit at the register like a manager, with bobbed hair." Rochel would beg Aaron, "Let me live, don't bury me in a drygoods and don't bob my hair." He would laugh and kiss her and it would be quiet until the next time. We were glad to go and come back; I always gave the chauffeur, Royal, a dollar tip.

Rochel refused to give up the restaurant exactly because she could have been a real "manager" no place else. On Passover and on the Feast of Lights, and sometimes in between, we would close the restaurant and pull down the shades. The tables would be put together and Aaron would come with Rhoda and the four boys, Pauline and Hannah with theirs, and Milton until he went to Palestine; and sometimes Laib and Gitel and theirs, and all the Kalmenitzkys from Rhoda's side, Ida and Lena and theirs, even Moey all the way from South Brooklyn; easily fifty people, often, the restaurant filled with our best fruits. They would go promising "not to wait so long until next time," but when they came it felt a bit like Golinsk again, like the synagogue on Sabbath where we walked the hardest path to the greatest joy, ignorant of the world being round or indeed of any history (being history ourselves), putting the world aside one day of the week, keeping our faith in something better known. Yes, exactly; seeing how our fruits had put the world aside to come back to us I would say to myself secretly, "Aaron comes back, too. He, also, wants something better."

Who was I to criticize? Other tailors had become manufacturers, other restaurant-keepers had built big hotels but all I had done was "run away from chances." The first year in America I could have become partners with Zalman Tekulsky in Broome Street; he would have taken me in for a hundred dollars and I had it; but after I hurt my eye I was afraid I'd go blind. I stopped being a tailor entirely, putting my hundred dollars into a chicken-farm Utopia in Jersey where one had to choke the eggs out of the chickens no matter how wonderful the farm life was according to the platform lecture they gave me in the Baron de Hirsch farm school. We had to eat so we opened a restaurant, I in the front and Rochel in the kitchen; and so we lived most of a good twenty-five years; in all that time nobody had to tell me I "ran away from chances." In 1910 Aaron brought me some kind of a Rubenstein; he had half a loft in Canal Street and a dozen machines. "Why not?" Aaron said. "I'll lend you fifteen hundred, Rubenstein will sell and you'll be in charge of the shop. You won't have to sew a stitch, just watch the operators." I tried it for a season. We leased the restaurant and took a flat, the two of us, in Jackson Place, Brooklyn.

It was a year for velvets but Rubenstein bought velours and with everybody else busy we played pinochle with the operators. Rubenstein didn't like the price I got for the velours and we had fights; I criticized him for buying them in the first place; then he went to the bank and took money on Aaron's signature to buy velvets but by then everybody else was closing out and buying goods for the spring. Aaron said, "Well, it's only one season. Wait, you'll see." Meanwhile Rubenstein became disgusted with his brother-in-law and fired him just at the time we needed a quick shipment on two hundred coats for Lipitz in Alabama. Rubenstein said to me, "Sit down now at the machine." Truthfully speaking, I had never worked a machine and had no wish to learn; my eye was weak again, irritated by the dust of the city. So I said to Rubenstein, "My son's money you're entitled to but my eye I'll keep."

"Who needs you to stand around like a manager?" he roared at me. That night I came home and said to Rochel, "It's good we only leased. We're going back to New Roseville." When I told Aaron he said, "Let me talk to Rubenstein," and from the way he spoke when he brought the dissolvement papers I could see he took Rubenstein's part. "Agh," he said, smiling at me quite gently, "what do ya expect? America!" After that Rhoda began her campaigns to take Rochel "out of the kitchen" but Aaron made no mention of any business where I would be the main thing. It was always "so Mama should take it easy," and so on, with "Papa is no businessman" under everything; which was true. This meant little against the feeling that I had reared Aaron into making this mistake. Hadn't Aaron since the age of fourteen conducted business on the Sabbath? When times were hard and there wasn't enough in the restaurant for ourselves much less for customers and I rode a rented wagon peddling anything I could get on consignment, hadn't Aaron gone out on his own while I took my Sabbath nap? Rochel had said, "Shim, you've got to stop this," but I had not; there were piles of "I had nots" until one couldn't talk to Aaron any more, coming home with his cigars and twenty-dollar gold pieces and order books filled. "You're a baby of sixteen, do you have to smoke cigars?" Rochel begged him.

"Only for business, Mama, so I'll look older," he soothed her. "I gotta smoke 'em home to get used to 'em."

It used to puzzle me that I who had never stopped cherishing my father, who had striven to be father to Laib before I had my own children, should have been of so little inspiration to Aaron.

Rochel used to sigh, "Ay, ay, America!" "Why America?" I would ask. "If the boat stopped in Africa instead of America, you'd be saying, 'Ay, Africa!' No, it's me, Rochel, my fault; everything."

"You blame yourself too much, Shim."

"I made mistakes," I said, secretly agreeing with her. "I shouldn't have been so afraid for my eye; I shouldn't have been afraid to give Aaron a few hard slaps across his behind once in a while . . . there's such a thing as too easygoing."

"To me you're the best, Shim."

"Ah, well," I said, kissing her hand, "you were always easy to fool."

Do I illuminate or do I obscure myself? Failures often take themselves wrong; even from my vantage point it's a ticklish stitch. With the frivolous failures, the chance-takers, the trumpers, the squeezers, it's something else; these blind themselves purposely so they won't see themselves changing into smaller and smaller coin the more they change their dollars into the higher and higher thousands.

Very well, it's sour. But just for the joke of it, when you are alone and undisturbed, say in your room in the middle of the night, think if failure could ever be success; and when, and how.

Don't be afraid. It won't be "the wrong time." Such a time never existed. What grows, despite the evils in which it finds itself enshrined, grows often with the highest springs.

Ask the failure the secret of success; the queerest thing, exactly.

7. *Laib-Shmul*
(1840–1899)

IT WAS HIS INTENTION, SAID RABBI BUNAM, TO WRITE A TREATISE UNDER THE title, "Man." It was to require only a quarter of a page and the whole meaning of man was to be included; but after consideration the rabbi changed his decision, lest his treatise lead to false commentaries.

Thus I contain myself.

8. *Tzippe-Sora*
(1827–1898)

WHEN BRAINS WERE MORE IMPORTANT THAN BEARDS, THEY LISTENED TO me; when Yeersel took eight and ran to America. Some said nothing, some said it was time to run all together. I said let fools from other towns run and be killed, we'd stay in Golinsk and bribe them again to let us cook illegal alcohol and pay the official fine of twenty-four hundred rubles. It took time for them to swallow but it ended as always, they waiting to be told what to do.

The next day I went into my dirty haggles with Rezatskin, Selenkov, and Vassily Buzarov, thirty rubles a month to be advanced us to buy grain for the distilling, we to find the places to sell, they to keep the accounts in their own book and with their own official arithmetic, and every day Buzarov to come and take away the money collected — the usual situation, we to cheat them half as much as they were cheating us or we'd be paying them until we died. But nothing could be started until the soldiers got out of our huts and I told Vassily to give the Squire a prod, for a word from him to the Colonel Commander would make the soldiers disappear. "The Squire is not smiling lately," he said. "Petersburg turned out badly this time, heavy gaming losses. He sits behind a closed door, Tzip, but I'll take a chance anyway."

Back an hour later with a grunt, "Ekh, he's disgusted, irritated. He's lost that Varya of his, her traits amused him. I'll let you know what," he said leaning down to me with his tongue out, "I think if that pretty one of yours around here, Baylah, should go herself and ask the Squire to remove the soldiers, nicely, intimately — ?"

Remembering Nochim's Lenka I advised him to think of another way because Baylah was with child so he praised her face and gave me a sly push on his way out. Enough, I ran to the girl and told her not to talk with Vassily, not a word. Then we put her to bed, her mother and I, swelling her falsely and shrewdly with pillows since the crow would certainly come to circle around her. He took looks and said, "A shame."

That week a new piggishness entered our lanes, the soldiers remaining, no work anywhere, nor for us nor for them, the hole in the zero growing bigger and bigger. The silences in the huts were worse than the loudest wailings and Baylah in her bed heard both and said nothing and thought only of her Nasan gone and her misery piling; and one morning where is Baylah? Not in her bed. The second morning and the third, the same; and on the fourth we woke to see the soldiers marching off. I ran to Vassily with her father and brother. "Why does the sun set?" he asked in a lazy tease. "Because it is time. Sh, when the bear sleeps don't sing him songs."

"He got Baylah for the Squire!" yelled Hertz in Yiddish. What else could I do but push him out, away from Vassily who was saying, "Much to do, cry later! Back to your side, the minutes fly, promises are to be kept! Fines must be paid!"

And Baylah our second Lenka; not seen again, or why.

We worked after that in a deep gully, Laib-Shmul and Hertz mixing the mash, Zisha cooking, Asher tending the horse, boys chopping wood, everybody doing something, and whoever could stand in the market with something tried to make a penny, and the women and children steady in the fields. We were to make six barrels a week, each barrel twenty gallons, the price as near to four a barrel as we could get, and that's the wheel, as we said, that we danced upon — "not falling off and not staying on." The fullest burden of the selling fell on my daughter Dvoora and myself (hers a good nature under a face too hairy, held herself haughty, remained without a man and taught herself to read and write, making herself delicate and lonesome), and together we rode the wagon through the worst side-roads looking for buyers, sometimes leaving a barrel or even a jug and taking anything broken but fixable to sell in the market.

So it went into June and a new style came to our lanes, one warned the other to speak quietly for somebody was always trying to get a little sleep at any hour. I became the leader, the daily decider, an honor impossible to like.

One night Laib came with news, his Uncle Mottel had been heard from by a letter he sent to one of his "Heaven" ladies, telling the boy his fiddle was in the cellar there. Great news, but not for me; then he said, "I'll get my fiddle, Tzippe-Sora, and go on the wagon with you when you look for barrel-business, and I'll help sell many barrels with my fiddling, Tzippe-Sora, and once it's seen how my fiddle has a use then the landsmen won't mind my playing it openly in my own hut!"

Could it harm? I allowed it and once rode with him far, nearer to Pukop than Golinsk, to a large place, no run-down vodka station but a country stock exchange, a tavern where banditries are housed and stolen goods haggled over. The man yelled us out but the woman heard us say we were from Golinsk, and spoke of "Onion Nose," the nickname of Nochim. Thus reminded, the man became angry and shook me with his big hand, demanding why I had come so far "to find out something." Wishing to avoid any Nochim connection I spoke of Laib as a talent, of how I was trying to get him money for eyeglasses so he could learn to read music. He told the boy, "See this hand, Squinty? I've broken many a bone with it! Say why you're here — the truth!"

"I've seen stronger hands on better people," said the brazen Laib. "I have an uncle who could break you in one spit."

"Fine, bring your uncle."

"He's gone. But if you ever meet Mottel-the-smith of Golinsk, try him!"

With the mention of Mottel, a new sun in the sky! The man said, "Mottel's your uncle? Here perhaps a month ago I saw him take three and then three more, a Jew to watch!" So, in a quick joviality, glasses set before us, a new customer — Yegor described with a sportsman's passion every move of Mottel's when he piled up six; and when alcohol was mentioned he fell easily into a bargain, settling for a barrel at three and a half and the same steadily all through the summer, ten barrels a month. And always when we'd go away after delivering he said, "Bring the boy again, I liked his uncle."

Ten barrels a month and quick pay; and I imagined I was really dragging two skins from one bear. He even insulted his landlord to me, how Vlad Ryba piled the rent so high ever since Yegor had sold crucial strips of land to him. This and more; too friendly for my taste; and when I stopped imagining and thought a little, I feared he'd turn, as he did.

Yeersel's first letter arrived in July, sent to Dvoora by a Minsk relay; the news that four of the eight had gone all the way with him, no names mentioned, with a word that Yeersel wanted his daughter to marry her choice, meaning Shim, and think of a new life "afar." This caused a two-week excitement and wonder. Which four well and safe? But a clear hint that all of us should run away to America. Talk of running rose among the youngers but the elders feared it, I also. My heart knocked with the doom of my sons Yussel and Yakov surely lost now and my Mayer long dead in the Crimea, food from my own mouth I had sent him, and a blanket and pillow against his army misery. I spoke against running and half never arriving and the other half to be among strange enemies. I said, "Whoever gave us teeth will give us what to eat. No bargains in America, the whole world is one town."

Bosha opposed any wedding of Rochel and Shim, giving them the same steady answer, "Too soon yet. It's easy for Yeersel to say because he doesn't see what is here. Love is sweet but tastes better with bread, and do you want children like our others are?" And every day we heard new gossip in the market. First, that Baylah was traveling with some captain, then that she was in Petersburg, sent by the Squire to have her stomach flattened, with her consent, studying also how to be a fine lady; and then it was further said that if we wanted to find Baylah we should look in the forest for a mound and she'd be under it. Every day something else — once Hertz found Laib-Shmul's chicken-knife in his son Avrum's shirt. Avrum screamed he would kill with it in vengeance over Baylah. I gave Laib-Shmul a few words for letting the knife into the boy's hands, but he said, "I gave it to him," and I told the others to watch Laib-Shmul carefully.

Watch today, watch tomorrow — on the fast day for the destruction of the Temple in the Jerusalem days, we had a nearer cause to mourn. The crazy partnership between Avrum and Laib-Shmul broke into something larger, Yesse, Frayim, Sholem, and Zagzaigel joining them one dawn after the gully-work; and they ran away without a plan, some even without boots. In two days Laib-Shmul was back, the others caught in the woods by soldiers on maneuvers, behind bushes, seeing and falling upon them. Selenkov told me it was a lucky thing they weren't conscripts. They would be kept in jail, merely, until they were of army age. The Squire made Laib-Shmul his new pigsticker, a joke; and soon we saw him on one of the Squire's wagons with a row of gutted pigs hanging behind him. It was Asher who shouted, "Don't stay there and kill pigs, better death!"

"Pray for me," Laib-Shmul called as his wagon passed. Poor fellow, my son-in-law, a fool with noble motives; when he killed a chicken it always hopped, and when he wound a clock it always stopped. After this everything worsened, five men less for the gully-work then, and for the fields and market, and the rest grew weaker with a soon October and a new conscription. Quarrels began. Zisha said he didn't dare wish for health, only for potatoes. When Maisha said The One Above would provide, Bosha answered, "If only He'd provide until He provides!" Fathers and mothers blamed each other, and other fathers and mothers for their sons' betrayal, and tempers rose all too easily even though Maisha kept begging us to be less proud. Our afflictions came from love, he said, and could not therefore be in vain. They were meant only to arouse our penitence, he tried to tell us. Old Zelyeh gave him the answer, "I am penitent enough to die. Only not here and now." Then a newborn choked to death and a lad of Vremya and Hatzkel's could not stand the dysentery, also a girl of Daneel and Lippe's, and on the second day of our New Year Zelyeh fell of a stroke in the synagogue, receiving half his wish — this and more which you can understand without my saying became the harvest of our months of straining. Then less quarrels, more silences until I feared a second senseless running and I said the same thing all the time, "Hold. The more we pick and choose, the more we'll lose. Remember the ten barrels a month we're selling Yegor, and remember we're paying the fines well enough for them to leave us alone. Hold, hold!"

But Yeersel's second letter pushed them even stronger for running. "Why not?" they asked themselves. "Dying's dying anywhere."

"What God controls is often vague," I pleaded, "the rest a blind tapping of walls! Time for other tries when there's something in our pockets that buys!" But I did not hope to tie them down with proverbs.

Into this pot was thrown a wedding. One morning Bosha called me inside. Her lamp was still burning and Shim and Rochel were there, both hot with the mother to let them marry. "Help me," Bosha said. "Show them the tears they wish to buy!"

Shim said, "What's left here, Tzippe-Sora? I'm sixteen and it's nearly October. They'll take me for a recruit! They'll say I'm twenty-one after a single look at me, haven't they done it before?"

"Yes, and Papa said yes," Rochel cried.

"Before you take Papa's advice why don't you look the devil in the face?" Bosha demanded. "What if Shim never gets to America and you're a widow?"

"As God wants it, Mama, let it be!"

They went outside together and I saw how it was. They were not playing love. "They're fated," I said to Bosha.

"They're children."

"No more. Bosha, let them marry and he won't run so quickly. He won't go without her and won't let her go with him. It's a deep hot love there, clear?" With this and more I trussed her down into saying, "Ay, how hard it is to see, sometimes, how the best horse needs a whip, the wisest mother some advice, and the purest daughter a man. Let there be a wedding!"

Ay, the wedding, hiba-hiba! Nine o'clock at night, the synagogue warm and crowded; all of us tried for a joyous moment. Reb Maisha stood under the canopy with them and gave the seven benedictions, and the candles went down softly. I remembered my own husband Bencha of long ago, how he hummed hymns while I wept for nothing to eat in the house, and also how we would pick berries together, he sly with his hands and so loving a man, sometimes making me sick and sometimes well again. Ay, Shim and Rochel married! Everyone shouted "Lucky day" and danced while Laib played his fiddle, and we sang and clapped hands and drank from a special barrel brought up from the gully, and all of us hoped Shim and Rochel would remain as they were for a while.

Mothers began carrying sleeping children home, the dancing slowed, and some of the men kept close to the barrel. The wedding could have been said to be over when they came from the other side into the synagogue, a dozen peasants lurching in and Vassily Buzarov among them calling out, "We heard the noise, are we guests?" The peasants went straight to the barrel, not for the first time that night. I asked Vassily, "Why this?" and he shrugged, "Give them a drink and they'll go. I tried to hold them."

Like the devil they went, our men sobering as they to the opposite. Hertz and Zisha took the bride and groom out, against any wedding-night tricks; meanwhile our guests grew curious and climbed to the altar to open the Ark and examine the Scrolls, dropping them. One put his head into the little room we had off to a side, and that caused the woe. With a tight finger he showed his brothers what a big prize he had found for them, two whole full barrels of our homemade alcohol; after that, what else but to open them and swill?

How did it happen the barrels were there? Laib told me, whispering, "Yesterday when you were sleeping Vassily came and said he needed two barrels and I went to the gully with him and put them in his wagon. He said he would take them home but then remembered he had to be with the Squire. He told me to leave the barrels in a safe place for an hour. Safe? Where is safe?"

"You put them in here, in the synagogue?"

"Ay. . . ."

And Buzarov not back for them? It smelled of a mesh to me, a two and two in my head. "Vassily," I said, "what can make them go now?"

"Give them a present, the two barrels. Go out, all of you, leave me with them. It's all right."

Done; and in our huts we waited, but not long. First there was a great laughing and yelling, they still holding to their drinking. We watched from our windows until we saw, to the last, a true nightly day — torches, the wood flaming, an explosion, and the synagogue flaming; the Scrolls unsaved and everything a smoke.

Laib was held to be the villain. All fell upon him, even Maisha, for using the synagogue as a store for contraband. They called him a second Mottel, a belittler, a defiler, and held morning prayers in a clearing. We had to go to Yegor's that day to collect what he owed, and Laib wore a thick coat, and I saw a tight bundle next to his fiddle.

"Where are you going, Laib?"

"Away."

"Why?"

"It was my fault, but no sin. The Evil Eye's on me, that's all."

"I didn't know you and the Evil Eye were such friends, Laib."

"Never mind jokes. . . ."

"I'm serious, Laib. Just for the sake of the Evil Eye you're leaving your brother to roam the enemy's land, helping them to kill you?"

I stopped the horse and kissed him. "Forgive them, Laib. They called you names only from too much pain. Imitate your gentle father, may he rest, and think of how the next one might grieve."

"Papa never imitated anyone," he muttered, "and neither will I."

But this was said with his fire going down and had I ever gotten back to Golinsk he would have been with me. In Yegor's tavern something waited.

It was a different Yegor, the real one. "He's here," he whispered, "behind me in the corner, Tzip. The one with the cheeks, a new tax man. He's been waiting two days."

"Your papers," he asked, coming to me. "Your permit to sell."

Laib waited outside on the wagon and I tried what should have worked. "I have my papers, sir, but they're home. Let me drive by tomorrow and you'll see such papers, sir! You'll count, may I say, to an interesting number!"

Quite with respect he seemed not to hear my offer. He said, "This man has confessed he bought from you without paying for tax stamps. Admit you sold, admit!"

I wailed to Yegor, "What have I to admit? Confess for yourself, not for me."

Well, words; but I saw I was sold and I let the tax man lead me out. He examined the wagon and the horse, hopped up next to the frozen-eyed Laib; and so I fell into the correctest hands.

In the Pukop jail they kept me separated from Laib; what they did with him I don't know. They brought me in time to a judge with the beard of Moses. He asked if I was guilty and I said yes, it was my own doing entirely, the boy was innocent and the landsmen did not know what I had done. Once given his pass, he played the light-bearer with me. "Speak anything, woman. It's your right."

"Excellence," I said, "I have no bad word for anyone, especially the Golinsk officials."

"Strange you speak so highly of them, woman. They say you're the coldest shrew of a bandit."

"Then, Excellence, maybe we're all mistaken."

"Ah, we have a wit here," he laughed. "I ought to put you into some pockets around here to lighten the legal tedium!"

"If so," I smiled, "they'd have more law in their pockets, perhaps, than in their heads."

Again my fate-maker laughed. "How so shining a wit, to have fallen so low!"

"Yes, Excellence, it's a pity. Or is the world itself too high? Yes, difficult sometimes to push the world away with the hands. Often a knife is needed."

His brow became cold and smooth and his face returned to itself.

Sternly, then, he said between times of lip-smacking, "Those who assign their crimes to bad luck forfeit mercy. You have equaled yourself with any animal. You wanted money, I see, for a serious and decent motive, and *that* was how you hoped to disguise your crime? Did you not attempt to corrupt your betters? Yourself certainly — but I ask, what of your betters who must nourish our motherland?"

This and more; the end being seven years for liquor traffic, seven years for attempted bribery; seven years for both, together; a little present from my polite barbarian of a judge.

It was neither good nor bad in that Nikolayev Prison. No markets or Squires, and some politicals taught me reading and writing a bit. In prison one slips away from one's self, losing even one's own stink; and what's outside is soon lost without caring.

Letters from Dvoora stopped after the third year. In the beginning were mentions of runnings in twos and threes (whether good or bad left unknown or unsaid, whether the children taken or hidden, where left or retrieved, not written), but that Maisha died, and Asher and Naftoli-Dovid; and in '88 the stricken Squire heaved up the cemetery for oats. And after '89, no more from Golinsk.

All my joints stiffened in Nikolayev. I turned so like rock that I could not hold the crutches after a year, and the last few I was never off the pallet. Then after the seventh year they let me go to be carried by a rabbi's friends to another pallet in Odessa's Moldavanka but I became too great a burden there and they carried me up the shore to Limon, on the Sea.

I sat on the sand begging pennies to buy the medicine-mud in that resort of the sickly, among others crippled stiff but in booths and with nurses, carriages, and parasols. And I sat five years in that last market of mine, my crutches on each side of me, my hands out. I grew into a landmark there, each summer being recognized by the poorer. Often in the heated middays I lived in dreamlets of my children dead and away, always pleased my husband Bencha could not see my ending, always in the sun and always burnt by it but never warm.

The cleaner dirtied me. Theirs was a low guilt, my own much higher. See by what doubtful roads I returned to myself, let others blame the villains; I say there are higher blames. But since nothing ends or comes too late, and happy the generation wherein the clever listen to the fools, here, to the last, is my only song:

> When the wind of pigs thickens the air,
> And it stands even whether to run or stay,
> Neither fear the exodus
> Nor look to bribe the pigs away.
>
> If you'd run, make the bold step quickly,
> And if you'd stay, still your own place loving
> For all the foulness of it there,
> Stay. But clean the air.
>
> I only bribed,
> Held I was right too long,
> And became wrong.

9. *Laib*
(1874–1932)

I'M BACK, I DIDN'T FINISH:

Me, Uncle Mottel, the fiddle. The whole idea of chasing a music rolling down the Squire's hill one hot summer night, and the effects . . . Varya, her perfume in the synagogue, Nochim sending her away, Kluzanov's goat upon me; then the assembly, the conscriptions and the eight running with Yeersel, and Berel grabbed for Siberia. Also the soldiers, the end of Baylah, the synagogue burning, Tzippe-Sora folded away in the Nikolayev Prison.

All right; arrested at Yegor's tavern with Tzippe-Sora, held separate from her in the Pukop jail, brought back to Golinsk the next morning in the wagon of Vassily Buzarov, he explaining on the way, "We didn't want this trouble. While she did her crooked business in our own neighborhood, we could look the other way." But the local gentlemen had now put themselves on guard; all I would have to do, Vassily pointed out, was "explain how she alone pursued the crime"; in other words, hide the bribery of the incorruptibles. He pressed to no immediate answer, in Golinsk taking me to the village hall where Kuizma Oblanski gave me a wooden cell in the basement all to myself.

A few days passed, they trying to make me answer their way. When left alone I would play fiddle and try without success to think of reasons to do as they were requesting. Rezatskin brought the Squire to me, Konstantin Andreyevitch Konayev, who spoke quizzical threats as he walked back and forth in the little room, his boots shining from under his coat. Though not much taller than our Nochim was he carried himself with the set of a giant in his own mind. I feared he would not see my fiddle in the scanty light, and step on it. Seeing me pick it up he asked where I had got it.

"From my uncle."

"You play it?"

"Yes."

"Who taught you?"

"Varya."

He said he'd like "to hear a bit of Varya coming out," so I did a gypsy piece I remembered from that summer's Pukop Fair. "Rezatskin," the Squire said with charitable languor, "I've heard worse from better players. Isn't it our duty to pluck a flower out of the weeds, now and then?"

"This one doesn't pluck," the sour clerk replied.

"Here's a boy, a fiddler. Let's take him for tutoring instead of sending him back to Pukop for the trial. We'll notify the Pukop Council officially and I'll be dining with the Colonel Commander in any case. It is interesting!"

Rezatskin's eyes shone. "You are the one for the Tsar to keep on his right hand," said the clerk with relieved snivels.

"We'll take him up the hill tomorrow," he announced while buttoning his coat. "Yes, you will play, you will do nothing but play your fiddle. Yes, Petersburg, I'm coming."

I heard him telling Rezatskin as they went, "Hot water in the barrel for this boy — to the brim."

Very well; chosen for a hobby then, for amusement in an elevated manner. The Squire gave himself something interesting to boast of to his Petersburg intelligentsia; he had a protégé and he would show them that even in the distant nowhere of Golinsk there lived one who knew how to extend a hand to anything artistic, be it found even in a small Jew. So it started, between him and me, and how it finished I would not have believed even if I read it in Balzac. Yet, ridiculously, it *did* happen. Understand — since the moment he had married, the Squire's days had stretched themselves before his face like rubber bands which snapped back and stung. With every sunrise another soldier had been added to the army of his enemy. The longer he had waited for Arkip Apollonovitch to die, the longer the inheritance had eluded him; year after year he had felt merely older and further from his true era. Arkip Apollonovitch's prepared tomb had remained empty; and who knew when his own dozing paresis would wake for breakfast? Meanwhile there had been no entry into those comptroller's halls where crudities could not live, where the graceful possession of unlimited funds filled the air with wondrous chemical lifts causing love to fall like rain and muffling the sounds of all clocks. Hating the ruble-pinched infestments by which he was surrounded, the Squire had filled his days as one fills a swamp until he had seen in me the means of being accepted by the aristocrats of Petersburg. It had been a modest wish. He would have liked to have been remembered as "self-emancipated from provincialism," "a savior of genius plucked from offal," "our little patriotic Konayev" — on such terms hoping to be displayed to foreign ambassadors at official parties as an amusing but relevant example of true Slavic strivings — with perhaps, due to the connection with Arkip Apollonovitch, the luck of some expense-paying post thrown in. However, Arkip Apollonovitch had not yet sent him the crucial letter revealing a need of help for an epochal loan which would transform this original whim into the project to bring him all he yearned for, and while Arkip Apollonovitch still lived. Fie on Petersburg footmanisms! Little neglected Kolya from Golinsk would get him his loan, make him a Duke! What rewards! And the trump? Me; my fiddle was supposed to win the opera singer who held the top card, but more about this later.

After he left me alone in the basement-jail, I tried to cheer myself up by reminding myself that jail was jail, and that if I was to be his personal prisoner he might think to drop a little mercy on the other side of the road.

Deep October was hurrying to winter when I became a member of the Squire's menagerie. The time he occupied himself in Petersburg, about two weeks, I was put among the servants in a place over the stable. My main comrade was Vassily's fifteen-year-old son, Ossip. Short for his age and fat (the cook Lubenka his mother), Ossip cut wood, chased the cows home, and looked to make use of me in a way that showed something not bad in him. He said he would catch a bear cub during the winter and teach it tricks. He would take it to the city. I would go along and play the fiddle while the bear did tricks, including dancing. From Minsk we'd go further, even in the winters we'd have a gay city life, the bear dancing on skates in fashionable winter parks, and after that we would join some circus and become acquainted with life as it was not seen in Golinsk. "Well, fiddler . . . do you agree?"

"Catch the bear first."

Ossip wanted to jump in with the coachman's daughter. Her mother was Natalya, the chief maid, and her father was Rodion Kluzanov, Pig-Simple's brother. Sashenka happened to be a strong and well-contained young lady, alert for her fourteen years, and she found it easy to ignore his teasing. One day he said, "Be good about something and I will show you how you can see that other one of yours here, the pigsticker, fair?"

I replied eagerly, "What's fair?"

"When Sashenka comes to clean your alcove, go to a certain place and there he'll be."

"And if it's said to be my fault?"

"Your fault," he said disgustedly, pushing me to the floor with his ham of a hand; but at least I had found out that Laib-Shmul was somewhere about the manor.

After a few cold evenings they allowed me to sleep on the floor of the Kluzanov kitchen. I heard them cursing "the Madame" more than once, so I asked why the Squire's mistress was so hated. Sashenka explained, "Madame is not the wife, she is the governess to the two girls."

"But they're old enough to be married."

"Old enough and that's all."

Between Sashenka and Ossip I learned that Madame was the aristocrat of the servants. She lived in the main house and called the mistress

"Tatya." A girlhood chum, she had broken a hip before Tatiana Arkipovna's marriage to be left with a bad limp and a tiny income after her father died, remaining a lonely seamstress in Smolensk until Tatiana Arkipovna had remembered and rescued her. Given a proper home Madame "helped" prepare the daughters for married life. Sashenka dropped several jealous remarks about her. "She steals," said Sashenka with a spit, "all the time. Her room's full of little things, that's why she doesn't allow anyone in to clean. In case she's left out of the will."

I'll go a bit ahead and say that Leta and Lilli were no prizes, in fact innocent freaks around which Madame manipulated her self-advertised expertness in the husband-catching game. By her own testimony she had visited many fashionable spas with her sick father and had absorbed methods. Each summer she would plan lantern balls for the officers up for maneuvers, bitter failures resulting, and then spend the winter planning for the next summer. Madame's main activity in addition to providing the house with noises passing for female whimsies was her habit always of spraying the girls upon the slightest excuse with the perfume sprayer carried with her at all times. The house acquired some stale hints of a garden smell. Madame's bad hip made extra use of her arms necessary, some touch of grace and gaiety to her movements. She always prepared the girls' entrance into a room by making quick *stt-stts!* in the air with her sprayer, her arms moving upward in circles.

Early one morning a week after I arrived, Ossip told me I was wanted in the kitchen of the main house. A tall blond lady of about fifty was there and gave me a coat with a double row of buttons. "This was Leta's," she said. "Put it on." It was tight at the waist and snug in the shoulders, but warm.

Seeing she didn't limp as she went back into the house, I knew it was Tatiana Arkipovna. Three heads taller than the Squire, her face lay hardened in hollows, a strong and regular expression to it, full lips, eyes wide apart, a thoughtful nature.

"They're madly in love," Lubenka said in a satisfied tone, "he with himself and she with herself," bending to pick up wood for the stove and hurl it in. Natalya nodded, peeling apples into a pot. "Sashenka went the last winter in chills and sweats, and she had the coat upstairs all the time, twice a week saying, 'Natalya, remind me about Leta's coat, it will do for Sashenka.' A whole winter of 'Natalya, remind me.' A good warm coat! Ekh, her word was warm," and she spit into the apples.

Lubenka and Natalya insulted the girls without pleasure. They were ugly, stupid, dirty, backward, and helpless. "And let the country be invaded," Lubenka finished, "from the north, south, east, and west every year for fifty years and they'd still be virgins."

Having now a warm coat I yelled to Ossip against the bugs and stable filth and in favor of a bath. Vassily told Ossip to build a fire in the yard and fill a barrel with warm water, down in the barn. The luck went further. Once he started the fire he turned the job over to Laib-Shmul and went off somewhere. No longer rough, burly, gruff, he had gone to all straight lines, the quick-to-boil melted out of his eye, his face reduced like a bear's carried to some tropical place, his beard longer but thinner. Saddest of all he spoke with a mouth half opened, a stone in his ear, nothing but a mumble coming out, his head to a side. But I could speak to him in relaxing Yiddish.

"Laib-Shmul, anything heard about our side?"

"Only from the simpleton. Arkady. Comes begging sometimes from his brother here. It's true? He put you here to fiddle for him?"

"Better than jail, anyway. Anything of Shim, Laib-Shmul?"

"Ay, a done thing," he said in wonder. "God moving the hands of a simpleton to take a Jewish body to Minsk in a wagon, free. In Minsk they say they have places for ship-tickets."

"Shim? On the way to America?"

"Not Shim, Rochel . . ."

"Rochel running to Minsk?"

Laib-Shmul nodded, his tragedy to be where he was. "A week ago, or two."

"And otherwise?"

"Sickness, burials. Arkady says many things, who knows what to believe?" A momentary shine of the old Laib-Shmul came out. "I'll run anyway, in winter."

"Who can run in winter, Laib-Shmul!"

"Ask who can chase in winter?"

"Wolves."

Ossip returned with fresh pants and a blouse. Laib-Shmul rose from his squat and trotted off without another word.

Towards evening Vassily Buzarov took me across the yard into the main house. I followed him through the kitchen into a dark wide hall. "Up," he said, pointing to the grand staircase. "There's been a letter," he added in a puzzled way. He took a candle from a stand to one side of the massive balustrade and led me two flights up to the room bigger than any of our huts, the bed as high as my shoulder.

"He says you're to live here until he comes. The closet is in the hall."

The first thing was to go with my candle and look at the toilet-closet in the hall, a new thing. It had an enameled pot with a removable seat-rim and special handles to make it easy to carry out. Back in the room, going about from corner to corner with the candle, I saw the stove and how big houses were heated. It was a stubby one built into the wall between colored tiles on both sides for about five feet and to the ceiling, to hold the heat; also a wood-bin and a poker, and the stove had been fired. Next, opening the packages; it was a wardrobe that fitted almost perfectly, warm drawers, socks, boots, a cadet-type suit and a gray overcoat with an astrakhan collar and cap. I put the cap on and went to the mirror, quite seeing myself in the big sled, being carried back and forth on the Squire's hill, already a member importantly connected to the main reception hall running the length and half the width of the stone lodge with "his" sitting room, "her" sitting room, "the Gallery," and on the second floor various bedrooms and the suite for guests. My own room was on the third floor down the hall from the Squire's private study. I did not think whether this was good or bad, only that such was my location in the house I never dreamed I would enter. From the outside, with its rows of wide windows divided into small regular panes by wooden molding, and its columns of painted logs in groups of three at the corners and middle, clear up from the second floor to the roof, I received an impression of official and luxurious relaxations taking place in it. Later, seeing other truly imposing buildings, I could remind myself that the paint on the logs had been a tasteless reddish brown, and peeling, and that the house could have been at best a first-class boardinghouse, depending on the neighborhood. Yet it had its own touch, a stoned promenade going almost all the way around the sides.

Ossip and Sashenka took hours the next day to prepare the room next to mine. During the night I heard horses.

Ossip came with wood in the morning, nodding energetically. They had arrived. "You're to stay here till called for breakfast, it's to be downstairs."

I dressed myself in my new clothes with the braid on the jacket and heavy horn buttons. I resembled a young cadet. The boots threw a high shine and a genuine silk stripe ran up each trouser-leg.

After a long half hour Vassily opened the door. "Bring the fiddle," he said, dressed up himself in his official steward's coat of gray with a tail in the back. We went to "his" or the big sitting room next to "hers" or the one that measured about twenty-five by twenty.

It was empty. Vassily told me to wait and not touch anything. The heavy green velour portieres had been drawn before only one of the six French doors facing the promenade. I sat in a chair near the round table set for six, aware in the miserly light of various furniture in heavy woods that appeared never to have been moved since put in. Animals' heads hung from the walls, mats and fur skins patched the dark floor. The blue cloth of the breakfast table caught the sunless light from the promenade and threw it against the heavy dull pewter.

Without seeming to notice me — the Squire was saying something — they came in, the five of them, and took their seats at the table. In the middle of what he was talking about the Squire threw a pointing finger at the chair next to him, nodding to me the while, and I obeyed. Like the Squire, Dr. Ostrov and Stanya Parsov wore riding clothes; a smell of personal leather rose from them but my eyes rested first on Ernst Glueck's beardless face, the spectacles firm on his pennant of a nose, his head clean-shaven in the direct German style. The face of my tutor depended on the pointed chin, a face of energetic thinness and strict with the yearn of a fish's swimming searches after deep wants. It was smiling and nodding with careful grace, and there was something dishonest in its humility, a secret condescension.

Natalya and Sashenka in fresh aprons were serving from trays — eggs, fruit, honey, three kinds of bread. Dr. Ostrov was inclining his head toward Father Semyon making some discreet prayer before the meal; Stanya Parsov had meanwhile finished spreading his napkin over his scarf, which he did not wear every day. The priest done, Dr. Ostrov turned to the Squire. "You are jolly this morning, Kolya."

"Yes, my stomach is excellent now. Serve yourselves, gentlemen. Natalya, fill the boy's plate. Oh, before I forget, what do you suppose Prince Rogovin's nephew has been up to?"

This became another monologue on his Petersburg adventures, of no interest to anyone but himself but listened to none the less. Stanya Parsov desired primarily to settle the matter of the field he wanted to buy from the Squire and Father Semyon wanted to fix times for my religious instruction. As for Alexander Voyinevitch Ostrov, remote and boyish for his fifty-odd years, the tall bald bachelor concerned himself with studying his patient whose paresis always interested him following one of the Squire's "Petersburgs." Dr. Ostrov wore only the slightest mustache. He had come to Golinsk seventeen years before with no wish to practice his profession. Of a family with means, it was said, he read and wrote voraciously, mostly by night in the winter, departing every spring, no one ever found out where, to come back again in the autumn.

Since the Squire managed to eat for two without stopping his flow of words, breakfast was soon over. Passing cigars, the Squire suggested a walk on the promenade before "the principal business." Holding my fiddle I followed them through the French door. Outside a mist almost fell, everything stiffening for winter, settling into itself for the coming freezes. For a moment the Squire turned away from his party to make a brief vomit over the side, joining us and falling easily into stride in a casual maneuver showing this stomach-habit to be a regular, expected thing. I found myself beside Father Semyon. His robe had a gentle fall, the baby-curls of his thin brown beard almost touching his crucifix, the peacefulness in his eyes containing that ironed-out childishness so striking in old men. He had something of Reb Maisha in him, free as he was of any cause to probe his vacuum. The difference between the priest and the beadle lay merely in the source of each's certainty, Father Semyon's from the most faithful logic and Reb Maisha's from his mature grasp of infancy. Father Semyon was trying to turn the Squire's attention his way, saying, "It is interesting, Konstantin Andreyevitch, to see you hope to accomplish things with this boy's fiddling. You must not forget, meanwhile, the freeing of his soul."

"He is yours," the Squire replied with a wave of his cigar, and went back to whatever he was in the middle of.

"Well, Squire," said Stanya Parsov, who had anxiously been hoping to throw in a word, "when shall we sit down about the field?"

"Yes, I mean to, promptly next week."

Parsov said nothing for fear of its raising the price. He had come for nothing, spoke then of having to go down to the market, but the Squire urged him to say "for the concert, Stanya, open yourself to a finer thing." The middle-peasant reluctantly followed us into the main reception hall, annoyed no doubt by the carelessness of the dilapidated gentry, but still with the look of a patient diplomat. Very thin, and prim in his movements, Stanya knew how to employ his wishy-washy appearance in the driving of a bargain. In my experience one got from such adversaries only hernias, yet he had occasionally tried to be nice to my father.

In the main reception hall the Squire took a cavalry bugle which hung by a red cord on a nail near the great fireplace and put it to his lips, giving a blurry do-me-sol-do.

"Ah," said Glueck, the Squire explaining it was from the old army days. Ossip came running and was told to open a few French doors.

The hall revealed itself as an informal tomb of grandeurs, heavy with rugs and blue, green, and pink lounges in the French style but corrected to do away with fragility; and there was a love seat in imitation of a boat, with double prows, and a peacock-painted sled with a canopy transforming it into a kind of throne. The lamps lay about, willy-nilly, and I saw tapestries, busts, pedestals, and footrests everywhere. The main chandelier measured about five feet across; it was made of thousands of pieces of different colors of glass, gilt fringes hanging from it and from everything and everything in a condition for a bargain auction. In one of the corners, flanked by French doors and turned to an angle with the room there stood a hippopotamus of a spinet, solid mahogany, at least eight by five feet, on legs a foot wide and carved in designs of descending folds so that they seemed to have oozed down to the floor and cooled there like lava.

A new violin case lay atop the spinet. The Squire took my fiddle from me and threw it to the floor, purposely stepping on it as he led me to the spinet, calling "Sit" behind him while he opened the case and put the new fiddle into my hands. Glueck examined it, whistling approval and praising it as a real old-timer, with a careful laugh of professional pleasure when the Squire gave it to him to tune; which he did without referring to the piano, his display of perfect pitch wasted upon our patron. Glueck then handed me the fiddle and bow and I realized I was expected to play. I raised my eyes. The Squire sat about fifteen feet away from the breakfast guests with his arms folded, his cigar clamped between waiting teeth. About halfway into the great room I saw the women of the house, Tatiana Arkipovna large and clumsy on a pinkish love seat, her dress a smooth sandy color with lines of tassels at the hem, neck, and sleeves, a quick impression of festive harness on some old circus beast such as pulled gypsies' wagons; then Madame with the girls on a separate lounge, Madame between them, her small head nodding, her spectacles quite small too but extremely thick, her hair pulled flatly to one side, her dress full and of a dark color making her appear even smaller. Leta and Lilli were not large girls, yet they towered over Madame. I had merely a glimpse that way. Glueck had sat down at the piano and was giving it a couple of brushes, whispering, "Anything. I will follow."

I never liked playing solos. The one thing I hated about professional fiddle I had always to put up with, always pushed to solos. I played two numbers learned while going around taverns with Tzippe-Sora, first a fast Cossack strain changed in the self-teaching and then my favorite gypsy one, heavy and slow on the G to begin with, thick with schmaltz, going faster and faster moving over to the E; Glueck's piano grew louder and louder behind me and I worried that he was purposely drowning me out because I was so bad. This helped, my fingers flew until it was over. Madame gasped ambiguously. Father Semyon leaned to say something in Dr. Ostrov's ear. Tatiana Arkipovna stood up, said nothing, moved to the exit, the girls and Madame following, nothing heard so far but their pattering feet, Madame making quick swivels of her bad hip. A mysterious silence; I put the fiddle on the piano, Father Semyon looked for a place to drop his cigar ash and Stanya Parsov simply rubbed the back of his neck. Then I heard Dr. Ostrov say, rather elaborately, "Kolya, are you sure it will be worth your while?"

Insulted, the Squire walked to the fireplace with his full military strut, tossed his cigar into it, turned, clapsed his hands behind him and demanded, "And may I ask what you are sure of?"

It left him like a shot. The doctor said, "You will break a vein, Kolya, if you continue shouting."

"Yes, sure that I will die." His brow livid now, the Squire turned to Glueck. "And what have you to say?"

Glueck kept his head down, making a basket with his fingers, looking at them as though into the vessel of his fortunes.

"He will play, Squire."

"He plays now."

"No. But he will play."

"And when?"

"We will know better in a few months."

"Oh, the devil with it then. Go find yourself a train."

He kicked a footstool and started to walk out quickly. Dr. Ostrov ran to him, holding his sleeve. In a panic Glueck called, "Squire, you misunderstand." And then wetting his lips for the lie, "In a few months we shall know if it's another Auer."

The Squire whirled and ran back. "Stupid German," he smiled, shaking him by the lapels, everything sunny once more, "let him be the twentieth of an Auer . . . you see, gentlemen?"

"In that case you are to be congratulated," the doctor remarked with professional irony.

Alone with Glueck, I asked, "What is an Auer?"

Winter soon took charge. My eyes opened between six and seven at this period. It would be dark, I would light the lamp, throw wood into the stove, dress, then look over some music for a while — the easy stuff in De Bériot's *Etudes* at this time — or perhaps go into the hall to look down through the window at the ice-rutted barnyard in the rear. The lamp in Rodion's would be lit and I thought different things, what Laib-Shmul might be up to, what new excuse to give Father Semyon for not going to church if he'd visit that evening (he came three times a week), or of how someday I might be able to sneak over to the other side and see what was what.

Or sometimes I'd knock on Glueck's door, very lightly, and if he said to enter we might run down some music together, the day's goal; by this time Rodion would bring breakfast and half an hour later Glueck would be tuning the fiddle. Sometimes we worked in his room and sometimes downstairs when the piano was needed, not often during the first few months. All morning we'd drill, he playing along on his fiddle to make it more interesting. After the midday bite he would write letters or work on his composition while I followed my orders to lie down with my boots off. This Glueck called the "period of drinking-in" during which according to his theory all the work of the morning soaked into me. After that we went out for air if it wasn't too cold and windy, both of us in boots, he in his city-style overcoat with a fur lining and loops and I in one of the Squire's old cut-down bearskins, very heavy, wearing the astrakhan cap with the ear muffs lowered. Near the conservatory we made ourselves a sliding pond and sometimes took the old sled that used to be the girls'. We saw it in the conservatory, and rubbed the rust off the runners with stones. Glueck would steer. Down the road we'd go until the turn at Dr. Ostrov's. I'd yell, "All the way down," but he'd pull into the doctor's yard and remind me that I was not allowed to go as far as the highroad, "orders of the Squire."

By the time we'd be upstairs and thawed out the light would be going. For a couple hours more I'd play as Glueck listened while at his desk putting more work into his composition about which so far he remained tight-lipped. He would call, "Good," or "Not good" or "Over again," his head bent low to his scratching pen, until my fingers wouldn't obey any more. "Well, enough. We mustn't strain," he'd say at last, and it would be long deep dark outside, about half past five. The main social activity came at seven, supper, which we took with the family down in the dining room. Until then Glueck made me lie down on the bed with my boots off and sometimes he came and sat next to me and talked about Petersburg, even getting his guidebook and showing me places on the map of it through his magnifying glass, explaining the different places. This somehow always turned into musical topics, he going into how it was natural for me to be having troubles with notes and the theory and the new uncomfortable positions of the fingers; in general, a harping on the value of correctness illustrated with stories about musicians and composers, with descriptions of how certain of the finest music had been constructed, all given out in a dry carpentered way, sensible but narrow.

Once in a while at this hour the Squire poked his head in. If it wasn't the Squire it was Father Semyon coming to make himself popular with me. No hells, no brimstones, only smiles and pats on the head and little candies dropped into my jacket pocket. If it was a Father Semyon day he'd go from me to the Squire's study until Vassily downstairs would ring the bell. Glueck and I would wait standing in the **dining** room behind our chairs, for the entrance. Whether alone or with the priest, Konstantin Andreyevitch never clanked himself in without making some small military noise either with the spurs he didn't take off or his pistol holster banging against his thigh (sometimes after supper he indulged in shooting from the promenade, throwing a coat over his shoulder and going for the bare branches), and sometimes also when reviewing business matters with Vassily in the Gallery he would wear his dispatch case on a strap. The thank-you prayer would be said either by him or Father Semyon; then Natalya and Vassily would begin supper, Vassily bothering only to serve from the bottles on the sideboard which the Squire had already touched in a test of the temperature. Madame supervised the girls' portions while Tatiana Arkipovna, if the priest was present, started him on his favorite subject, the building of a new chapel where he would be after he died, and though he never came out bluntly, "also our worthiest people." Tatiana Arkipovna spoke of this with all the reverence she could muster, the Squire wanting to shoot her, he being extremely touchy to hear about death in connection with himself which Tatiana Arkipovna knew quite well. Witnessing these byplays of fun I took them for the sensible concern of a nice lady in a matter which had to be attended to. Now I will jump forward; here is why she hated the Squire so sincerely.

When Leta and Lilli had been small the Squire had brought a genuine Frenchwoman from Petersburg, as he said, for purposes of thorough education, the girls at eight and five having shown no talent even for counting numbers. Tatiana Arkipovna had not suspected why the girls were so backward until she found the governess, a determined woman of brazen views who smoked little cigars, doing more than smoking with the Squire in the privacy of his study. This led to explosions in which her father also participated and it came out at last that for many years the Squire had been suffering the most serious physical consequences of his bachelorhood's sexual propensities, which explained why after the births of the daughters he had avoided further tries with Tatiana Arkipovna, confining his bed-activities to sorties outside his own house. This had caused Tatiana Arkipovna to enter into a controlled melancholy out of which she had finally taken to Madame. Now Tatiana Arkipovna had persuaded herself to adopt Madame's superstition about the girls, that indeed the two miracles would arrive, their husbands; Tatiana Arkipovna had forced herself into believing Leta and Lilli were perhaps not corks on a vinegar sea being eaten away by what kept them afloat. Far from easy to look at, smudged carbon copies of their father, they lacked almost entirely the characteristics of female development, of normal height but without any normal growth of intimate parts and ignorant of why this was so.

Lilli always seemed to have a cold and to eat with difficulty, the shine of her small eyes and her lack of neck reminding me of a shaved eagle — a fat slow clumsy girl, totally on guard. Leta, the elder, had a flat narrow torso planted on her hips like a pole on a barrel. Her head stood heavy on her spoolish neck, her square chin pulling like a weight at the tired bulging eyes of one unable to cope. But her small sharp-fluted nose was good by itself though lost between the squirrel's cheeks inherited from her father. Only her brownish hair separated itself from her, a paradox, the shiny thickness crying vigor and a desire to collide.

Occasionally at supper Madame intrigued the Squire into words, and laughter sometimes visited the large dim dining room. But the overbearing mood, however punctured, maintained itself. We would rise from the table, Madame producing her sprayer to make her *stt-stts!* over the girls' heads and out we'd go, each to his place.

Once or twice we were allowed to look into the Gallery, filled with many versions of the same picture, gypsy girls in barrels or floating among the stars or outside of tents, holding flowers or with their fingers to their chins, and always it was summer and always parts of their busts showed. The remarkable thing was the big painting of Tatiana Arkipovna's father, Arkip Apollonovitch Rezin, showing him at a table, holding a quill pen in one hand and a riding whip in the other, the Squire explained, signing the document making him a member of some corporation. Long boots brought out Arkip Apollonovitch's tallness and his narrow-bearded face through shadow-trickeries had been given the set of one ratifying something historic.

After supper the hardest part of the day; for more than three months. All through the day the routine carried me, I had much to learn and remember, easier to forget what couldn't be entirely forgotten — the other side, my brother, the landsmen, Laib-Shmul nearby — and at night these came closer than the world of notes and scales. Glueck forbade me to play my songs in the old finger positions and at night I did not wish somehow to play as he wanted me to, like a dentist with calisthenic picks.

Out of despair I began bothering Glueck after supper, going into his room with a "Don't stop your work, please. I'll just sit." He would have his nose in a letter or his composition and I would be in the chair near the stove.

Another time — "Glueck, where's your father and mother?"

"In Petersburg."

"What do they do?"

"Keep a shop."

"A bake shop?"

"My father fixes instruments."

"Have you brothers or anything?"

"I have brothers and sisters. They went back to Germany. I shall remain in Petersburg. I have my place in the Maryinsky pit, I am not disliked, and . . . so."

"But you left it."

"Only for a while."

"To come out here?"

"For a little change."

"But why do you want a change when you like Petersburg?"

He laughed. "Shall I tell you a secret, Lev?" (Using a Russian version of my name.) "Very well, it's because of a certain person."

It came out little by little. Anya was the daughter of one of the 'cellists at the Maryinsky Theatre. It had been her ambition to play the harp but doubting her talent the father hoped she would capitalize upon her attractive figure and simply marry well, discarding her harping ideas. Glueck allowed himself to compare her to a tulip passing

from budding to opening fullness. He had for her birthday taken her
to the Summer Gardens where they had danced and listened to a
fortuneteller, and coming back on the ferry he had revealed he was
composing a sonata for harp and violin. She promised to play it with
him the day it was finished; but when he came to her house with the
manuscript she was not there and her harp was not there. But she had
left a note.

"Where was she?"

"She went to Novgorod."

"Why?"

"Because she bought a ticket to Novgorod." He touched his spectacles with one hand, adjusting them.

"What is a sonata, Glueck?"

Immediately he launched into the explanation; and so it went.

Coming to the middle of December (if I stop to throw stones at
every day I'll arrive nowhere), military sleds from Pukop began making
their way up the ice-rutted hill. Officers would stay with the Squire in
his study until twilight and once even the Colonel Commander came
and had supper. There was nothing military to him except his abrupt
style of drinking. Tired and bald, he suggested a shelf-climbing libra-
rian with a wide seat. At the table he and the Squire discussed the
sending of some members of the regiment's band to play for the Squire's
usual Christmas ball. The details were agreed upon and the Colonel
Commander went off, but this was not the last of the military sleds.
Preparations had been under way now for days. Tatiana Arkipovna
and Madame walked about with eyes red from sewing dresses; the
servants never walked but hopped, Lubenka and Natalya cooking and
baking into the night, and even sour Rodion adopted a restrained look
in order not to endanger his Christmas tip.

Ossip came back from working in the village for a few days to help
along. He had something to say. "And soldiers are out every day now,
hunting your Jew-conspirators."

"We don't have any conspirators, that's a lie."

"Think they're in the woods just to freeze?" he demanded. "They're looking for the Avengers . . . Jews going about slitting throats. Near to Christmas is when they like to."

Laib-Shmul had mentioned these "Avengers" too but Vera Zasulich had been executed more than five years ago. "It can't be, Ossip."

"And if there's proof?"

"That's a lie!"

"Then where's Laib-Shmul, eh? Gone to the Crimea for the winter?"

"What about him?"

"He's gone a week. Persons without coats don't stroll off in the winter without knowing where they're going, clear? Oh, he'll be found with the rest of them!"

Laib-Shmul had gone out of desperation as he'd predicted to me. But I kept still; I couldn't be absolutely sure Laib-Shmul didn't know more than he'd let out; I wavered between being angry and proud for him. Out of touch with our Jewish calendar I wondered if the Feast of Lights had arrived, the yearly celebration of Judah Maccabee's victory over the Syrians out of which the Jews won back their Jewishness and created a country for a time. The Feast of Lights fell often near to Christmas and perhaps . . . no. Russia wasn't Syria and we weren't Judah Maccabees and furthermore we would not go around just slitting throats.

Hearing the news from Ossip caused me to become steadily listless. Some Feast of Lights; the few left on the other side no doubt colder and hungrier than ever while I lay like a prince and my brother so trapped, old enough to be called an Avenger himself and slammed for it if it pleased them. There would be soldiers about for the Squire's ball, drivers and hostlers as well as musicians, and these would need holiday sports and I knew where they might look for it.

Seeing I was depressed Glueck asked questions and I let him know. He said it was sad but "one must adopt the healthiest view."

"Show me the health in it."

"You are going to be a musician. Music always arouses the cleanest, healthiest feelings. Say this to yourself: 'I shall arouse the finest feelings in others, my fingers doing it, on my fiddle.' Believe in your music, believe it won't hang in the air. Believe it will draw out the best feelings of those who will hear it. This is the creed of artists — to ventilate the human heart. Believe this and you will feel better, Lev."

I wanted to believe it so much that I fell into a rage. "Lies and crap, crap and lies! Murderers are murderers, music or no music! Don't choke me, choke yourself!"

I ran to my room. All night a thought waited for me to wake up. Before dressing in the morning I went to Glueck. "I'm sorry I insulted you."

"Very well, then," he said, "clear weather . . . and this morning we start on something new."

"What?"

After breakfast, as usual with something new, he played it first. It spoke to me from beginning to end. "What is it?"

"The *Ave Maria* of Schubert's."

"Schubert?"

"Franz Schubert."

That name, where before?

I remembered. Uncle Mottel, the time he was in the army, the soldiers giving it to him over the Jew Franz Schubert. "Wasn't he a Jew, Glueck?"

"Schubert? Never! Do you know what *Ave Maria* is?"

"No."

"It means 'Hail Mary.'"

"What Mary?"

"You are an ignorant boy this morning," he replied lightly, "to have forgotten what Father Semyon has been telling you."

Then it was not so. The soldiers had said it to Uncle Mottel just for fun. I pointed to the music on the stand. "This is Schubert hailing Mary?"

"Do you like it?"

"Very much."

"Come, the beginning."

"I don't feel well."

"Lie down awhile."

A nice how-do-you-do . . . because Schubert was not a Jew my uncle had been whipped in the army. But it sounded as Jewish as it was beautiful. Hearing it only once brimmed me back to my deepest oldest sureties. Lying in this mix I kept muttering, "No, it's ours, it's ours."

I heard Glueck entering and pretended I was asleep. He shook me. "Lev, the Squire wants us."

I sat up, saw Rodion outside in the hall.

"We mustn't keep him waiting."

Rodion took us down one flight to his bedroom. It took fifteen steps in the room to reach his bed. I noticed the softness of the carpet and his clothes on the floor in a line as though he'd undressed while walking to the bed. The stove was a gay white, a smell of pomade about. A lamp burned next to him on a small round table, the blinds as yet not opened. The Squire lay comfortably on his back in the manufactured dusk. He wore a nightgown with a round collar, his knees up, hands clasped behind his head against the mound of pillows. He seemed older and more tired than when he was up and about, but with an aura to him of being somehow a boy actor made up magnificently well to play a certain Squire. Many times in that house I experienced similar confusions, out of my inability to piece up what was really going on there. Out of the corner of my eye I had a glimpse of Vassily Buzarov seated on the pot in the toilet-closet with his arms folded; just sitting, quietly, like waiting for the show to start.

"Good morning, good morning." The Squire stretched himself as Glueck clicked his heels and bowed, a paper of some kind in one of his fists. "See, a letter. . . ."

"Ah," beamed Glueck.

Folding his letter carefully the Squire announced that his father-in-law would be visiting for a week in April. This was said with deep thoughtfulness, as if a speech in explanation must follow. After some deliberation however the Squire contented himself with asking, abruptly, "You are fond of your Glueck?" I nodded. "As you should be. You will continue to follow him in everything and it shall be worth the expense. Arkip Apollonovitch will see for himself how we have not been sleeping through the winter." His voice rose to command. "We'll show him how one needn't travel to Paris to be entertained, he'll see I don't belong banished in the provinces, I'll give him a welcome of the finest music. . . ."

The Squire smiled and Glueck added a fawning grimace to the joke, saying, "Lev is quite intent, without fault," but the past few days were too much. I began to cry that I wanted my brother. The words tumbled out and I cried simply to cry.

Vassily rose from his eminent seat and came to lead me out. "Wait, who's the brother?" the Squire asked.

Vassily told him, mentioning how we'd been made orphans the year before. Glueck threw in, "He has been disturbed," and the Squire waved his hand, using a generous tone. "He'll have his brother, then. Go bring him for a visit, Vassily."

Back in my room Glueck washed my face, soothing me with congratulations. "See, Lev? The Squire isn't stone, your brother is safe!"

"Glueck," I asked, too dazed to probe any new turns, "what was Vassily doing there?"

"Warming the pot-seat for the Squire."

Waiting for Shim I wondered what made the behinds of the mighty so cold. It lay beyond me that there was a whole philosophy of pot-warming and that the Squire himself was warming a pot for the colder and mightier behind of Arkip Apollonovitch.

The day passed; no Shim. At supper Vassily went about all in sighs, making small clatters. Controlling his drunken condition he said that the hill had been very bad, the horses falling twenty times on the ice, and that my brother was sick anyway. From the look on my face the Squire saw I thought Vassily was lying. "Well," he said with an assuring shrug, "when a brother is sick he should be visited. Take him tomorrow if the hill allows. And Vassily, put a few things in a sack. Bread, potatoes. Don't leave him out of sight, however."

Vassily, Rodion, and Kuizma Oblanski rode me to our side about noon the next day, my feet on the lanes for the first time in over two months. On the way to Dvoora's where Shim stayed I noticed how many huts were empty.

The first thing I asked Dvoora was, "Where's everybody?" It was hardly warmer inside than out. "Shh," she said, pointing to Shim bundled in ragged covers on the cold ground; nothing there but a table, a chair, and a miserable little stick-fire in the center of the room.

Dvoora did not seem surprised to see me. "If we're here, let's get wood," Vassily said to Rodion as an order. He went out and I dropped the sack in my hand. "A few things, Dvoora. But where's everybody?"

"Where everybody is, you'll have to ask a better-informed person," she replied, her quickly aged eyes narrowing. "But those few who are still here you'll find in one place, praying. They warm one another."

The wind blew through the chinks. In my warm sheepskin I had to look away from Dvoora. She was not so much dressed as bandaged, wrapped in rags on the arms and feet, her wool petticoat open with holes, the thinnest of shawls over her ripped leather vest. Feeling her eyes on me I went at last to Shim. He seemed asleep, or at least not awake. I took my coat off and put it over him.

I heard her spit. "Who needs you here with your dishonest worries, Laib?"

"What's the matter with Shim?"

"I'm not a doctor but I can tell you."

"Don't be angry."

"Anger is good, we fill up on it."

"I brought bread and potatoes."

"A good thank-you."

"Dvoora," I began, but she hobbled out clumsily, hate-bitten more than frost-bitten, saying as she left, "Ay, I just cleaned the house."

I bent down before Shim and kissed his forehead. His face seemed smaller the way death makes them. "Shim, it's me."

Rodion just then entered with the wood, threw it with a noise to the floor, kicked some of it into the fire. The commotion flicked him more awake. "Who are they?"

"Buzarov, Oblanski, Rodion Kluzanov."

His hand touched my coat over him. "Fine goods," he murmured, his tailor's fingers judging it automatically.

I said nothing. In the silence I heard his confirmation of me as an outcast just like Uncle Mottel. "I brought bread and potatoes," I said after a while, still kneeling over him. "Are you warmer?"

"Rochel is away," he whispered.

"Laib-Shmul told me. Did she go alone?"

"The priest sent him to Minsk to sell goats. I saw him, Arkady, he'd made himself into a friend. He said he'd take Rochel too." He breathed longer now between words. "Minsk, there they have societies. Minsk . . that's the whole trick."

"Any news from her?"

"No."

"Get well. After the winter you'll go to Minsk, I'll help you. Just get well."

He turned his head away. "Eat your dirty, I'll eat my clean."

I looked with a visitor's eye at the pest-eaten walls, free of remorse, satisfied to be cast out of this. The recipe of my life yielded its first hard crystal; something in the world was polluting everybody when it was not cleaning them, never letting them stay the same, dizzying them into spontaneous turns and then making them get used to it.

When Dvoora came back Vassily ordered me to take my coat. I said good-by to Shim. He made believe he did not hear me. I told Dvoora I would come again. She said, "Burn in your deepest throat."

Vassily picked up my sheepskin. Bending and kissing Shim, I put it back. "Get well," I whispered, "you know why."

Waiting to hear something out of him I heard Schubert in my head, the *Ave Maria*. But I belonged not here and not there, and my brother said nothing.

I felt better on the way back and every evening Vassily said something about Shim feeling better. I dived into the job of mastering the *Ave Maria* with results so pleasing that Glueck gave full reports at the supper table. For the first time my tutor allowed himself to be the bird who tested his wings, and was so pleased he didn't stop whizzing around. His new suppertime personality caused Leta to listen without eating, a steady look of pleasure on her face, her eyes never off of him. Madame noted this quickly. The next night the same; and Madame vied with Tatiana Arkipovna in recalling memories of Moscow concerts and balls, involving him in comparisons with the Petersburg variety and generally managing to lead him from the subject of me and the *Ave Maria* into more sociable fields. It was here that Glueck became classed as an eligible as it was that Leta first showed something of an ability to have a "crush."

One night Vassily said Shim had gotten up on his feet. I told the Squire I wanted to see for myself. He replied, "You cannot cross the road any more, Lev. Kuizma Oblanski has it that they've made you their main enemy over there. They're waiting for you with clubs and stones and I won't have your fingers hurt."

"I won't play if I can't see Shim," I said boldly.

The Squire ran his finger along his gums, cleaning off bits of nuts. "If you don't, you're no good to me and I'm sure they'll give you a fine welcome in the Pukop jail."

Whether this was only his child psychology I didn't try to prove; I kept quiet and that night the worst blizzard of the year began, canceling the Squire's ball. A barn wall collapsed, pigs and chickens went, roofs flew off in the racing winds. During the first day of it the Buzarovs and the Kluzanovs moved into the main house, sleeping on the kitchen floor and in the Gallery. With plenty of wood in the cellar, meats taken from the smokehouse, and water gotten from a drift that crashed the glass roof of the conservatory, the snow shoveled in buckets through the door, the house was comfortable except for the waste-smells from the barrels in the cellar which little by little spread through the first floor. Madame produced extra perfume sprayers and everybody started making *stt-stts!* Glueck and I kept mostly to his room upstairs, the *Ave Maria* more on my mind than the blizzard.

I did not observe the drinking but Glueck did. By the second night of the blizzard, Christmas Eve, the servants were staying good and tipsy and the Squire along with them. Even Madame and Tatiana

Arkipovna fell into it and Leta and Lilli made up some game of giggles between them at supper; a huge banquet. Glueck was careful to avoid vodka, sticking to the wine though Madame urged him to all kinds of toasts. And Tatiana Arkipovna said, "Come, dear Ernst, it's Christmas," in the jolliest voice imaginable, a new side of her rising.

In the kitchen they were singing; Vassily almost dropped the roast coming in with it. Everybody laughed and Vassily dropped it purposely. Already drinking from the bottle, the Squire forbade Vassily to pick it up and ran for his hussar's sword, returning to make running attacks upon the roast. To Glueck and me this appeared dull but the others hailed him.

"Kolya," cried Tatiana Arkipovna, her face flushed, "go put on your full uniform! Blizzard or no blizzard we'll have our ball, let's all be young and dressed up and make believe it's Moscow!"

"And Ernst shall play," Madame cried, throwing her hand at him in a modest imitation of the theatrical way, "and we shall dance. Come, girls, into our white silk!"

"And you," said Tatiana Arkipovna with a sudden point at the aghast Glueck, "you into your best also!"

"A member of the family!" Madame ventured gaily.

"Not the boy," the Squire said, "he mustn't be wearied, more important matters are waiting for him. Take him upstairs, Glueck."

I fell asleep, not for long. The wind woke me and then the hailstones. Downstairs I heard the piano, something very fast, and noise. Then the piano stopped and Glueck soon came in. "Laib. . . ."

"What's the matter?"

"He says he wants you."

On the way downstairs, because of the fatal set of his face and the pleated shirt and white bow he wore, he looked not only like the waiter who has just spilled soup on a customer, but the customer as well.

The closer we approached the main hall the crazier everything sounded — laughs, yells, giggles, poundings, a tide of roars and thumps of weights falling, and above all a senseless ugly pounding of the piano, low and high, low and high as though it was being clubbed. One look was enough. Leta sat at the piano, her fists flailing down, her face reddened with wine and triumph while Lilli squirted long *stt-stts!* at Lukenka and Natalya asleep next to each other on the floor near the fireplace. At the same time Madame was trying to teach Rodion something like a minuet, both pounding their feet and stumbling against each other while Tatiana kept calling, "Again, again."

It wasn't unpleasant or shocking, lacking connection with anything pleasant or customary. The room seemed to be hanging in the air, holding itself perfectly well together while managing to be part of something elsewhere. The Squire was adding his own touch. Circling the air with his sword, he was riding his noble steed Vassily about the room and dealing various deaths to pillows, cushions, lamps and entire sofas, calling out the charges with the bugle in his other hand as Vassily negotiated a crawling tour of a big square marked off by four bottles, stopping at each for a long swallow. Wearing his hussar's uniform the Squire kept shouting, "Don't be still, Tatya, stay noisy," she obeying. Nobody stopped, nobody grew tired; it was a coda refusing to end, the same over and over. As Glueck pushed me into the room, the immense chandelier gleaming over my head, I remembered those moments in Profim's "Heaven" when they had let me for a show with Arkady's goat. Glueck pushed me toward the fireplace where it was warmer, then went to the piano for the fiddle. No one seemed to see I was there.

"Anything," Glueck said with a raised voice, to be heard. "You're to play, he wants it."

In my nightgown I played the *Ave Maria,* closing my eyes on the long notes, hardly hearing them myself in the beginning. First the piano stopped pounding, then Tatiana Arkipovna subsided. Toward the middle of my playing it the first time, the room touched quiet and stayed there, the storm outside meshing with it in a counterpoint. When I finished Tatiana Arkipovna called, "Again," her voice low, a need in it, and I saw the Squire kneeling. "God be thanked," he said, moaning religiously.

I played it again. Lubenka snored next to Natalya, Leta ran to her mother and Madame to Lilli, Vassily eyeing a nearby bottle and Glueck encouraging me with pleased nods. A short while before the room had been evilly squeezing itself. Now it was some place of holiness to them, because of my playing. The Squire got up when I finished and came sobbing to me with healthy tears. He put his hands on my hips and spoke with wonder, "You will do, Lev, you will do." He kissed me on the mouth, his fumes choking me; the act of a drunkard turning toward his good side, a rusty impulse. Here, as though hit on the head by a halo, Leta ran to Glueck and threw herself against him, hanging onto the lapels of his coat and blubbering, "Teach me, teach me too," the eruption causing him to writhe with polite control. Tatiana Arkipovna hurried over, happily taking Leta's hands. "But Leta, girls do not do the violin. See, you are hurting Ernst's jacket." Leta threw off her mother's hands and clung to Glueck with a desperate strength until he said, "Miss Leta, perhaps the piano. . . ."

"The piano, the piano," she said, looking at him and going all loose, a hunger in her eyes not missed by Tatiana Arkipovna nor Madame who had by then come over.

"There, little Leta," Madame cooed with her best syrup, "you shall play the piano and our dear Ernst . . ."

"We'll start tomorrow and prepare the moment now," Tatiana interrupted, holding Leta by the shoulders and starting to turn her away; but Leta turned herself to Glueck, shot herself up on tiptoes and gave him a quick peck on the cheek before running out of the room, followed by Madame with Lilli in a giggle.

"You have made the child happy," Tatiana said flashingly, smiling at the astounded fellow, her own cheeks paler now. "Good night," she said in a new way, the words elbowing themselves through other, more exciting thoughts.

Vassily began uprighting the furniture and glumly the Squire pointed to the sleeping women. "Drag them out, Vassily." And to Glueck, "For heaven's sake take him back to bed. He's cold in his gown." As we left I saw him turning to the fireplace, getting ready to pass some water, his cavalry bugle hanging from his shoulder, the cord under an epaulet.

In the hall I asked Glueck why the Squire had knelt and he said, "You reminded him it was Christmas. You see, don't you? Lev, music always arouses the cleanest feelings, it is supreme."

The blizzard left more than snow. Each evening before supper Glueck gave Leta her lesson at the piano; new sounds, Leta's bruised tinklings and Glueck's calm correcting ripples. A week passed into the next and the next, hints of changes peeped out of the winter gloom, the buds of that crazy spring — new bright ribbons in Leta's hair, a lightness to her step as she went to practice after supper, a variety to her, sometimes braids, sometimes her hair rolled up into a shy crown; and once I saw Leta outside the dining room before supper, biting her lips to make them redder.

Supper changed; gone were the silences broken by gruntings and sippings. We had conversations, a façade of domesticity, chatterings about changing the positions of pictures in the Gallery, of replacing draperies in the spring, of converting the conservatory into some kind of a summer sitting room "for the girls," Madame agog with letters to various stores in Petersburg. Through all this Leta would take long looks at Glueck every time she put a glass to her lips. It was fairly plain. The women were plotting the match. Tatiana Arkipovna took care to hook Glueck into descriptions of the musical life in Petersburg, spoke of "giving up the estate here" and settling in that city "when the right time came," Madame meanwhile making exclamation points over Leta's head with her perfume sprayer. Not entirely crass; Tatiana Arkipovna retained a portion of her reserve, nevertheless pushing herself further than she imagined she could.

Glueck acted as if everything went over his head. One morning when we were resting a minute I said, "She likes you."

"She?"

"Leta."

"A child. . . ."

"She bites her lips to make them red. I saw her."

"Ah," he said, "nature has plotted against her too well."

"They'd make a king of you if you married her."

"If I married her?"

"They're throwing a house in Petersburg at you. You haven't noticed?"

"Impossible . . . she's as strange with me as I am with her. Relieved to see a face as ugly as her own."

"Glueck, I've seen matches made. . . ."

"Now we'll go back to our *Etudes*," he cut me off.

For the rest of the day he failed to correct me as much as usual. When it came time for Leta's lesson he asked me to tell Madame he would not be coming downstairs. "These headaches of mine," he explained. "They strike me a few times every year and then go away, sometimes after only a day . . . nothing to be done about it but rest and drink plain tea."

This was said for rehearsal purposes. As the wife of a tailor always having to fight for a price my mother used to listen carefully to the speeches my father tried out on her before giving them to his customers. She was quick to detect overlapping vibrations, unnecessary bravados, anything which might wrinkle the total plausibility and especially the greatest giveaway of the worried man — too many different faces being made while much was being said too quickly. Having observed my parents in this activity for so long, it was easy to see Glueck was only playing sick. "Here's a better idea, Glueck. Just say you are already married."

"No, I must take care," he sighed, too upset to deny anything. "I must be aloof, somehow, without offending. The girl is freakish. How foolish and blind of me, I am not ready yet to be dismissed. . . ."

"Well, I'll go down and tell it to them in your way."

"Thank you, Lev."

I performed my mission in the ladies' sitting room. Madame made piteous gasps about "our poor chronic" and suggested to Tatiana Arkipovna that Glueck be tenderly nursed "at all times, not to feel forsaken." A samovar was ordered to be sent up to him and Leta ran into the kitchen to make sure everything would be just right. For her more than a piano lesson was being missed. Within her arrested and ignored spirit lay something pushing her to conquer the handicaps of her body, an extraordinary natural effort to be like others.

"He will need poultices and medicines to sleep," Tatiana Arkipovna said pleasantly, putting down her sewing and standing up.

"I think I have some good things too, I'll see," said Madame. Tatiana Arkipovna told her this would not be necessary. "Stay here with the girls," she ordered. There is a certain calm in many women behind which may be found a crouching power that waits and waits, knowing it can pounce but once, and only for a kill; such was Tatiana Arkipovna's.

I left her at her own landing and flew up to ours to report to Glueck already undressed and in bed. "It's all right, very good, they're worried," I told him in a gross miscalculation.

Glueck's imaginary headache became soon real. He had thought to make a fortress out of his bed but the women came at him in waves. Tatiana Arkipovna smiled herself in with pills and poultices, Madame made herself the girls' escort "to prove to them, the little dears, that he wasn't dying, now they'll sleep," spreading it hard and thick a few times about "the big one especially, you never saw anyone so upset." There could not fail to be complications; while setting down the samovar on the writing desk Natalya stumbled, the inkstand tipping over some fanned-out pages of his precious manuscript, a concerto; and when he groaned Leta knelt and held his fingers against the pain, begging him to accept the doctor. Madame meanwhile made her little *stt-stts!* around the bed as though anointing them with a double halo. Tatiana Arkipovna insisted on making him take three kinds of pills, and after the pills came a poultice and then a glass of tea, all this with Leta before him, holding his hand and mumbling "the doctor, the doctor."

As she lifted the girl away from him Tatiana Arkipovna said, "You must conquer this, Ernst, you are needed." She touched his cheek, coldly possessive in her dignity.

I met the Squire coming down the hall from his study. "Why the noise, Lev?"

"Glueck's sick."

"Impossible!"

Washing, I heard the Squire being cheery with Glueck. "An impossible time to be sick, Glueck!" he shouted. "You have no idea! No time to waste! We've matters to settle — the moment you're well!"

From Glueck, a moan.

At supper things began with unusual spirit. Glueck's illness had expanded itself into a family event of immediate gaiety (though Leta kept saying the doctor should come, he might be dying). The Squire directed her to shut up but Madame said comfortingly, "Oh, he is not really ill, we are happy to show him our wishes, to care for him, to surround him as never even in his own home. No, Leta, we must be cheerful, anything may happen. . . ."

Tatiana Arkipovna reminded Leta to be thoughtful, to let Glueck see nothing but smiles, to conceal all worries, "to show we are fondling him as a baby." There was more of this until the Squire said, "What a fuss over a headache!"

"We wish for him to see one dear heart beating faster because of his pain."

"Oho," the Squire said with a wink at me. The happy mood of the others disappeared when he added, "Well, there it is . . . next they'll be tossing her into bed with him, these two."

"Come, girls," Madame gasped, seeing the Squire was bringing up his larger cannons. "Papa's not himself again."

Tatiana Arkipovna closed the doors, after Madame and the girls had gone, a burn of hate in her eyes as she came back and stood over her husband. "Do sit," he said, nibbling on something, "it hurts my neck to look up at you."

"Kolya, you must listen." She took an apple from the bowl and spoke in reasonable tones. "It is not Madame. Leta found it for herself. She loves him. Kolya, it is so. She has confided in me voluntarily. She is awakening."

"Give her a medicine to sleep."

"Kolya, please — "

"Don't you see the cruelty? Who would ever want her?"

"God has given Leta a chance. We cannot be blunt, Kolya. She *wants* him. That is the blessing."

"Well, let her want the Tsarevitch. You care for her? Spare her feelings, men do not marry sexual cripples. There's no price on it."

(She cut the apple into small strips with a horn-handled knife, speaking the while.) "You haven't studied him. He is shy himself, gentle, enough of a child. One of those who lives in his heart, a little bit priestly with his music. Women are strange to him, he is afraid of them. But to be worshiped, to be taken for a god as Leta takes him, to be supported in his career as my father will do . . . Kolya, please, it is sinful to interfere. And you, Lev . . . you are a child, you are not fooled. Leta is pure!"

She waited for the Squire to reply, cutting the apple into smaller and smaller bits. He drained his glass slowly, enjoying his triumph, a smile hardening itself. He said nothing. "Please give him a chance to become used to her. Please, you must not interfere, Kolya, with any of your jokes."

He stretched his smile until he had to make a sound, the words oozing out with careful laziness. But he sighed first. "Well . . . how fortunate Leta is Leta and not Tatya, the girl sent to Moscow . . . and our Glueck is not that young bookbinder who took the sensible way out . . . this way, Leta won't marry to bury herself. Better not to marry at all than your way, Tatya. . . ."

The reference to certain facts as yet beyond me caused Tatiana Arkipovna to lose her calm and to stiffen, the knife in her hand loosening, then catching it again at the blade, tightening, the pain not felt. The Squire reached over and took the knife. "There," he said as she looked down at her hand, the scratch rising, "you hurt yourself."

In the quiet as she kept her head down I said, almost whispering, "Mistress Konayeva, but he has a sweetheart."

"It is a lie."

"Go on, Lev. . . ."

"It is so," I said. "She is in Novgorod, he's spoken of her to me. He came here for the money. He wants to bring her to him, with a new harp."

"Shy," the Squire mocked easily, "a child, afraid of women. . . ."

"I will hear it from his own lips," she trembled. "And if it is so, he will leave!"

"But he is under my orders, Tatya," the Squire said. "I have a use for him here."

"He will leave this house." She brought her fist down upon the cut-up apple. The plate cracked.

"No, he will stay."

"Then I go. We go," she said, her voice low and flat, as though to a corpse.

"As you wish. But I've no capital for trips this winter, you'll have to find the money."

"I'll write Father."

"Send my love."

She dropped her head, covering her face with her arm, lips touching the tablecloth, her words rising in a mumble difficult to hear. "How dare you? . . . is this your pleasure, am I amusing you?"

Taking an opened letter from his inside pocket, the Squire waved it, saying, "No, Tatya, it is business of the highest order."

"Yes," lifting her head and hurling a smile, "to be a peacock in Petersburg. . . ."

"This is from your father. See how long it is." He waved the two pages at her, closely. "Both sides covered. . . ."

I didn't catch all of it. But enough was plain, though not immediately. The Squire took this letter as the biggest single chance of his life. With a singsong relish he read off his father-in-law's sour summary of a disappointment in Paris. Arkip Apollonovitch had been maneuvering for an important loan which would give him control of God-knew-what, but following the Panama Canal swindle the Bourse held tight and Arkip had wasted four months until at last he found a willing party; only the party's mistress, an opera singer, unfortunately put her foot down against the old man because of a remark he had made to her about the Jews, without knowing she was one. Good-by to the great loan and also the possibility of a dukedom; tired and disgusted, he ended by saying he'd be in Smolensk that April and would probably come to Golinsk for a few days.

Tatiana Arkipovna paid merely the slightest attention, but as the Squire put away the letter he said, "It's the bull's-eye this time and my sights are fixed higher than the Petersburg canaries, you may be sure! For this reason, Tatya, keep your bloc from bothering Glueck any more!"

She laughed, the croak of the defeated in it. "I have better for you. Until I leave this house I'll never step from my room, Kolya, never." She stood towering over him. "Should I see you once again, it will be your end." She threw her hand against his chest with such force that the chair fell backward, toppling him to the floor; then she hurried out.

Vassily ran in from the kitchen. "What was it, Squire?"

"My wife has had an accident," he said, coughing in his laughter, by then whirling in his own mania, Glueck and I sucked into it. "We can't wait," the Squire said, getting to his feet, "we'll settle it now."

Glueck was sleeping. The Squire strode to his bed, ripped back the covers, and slapped his flat belly. "It's a joke, dear fellow," he said to poor Glueck so wrackingly awaked, "and now listen, sick or well . . . when do you suppose we might go to Paris?"

"Paris . . . ?"

"Give your most careful answer."

"When you wish."

"I've a letter from Arkip Apollonovitch in Paris," he explained in the manner of those who imagine their thoughts are graven upon their foreheads. "Now don't grope, think carefully . . . when will our genius here be ready to charm the heart of a certain Jewess of an opera singer, make her embrace him, melt her heart?"

Glueck replied with a gulp.

"You, a Petersburg expert, and you cannot reply?"

Seeing himself fired in the next minute, Glueck gave him what he wanted. "It is a matter of work, a concert, a program. I would say, if you are meaning an informal concert before knowing persons . . . perhaps in three months . . . the freshness, the devotion is there, crudely yet . . . yes, three months."

With a second slap of Glueck's belly the Squire cried, "Get well! Arkip Apollonovitch comes in April and then we go to Paris, *à quatre!*"

Tatiana Arkipovna entered immediately into her pledge, allowing only the Madame and the girls to visit her, they soon becoming companions in exile. The servants were admitted once or twice to clear the room of accumulated refuse, used dishes and what-not, bringing the Squire stories of how she would hide under the covers, the room a perfumed stench. This could not fail to be noticed in the town, the servants leaking it out, many stories being told. Every day for two weeks Dr. Ostrov and Father Semyon arrived in hopes of being admitted to her presence. They would stand in the hall outside her locked door, begging, the Squire shaking his head and saying, "You see, it's a massive tantrum." But the door opened at last and the priest and the doctor did not emerge for two hours after which they closeted themselves with the Squire in his study. The next day Rodion drove them off in the big sled, the four of them, and that night the Squire made a dry announcement, "The ladies have gone to Minsk where they will stay until April." Vassily informed Glueck and me more fully. "The doctor thinks her senses are going," he said. "She refused to leave without the other three, however."

"What does Dr. Ostrov say of the Squire?" asked Glueck, whispering.

"An old story. From putting his foot into it too many times, as is said."

Ostrov and Father Semyon continued to visit but the Squire refused to allow Father Semyon to continue his baptizing campaign. "We are too busy here," he assured the priest, "it is crucial that he not be baptized yet."

Father Semyon began a severe lecture. "Konstantin Andreyevitch,

you choose a poor time to oppose the will of the Lord our Father — "
but Ostrov pulled at his sleeve, and soon visited more and more by himself. The Squire would greet him from the third landing, shouting
down, "Ah, you're here. Well, go away," and then run nervously to
him, almost tripping sometimes on the steps, to ask about Tatiana
Arkipovna, thanking him for the news, and always ending the visit in
some abrupt way yet not before the doctor had counted his pulse and
warned him, "Kolya, you must restrain your enthusiasms or you will
take a stroke."

Actually the weeks of our upside-down existence since Tatiana Arkipovna's withdrawal had but one meaning for the Squire — to press my
musical mobilization to the utmost in preparation for the epochal storming of the Jewish opera singer's Parisian barricade. To keep his vision
clearly before him the Squire required us to sit nights in his study,
whole nights. We slept when we could and ate at all hours, never in the
dining room any more, our only chance for air being a walk on the
promenade towards evening. Less and less the Squire left his study,
leaving Vassily to decide all estate matters, throwing himself into his
project as a father dives into the pool where his child is drowning, running about all afternoon in robe and slippers, popping into Glueck's
room or wherever we were working at least four times an hour, listening, criticizing, approving. Sometimes he read aloud, with gestures,
drafts of letters to Arkip Apollonovitch detailing our progress, or long
passages from *Oblomov* to prove he had emancipated himself from his
unpatriotic sloth. Only towards evening did he dress and after some
bottle-work usually changed into his hussar's uniform or his salon garb
or his formal hunting outfit of red coat, high silk hat, and shiny
boots with turned-down red cuffs for the climax of that particular
twenty-four hours, the midnight-to-dawn celebration before us in his
study.

We saw only Rodion and Vassily, their wives too superstitious to
leave the kitchen; and they kept Ossip and Sashenka away from us.

Some weeks after Tatiana Arkipovna's departure Stanya Parsov
climbed up to the Squire's study. The Squire made short shrift of him.

"I'm not selling. Good-by, Stanya, come back next year and I'll give you the field."

Parsov spread the news in the markets that the Squire did nothing but rave since his wife had left, "and with two streams of froth," Vassily reported him saying.

The main thing now, I was being drilled for "an hour's informal concert before the Jewish opera singer." There I would run prodigious gamuts supposed to make the lady forgive Arkip Apollonovitch's insulting remark against her people. It was perfectly clear within his preposterous head that somehow my fiddling could persuade the woman into believing that not only Arkip Apollonovitch but his entire family actually lived only to devote themselves to Jews; impossible, therefore, for her to block the great loan any more from her influential protector. Ah, what a triumph for the Golinsk branch! The old man made into a duke, you see, by the previously regarded little pimple! And out of it all, the Squire would receive a just reward, a slice of the inheritance right away! Then hurray, and let the old man live to a hundred and fifty!

Since she was in opera, various arias had to be included. From his trunk Glueck finally selected "just what will overwhelm her and what you will be able to play well," the "Evening Star" and a potpourri from *Russlan and Ludmilla* to promote the Russian side, "Wonderful Dream," "Shining Star of Love," and "Oh, Field." My lack of command made me feel defeated in advance but Glueck imagined he remedied this by playing along with me and having me copy his touches. However, in time I could put in my own, and with *Ave Maria* mine from the start these grew into pleasures.

I had a big never-absent headache. I was supposed to dazzle her down to a melt by the Beethoven D Major sonata. In the beginning I believed it was something Glueck composed to show off in Paris with. I watched him writing it out. He said the D Major had been composed by Beethoven for 'cello and piano but it was his thought to alter the 'cello part to violin. I would be able to play it well and my concert would be imposing. This I accepted without believing; in America I saw he wasn't lying. Glueck had made a most respectable transposition into A major, bringing up the piano part so the counterpoint came out not too tinkly and also simplifying the piano harmony to make my violin part stand out better. I told him I could hardly read it; if I practiced ten years I'd never stop making mistakes. "Nonsense, four and a half months ago you couldn't read a note and look where you are!"

Meanwhile every night in his study the Squire continued to worship himself sincerely before us and with complete freedom. Having at last admitted his true religion nothing in him could be unimportant. Sitting at his desk in his great tall chair he unwrapped all the dusty ancient bandages of his mummyhood, fearless against humiliation and without the need to be contradicted. With his hussar's cloak draped over his shoulders, the dogged commander unbothered by the rigors of field headquarters, the bottle always near to hand, his eyes saw again what lay in the far-gone days of his faithlessness. He shook his sins out of him, his little nasals whirring with small trembles as he renounced those years, even the ones furthest away, when the world was a closet filled with wonders and he too blind to go and open it. I cannot reproduce his repertoire of rigmaroles but here are a few samples, not word for word yet more true than word for word, because I wasn't listening that way. About '61 —

"I remember old Buzarov, that's Vassily's father now. He could tumble a bull off its feet with one push of his boot. It was in this room he told my father that the proclamation was up, the day set, the rules there before everyone's eyes. My father drew old B. to this window and looked down upon his souls, whole thousands of them covering the hill, all their hats off, singing as though in the church to thank Father for giving them the land. Father said to me, wearing his favorite tie, a bow made into doves' wings, 'From hence onward we shall be striving. You will be teaching yourself a new word — "forward" — the people are no longer a theory.' Father turned his face to old B. and asked if he would like to spit upon it. Old B. fell to tears and this angered Father, he took his revolver from the desk here and swore to shoot, but old B. shook his head merely, sobbing, 'Shoot, Andrey Fedorevitch, I cannot,' whereupon Father hurled the revolver out of the window and then spit in the direction of old B. 'This is what we shall be doing for the rest of our lives,' he said to me. 'Prepare yourself, Kolya.' Then he went downstairs. I experienced a wrench, wanting a harmless willy-nilly about me, no angers, no difficulties . . . I was not fit for the times. 'Forward' is a ship that rides on blood, I was gentle, I sipped Pushkin. Well! With brothers in the army long gone from the estate, what was I? Just my mother's, the one that was left and out of love I allowed her, as they say, to comb my bald head every morning. In two years they both died, I came to Moscow for the winter, and that's the Tatya of it. Kept from anything higher I drank, others were amused by me, I was a dwarf among giants, I led pageants of disgust, debauched myself clearly — and for what? For the gone willy-nillys, for the old dear tediums, to wait ghoulishly for Arkip Apollonovitch to die! But that's over! Now I have with what to strive! I have become quite orderly, I care not that the orchards are dull, the fields poor in the market, the grapes never right any more! Let the roof leak, the lamps stink! No, in the honesty of my plan I can pronounce the word 'forward' with joy. When Arkip Apollonovitch comes next month and hears what I prepare for him! What prizes he'll yield! The world will see me!"

With this and more the Squire burned himself for sparks, until again on the following night. One time he revealed "the Tatya of it" — a tomboy girlhood, her father mostly away from the estate, the daughter scorning the dainty manners of an heiress, growing taller and stronger, drinking vodka by the glass like a man; engaging in intimate frolics with peasant boys, storming, laughing, insulting her father's important people and finally managing to be sent away from the estate. To stir her aunts and cousins into frenzies she had compromised various visiting uncles; hoping city life would polish her down, Arkip Apollonovitch remembered a second-class aunt in Moscow and sent Tatya there for a winter. The aunt gave her books to read, took her to teas, museums, and balls. The dressmaker lived nearby, out of which a confidential friendship grew between herself and the dressmaker's daugh-

"Eh?"

"Who are they?"

The Squire was on his belly. In this position his words seemed to fall out to floor. "The Avengers . . . sh."

Natalya found the courage to crawl next to him. "Dear Konstantin Andreyevitch," she begged, "everybody loves you, you are safe."

I knew he was crazy and I didn't see any good news in it.

In a minute or so he said, "Nnnnnnow . . . fire."

I only fired once. I didn't know how to reload. They each fired about six times, the glass shattering; we heard shouts from anear, "Enough! They ran away!" I recognized the voice of Dr. Ostrov, somewhat highly pitched and neither irritated nor friendly.

"Good," the Squire said, standing. "We didn't need reinforcements."

When the doctor and the two others came through the unhinged door the Squire stood quite calmly explaining "the action " The doctor kept nodding while holding the Squire's pulse, his head cocked to a side, a dead piece of cigar in his mouth. "Come, Kolya," he said, leading him to the door, "you'll tell me everything upstairs." They left the room in a most natural stroll. When they reached the stairs Dr. Ostrov told Rodion and Vassily to carry the Squire up. The Squire protested, "No, I am not even scratched," and without warning fainted and shook in it.

The doctor did not come out of his room for an hour. Glueck and I waited on the landing. "He will be in bed a week," Ostrov told us at last. "I'll talk to Vassily, he'll know what to get from Yushin."

"Is it a stroke?" Glueck asked.

"A stroke of luck," said the doctor drily, hurrying away; a curious reply.

The next evening Dr. Ostrov brought Tatiana Arkipovna and her female train from Minsk.

She walked past us in the hall, straightly proud and up the stairs with a sure balance. She carried a small box or two, and she showed us clear eyes and how she must have looked long ago, seeming to have come from a thrilling vacation. Madame had apparently retrogressed, he

ter then occupied in a secret flirtation with an apprentice bookbinder, a frivolous dispenser of charms. Tatya invited him to the aunt's house to bind some books after which he visited when the aunt was absent. Within a month Tatya's first and last love fanned up and down; there was to have been an elopement but at this point the friendship between her and the dressmaker's daughter ceased being confidential. The apprentice bookbinder told the dressmaker's daughter who told the aunt. The fellow disappeared, promising to return. Tatya soon learned that the aunt had given the lover a hundred rubles to go away. She took herself for a stone and tried to jump from a window. In this condition she met Konstantin Konayev at a ball. They were suited, sharing negative needs, he for an heiress and she never to be happy and never to go home.

The nights droned away. He kept up with several of the polite magazines, remaining languid and authoritative on certain topics, up to the moment of twisting them into his mania. In this fashion he once sermonized, "After all" (with a look at me, I had seen him only as a hater of my people and now he would enlighten me), men like Arkip Apollonovitch and by adhesion himself, "had the mission of raising Russia from the pesthole of Europe to an example before the world." Before this could be done the Jews would have to be conquered since they refused to renounce their "heathen gall," by which he meant our history, "preferring to remain scavengers, to cheat and outwit and kill, forcing methods not yet enough harsh to curb the pollution of the honest peasantry." There existed some good individuals among us but these were "helpless against the making of meadows into latrines." He insulted, with patriotic phrases, wealthy and powerful Jews, such as the Vysotskis and Brodskis whose existence demanded the control-ment of "the Golinsk gnats" which must never be allowed to graduate into the fraternity of "poisoners of the mass"—interpolating various frauds about how rich Jews were contributing sums to subsidize roving bands of "Zasulich Avengers" killing and burning throughout whole provinces—though of course Vera Zasulich had been hung long ago for her part in the assassination.

It got to what the Squire never allowed out of his mind. The history of crusades demonstrated how nothing inspirational was possible "without the firing of the youth." It had to be the duty of such as himself to snip the Jewish fangs by taking the best of their youth away from them. However, the expropriation must not be gross; youth in whom appeared some possibility of bettering should be molded for proof that in Russia even the Jew received a place of worth, and a hand. Here the Squire grew wholly emphatic, his eyes shrinking and his words spittling in a monotone rant. "Two struggles! The dull daily, the spooning down to the people of the anti-Yid medicines! And the other, proving we are no longer devotees of kvas and radish but farmers of the spirit, Glueck! Yes, reapers of Pushkins by the rows, out of Jewish weeds!"

He had carried himself past the opera singer, Arkip Apollonovitch already a duke and himself long since possessed of the spoils due him for accomplishing this; and during such moments he convinced himself of his future commemoration, with parades, as a cleanser of the stable, a Russian Hercules.

The sun was stronger, everything winterish in drips, the roads canals of mud, and you could walk outside without buttoning your coat. The domestic props began to be replaced; Arkip Apollonovitch would arrive in a few weeks; the house had to be pulled together. Meals started being served at regular times downstairs though supper still did not come before ten.

Ossip began requiring many private conversations with me. In between his boastings about his friendships with a few of the ladies who worked in his Uncle Profim's "Heaven" he gave me news about our side that put weights on my heart. Through the winter, a funeral almost every week: Faiga, Naftoli-Dovid, Asher-the-Sour, Pesha's Fendel, Shprinza's Zish, Yeersel's Bosha and their Mayer; also children whose names he did not know. Of the nineteen huts only two now were being lived in, the land-rents unpaid as well as the fines of July, death foreclosing mostly ahead of the Squire, the junk in the empties taken for whatever could be realized. And what about the last two

now? How many were alive I could not guess; the number had to be tiny if only two had people in them.

"Do you hear about my brother, Shim?"

"They say he stays away, sewing in places for a bed and a bite."

I kept hoping this meant he had managed to run away. "And what will be done with the last two huts, Ossip, do you know?"

"They're no good until it's warm again. Maybe my uncle will rent them from the village, next maneuvers, and fill them with girls for the soldiers."

According to him the villagers were gossiping that the Squire was dying, that his wife was crazy, that Glueck was not really a music teacher but a fortuneteller with an evil eye who was persuading the Squire to sell off the estate in pieces and that the one behind the scheme was Stanya Parsov.

The night before the return of Tatiana Arkipovna the Squire suffered a serious knock. While enjoying one of his monologues, pacing up and down in his study, he happened to look out of the window. He shouted, "Danger, they are here, everybody take arms," and ordered us to follow him to his sitting room where the rifles hung. There he fired shots to wake the household. When they appeared he explained that the enemy's line lay along the near side of the stream and gave each of us a rifle, with instructions to Rodion and Vassily "to make a careful count of their bonfires."

By an exchange of rapid glances between them after they made sure the Squire was seeing things, Rodion and Vassily took themselves outside "to reconnoiter," in this way to fetch Dr. Ostrov. Meanwhile the Squire had us lying flat on the floor with rifles, even the women. Every few moments he would speak in some intended tone of assurance to remind us he was our general. "They're clever, clever . . . but wipe them out when they come creeping with their brands. Listen! Hear them? Ossip, you have good ears! Do you hear them?"

Ossip thought it over. "I'm not sure, Squire. Your ears are better than mine."

By now I was able to speak. "Squire," I whispered.

small face betraying indications of new worries piled upon the old, but a stiffer pride in owning them. Lilli looked as before, her bonnet in a slant as she cried she had lost something on the way, nothing to hear outside of a baby carriage. Leta had taken some of her mother's entering dignity and color, walking quickly and gently past us half on her toes with no more than a quick smile at Glueck's bow. Her cheeks were red with more than the cold air, the girl happy to be young and near the one for whom she would have died.

The rupture of our routine that day gave me unexpected time to think; and this happened more and more until Arkip Apollonovitch came. By peering out of my window at a slant I could see an angle of our huts, patches of brown dotting the gray-white fields of soft wet snow, the generous air preparing the end of our locked-in winter life, and I would have taken any chance, no matter what the punishment, to run across the highroad and see which of my own were left and if my brother would still not talk to me. But I had visions of faceless women screaming, "Back, back, you murderer," and no heart to hear if the real faces would speak differently. For themselves they would be right, I thought, overestimating the depth of my estrangement. In this mood I played *Ave Maria* sometimes; it sounded mostly "theirs."

I was playing it when Glueck returned from an interview with Tatiana Arkipovna. For all his slight build he never moved easily in a controlled flow, more like nailed together at the joints, yet here he almost danced to where I stood, taking the fiddle from me and giving it several happy rips of pure improvisation, more astounding to me than the time my nephew Aaron's wife Rhoda lost a bet and paid it to him by kissing him in the behind at their twentieth anniversary party.

"I'm happy," he cried, skipping as he played, his small coattails flapping, "it went well, excellently! I'm to give Leta lessons again but Tatiana Arkipovna will do the rest, she said. I mentioned I had the highest feelings for the girl but only as a pupil and friend . . . which she's to tell Leta . . . an amazing woman! Leta will know from her that it is useless to hope. She promised!"

"She has changed?"

"To her true self . . . the rest in Minsk has done her good. She's at peace, Lev. And I too! Come, let's work!"

The piano lessons resumed, Leta in a controlled calm, Glueck gay at the table, Madame glummer and bitten inside, Tatiana Arkipovna blooming, visiting her husband in his room twice a day for an hour; and she let us know she approved the plan to render Arkip Apollono-vitch a service, spoke of leaving the girls with Madame and traveling to Paris with us; and the day the Squire rose from bed she greeted him with the loveliest surprise; he was delighted! The family a family again!

Dr. Ostrov learned of the surprise at tea, kissed Tatiana Arkipovna's hand, said, "My dear, you have added twenty years to your husband's life," smiling in a gleaming manner. And what was the great surprise? The first morning the Squire joined his family at breakfast, leaning on a cane, looser about the face, he asked, "Where is Madame?"

"Where indeed," from Tatiana Arkipovna with a girlish giggle.

"Sick, I hope."

"Ah, be more charitable," from her, "say you'd want her to enjoy her holiday."

"What holiday?"

"I made it difficult for her in Minsk, I was a baby there," Tatiana Arkipovna murmured with a rosy smile, "and since she's to be alone with the girls while we're in Paris I thought she ought to have a little trip too. She's with her sister in Smolensk for a while, Kolya, until you say we leave for Paris. Poor Vera hasn't seen her sister in years."

"How nice," said the Squire, "to come down in the morning and see Madame among us, but how delightful it is to know she is in Smolensk!"

Calm agreements, shared joys . . . he obeyed to the letter every Ostrov instruction, napped or read the whole afternoon while Tatiana Arkipovna took a horse for gallops when the sun was high, the snow almost gone; even telling Rodion to saddle the two slowest horses for Leta and Lilli, teaching them all over again in the field beyond the summerhouse. In this atmosphere Leta betrayed no discontent, neither plying Glueck with her old look of waiting to be harnessed and ridden nor allowing him to discover why. And so it went, nothing ceased on top. On the Monday before the Thursday that Arkip Apollonovitch was expected Tatiana Arkipovna urged Glueck into a concert for the family; I played what the great guest would be hearing except the scherzo of the Beethoven which I could not tame. She cried "Bravo!" and the Squire took great heart from it, the excitement whirling in a glow. Deep knocks were preparing themselves, however, the house never a house again but a casino of obsessions, a place of endings.

The telegram arrived on Tuesday. The Squire inspected Rodion's boots and coat for fifteen minutes, the carriage and livery polished spotless five times, and at dawn Thursday Rodion clattered down the hill to bring the guest from the Minsk depot. That afternoon, another telegram from Arkip Apollonovitch; delayed in Petersburg until Saturday. Again waitings, inspections, polishings; and I too. "It gives them more time to be ready to play for Father," Tatiana Arkipovna told her restless husband. The Squire insisted we work like horses and Glueck spent most of the next days trying to get me even with the Beethoven but he had to give up. Perhaps next month, he decided, when we were already in Paris I might have mastered at least the middle movement. Meanwhile he shined me up on the Glinkas, the Schubert, and the "Evening Star." Dr. Ostrov did not fail to visit every day, giving the Squire encouraging chats and then retiring into private with Tatiana Arkipovna. She possessed her usual braveness when she reappeared, yet she smiled with an inner paleness. I said to Glueck, "The Squire is going to die."

"Nonsense."

"Do you suppose she'd be sorry, really?"

"Yes, a bit. Her deepest sorrow is pledged to another cause however. Since we have grown close, I see it. She mourns being denied her own son, that's why she's fine and tender about me, somewhat secretly, it's true . . . if you knew what she's accomplished for me . . ." He sighed, then with happy risk, "I must tell someone, you won't repeat?" I shook my head. "The woman is a jewel — a second mother."

"What did she do for you?"

"I may stay here as long as I wish," he cried youthfully, "as a son to her and a brother to Leta! Oh . . . now you'll see me compose! Do you understand, boy? Suites, operas, symphonies! And conduct them all myself, in the Hall of Nobles!"

"You're happy."

"My life is saved!"

Then, the great Tuesday; and with it a weary annoyed Arkip Apollonovitch anxious to leave before he arrived, trailing behind him a certain Kremenko, a little person of indeterminate age and magnificent blandness carrying several dispatch cases and wearing a shock of a diamond on his pinky finger; something of a butler, more of a secretary, and mostly the old man's assassin of those irrelevancies hovering in swarms over brows contemptuous of halos, brows already graven on top of their self-erected monuments. The first meeting downstairs must have been of the briefest; Glueck and I saw the carriage coming, from upstairs, and shortly afterward we heard them on the landing just below us. We had a glimpse of Arkip Apollonovitch as he made the turn towards the guest suite — tall and spare, incredibly straight for his over ninety years, no beard, a starved eagle's face, it seemed, of cherubic structure planed thin by a life of the sternest flights; some giant of a bird from another time flying the continents from peak to peak, austerely avoiding the jungles, satisfied only when alone and above. This was his everyday face, the full red lips and russet cheeks of his picture hanging downstairs in the Gallery the artistic embellishment he had not been able to abide; why he had gladly given away the picture. He sent out Kremenko to inform that he wished to see Dr. Ostrov but no one else until the next day and that no food should be prepared for him.

Dr. Ostrov paid his call. The Squire forced him to stay for supper in order to receive a full explanation of Arkip Apollonovitch's exclusivity. Kremenko failed to appear downstairs when the bell rang, taking his meal in the guest suite also from the store carried with them. He called for hot water which Vassily took up, returning to report that their supper consisted of a special brew of tea and herb-root from their own samovar together with clabbered milk mixed in a bowl of plain white cheese with a garnish of raisins and almonds. Dr. Ostrov said approvingly, "He eats like a peasant."

"Is he ill or tired?"

"To say he's ill would be incorrect, Kolya. He is ninety-four or -five."

"Please, Alexander Voyinevitch, say straight out . . . is there any danger of his . . . ?" The Squire bit his lip sharply and not entirely without pleasure. Dared he hope the father-in-law's time had arrived? After all had his long-nursed project turned unnecessary?

"He's prepared, bodily, to expire," the doctor said carefully, "but this has been so for more than twenty years. Don't upset yourself, Kolya. I simply reviewed for him our little ailments here, in which he took a fatherly interest. He is relieved that the worst has passed. He took cold on the train and wisely rests in order to give his best self to the family tomorrow. Besides, his Georgei advises me he has a number of decisions to certify and telegrams to compose."

"Yes, that's Father," Tatiana Arkipovna said without bias.

Three times the next day Rodion was sent to Pukop with telegrams. It went into the afternoon, and still no summons from the little Kremenko. I fiddled in the main reception hall, Glueck filling in at the piano. Tatiana Arkipovna took the girls for a gallop, it being almost balmy that day, and as the sun slanted we saw the Squire and Kremenko step out to the promenade together, Kremenko democratically accepting a cigar without modifying the gestures he was making in the course of his establishing some point or other. The brusqueness of his steps and the vigorous casualness with which he was waving the hand holding the cigar, together with the smiles of self-evident shrewdness playing on his face as he pronounced what through the window-glass appeared to be informal observations of an epochal nature, made Glueck remark, "The Squire is contented, for once, to listen."

That evening after supper, the formal welcome; the family must have been with him about half an hour when Glueck and I got our summons. They sat in a ring about the bed, the Squire at Arkip's feet, one leg over the other, his arms folded across his chest, a cigar in his mouth; Leta and Lilli on a bench together near their mother, their hands in their laps like the girls who go to dances but don't dance; and Tatiana Arkipovna, a young tilt to her in the lamplight, leaning forward listening to her father, the skin tight upon her cheeks taking some of the pink of her dress which rustled at her smallest movement, and allowed a visible rise and fall of her bosom; no sign on her strong face if her father's words had touched her or if like him she was standing on the ramparts. The bed was a litter of documents and ledgers which Kremenko unobtrusively cleared piece by piece, examining each one carefully before placing it in a small trunk filled with similar material, the old man talking along meanwhile though having noticed Glueck and me standing at the door, a good twenty-five feet from him and to one side. We were allowed to remain there until Arkip Apollonovitch finished.

"It is interesting, I suppose," he was saying in a voice well reined, the breaths paid out carefully like coins taken from a purse and laid one by one on a counter. "But not for long. It is always the same at spas. The pilgrims come; everything is planned by the watch. They stand in their bathes, looking about to see if anyone is cured. It should be a pleasant life, in the summer. I will go to no more spas. No cures will be made on me. Many of them are genuine but not from the bathes. You see gentlemen on the benches in the morning waiting for their time, conversing on topics considered *au courant*. One speaks, the other listens. They meet in the afternoon, waiting for their time to bathe. Now the morning speaker listens while the other talks. For this they return every summer to the spa. For the curative *bon ton*. . . ." He stopped. "And who is that?" he asked quietly, pointing to Glueck and me. Glueck came forward, gave him a full bow and a loud click of his heels. "Ernst Glueck, sir, of the Maryinsky Theatre, Petersburg."

"So you are the boy," Arkip Apollonovitch said, indicating with his finger for me to come forward. "I thought I heard a piano downstairs, and not poorly."

"He plays the *violin*, Papa," Tatiana Arkipovna said.

"You must hear him," from the Squire, with a defensive puff at his cigar.

"Yes. Well, Georgei? Before we go to sleep what have you forgotten?"

"Nothing," Kremenko replied, congratulating himself with a smile.

"I would like," said the Squire as the ladies rose, "a minute privately with you, Arkip Apollonovitch."

"Yes, yes. Tomorrow, Kolya."

"It is of first importance to you, Father."

"Yes," the old man threw into the Squire's trembling aggressiveness, "tomorrow, then. Tatya . . ." He motioned to her to sit again. "We'll see what's left to speak of."

Good-nights were said stiffly, the Squire bearing up against having to leave with Leta and Lilli.

On the morning of that Thursday Glueck and I were fighting with the Beethoven downstairs in the main reception hall, the day rolling warmly to noon, the trees losing their winter gray, the bark darker, the brown ground lightening with promises of soon green, spring still with its eyes closed but yawning; and during a short rest as I put my bow to the resin Glueck opened the French door near the piano, sampled the refreshing air that entered. We left the door open, returned to the Beethoven not aware immediately of the voices on the promenade, when they began or whose they were. As we played there seemed mixed into it that other sound, at first sensed as a discord, extraneous, then as voices, clearly people talking on the promenade, two. Our eyes slanted to the door; but no one, the voices continuing *agitato,* the piano angled to the meeting of the walls; we were unseen.

Glueck's eyes met mine, we stopped playing, we listened. The woman was doubtless Tatiana Arkipovna, her tones urgent and even pleading, her tempo quick, her volume conspiratorial but carrying. They stood at the corner of the promenade just to the side of the French door; at first the voice of the man remained a mystery. Not his public voice, no professional control in it; all feeling, the voice of a man with a woman important to him.

"Tatya, there's no danger."

"I'm afraid."

"Dismiss it. I've explained it to him. Arkip Apollonovitch will *not* touch off Kolya."

"He says he will not. I'm afraid, Alexei."

"Don't tremble. . . ."

"But Father hates him . . . more than I do. . . ."

"Not enough to brew a stroke in him. Tatya, it is all right, please . . ."

"But I've sinned, sinned — "

"Not us, never that. Let God be judge. And I swear your father won't give him a blank 'no.' "

"You are wrong."

"He'll put him off, leave Kolya his hopes. Kolya will never know the truth. We spoke of it only just now."

"I shouldn't have told him Kolya's scheme!"

"He knows he *must* leave Kolya his hopes. The man is your father, not a murderer."

"Promise you won't let him die, Alexei . . . ?"

"You think I would?"

"I would not be free! Yes, I spoke against Kolya to Father, with malice. . . ."

"False conscience, Tatya. Your father and I would not be murderers. . . ."

"And I, Alexei . . . ?"

"No, darling Tatya, it is all right. . . ."

They moved, their voices trailing away, around the other side.

"Glueck!"

He stared ahead, fiddling with his glasses, gulping like a hooked fish. "Sh."

"What was it?"

"Nothing."

"Not *her* . . . and the doctor?"

"Sh!"

"But it was *her* and the doctor. . . ."

"Sh!" he repeated savagely, against his panic. "Whispers are deceiving, ears make mistakes! No, there is an explanation!"

We went back to the Beethoven and Glueck hurled himself into the piano part. But the harder he pounded the keyboard, the more he thought about it. Tatiana Arkipovna with a *lover?* So great and warm a woman speaking secretly against her husband's Parisian scheme to her father, knowing it might kill the Squire if Arkip frowned upon it? Twice never! Not she who had risen above herself to protect him from her own impossible daughter; no, ears must be mistrusted, whispers flung into the wind.

At lunch the Squire was gay, quips radiating from the great central news given him by Kremenko an hour before. Quite rested now from his journey Arkip Apollonovitch would be leaving his bed that afternoon, take some air, and listen to how I played. "First he'll hear the boy, then what I propose! On guard, Tatya — to pack for Paris at any moment!"

She appeared to be pleased; no sign of her depths. The talk ran on and until Leta spoke I thought I alone noticed the absence of Glueck. "Mother," she said, "does Ernst know we are eating?"

"He is late."

Late and more; he did not appear at all. Finishing first as usual the Squire gave his mouth a careless napkin-wipe and said, "I'd better hurry him, Kremenko didn't say exactly when Papa was coming down."

He strode out with pleasant quickness, sure the sun shone for him that day. He wore a hard collar and a frock coat, adding a typical touch by putting himself under a turban of ivory silk adorned with rhinestones and a couple of gay feathers, a trophy brought back years ago from a pseudo-harem in Petersburg. Tatiana Arkipovna pushed her tea glass away, she had something to tell Grandpa. Not wanting to be left with the girls, I went upstairs too. As we climbed her face lost its clean lines, her emotions melting them waxenly.

I left her at the second landing.

Glueck's door was closed. I heard the Squire talking to him all buttery and jolly but I didn't catch what Glueck said. In my room I stood looking out of the window until the Squire left. Then I went to see what made Glueck miss lunch.

His trunk with the lid up stood in the center of the room, his closet door was open, and his worktable always so piled with books and papers and music manuscript now sat bare of everything but dust, Glueck leaning forward on the chair, his legs spread, his head bowed. A second look and I saw he was packed.

"Glueck?"

He raised his head, looked at me, and removed his eyeglasses, putting them on the table. I had never before seen him without them. He appeared fishier, hungrier, younger, and completely stunned.

"Did anyone die, Glueck?" He shook his head. "But I see you're going away for a while."

"Not for a while." He went to the window and looked out, then started rubbing his palms against his temples as though his hair would not stay down. But he had hardly any, keeping it cropped so close.

"Glueck, but aren't we playing for the old man this afternoon, and aren't you needed for Paris too?"

"There is no Paris," he said, all blank. "She went to her father and exploded Paris. Now she waits with her lover, the doctor," and here he allowed himself some bitterness, "for the husband to die."

"Glueck, it sounds impossible . . . you're sure?"

"You're too young to know these things." With his hands to his brows and his elbows before his face, the words came as though from behind a shield. "You heard them on the promenade but you didn't get the meaning."

What could I say? All I thought was, "Paris is exploded."

When he turned from the window the sobs began. He tried holding back, then did not care. "I was to be a brother to Leta, a brother . . . stupid me, me she thought to deceive even more than the other one! I took her promises, took her for my second mother . . . took what? . . . a harlot, a murderess. . . ."

Saying the last words passing the open trunk, he slammed the lid
down hard and stopped pacing. "Yes, I'm young," he reminded himself, with temper, "too young to marry a Leta . . . and live among
trash . . . and compose trash!"

"You are leaving. . . ."

"Tomorrow, early. They'll know before supper . . . yes, and I'll
miss you. . . ."

Afternoon, the main reception hall, two o'clock. Command performance for Arkip Apollonovitch.

Enter the Emperor of all the Konayevs, on a cane, in a black velvet
gown with tassels, followed by Kremenko with portfolio; and the loyal
subjects rose, the Squire now without his turban for the solemn occa-
sion, Lilli limp with boredom but Leta aglow in advance at the triumph
of her chevalier standing beside the piano, one hand upon it, with the
most dignified and artistic melancholy; present also, of course, the
suffering Tatiana Arkipovna saved from the Squire by the doctor become her paramour in Minsk; yet already she was close to a new and
steeper fall. She clasped her hands, her proud head dropped in a charming bow, she smiled to hide the pain of her fear's clutch. Then un-
expectedly there the paramour himself, fresh from a healthy gallop
across the fields, suffused by a cheery shine from his bald head to his
brown boots. Clear is Ostrov's conscience, teeming with virtue is his
sin. He keeps wife and husband somewhat alive by means best suited
to each, deriving at last satisfactions both professional and personal,
the right spice balancing his Golinsk life.

And finally there was me, the ignorant hub.

Arkip Apollonovitch lowered himself, the rest following. He pointed
his cane at me.

Glueck put himself at the piano, his face wearing the concert mask;
he began the introduction to the Glinka potpourri.

I played, the air about me thicker and heavier, the notes striking some
wall a foot away and bouncing back. I was surrounded, nothing flowing, I was to my neck in notes. When it was over — silence.

I looked up. The room was shivering. I blinked my eyes.

Glueck began the *Ave Maria*. I came in at the right place, keeping my head down so as not to see the room. I closed my eyes on the sostenutos, played according to practice, no Laib in it until about half-way, the music then forcing me to forget them all. There were no notes, only sounds.

When it ended — again silence. I saw the Squire's mouth working. He had many words to say but kept swallowing them until Arkip Apollonovitch spoke.

Leta stared at Glueck, the Squire and his wife at the old man, Kremenko threw a noncommittal grin at Ostrov and Lilli said, "Mama. . . ?"

Tatiana Arkipovna replied with a quick understanding nod and Lilli dashed out.

Arkip Apollonovitch tapped the floor with his cane. The Squire interpreted this as applause. "Ah, Papa," he cried, "I see you're convinced!"

"You haven't been idling," with an honest nod, "he plays well."

"Well enough for anybody?"

"Well enough for me," said Arkip Apollonovitch. And the Squire's heart leapt as Arkip Apollonovitch added, "Indeed well enough for anybody."

Arkip Apollonovitch prepared to rise; in a man of his age and height this took time. Tatiana Arkipovna threw an appealing glance at Ostrov.

The doctor stepped close to the old man, his own back to the Squire, and helped Arkip.

Meanwhile from my angle I saw what the Squire could not. Ostrov caught Arkip's eye with a slight head-shake of warning; Arkip's lips moved in recognition. When he was fully up and Ostrov had stepped away, Arkip faced the Squire. "You have something, Kolya. What are you going to do with it?"

"That's it, *exactly!* I haven't been at a pastime, Papa! I *know* what can be done with him, superbly!"

"That should be worth hearing," said the old man, calm in his ruthlessness. "We'll talk about it, sometime."

He turned away. Kremenko stepped forward. "Don't forget the telegram," he said pointedly.

"Yes, the telegram," with an annoyed rumble. "Tatya, it is unfortunate. I must be in Moscow Sunday."

"Then you leave tomorrow," the Squire gulped. "Well . . . in that case," grabbing his nervousness by the throat, "we should have our talk immediately, Papa!"

"Why immediately?" from the man not too senile to be unable to play the fumbler when it suited him. "Later, Kolya, when it is time for good-nights. . . ."

"Papa — I speak with firmness — allow me to expose the purpose of my months of work. The boy is a Jew; five months ago he could read not one single note of music. Hearing him play, just any way, I decided to bring him along, got him his tutor . . . at first for just-so. But then, with the most serious purpose after you wrote in December concerning your dilemma about the loan . . . your letter from Paris, the loan, that opera singer blocking it . . . ?"

"Well, yes," with a beetling of his brows, baiting his son-in-law, "but how does it follow?"

"Papa . . . this fiddle-kid of a Jew will melt her determination to block you with her prejudiced thrusts, allowing he who monopolizes her favors, your friend . . ."

Arkip Apollonovitch waved his hand, an implication of equality granted; two gentlemen sharing discreetly a certain little fact. "Hn, to use the boy on her. Is that your thought, Kolya?"

"Let her turn her back upon a hundred Arabias, Papa, she cannot refuse *this!*"

"I'm no judge of these points."

The Squire paled, Tatiana pleaded with a stretch of her neck and a gasp and the old man dropped the right card. "I'll give it thought, Kolya, the approach is shrewd." He imitated, with a twitch of his lips, a veto in the Squire's favor. "Yes, I might have Lev play for people who know these points and who know *her*. Then we might try him on her."

"Shall we plan for Paris?" the Squire begged.

"Yes . . ."

"Leaving when?"

"I drag myself first to Moscow. I'll telegraph from there."

"Victory," cried the Squire, lifting his arms, leaving Tatiana Arkipovna half happy.

A bit of air on the promenade with Glueck, he in his own silent writhings; announcements of twilight, the bare branches more in a wave, the fields in a darker key; it was a reprise of November before the snow. Inside as we went to take our coats up we found Tatiana Arkipovna at the staircase, an uncertain sentry.

"Ernst," needing breath, "a moment . . . ?"

She led him to her sitting room, the door closed.

In my room, nothing to do. I looked out toward our huts, watching for the sight of a speck down there. The piece of lane I saw remained unpopulated. What was it like in Paris? How far from there to America?

Dark enough for the lamp. Where are you, Glueck? Please God, I know You're busy and angry at me. But don't let Glueck go. I know You're on Shim's side too but listen. Don't let Glueck go and leave me here.

A noise. I stumbled to Glueck's. He was there, lighting a lamp. "Glueck. . . ."

"Go away."

Deadly said, hostile. "I'm afraid, Glueck. Please don't go."

"*You are all crazy here!*" he shouted, the pain in him more terrifying than the unexpected noise of so contained a man.

I jumped away. He ran to the door, slamming it closed. "Excuse me, boy . . . I did not mean . . ."

"Don't go. . . ." I begged again.

"*Crazy, crazy, crazy!*"

All right, I won't keep you waiting. Now to the comic finale, all brass and percussions, the HAH–HAHS and BAH–BOOM–BAHS after one another like cats and dogs. I was too near it to be entertained.

After supper that night which Arkip Apollonovitch attended with Kremenko in honor of his departure the next day, there was no question any more about Paris. Hair would grow on the palm of my hand before the Squire would ever bring me there and he was the only one who didn't know it, leaving out the girls. Hearing Glueck's yelling, Tatiana Arkipovna had thoughtfully sent straight for Dr. Ostrov to administer a sedative.

He stayed for supper, and it was his behavior that convinced me.

With the finish of the eating they sent me upstairs. I peeked into Glueck's; he was asleep. It was after nine; I wasn't sleepy but I went to bed too.

I couldn't stop thinking about that supper. The more I thought, the surer I was. In the first place only the Squire drank more than one glass of the special champagne brought up for the celebration, and he alone rose to make toasts. Each time he lifted his glass and proclaimed his loyalty to Paris, to opera, to music, to Arkip Apollonovitch — "to our dearest Papa, who indeed will sit where the right hand of the Tsar may touch him" — though he drained it the others merely sipped; and here took place jolly eye-plays between Kremenko and Ostrov, even a wink, Arkip Apollonovitch himself remaining impassive, excusing his hardly touched glass on the principle of diet. When the Squire allowed himself to ask about where we would be staying in Paris so he might write for rooms the old man quite reasonably explained that Kremenko arranged everything; and though the Squire approached the question from several different sides Arkip Apollonovitch parried telling him even the name of the opera singer whose opposition was to be removed. In all this Tatiana Arkipovna kept silent, her face holding a steady reddish touch. When she looked up from her plate it was only to glance worriedly at Ostrov who pursued a steady campaign with napkin, glass, and fork in order to camouflage his constant pacifying looks in her direction. Through it all, Arkip Apollonovitch quite calmly disposed of his dish of cheese in clabbered milk, patient in his role of honored patriarch and benefiter of the Squire's keen plotting in his behalf, a little tired, considerably bored, and finally annoyed when the Squire brought up "a matter of some embarrassment, Papa," the problem of his "possibly" being unable to "shake free a couple of thousand" for the trip. He asked "while we are talking about it" if it would be too much trouble for Kremenko "to leave a draft" before he went to bed since "in the rush of good-bys in the morning" the matter might be forgotten "by all."

Arkip Apollonovitch looked up with weary scorn. A well-digested laugh rippled from Kremenko which the Squire returned as a gesture of "that's how it is sometimes with country squires."

As Arkip Apollonovitch paused to choose his words Ostrov remarked, "Don't fret, Kolya, these things are understood."

"Yes, don't flap your wings so hard," said Arkip Apollonovitch drily, "or you will be too tired to fly."

"Exactly," smiled Kremenko, lifting his glass; and the Squire, relieved, drained his own. As he did this Ostrov delivered his telltale wink to Kremenko, whose urbanity absorbed it immediately, his lackey's eyes twinkling semi-preciously over his glass.

And then there was Leta. She had not been told what had sickened Glueck but Ostrov's coming to treat him drew all sorts of questions out of her which Tatiana Arkipovna feared to answer. "He has received bad news of a family nature," was all she said, Ostrov meanwhile assuring Leta that Glueck would be himself in the morning. "It is nothing, you will not even skip a lesson," he told her. She failed to content herself, asking more questions until the Squire ordered her to stop chattering. As usual, nobody thought to pay me any attention; I wasn't supposed to know anything or be anything but a piece of special wood. The best I could hope from the Squire would be my return to the other side of the road to starve among the bitter survivors of the winter, laughed at and hated even by Shim. If not that, he could toss me to Pukop where they'd handle me for my part in the bootlegging, but whatever — it would be far worse than running.

And now, soon spring, was the time for it.

All right, run where? I tussled with this and came to . . . Glueck. With *him*. To Petersburg, why not? And once in Petersburg I'd figure out the next jump.

What now? To put it to him, convince him to testify I had to be taken along, that my fate lay with him. When all this? In the morning? No, too late. All right—then before morning.

Now!

It was late, the house very still. It felt late enough to be near dawn. Better wait till then? Glueck might be annoyed to be waked in the middle of the night. No, let him know it was important enough for me to wake him, let it be now.

I tiptoed into the hall, felt for his doorknob. It was pitch black there, I couldn't find it, my fingers touched nothing. I stepped closer, found the wall, ran my fingers along it to where the door should have been; nothing. Where was I?

I didn't know what I heard. A sudden flow of cold high whispering on the other side of the black air, where the door should have been. It took a few seconds until I realized the two things. The door was open and someone was with Glueck, the room dark, the shutters closed. But *who* . . . ?

Nobody; just Glueck talking to himself in the middle of the night, like me.

I stepped in and with my second step recognized her voice, Tatiana Arkipovna's, coming from in or near the bed. I sunk to the floor, to the carpet, out of possible sight.

Instinct helped me. I remained motionless.

Her voice held itself cool and certain with a confident fencer's poise, the thrusts small and almost merciful. "You must reconcile," she was saying. "I know your suffering. Long ago I loved hopelessly. I remember every hair on his head but see, I have reconciled. Ernst, had Anya loved as you believed, no words of Madame could have made her send that letter to you."

"Tatiana Arkipovna, *please*. . . ."

I wanted to run out. Some people can listen while their ears are being cut off — thieves, storytellers, race-track specialists, and real-estate men — but not a kid where he didn't belong, in the middle of the night, his own pressing mission derailed by an incomprehensible circumstance — nor could I treat myself to bystander's sweetmeats or attempt to siphon out what might be good or bad for me. It was a dangerous mishmash and I trembled that I might learn what it was all about and that I might not.

I didn't move, just gave in to it like a bee swooping up from its inside nest against the screen at the window, its feet and wings seeking the crack through which it had entered. I began to follow without trying.

"Ernst, for your own sake do not go to Novgorod."

"Anything else, Tatiana Arkipovna — "

"Say 'Tatya.' "

"Tatya . . . but I must face Anya."

"Ernst. . . ."

By the rustles of her dress here and the soft lower scrapings, I judged she was on her knees at his bedside. "What you refuse yourself, do for me. Stay for my sake, spare my seeing your ghost when you return from Novgorod."

"You are right! I am a fool, but I must go."

"Forget her, reconcile, stay with us, with me. You shall miss nothing, you will be happy."

"The kindest soul in the world speaks, you wish to save me. But I wish to save myself."

"You refuse me?"

"I cannot refuse myself."

"Yes, you *do* refuse me."

She raised herself to her feet in a great rustle, jumping in with him, and her steel rang; she lunged for her one killing chance. "I beg no more, I command. Must I say it?"

"Tatiana Arkipovna," came his horrified gasp —

"No, it is you who are blind." She gave it to him without cajolery, on strength and will alone. "I sent Madame to Novgorod, I wrote damning letters to your Anya, I, I, I . . . my wish from the start, Ernst, to have her away from you! See, I am honest."

"Oh, lady dear," Glueck whispered from his innermost cosmos, "think what you are doing, you are not well tonight."

"I am well, well, well, excellently well!"

"No," he wrenched from himself, "you are overcome, you are telling little stories, it is only your motherly sympathy."

"You can't go. She'll take you back. I counted on your pride, on your need to be comforted!"

"Lady, please," sliding into hysteria as she clutched him to her, "don't urge yourself, you do not mean this! Forgive me," he blurted, "but isn't there the doctor?"

"Yes," she said in a lower tone, her words fighting up from her throat, her body moving for him, the bed rumbling, "Yes, I've beaten Kolya at last but I'm a mother! Lilli is lost, the nunnery waits for her. But Leta can be saved — and what's the doctor if she isn't?"

Sobs from her; and from Glueck, wrenching tears of fright. "You are so terribly ill tonight, lady . . . come, let us take a walk somewhere, calm ourselves. . . ."

"Ernst, you cannot go away."

Said as a fact, it calmed him. "Very well," he soothed with cunning suddenness. "It is settled. Do you hear? I stay. Now let us compose ourselves," he sing-songed as to a child, "and in the morning — "

"You will stay?"

"I promise. It is over. I cannot demolish you, Tatiana Arkipovna. . . ."

She pulled him to cover her; in the dark I heard his gasp. "See what's yours, I'll send Alexei away, by God! You have me in a double love, Ernst. You will see. Whatever Leta fails you in, *I* provide!"

"Tatya, my God. . . ."

"Ernst," she half-groaned, "marry her, marry her — what she cannot, I will!"

"No," he shouted, her purpose hitting its hardest into him; and there began between them half a fight and half a rape. He twisted, gulped, her hands at his neck; he freed himself, shouted; she kicked and shouted back. As the noises rose I crawled outside. I saw a low glow on the staircase, heard steps; from my room I watched it come brighter in the hall. The sounds next door leapt into tragedy; Glueck screamed, then she; and then the Squire and Kremenko appeared at the head of the stairs, each holding a candlestick.

In the moment after the two entered Glueck's room, the bedlam augmented itself. The Squire screamed something at Glueck, and he back, and then Tatiana Arkipovna, the three all at once in a jumble of hatred spewing out just partly in words; and like some crazy kind of whipped cream on top of it all, the fluttering wavy laughter of the spectator, Kremenko.

I shut my door against it. Was this what people grew up for? How did I get into it and how was I ever going to get out?

The wall between the rooms did not hold them away from me. The Squire screamed something. I heard a flat sound like a stone hitting the wall. Her scream followed and the louder thump of a person dropping like a heap, Kremenko's amused chiding tones coming in a skippy and muted obligato.

I opened my door to run I knew not where. Light rose again from below. Others were climbing the stairs. I drew back inside, leaving a crack in the door. It was Leta stumbling up, followed by Arkip Apollonovitch making slow progress with cane and candle. Leta flew into the room to be greeted by her father. "Ahhh," he whined, bitterly satisfied, "now you see your rival! *She* wants him, Leta — your Mama!"

A paralyzed silence, and from Leta a noise not animal and not loud. Her feet pattered, she jumped toward someone with a wail, and Glueck moaned. "Yes, good!" the Squire spat. "Strike Mama — "

A subdued scuffle for a moment, and then Tatiana Arkipovna's broken sobbing as Arkip Apollonovitch walked into it. "What have we here, Kremenko?"

"Tatiana Arkipovna has reverted," he announced in bulletin style.

Imitating, the Squire said, "She hopes to marry her lover to her daughter in the French fashion."

"You lie," Tatiana Arkipovna replied. "It is Alexander Voyinevitch."

By then I had inched myself toward Glueck's door; from her announcement I expected new explosions. Yet they continued quietly, grossly intent. I peeked in; a lamp had been lit. I saw them arranged like actors at about five minutes to eleven — father and mother facing each other across the middle space, the daughter with her head against her father's chest, his arm about her, his back straight as though posing for a grand portrait, Glueck sitting in the bed between them, his glasses off, his eyes shifting from one to the other, Arkip Apollonovitch smiling publicly and sneering at them inside; and Kremenko off in a corner, his pinky diamond throwing tiny sparkles as he fiddled with a cigarette, the two candlesticks on Glueck's writing-table nearby spilling something stupidly religious into the tableau — a play of the old school, exactly one of those dull logical dramas massacred by students in extemporaneous classroom translation and no longer performed any more. Only it was a matter of lives being changed, theirs as well as mine, all of them in gowns and night-robes and all so intimate and heartless.

"The biggest ball of twine unwinds," said Arkip Apollonovitch, leaning upon his cane. "Still lovers upon lovers, Tatya? I cannot blame you entirely," he added, sniffing amusedly to himself. "It was a poor life to begin with . . . though our young professor might be asked what he hoped to gain."

Glueck returned his bricklike glance with a hopeless shake of his head. "It is a sickness, sir, a sickness!"

"Perhaps we ought not to take her to Paris," said the Squire to the old man in a bravely man-to-man way. "It might be healthier for her to stay in Minsk again, meanwhile."

"Paris," said Tatiana Arkipovna, scornfully.

"I thought you'd agree, Tatya." The Squire shrugged, Leta's head against him moving a bit. "I am willing to provide you with Alexei, if he is so good for your health."

"No," she replied. "I can't leave you that, Kolya."

"You may come also, if you insist."

"Tell him, Father," she said, "there is no Paris."

"Ah, Tatya," the Squire parried easily, "you are too demanding, even for an only daughter. . . ."

"Say it, Father . . . I don't care," she ranted suddenly, "I don't care!"

"Sh," cautioned Arkip Apollonovitch. "I leave for Moscow tomorrow; we'll say nothing about Paris *now*."

"Well, Father? Are you? *Are* you taking him to Paris?"

"Tatya," he smiled, "don't be a bad girl. . . ."

"But you are not," she said. She pointed to the Squire, shaking her head. Arkip Apollonovitch lifted his cane in the direction of Kremenko, then moved it toward his daughter in a commanding arc. "Let us keep our heads," he told Tatiana Arkipovna as Kremenko moved behind her and attempted to escort her out. "It is late, we'll review everything in the morning. . . ."

She threw Kremenko aside with a shake of her body and a fierce thrust of her arm, her face as hard as marble now, drained of its fluidity, her large features regularized and made even beautiful in a chilling way by the murder of her last inner doubts.

She had been forced to choose to win. "Let him know Paris is a fraud," she said with a great sob of pity for herself, "that there is no opera singer to be wooed with a Yiddish fiddle—"

"Stop it, Tatya!" from the Squire.

"—that you got your loan last month, Father!—"

"Stop your ravings!"

"—that you had her sent to Dresden, Papa, and while she was away you persuaded your friend about the loan! Tell him all you told me!"

The Squire pushed Leta away and stepped closer to his wife. "Ah, Tatya," he said, close to tears, "I can only forgive you. You are miserable, ill . . . I agree with Papa, it is not your fault entirely. . . ."

"Save your tears! You can do nothing but wait for Papa to die."

She said it quietly, and after she said it the words stood in the air as though written. She looked about her, began sobbing not quite for herself alone, and ran out, passing me quickly in the darkened hall to fumble her way down the stairs, her sobs diminuendo and out.

In the room the Squire said, but as a question, "She is out of her mind, Papa. . . ."

"It is bad," the old man said. "What, Kremenko, makes the least thing so difficult these days?"

"At night," answered the lackey drily, "what is easy?"

"No, Papa," the Squire urged, unsatisfied, "she spoke madly, of course? You didn't . . . ?"

He could not push himself to finish the question. I did not see Leta in a corner, but I had a view of Arkip Apollonovitch's face, something monumental in it, grave and decided, a face fixing itself down upon the Squire with a dignity to be admired had Arkip Apollonovitch been facing his executioner. But it was the other way around and though an overdue and guilty love for his daughter might have moved him to press the button anyway that shot the current, it was nevertheless *his* button and *his* current. He had done it so many times that one more hardly counted; and besides, he disliked the Squire personally. "You must not be Paris-minded, Kolya. You have affairs to regulate without seeking distant engagements. The loan was made and that's the end of it."

"The loan was made . . .?"

"Yes."

"When?" said the Squire, turning to Kremenko, hoping distantly. Perhaps from another, a truer answer. . . . But Kremenko said, "Last month, Konstantin Andreyevitch."

The Squire said nothing, breathing deeply, then drawing himself to his full height of some five feet. He attempted at this last to leave the field with some remnant of Staff dignity but near the door he stopped, tried not to stumble and fell anyway, lying in a steady shake of trembles, stricken.

Often I tried to imagine what he thought as he lay there but it was useless, unnecessary.

The house became both a cemetery and a depot of departures.

The servants were roused, lights broke the night, and sounds;

Vassily carrying the Squire to his bed, Rodion hustling on horseback
to fetch Ostrov, Natalya and Lubenka meanwhile sitting with Tatiana
Arkipovna on Kremenko's orders until the doctor came.

Leta remained in Glueck's room, preventing me from begging to
be taken if not to Novgorod then at least as far as Minsk; the fiddling
was over and with the Squire and Tatiana Arkipovna so ill Vassily
would surely return me to Kuizma Oblanski who would dutifully
carry me back to Pukop and they'd have me for good.

If only Glueck would do it, if only as far as Minsk! I'd pawn my
fiddle and go straight to a synagogue where they'd surely help me to
one of the illegal wagons going over the border; in Minsk I'd tell
them about Shim and they'd tell me how I might find Yeersel in
America and sooner or later I'd see Shim again. How queer to be
thinking this when he might be just across the road yet impossible
to get to; perhaps he had drifted away long ago and was in America,
waiting for me. I promised myself I would try to make sure about
Shim. With such a spinning in my head I dressed myself, anxious to
stride to the beginning that waited, fearful of never getting to it but
determined to unbury myself from this debris.

I heard Ostrov's angry voice cutting over Kremenko's purring tones
on the landing below, and Leta finally left Glueck to hurry downstairs to the doctor.

Glueck had a damp towel about his head and was closing his trunk
as I entered. With a wild annoyed look he asked why I was dressed,
as though it constituted an obstacle to his plans. I almost saw my words
bouncing from his emergency turban.

"It is childish," he dismissed my idea. "I'll be riding to the Minsk
station with the old man and Kremenko, and if I decided to ride alone,
later, Rodion would never take you anyway. You're a good lad," he
said, seeing me already part of the past, "here, take your music, keep
it as a treasure, work at the Beethoven."

I told him they wouldn't let me play in jail and it made me cry.
He wrote his address in Petersburg, promised he'd see "what could be
done officially" about placing me in the Conservatory. I couldn't stop

crying. He said he'd talk to Ostrov who would "protect" me until he could "enlist the influential Jews" around the Conservatory. That didn't help either. Finally he gave me a five-ruble note and made me promise to "behave properly, if you make yourself a fugitive no one can help you." During this he dressed himself. "We'll say good-by later. I'll go down now, Lev, to speak to the doctor. Ugh, what horrors!"

All very nice and German; nothing for me to do but sit in jail practicing Beethoven until he got back from Novgorod and waited in lobbies to talk about a nobody of some small town. It took a month to find out whether the government knew you had been born; how long would it take to fish me out of the Minsk district, even granting they wanted to? By then I'd be shoveling snow or mud or rocks, old enough for the army while in ten minutes Vassily could throw me to Oblanski and before the day was out they'd have me locked up in Pukop. Nothing doing. My greatest friend was distance. I would put distance between me and my enemies. The worst that could happen was getting caught by distant police and maybe with my fiddle case and fine clothes I could give them stories, say I was lost. In this way I kept my courage up.

The thing to do was to get out while it was dark, and down the hill without being seen. Once down I could cross and stay in an empty hut until I saw a light going on; I'd make sure where Shim was and if still there I'd get him to make the try for Minsk with me. Or perhaps I would not wait for a light to show, but wake them up; the quicker the better and then away, with or without him, down the highroad until dawn. And after it got light, through the woods then alongside the road, circling around Pukop when I got near it. I'd wait in the woods until dark and take a chance on getting to Rabbi Sussya's synagogue while they were still at evening prayers. One of them might help me to Minsk and I had Glueck's five rubles; and in Minsk the fiddle could be pawned for wagon passage.

Going alone would be safer. In one way I did not want Shim with me but in a stronger way I did.

The first time I thought it all over it seemed simple and good, the second time not so simple or good, the third impossible. To begin with, just getting out of the house . . . I almost gave up.

I remembered one of my father's sayings, "Take the scissors to the goods, not the goods to the scissors"; cut for a purpose, not just to cut. I never accepted it as much of a saying and my father said it every time my mother complained, which was not often but not seldom either. My father was never much of a fighter, a doer, a maker; he did not express leading ideas and he distrusted daring; but in the face of danger he held. Danger was a customer to be out-waited and out-haggled and so was my mother's complaining. My father would fix a sad eye upon her, knowing my mother never complained unless something really hurt her, and his eye would be massive with contempt for the regime in which we were trapped. With patient stubbornness he held against this, confronted the Evil Eye with his own, achieving a loftiness, an untouchability of which he was unaware. Remembering his look as well as his saying, I took it was a sign of nothing being worse than sitting still while the Evil Eye was roving.

It was like watching myself putting my music into the fiddle case, my astrakhan cap into the overcoat pocket — also pawnable in Minsk — like someone else leaving my room. On the landing I peered down and saw a swatch of light. I started one step at a time, keeping to the railing where the carpet was thicker. Leta or Tatiana Arkipovna screamed; feet ran toward the sound. I timed my jump to the landing and hurried down, leaving by way of the unlocked French door near the piano in the main hall, then from the promenade to the front steps, across the carriage-way, and downhill through the trees.

A hard half-mile for a boy in my situation, until the wind blew more strongly against my face and I heard no more branches crackling.

Now that I was down I had to watch out for their back yards, find the downhill road and slide past the sleeping huts. I saw the first gray splotch in the sky. It couldn't have been so late, but it was. Without thinking of the noise I ran the last few hundred yards down the middle of the hill road, jumping into the carriage stop whose sides and rear wall hid me from any early peasant on their side. Like any traveler I sat down and caught my breath. In a few minutes I'd know how I would be going, alone or with Shim.

I was about to stand when I heard, not near and not far, a noise of rocks rolling down a hill and bumping into each other. It came from the highroad, from the Pukop direction where the ground was level, louder every moment and less rocky too, and with increasingly complicated clumps yet altogether orderly. Not until it was almost up to me did I translate it into horses; many, in formation. Just horses, no carriages.

I threw myself back where the walls met. Enough light to see them pass, the Tsar's proud cavalry, the horses dim and large and prancing, the soldiers riding them slumped, some shaking like jelly in their saddles, doubtless half asleep. Here and there a gray horse in the faint morning gray, the others brown and blended into forage uniforms, the hooves whushing as they fell into the thicker mud around the carriage stop. Thirty or forty feet past me, I heard the order and the rustling down of the hooves. I gambled with a one-eyed look and saw them dismounting.

Lamps were lit and carried. The platoon divided into three groups, one going to the huts on our side, the other moving up the road on foot, the third remaining and lighting cigarettes.

Good-by, Shim! And hello to what?

What were they doing there?

It got lighter with every passing second, and the Evil Eye was roving. I moved behind the carriage stop. Ten yards to my rear stood Verenka's tavern; the only thing to do was try for the yards, work my way partly up the hill again through the back yards, circling around the Squire's house to the drop far behind it where the fields stopped and the woods began. Once there I'd head in the Svutz direction, find my gully, and sit down to figure. The gully was safe. But the back yards weren't, people rose at dawn, it was past plowing time and taverners did business early.

How queer to be running away from the Squire while coming closer and closer to the house; I made the circle as quickly as possible for the ground was open from Ostrov's to the top of the hill. I saw the lights on the second floor, my feet slid faster through the soft earth and I gasped, falling when I got into the protecting underbrush. There was no doubt in my mind that I would be caught; only they would have to catch me. It was no deep trick but it seemed the hardest thing in the world to get to my gully and when I plunked myself down there, fiddle case and all, I felt like half a Christopher Columbus and half a Napoleon.

Sweating, muddy, I piled some deadwood and sat on it. The sky grew bluer. What had seemed workable in the dark now appeared crazier and crazier. In a panic I began considering going back to the house and saying I had gone for a walk. Who could have figured on the accursed soldiers? At least one thing; whoever they were after, it wasn't me. If they found me I'd say I'd gone for a walk. I heard their rifles a few times, individual cracks far off, and prayed it was only for fun or practice. The sun rose higher, time passed, and I saw nothing to do but sit. If I wanted to make it fancy I could throw in a lot of onions and carrots here, give you all my thoughts as they came and went, and so on. Just take it from me, I was scared and without hope but loving my father and remembering his look when my mother complained.

I heard more rifles, further away each time down toward Svutz, which gave me the idea they'd moved in that direction. Minsk lay on the other side, beyond Pukop; very well, I'd put distance between them and me, try making it to the Pukop woods, going slowly, resting; plenty of time until evening prayers and the dash for the synagogue.

It is pleasant to take a walk in the woods when you and nature are on friendly terms. Everything stands on display, the interesting poke of a bough, the unexpected clump of sweet berries, the busy scuttles of rabbits, the arias out of the trees, the whirr of wings. How nice, then, to walk in a sporty jacket with perhaps a cold chicken-leg wrapped in a pocket and with a rifle on your shoulder, ready in case something like a bear or a wolf should venture into your preserve. However, I was hungry and without the chicken-leg, and I carried no rifle but a violin case, and my overcoat was long and wet and muddy at the hem, and the rabbits looked like foxes and the foxes looked like wolves. Moreover in the thick woods to see the sun was never easy; I knew I had to keep facing it, when it started dropping, to be bearing correctly for Pukop; many times I'd come to a clear space and see it on my right or left. It would have been a relief to walk in clear spaces and sometimes I did, always forcing myself back into the woods, having to choose safety against false relief.

I rested more and more, trying once or twice to sleep. There had been no clear spaces for a long time, everything went uphill to the west and I had to circle around many hilly rocky nubs. The woods sat thickly there, the oaks and maples mostly only a few feet apart. I kept stumbling and stumbling up what could only be the darkening side of something mountainous. Not sure even of heading west any more, I had to get to the top to see; lost or not, that's how I felt, not remembering any such mountain near Pukop.

I'd been moving some six or seven hours. The fiddle case felt filled with rocks but I couldn't stop, so exhausted I'd surely fall asleep and wake up after dark if I took a rest. No, the place to rest was at the top; and if I happened to see Pukop everything would be all right. But more and more I started falling; once against a large rock, the fiddle case banging so hard against it that I was afraid to open it and examine the fiddle. Then came the last time that I fell. To protect the fiddle case I turned with the slip and hit my face on stones. I lay there crying a little while, got to my knees, and wiped my eyes on my sleeve. I was rising from the ground when something like a rock caught me in the back of my neck and everything went away.

My head lay in a woman's lap. The flame of a thick candle on the grit of the earth showed me the rough curve of the cave-walls rising briefly to a few crude log-splits blackened by old fires.

I pushed myself up. A mural of faces circled the candle at my feet, the four of them squatting and watching.

Two of them had hair cropped closer than Glueck's, their beards in stubbles, the familiar under something transformed. New things had stamped themselves on these features, reckless things, luxurious humor and efficient cruelty, the set of beginners at using printed thoughts.

It might have been the night that never goes away, when faces return for a little visit, refreshing and lifting you; everything puzzling beside the point because you are part of the secret.

The boy of fifteen, Timo, the mop of straight dark hair over his large wild begrimed face; he seemed hardly human, more bulldoggish. And Miss Faitoute, her old cheeks sagging above her high-necked gray blouse, could have at that moment been some wise and grumpy cat with its hair molted off and swollen to human parity, also part of the secret; never having seen them before they were immediately precious, by being with the other two.

Was this The Next World, that "life of night" so many times with ecstasy described by Reb Maisha at the learning-table? Was this where you felt the sun without seeing it always? My first thought was, "It *is*," I must have been elevated to the last heaven; for surely though their ears were larger, the eyes smaller, the cheeks very flat and their chins naked, these two melted-down faces belonged to Uncle Mottel and Berel-the-Ox. It could be neither dream nor in life but a true union of both.

They said nothing and I could not produce a sound. Sleepless since long before dawn, drained and wracked by what you already know, I thought again, "Yes, it *is*."

Without taking his eyes away from me Uncle Mottel put a cigarette stub in the exact center of his mouth as he always did. He lit it with the candle. As he put it down the spell dissolved to a weaker version of itself, less rigid and mysterious, distorted by living motion. I heard Uncle Mottel's quiet Yiddish.

"These are Timo and Miss Faitoute." So calm, yet not bored as he ever was, no more the words beneath his words saying, "I am weary of myself and everything"; it was Uncle Mottel but also . . . who? Who was he now? In Russian he said, "Timo, you struck him too hard."

"So he wouldn't make a sound," replied the boy.

Then in Yiddish, puffing, "Laib, don't be afraid."

I flung myself to his chest. Close to his hard body, his chin touching my head, I felt the spell wriggling off terribly fast. My numbness became pins and needles of questions clamoring to be heard, questions which could have only the most frightening replies. I shook with my sobbing. "Sh, it's not so bad." He turned me to face Berel. "Now," with a gentleness novel in so brusque a spirit, "you will feel better. Do you see who it is, Laib?"

"Berel, is it you?"

"He doesn't hear any more."

Berel neither smiled nor spoke. In the days of his beard I never suspected he had such a fierce Adam's apple. Now it was rocking up and down.

"See, Laib, how happy he is."

"Is this Siberia?" I cried.

"If it is," said Uncle Mottel, "Siberia has moved."

Impossible to call him "Ox" any more. Thinner, sharper-faced, Berel had surrendered his patience for some boon clamping a pride to his neck. He held his head as I have seen heroes of opera doing it, the easy rigidity flowing along the cheek lines and affecting the chin, but this was not on any stage.

I could not stop shaking my head.

"It is too much," Miss Faitoute said in a slow and nasal Russian.

From behind, a laughing sound; I turned to the last of the strange faces. She was younger; I'd had my head in her lap, and though not beautiful, she encouraged the eye to linger. Her face was fouled with dried mud, everything about it longish and settled but full, the mouth wide and definite, the lips thin promise-keeping ones. Her forehead perched narrow. Her hair looked coppery in the candlelight and she wore it parted to a side tightly against her head, twisted in

the back. Her mouth a bit open, she looked at me with an easy jolli-
ness that could become serious in a flick, her skirt hitched up and her
knees out, showing battered run-down shoes of the high-laced city style.
Despite her size and dirtiness and the splotch of a mole on her cheek,
some daintiness remained.

"I used to hold you in my arms when you were a baby," she said,
the memory entire in her eyes, the Yiddish made into a line of melody, full and vibrating in the contoured closeness of the cave. "Many
times, on the back benches of the synagogue. I'll show you."

I let her pull me close; she was strong, easily lifting me into her lap.
"Just like this," she said. Not for more than a year and a half had
I been offered anything motherly. I took it without shame.

"Me, too," said Timo, humorously exercising his adolescent lust,
"every fellow needs a mother."

"You need a wife more," was her light answer.

"Come on, Lenka, me next?"

I drew myself away. Lenka? Nochim's? ". . . You're *Lenka?*"

"It's me."

"Nochim's Lenka that — that — "

Too shy and dazed to finish the rest, how her father had carried her
out of the village after her time with the Squire, I tumbled off her lap
wondering why and how she and all these were so banded and near
to Golinsk. I said, "Your father died."

"I know it."

Looking at them one by one, I put my hands to my head. Everything was spinning too fast and out of fear it would go faster, I began
to fight for breath. "Water," I said.

"Water would be good," Lenka nodded.

Uncle Mottel said, "Water would be wine."

"It's too far away," Miss Faitoute said.

"I'll go," said Timo but not eagerly.

"You can't," Uncle Mottel said. "It's too soon. When it's darker
and the soldiers have given up."

At the mention of soldiers I heard in my head echoes of the morning and began trembling. The last I saw, Uncle Mottel was watching me gravely.

When the faint was over, my head lay again in Lenka's lap and Berel was not there. "Where is Berel?"

"You can't tell an old water-carrier what to do," said Uncle Mottel, patting my leg.

Again I thought about how gentle he'd become. "Uncle, I'm in such a mix. Where are we and what are we all doing here? Where did you come from, and —"

"Sh, there's time for stories. We'll tell them all, every one."

"I lived in the Squire's house six months."

He exchanged looks with Lenka. They thought I was out of my mind. Lenka was stroking my head, her fingers hardly touching my hair. A wave of dysentery went through the lanes when I was four or five and the kids lay in one diarrhea, me included. My father would kneel beside my mattress on the floor, stroking my hair delicately with his tailor's fingers. "You will surely sleep, Laib, I promise. How can you fail to sleep when Papa gives you the magic pat?" He would stop a moment for the effect and say, "Now I'll give you the magic pat that always makes boys fall asleep. A wise man taught it to my father, and he taught it to me, and when you are older I shall teach it to you. Now, see . . . I am starting and you will sleep . . . magic pat, magic pat, magic pat," he would say in time with his stroking, his voice going softer and softer and his fingers hardly touching my hair. Soon I'd be straining to listen and feel, and it never failed. I would sleep. Lenka's stroking my hair brought me back to this.

I whispered to Lenka, "When you stroke, say 'magic pat, magic pat. . . .'"

She did. I slept or winked and nodded, a layer of peace rimming me. Distant sounds of danger intruded several times. When I stirred I would hear Lenka whispering, "Magic pat, magic pat," as she stroked.

Then a few drops of water on my forehead, and a small nozzle to my lips. I drank. Uncle Mottel held the military canteen close. "There, better . . ."

Behind him Berel was speaking. His Yiddish was high, wavering, and not only because of his deafness. "They saw me."

"How do you know?" I saw Timo gesture, questioning.

"The bushes moved too much," Berel said to Uncle Mottel.

"We could go for the road, they wouldn't expect it," Lenka said, looking from one to the other. Berel crouched himself nearer, his eyes going from mouth to mouth, reading.

"It is a very poor chance, the road," Miss Faitoute said as an estimate.

"Yegor might fix us with a wagon," Uncle Mottel said. "The tavern isn't far once the road is reached."

It was hard for Berel to lip-read Russian, he deaf again not so long this time; but at the mention of Yegor he cried, "Yegor, no . . ."

Uncle Mottel put his hand on Berel's arm and spoke to the others. "If he was seen, he was also followed. And if followed, they would be shooting long volleys into us now. The road is sensible."

"Frenchmen would be throwing torches here," Miss Faitoute said. "Still, even if Berel is wrong about being seen . . ." She shook her head. "I don't agree about the road."

"Or I about Yegor," Lenka said.

"Uncle," I asked, "who does Berel say . . . who is 'they'?"

"Soldiers."

"Why are they looking for us?"

"Because," smiling, "someone told them to. Sh . . . you will know all about it some other time. . . ." He spoke to Lenka now, as though once she were convinced the others would agree. "Here is my meaning, regarding Yegor. . . ."

Now a monologue began which branched into a discussion held as quietly and with a sense of confidence as might be seen in students or book-lovers holding up idealistic points for examination and settlement. Surely it couldn't have been too dangerous a pinch we were in.

Squatting and puffing as he spoke, Uncle Mottel said Yegor was a peculiar fellow in some ways and it was possible to predict what he might do about helping us with a wagon. Owing to being a discontented tavern-keeper with paradoxical hatreds it was possible to get him on our side by means of the following stratagem: The peculiar thing about him was his excellent talent for crookeries higher than those coming his way; whenever he strived for richer prizes than what might fall into his tavern from off the road, his landlord Vlad Ryba always stood in the way; Vlad was his prime hatred and whatever would hurt him was good. Additionally, he had once admired Uncle Mottel in a fight and would listen to him and that meant everything, for what Uncle Mottel proposed was to go to Yegor and in exchange for the loan of a wagon reveal to him how he could damage Vlad Ryba most heavily with full safety to himself. "I will say to him," explained Uncle Mottel, "that I 'happen to know' about the escaped prisoner the soldiers are looking for, and that there is a band with him which would do anything against any landlord; in the circumstances it would be easy for Yegor to torch up Vlad Ryba's barn, report the theft of his horse and wagon, and the blame for the burning could be laid upon us . . . but by then we'd be far along on our way . . . yes or no?"

Miss Faitoute shook her head.

Berel said, "Wait . . . it is helping Yegor burn something? Do I understand?" Mottel nodded and Berel said, "No good . . . we would have to ride far, then . . . and you forget . . . I wanted to look again at Golinsk."

He tried unsuccessfully to hide his disappointment. Lenka said, "Miss Faitoute is right, Mottel." And to Berel in Yiddish, "We'll see. . . ."

"Having got him so near to it," Uncle Mottel said, puffing his cigarette hard, "it's bad to think of denying him his wish. But our best chance is Yegor."

"Uncle," I cried in fear, "he put Tzippe-Sora in jail, I saw with my own eyes how he threw the tax man at us!"

"I know."

"How?"

"Sh . . . well . . . looking at it another way, then . . . " He thought for a while, the others waiting, and he grunted a few times before he glanced at Lenka. "Maybe you, Lenka . . . let's see . . ."

He picked up a handful of stones and moved closer to the candle.

We all watched. "Here's the road," he said, making two lines in the dirt with his finger, "and here is Yegor's." He put a stone down beside a point in one of the lines. "Pukop sits towards me . . . very well, now here we are," putting another stone near his foot and away from the lines, "between us and the road, thick forest going downhill. When it's darker, we strike for the road. Here." He marked a line with his finger to a point on the road down from the tavern. "It's a good half-mile from Yegor's, about a mile from here to there through the woods. Next . . . we're in the bushes near the road, it is already dark. Lenka — you and Miss Faitoute will walk the half-mile to Yegor's. Miss Faitoute will be the tearful mother with a daughter just ravished by a soldier down the road . . . who paid nothing for the favor, clear?"

"That again?" Miss Faitoute replied doubtfully.

"Sergey swears it is your most sympathetic performance," Uncle Mottel smiled.

"We were lucky to win with it the other time," Lenka said.

"Not according to Sergey. But remember his criticisms, Lenka," he teased. "Don't cry too hard, simply sniff and look angry. Come, show me. . . ."

"Consider the soldiers," Miss Faitoute said. "Constables wouldn't be too important."

"When it's dark and a tavern's near that's where you'll find soldiers, not in the woods. It's an international trait."

"Enough nonsense," Lenka said.

"We'll be here," Uncle Mottel said soberly, tapping the stone that meant us near the road. "You will get the wagon, by what I know will work, and ride to us. It will be dark, but you will hear us singing Sergey's little song just loud enough."

"And we'll be in Minsk in four hours," Timo said.

Lenka and Miss Faitoute shook their heads but Uncle Mottel asked, "You know the song I mean?"

"*I had a King though I'm no good at chess,*" sang Timo through his nose.

"That's right," from Uncle Mottel. "And if you're not back in an hour, Timo and I will go to Yegor's."

The way he said it showed this was his best thought and Lenka realized it was up to her to say yes or no. Without answering, she crawled up to the front of the cave and lifted the pile of thick boughs enough to allow a glimpse at the outside. "Soon dark," she called back. Uncle Mottel began talking to Berel, combining gestures with silent slow mouthings. Lenka crawled back to Miss Faitoute and started whispering to her.

I said to Timo, "Please say what it all means?"

"They've done it before to get wagons. They'll go into a place with their story and complain heavily about somebody taking Lenka and not even paying. Miss Faitoute then makes an arrangement with some eager fellow, and it's to be done out in his wagon, you see? Once they're out there, he's unconscious before he can open his fly."

"How?"

"They choke him."

"But if they're caught?"

"They haven't been."

"What are you all anyway—robbers?"

"Ask your uncle."

"*Ay*," it went through me, "*they're Avengers.*"

I would have asked him about it immediately, but Miss Faitoute turned from Lenka and called to Uncle Mottel, "Very well . . . but look at the dirt on us, we should go first to the stream. . . ."

"That's right," said Uncle Mottel very softly, happy, turning from Berel and crawling to Lenka quickly for it was too low in there to stand up. "Yes," he said, touching her cheek with his fingers, "we must let them see how pretty you are."

She brushed away his fingers, her own lingering a moment upon his, then saying, "Over it once more," and again they bent to their lines and stones, deciding distances and times and searching their memories for landmarks. I was accustomed to the Golinsker way of chewing things over together, which was never quietly, soberly; here words were being counted as well as weighed as they estimated how they might live, without any fear in them that I could see. The morning already seemed years away, my months at the Squire's compressed into some crucial prelude. What was the fountain of their calm, I wondered, and who was Sergey? And how could they be anything like Zasulich's Avengers with Timo a gentile and Miss Faitoute from France so far away? As they settled the plan in each other's minds every moment stretched and teemed for me; I needed answers as much as I needed to breathe, yet whenever I thought I saw a chance to ask my questions something more important happened.

They appeared to be done with their diagramming and Uncle Mottel had picked up the stones, for some reason dropping them into his pants pocket, when Lenka said, "But perhaps we should better stay," her Yiddish framing a hope of winning a wagon by other means, "until later at night when there are fewer about."

"That's our time for traveling," Uncle Mottel replied, "and the quicker on the way the better."

"The safer the start, the better," replied Miss Faitoute. "We could snatch the wagon later."

"And be trapped by daylight?" he asked. "What a shame, after all the work of swinging Berel off the train! No, ladies . . . daylight must find us safely back in Minsk!"

Berel had read enough from their lips to understand and said haltingly, "All right, but a night here . . . just a night . . . I'd bring water, and I saw berries . . . and," he added with a shy twist of one side of his mouth, "to see Golinsk would be good too, having come this far. . . ."

Lenka shook her head at him and drew a finger across her neck but Miss Faitoute said to Uncle Mottel, "He wants to see Golinsk," making it sound proper that he should see it.

Uncle Mottel showed some annoyance. With much mouthing and pantomime in which Timo collaborated, he explained to Berel for the second time that it was impossible to complete their original intention, reminding him of his previous promise to get him back for his precious visit, here emphasizing that Sergey would definitely arrange it. Berel neither argued nor surrendered, simply saying in a mumble, "I wanted to walk down my path once more, perhaps see somebody," and I would have settled it there but could not find the words to let him know there was hardly anyone to see; let him believe his wife was alive, though the chances were against it; why give him that to carry?

Uncle Mottel turned to Miss Faitoute. "Come on, help me. We'll hardly get out of this, and without trying for Golinsk now."

"They'd grab us in Golinsk in a minute," Lenka said.

"Then convince him. He knows Sergey needs him badly for the Nizhny meeting."

"What Berel needs is also important," Miss Faitoute said stubbornly.

At this Uncle Mottel stood up quickly, forgetting the low ceiling, banging the top of his head against one of the beams. He swore in low tones, the words viler that way.

"Are you bleeding?" Lenka said. "Let's see."

"Not the point," he said harshly, shoving her away. "No," he said to Berel between his teeth, wanting more than anything to scream it, but controlling. "No, no, no," he kept saying, each time less angry, more begging. "No, Berel, no, for our own sake at least. . . ."

Seeing him so angry yet appealing, Berel blinked his eyes and turned his head away, letting his hand fall and rise and fall again.

Timo went first, removing the boughs, showing the approaching twilight. The others crawled out one by one. Uncle Mottel blew out the candle. "Now you, Laib."

"Who is Sergey?"

"A man. Go . . . we'll talk in the wagon, on the way to Minsk. How would you like it in America?"

"Are we all going, Uncle?"

"We're starting, now out. . . ."

"Why does Sergey need Berel in Nizhny?"

"If you were supposed to know, I would have told you. Now . . . don't be afraid, it's all right."

Again on the way . . . in the gray of the morning deepening now, under the same stirring of wind, dawn and dusk always the same to me after then, my personal intermission; only now soldiers lay against us in cahoots with nature. Crouching one behind the other we twisted through thick brush, Timo and Berel leading; we passed trees marked with rocks Berel had placed for signs of the way to the stream; and we came there safely. In the summer it would not be much; for a few weeks the water would run with a temporary roar to it, just going into May, into some tributary of the Berezina. It was lighter there, a crack among the great oaks, the water's sound marking the stillness of everything else, and we came to it as travelers from a faraway and ridiculous land of stupid turmoil, reveling in the sudden difference. Timo stripped to his bony skin and waded in to his armpits, shivering joyously as the water ran by him. Uncle Mottel squatted at the bank, put his hands in to his wrists, washed his face. Timo ran out and let Uncle Mottel rub him with small rocks until his skin reddened, and I gave him my overcoat for a towel. Meanwhile Lenka and Miss Faitoute were wading, their skirts drawn up high, Berel in the water to his knees washing their faces carefully with Miss Faitoute's shawl.

Timo threw my coat off and dashed in, unable to deny himself the encore, and went to Lenka after he had immersed himself, to shovel water up her skirt with his hand. She kicked him down and he did it once more, both laughing and hooting; and Uncle Mottel watching and enjoying but urging haste and less noise. I watched him watching Lenka becoming cleaner, the dirt being removed from her face by Berel, something most contented and admiring in the set of his neck and the clasp of his hands as he squatted not smiling but with his mouth open a little. When she started coming out of the water she took his blouse off and she sat by him and he dried her face and feet with the blouse, being thorough between her toes. When he was done, while wringing out his blouse, before putting it on again, she laid her cheek to his and said, "Smell me." He sniffed and she helped him with his blouse, saying, "You smell filthy," but gently. He shrugged the damp blouse down his torso, then touched her ear, and I saw it did not matter to them whether they were clean or filthy and it made me think they were married or wanting to be. Berel helped Timo dry and dress, Lenka went to Miss Faitoute. It was a family; this was home, soon they'd walk slowly back to their house and have supper and go to sleep in beds and it was crazy to think of sorrow, pain, and danger.

Out of that, I asked, "Uncle, why am I the only one who is afraid?"

"Because you are on your way to America and because you are a boy."

"Do you ever think of dying?"

"Yes," he said, giving his head a cocky twist and seeming surprised. He took the fiddle case from the ground beside me. "We'd better be rid of this in case of questions anywhere. It could be said you stole it. And there might be news sent of your escaping from the Squire meshing in with this pretty thing."

"Who told you?"

"There you were," amused thinking of it — yet with a deeper pleasure too, the picture of it holding a meaning I was too young to guess, belonging to the hard privacy of the denied — "like a baby in her arms, snoozing and waking, talking and snoozing . . . so it was the wife and Ostrov, the Squire butting himself in his rear with his own horns. . . ."

"Anything too about Arkip Apollonovitch and — "

"Who's that?"

"The father-in-law."

"Rezin, that's right. . . . No."

"It's the best part," I said eagerly, the harsh comedy beginning to dawn on me. But the women were ready and he stopped me by reaching for the fiddle case and standing up. "This can't go, what'll we do with it?"

Curious, the others watching, he took the fiddle out and held it up. "Nice. . . ." Then he gave a string a plunk with his thumb. "Remember that mandolin, Laib?" I didn't say anything; I didn't know when I'd ever be able to get another fiddle. "All right," he said, "now before we do away with it, why don't you take it and play something quietly . . . something like birds. . . ."

"Did I say anything about my teacher . . . before?"

"What teacher, Varya?"

"No, Glueck. The Squire brought him, he — "

"On the way," he reminded, "on the way we will exchange gists of everything. Quickly now. . . ."

"Mottel," spoke Lenka, warningly.

"It's all right. Let it mix with the birds and the water a little."

I did not know what to play that might sound like birds. I played the first thing in my head, without stresses, going easy on the bow: the *Ave Maria,* my favorite. The water seemed to rush faster to it, the birds stimulated likewise. A suspicious blackness had begun mixing into the gray light, twilight's grip loosened, and the sky appeared to be lower and fighting to stay blue. I closed my eyes, the tone sounding stiff, and I was sorry not to have played for him in the cave where everything had reverberated.

I felt his fingers on my cheek, and stopped in the middle. "It's getting too dark," he whispered. I opened my eyes. "It's good, Laib."

He took the fiddle and I handed him the bow which he put into the case. Out of the corner of my eye I saw Timo and Miss Faitoute kneeling beside each other, their heads down, whispering to themselves. Lenka came and put her arm about me. Berel looked at me with a little smile and said, "I almost heard it."

The birds still chirping high, I said, "I played it on their Christmas and the Squire also knelt."

"It's not the same here," Uncle Mottel replied absently. "He never walked."

He stepped a bit into the stream, the water running over the toes of his boots. In a high arc, spontaneously, he let the fiddle fly out of his hands. I saw it bobbing and skipping a moment, atop the little springtime river, and away; then, picking it up and clicking it shut, the case. He called softly, "Well, religious ones," and they rose.

Silently Berel followed Uncle Mottel's leading steps, the others behind in a single line. I stayed close to him until the brush ended. Coming to the edge of the tall trees Berel and Timo took the lead, we just behind. We went that way, through the unending thick grove, a downhill slant to our steps soon beginning, the light giving way more and more, and when it became almost dark I whispered, "How far?"

"Not far," Uncle Mottel said. "Don't think, hold my hand."

A shot burst from the left, then another from the right.

"Ho," Uncle Mottel whispered. We stopped. Lenka moved to us, the others motionless.

"Signaling?" she whispered.

"Maybe. Each to a tree. Not near and not far. We'll see."

Lenka drifted back to Miss Faitoute; I followed Uncle Mottel to Berel and Timo. He gave Berel a revolver I did not know he had. I heard Berel sigh; I could not see his face. They separated and stood each against his own tree, all but me; I couldn't leave him.

We waited.

Then another shot from the right and a second later one from the left, both louder.

"Signaling?" I whispered, imitating Lenka.

He took my hand and guided me to her tree. "Joining," he told her. "Take him. And no changes, the plan remains."

"And you?"

"I'll follow."

There was enough light to see the white of her teeth. She said, "But the soldiers . . ."

"What they'll do for me they won't for their God," he whispered. "They're only two, now all right . . . until I hear you singing Sergey's song."

She kissed him briefly. He said to me, "Do not be afraid, the night is our friend."

I would have kissed him but Lenka held my hand and was already in motion.

After a few steps I twisted my head back. A tiny bit of white stood out of the dark, the stub of his unlit cigarette doubtless in the exact center of his mouth. I could frame his face around it, and that's how I saw him then and again and again and no other way at all.

* * *

I never found out how Berel escaped from Siberia or who Sergey was or what common harness these five had braced themselves into. From them I received experience of the conduct of heroes and of how these grow like weeds over the world, it being the luck of history that promotes some to flowers. Such were these, unnoticed, but true blooms anyway.

Just for that it was never worth merely to put on clothes every morning and take them off at night, to eat and sleep and go to the bathroom for its own sake. The thing was to refuse to reconcile to what was held proper or worthless in view of the prevailing, ever to be contemptuous of such arrogant advertising. Thus I said No running from the huts and from the Squire straight to Uncle Mottel and No again later to my nephew Aaron in America, and now again and forever, No.

We made the road that time, all but Berel and Uncle Mottel; perhaps because of them, since we had shooting behind us.

We waited for them long in the bushes of the roadside, until Lenka and Miss Faitoute went back into the forest, refusing to allow us with them. So it was Timo and I after that, and if it wasn't off my point I could give you a cowboy and Indian tale of how Timo's ingenuity wormed us to Minsk in four days, he nourishing the mystery of Sergey to the last, silent to my questions "until we come to Minsk, so if we're caught they won't squeeze anything out of us." Our final maneuvered wagon ride ended in a Minsker open-air junk market. Timo said he had to go somewhere but would return; meanwhile I sold my overcoat there, and when Timo did not return at all I went into the first street I saw, muddy and lined with shops. One had a sign with Yiddish lettering; I looked inside, I was beckoned, and that began my longest journey.

The rest you know from before, how I could not put myself over to my own deepest loved. The grief and anger holds, but I tell you this:

Nothing is ever forgotten, everything is remembered, and this makes everybody a relative, you follow me?

10. *Mottel*
(1848–1887)

Except after it was too late, I segregated myself.
I segregated myself from the segregated and the segregators both.
From man I flew, as from God.

Indifferent to death I feared life except after it was too late; fighting movement with inertia, remaining restless and stationary.

I lived by No and it was insufficient.

Lenka and Sergey; finding them by apparent chance, they showed man to me by the tracks of his trail. I went with them for no honor, victory, or survival—too late for me to drink the use of man, the wealth of blood and brain—but to abolish such as myself.

By accident, it can be wrongly said, I helped push my nephew Laib to America. Yet nothing happens accidentally, only surprisingly. The inevitability is masked.

The face of it was and is more than ugly. It blew arrogant winds over fires denied water, carrying the unburned to other fires.

Its exhalations blew pieces like myself into holes and corners until the flames found them again; or a curving gust flew them to other traps, the winds whistling in an imitation of eternity.

In this climate, say the learned clothed apes, it is possible to sew sails that can accommodate these winds, using needles ground fine out of the bones of the less cunning and thread woven from their sinews. Beware. This is the core of its victory.

Make no friends with those winds, nor compromise with its fires, nor trust in water.

Make friends with the earth.

Afterword

By Wallace Markfield

HERE we see force in its grossest and most summary form—the force that kills. How much more varied in its processes, how much more surprising in its effects is the other force, the force that does *not* kill, i.e., that does not kill just yet. It will surely kill, it will possibly kill, or perhaps it merely hangs, poised and ready, over the creature it *can* kill at any moment, which is to say at every moment. In whatever aspect, its effect is the same; it turns a man into a stone. . . . He is alive; he has a soul; and yet—he is a thing. An extraordinary entity this—a thing that has a soul. And as for the soul, what an extraordinary house it finds itself in! Who can say what it costs it, moment by moment, to accomodate itself to this residence, how much writhing and bending, folding and pleating are required of it?—Simone Weil

At sixty inches I stopped growing; year after year in my youngest manhood the recruiting clerks would measure me. Some tried to stretch me; one of them made a change in my nose with his pistol butt and I never wore the Tsar's uniform.—Nochim (1834–66), in *The Landsmen*

For six, eight weeks, I put off reading *The Landsmen* in the smug certainty that it was yet another crudely written, sentimental celebration of piety and poverty, yet another ruefully nostalgic chronicle offering the everlasting shtetl population of *luftmenschen* and *schlimazilim*. (Rootless intellectuals and hapless fools.) Weary with the genre, anticipating, at most and at best, permutations and combinations of wonder-working rabbis, ritual slaughterers, sadsack yeshiva students, drunken horse thieves, chicken pluckers, militant socialists, and the single obligatory sweet-tempered gentile, I started skimming. How styleless, how stilted, I told myself! Why, who in nineteenth-century Eastern Europe ever asked questions like, "Can't you reach God though your boots are pinching?" Went "Hiba-hiba" when they laughed or lamented? Sang such songs as "If the wind of pigs thickens the air / Look not to drive the pigs away?" Talked in aphorisms and paradoxes? ("The cleaner dirtied me." . . . . "Happy the generation wherein the clever listen to the fools." . . . "Look for heaven and find only worse hells.")

But presently I came across:

> The sergeant cut sapling wood with his sword to make a small hot fire. Removing the handkerchief from the mother's mouth, he thrust the face and arms into the fire, keeping it hot with more wood until the skin had shriveled, more especially the arms. He drove the sword under her left shoulder blade as an afterthought of surety, wiped the sword with the handkerchief which had been in the mother's mouth, and threw the handkerchief in the fire. Watching the fire burn itself out, the sergeant felt the sudden press of his bowels and he relieved himself, and threw stones over the last few smoking embers, and walked back to the highroad.

I was grabbed and shaken up by this passage, but not only because of its consummate brutality. (From my grandfather, after all, I'd heard enough to understand that in Alexander III's army the revolver was too costly, too high-prized an instrument to use on a Jew.) What unsettled me, I must confess, was a glimmering, a presentiment, a hunch that I would soon have my hands full coming to terms with a talent too profuse to place or pigeonhole, an American-Jewish writer whose intensity and energy and singularity were light years removed from those forces and figures which, more than I cared to acknowledge, had shaped the roots and reaches of my own work.

For I'd never heard of Peter Martin, never so much as spotted his name in the explications and anthologies of American-Jewish literature. And nobody I knew had anything to say about him. After a score of inquiries, though, I turned up one critic who dimly recollected refusing an invitation to review *The Landsmen* for either *Commonweal* or *The New Leader*. "What can I tell you?" he told me. "Granted, it had the flavor and savor of authenticity, but authenticity was the last thing this young Jewish intellectual had on his mind in the 1950s. A thousand words on a bunch of lumpen, landlocked *Yidden*? Not with my exquisitely fine-tuned post-Stalinist, post-existential sensibility, my taste for dialectic and disputation, my grounding in the New Criticism! Let Lionel Trilling risk *his* tenure. My reputation would be made exalting symbolic, archetypal, quintessential Jews—kvetchy urban characters specializing in angst and alienation, moral undergroundlings who gave me a chance to plug the human condition."

From the late 1940s throughout most of the 1950s, God knows, my own mind was stuffed with similar notions. The writers I envied and emulated were Saul Bellow, Isaac Rosenfeld, Delmore Schwartz, Bernard Malamud, Leslie Fiedler, and Robert Warshow—whose Jewishness, I believed, gave them a wonderful kind of edge on the Zeitgeist, as though they'd been born a day older in history than everybody else. Each in his own way commanded a complex, embattled, sophisticated style which linked the idiom of the academy with the idiom of the streets, and collectively they constituted, as Seymour Krim has written, "the first homebred group of writers to bear the full brunt of Mann, Joyce, Proust, Kafka, and Céline."

This was the period of heady half-truths, when Malamud proclaimed, "All men are Jews"; when Fiedler, in a discussion of Negro and Jew, concluded, "There seems to be a transcendent, eternal Jew who lives in the consciousness of all peoples"; when Warshow, reviewing Meyer Levin's movie *The Illegals*, wrote, "The Jewish awareness of a long history often masks a refusal to recognize history at all"; and Clement Greenberg answered huffily that "the time is at hand to move out from 'It's hard to be a Jew' to Kafka's 'It is enough that the arrows fit exactly in the wounds they have made.'"

And even the toughest-minded *realpolitikers* gave an impression of seeking, like Isaac Rosenfeld, "the everlasting in the ephemeral things: not in iron, stone, brick, concrete, steel, and chrome, but in paper, ink, pigment, sound, voice, gesture, and graceful leaping." For the legacy of political insight and social criticism they'd conserved through the 1930s turned to ashes at news of the Holocaust. Still, they were left with a certain plaintive satisfaction: the world they'd seen coming had truly arrived. Something almost akin to euphoria—"Jewish vertigo," Harold Rosenberg called it—could be sensed in the prevailing mood of wanhope which invaded the avant garde; by 1950, at any rate, Delmore Schwartz was exhorting a symposium to "post yourselves on the periphery—the true center and community of marginal men who are homeless in the world. Sing from there the Jewish blues and find, amid the clamor and din, the roaring in your ears, a language commensurate with the unheard scream—a language which will bring joy alive."

In fiction, this language turned increasingly ironic, oblique, cur-vilinear and, at times, almost gaggy. ("Syntax," William Poster once asserted, "died around 1947.") To be sure, it was sensitive and responsive—so sensitive, so responsive that it cracked under the pressure imposed by themes of suffering, redemption, and transcendence, by characters expropriated from Dostoyevsky or Kafka and given to speak-ing in the cadences of Sholom Aleichim.

Though I all along had doubts about the impulse and thrust of such writing, I nearly always fought them down. My own work, after all, dealt with these themes, expropriated the very same characters and carried comparable cadences. (Sample: "Believe me, the face we seek is seldom, seldom the face we come upon. Anyway, *boyeleh*, we are all strangers, and it is only the mass grave of history which brings us together.") Thus, I felt bitterly irritated when Elliott Cohen went after "the herd of alienated writers" in a 1951 *Commentary* editorial. "Enough, more than enough!" he thundered. "Declare a moratorium on that multitude of marginal men." I promptly started a seething rejoinder— e.g., "Last night, Mr. Cohen, I dreamed I had been turned into a goat and was about to be dispatched by you into the wilderness."

But then, in the midst of some prodigious point about "self-styled legislators of literary taste," I rose and started rummaging through a two-year backlog of prestigious quarterlies. I found fifteen short stories by, among others, Calder Willingham, John Berryman, Bernard Malamud, and Paul Goodman. Eleven of the stories had to do with neurasthenic writers, consumptive tailors, unemployed cantors, and synagogue builders who *schlepped* about a metaphysical metropolis during a timeless depression; and in at least five I could have used footnotes from Martin Buber. And quite suddenly I was assailed by wild longings for the works of Sholem Asch and I. J. Singer and Abraham Cahan, for some straightforward, elemental accounts of steerage, sweatshops, and strikes.

Nevertheless, I suppose I'd have gone ahead lambasting Cohen. Only, before long I ran into William Barrett, then an editor of *Partisan Review*. He started praising a story I'd just sent off to the magazine, and I was delighted. For it was the first time I'd made connection in fiction with my own boyhood—mentioned movies, egg creams, and Big Little books, celebrated Chinese food and a certain crazy girl around the corner named Maxine. "*I* loved it," Barrett said softly. "The others. . . ." After a few silent seconds he went on to say, "The others felt it was a shade too peppy for the PR *Weltanschaung*."

Less than a year later, when *The Landsmen* appeared, most everybody who mattered to me was carrying on over the bits and pieces of Bellow's *Augie March* which were popping up all over the place—their exuberance, audacity, bounce, and joyous affirmation. "Bellow," Delmore Schwartz prophesied, "will show us the way back from flight, renunciation, and exile into our country and our culture: our America." And Elliott Cohen, as I remember, remarked, "Who knows? Maybe our American-Jewish writers might discern from Bellow that Huckleberry Finn is as relevant to their situation as Joseph K. and Alyosha Karamazov."

2

Peter Martin was no child of those cannibalistic literary times. Indeed, from what his wife, Ruth, has told me and from the impression I've formed staring and staring at his photograph—the wide, blond, affable face, the air of gentle earnestness and courteous, manly decency—I suspect it's just as well he never fell in with me and *mes semblables*. Where, after all, had he published? This schlocksmith, this

TV writer, this *Kraft Theater* Big Thinker, this easy-going petition-signing *PM*-style progressive! Inside of five fast minutes we'd have most likely called him a liblab or a left-wing middlebrow, had some good mean fun parodying Reginald Rose or Paddy Chayefsky.

It turns out that he was born, by crazy coincidence, no more than two subway stops away from me in the Flatbush section of Brooklyn. He was a big, strong, solidly-built, street-wise kid with speed to burn—what candy-store intellectuals used to call a "shtarke." (Significantly, I never thought to ask about Martin's Jewish background, nor did his wife make a point of it; I'd guess, though, that like any average middle-class boy in that red brick one- and two-family-house neighborhood, he picked up a smattering of Yiddish, fasted a few hours on Yom Kippur and dragged himself through the obligatory year at a Talmud Torah where over-worked, underpaid rabbis prepared you for bar mitzvah with a transliter-ated Hebrew paragraph and a hectographed speech.

He grew up in the 1920s on stoopball and running bases, Dixie cups and fudgsicles, rubber-band guns and air rifles, Abe Kabbible and the Katzenjammer Kids, "Og, Son of Fire" and Tom Swift, the Radio Rogues and "The Rise of the Goldbergs," William S. Hart and Leath-erstocking. "Our fathers wondered whether we were Jews or a new kind of *shaygitz*," the poet Milton Klonsky writes of that generation and those neighborhoods. "But because time—and America—was on our side, they let us have our way, which was more and more becoming theirs as well. For they, too, could smell the sweet keen smell of Coney Island frying in its own deep fat."

Coaches at Erasmus Hall High School must have adored this beauti-fully coordinated kid who showed such style at the plate and in the infield, who could have done at least the second-best breast stroke in Brooklyn if he hadn't pulled a shoulder muscle tossing the javelin. Teachers called him "responsible," "disciplined," and "scholarly"; after grading his themes they had a habit of adding phrases like "nicely written and admirably researched."

For he was something of a workhorse. When he covered sports for *The Erasmian* he made it his business to flesh out stories with oddball statistics and arcane analogies to Greek mythology; when he wrote varsity-show skits at N.Y.U. and Columbia he timed the laughs at rehearsal and discarded any piece of business which drew less than a boffo; when he fell in love with jazz he took jobs on seltzer wagons and newspaper trucks to pay for first pressings of Louis Armstrong.

I have an idea that he had little use for the graduate-student squalor favored by many of the writers I knew who saw dirt as one of the forms of liberation, that he kept his life and the objects about him in good bourgeois order. And though he started selling radio plays while he was still a college student, he never ran up against the blocks and self-doubts and recurrent failures of nerve which commonly exhaust the will and energy of writers who achieve early recognition. It was not Martin's nature, for that matter, to agonize long about "losing his soul" in the marketplace; he thrived on the endless revisions, the impossible deadlines, the ulcerous meetings, the captiousness of actors, directors, and sponsors.

Because he had a knack with people and an extraordinary flair for administration, executive jobs came regularly and easily. After a spell in radio soap opera (*Helen Trent*), he set up a TV story department at NBC. There followed nine years at ABC, then three more at CBS in addition to his own free-lance writing for *Kraft Theater* and *Philco Playhouse*. Doubtless his mix of talents might have carried him farther along in those early years of TV—the "Golden Age" when on any given week fifty original dramas with a claim to seriousness showed up on the small screen. Yet he appeared to lack that final dedication, that absolute commitment which corporations exact in return for wealth and power.

Besides, he had six million Jews on his mind.

3

Perhaps Spring Valley, the New York town he moved to in the late 1940s, was the worst environment for a writer with a yen to be the American Sean O'Casey. Once a mean way station on the road to the Borscht Belt, a sprawl of broken-down bungalow colonies, *kochaleins*, and chicken farms, it had turned into an etceterogenious muster of split-level developments, artsy-craftsy ranch houses, and Zionistoriented communes. Now solid business and gemütlich professionals joined with artists, poets, and academics to find a modern young rabbi for the Mies van der Rohe-style temple, form a Hebrew Study group, a B'nai Brith chapter, a Combined Jewish Appeal. "In the green pastures of Spring Valley by the waters of Nyack," Harvey Swados observed, "they sat upon their daises and wept. And why not? Who had a better right? After twenty years of assimilation even the alrightnick could sense America was no sure thing."

Along with everybody else, Martin sent money, food, and clothing to the survivors, and learned the new rhetoric of intergroup relations— those pious platitudes which would fit Buchenwald and Auschwitz within the realm of the explainable. But all the fund-raising dinners, all the talk by human relations experts about "mutual understanding," "healthful democratic attitudes," and "our common Judeo-Christian heritage" could never seriously engage him. He longed for continuity and connection. Perhaps he had in mind what Laib the musician calls "a history, a valuable history, a part in man's enduring chronicle: Golinsk, but more than Golinsk, more than the remembered dead, the living and the imperishable."

And nothing in the ironic folktales and gentle fantasies of Sholom Aleichim or Mendele Mocher Sforim or I. L. Peretz convinced him, any more than it did Laib, that "if Israel's eyes were on heaven you yourself could live in a barrel of crap." For the virtues of humiliation and abjection, suffering and privation, he presently discovered, eluded flesh-and-blood Jews who had firsthand memories of the Pale.

These were Spring Valley's old-timers—the *proste* or common folk whose "weird gutteral Yiddish" Henry Adams loathed when it reached him through a Russian railway car in 1903. Martin encouraged them to talk and to tell him how it was to live from day to day under the Romanovs. Now and then he found himself taking a few notes to show his wife and his two young sons; by 1947 he'd accumulated several Talmud-size ledgers spilling over with down-home shtetl details—the daffy stiff-necked caste system which put land- and hand-workers in the back rows of synagogues by the worst drafts; rough sketches of smithies, taverns, brothels, and garrisons; how much it cost to have a twelve-year-old maimed by a professional crippler so that he might evade Tsarist conscription laws; the duties of a beadle; the dimension and design of the cast-iron stoves which heated the houses of the gentry; when to petition a provincial governor or a local squire; the habits of wolves and peasants; recipes for kvas, candle-sugar, and garlic-carp; the way to mend a harness, patch a roof, set up a market, wash down the dead, cajole a drunken Cossack.

And so he decided to undertake a trilogy.

Through the eyes, skin, and nerves of some shtetl Jews, he planned to capture the whole dense oppressive complex of East European life just as this life was succumbing to the blows of history. One or two Jews would reach America, carrying a burden of undefined moral responsibility. For he had a past, and money was never enough to obliterate it, though money would be the most he would get from America. ("I think of my father's face," said Laib in America, "that painted by the right artist would cause a rock to blow its nose. Alas, even here the State has other plans for artists.") Hitler, only Hitler, would suffice to show his sons and daughters who they were, what they wanted, and how the world saw them.

All during the next year Martin immersed himself in nineteenth-century Russia. He wanted to know about . . . but what did he *not* want to know about? Pogroms and pan-Slavism; The Protocols of the elders of Zion and the Black Hundred; the Enlightenment and its effect upon the Russian masses; the Russian Orthodox teachings which linked Jews with Satan; the "League of the Russian People" and its secret fighting squadrons; the anti-semitic forgeries of Hippolytus Lutostansky; the trial of Mendel Beiliss; the deportation, in 1891, of 17,000 Jews from Moscow; the writings of Nikita Pogodin, who opposed "the profundity and magnificent violence of Russia to the frivolity and triteness of the West."

At first, Martin set up a murderous schedule for himself, writing from four or five in the morning till it was time for the then two-hour commute into Manhattan. When his health failed—doctors had long ago noticed a tendency toward embolisms—he arranged a three-day week with CBS. Even so, nothing came easy during the five years he invested on *The Landsmen*. He feared that his rage and grief would stay imprisoned in words, that those who felt nostalgia for Sholem Aleichim's Kasrilevke would be repelled by the unrelenting bleakness of Golinsk, by characters redolent of horses and wagon grease, sour milk and chicken entrails, that the pace was too lethargic, the plotting too intricate, the canvas too broad.

4

Little, Brown and Company was "not proud, but honored" to include *The Landsmen* in its 1952 list.

Angus Cameron, Martin's editor, wanted the salesmen to understand that they were dealing with "an American Turgenev."

All the same, *The Landsmen* appeared during mid-summer, a season then allocated by the publishing trade to brilliant first novels and other ordained failures.

The ruck of reviewers were alternately enthusiastic, lyrical, benevolent, sweet-tempered—and uniformly depthless. Frederick Morton, in the Sunday *Herald Tribune* was so overcome by "this rich exuberant pastoral" that he caught whiffs of "a puissant nostalgia hovering over the volume." Carl Ruckhaus, fretful about the "general reader" in the *San Francisco Chronicle*, suggested approaching *The Landsmen* as "an invaluable source of exotic ethnic information." Rabbi Abner Kessler, in the *Cleveland Call*, pleaded with "Americans of all denominations to put this book alongside the priceless moral texts of Drs. Joshua Roth Liebman and Norman Vincent Peale." Only Anzia Yezierska, in *The New York Times Book Review*, bothered to mention the Squire and throw in a line about "the powers of darkness"; she wound up "bewitched" by the Golinskers' "folk-wit as they laughed, sang, and danced through their many ordeals."

I'd guess Martin, like any first novelist, had armored himself against the possibilities of failure. But no armor, believe me, avails against the kind of semisuccess *The Landsmen* achieved. (Two modest printings; a Book Find Club selection; a nomination for the Pulitzer Prize and the National Book Award; and sales sufficient, though only barely, to keep it off the remainder racks.) By 1953, when his royalty statements showed more returns than reorders, he had stopped talking about "the gift of time, the year as my own man."

As single-minded and disciplined as ever, Martin went ahead with the second volume of his trilogy, *The Building* (1960). Withal, he managed, as was then said, to keep at the business of living. In 1960 he followed the television industry to the Coast. He sold a pilot script for a whaling series which never got off the ground and wrote for other shows. Then an old friend from New York involved him in one of those "He had the motive, plus opportunity, plus his fingerprints are all over the place, but he's anyway not innocent" courtroom dramas. It would star some unknown and be called either "Perry Mason to the Defense" or plain "Perry Mason."

Martin wrote a script, and the network offered him a contract as story editor for the series at $30,000 a year. He planned to lay aside part of each week's salary as a "freedom fund" until he had enough for a year's work on the third volume of the trilogy and a jazz novel. Driving to the studio to discuss the contract on 18 May 1961, Peter Martin suffered a heart aneurism and died at the age of fifty-three.

Textual Note

The text of *The Landsmen* published here is an exact photo-offset reprinting of the first edition (Boston: Little, Brown and Company, 1952). No emendations have been made in the text.

LOST AMERICAN FICTION SERIES

published titles, as of October 1977
please write for current list of titles